BLUE TEARS

BLUE TEARS

Through The Canvas: Book 4

NINIE HAMMON

STERLING & STONE

Chapter One

"I DON'T MEAN to rain on your parade," T.J. told Bailey, and she could see he was trying to say it in the kindest way possible. "But you figure that federal marshal fella's gonna be in his office today, it being Thanksgiving and all?"

She hadn't even thought of that.

As soon as she got over the shock of seeing the man who had murdered her husband standing in the background of the photo she, Brice, T.J. and Dobbs had taken at the Nautilus Casino the night of her birthday party, her brain had likely had only one or two synapses still firing.

Mikhailov was the reason she was in the Witness Protection Program, the reason she'd been shipped all over the country, the reason she had given up her little girl. The police had stashed her away until they could arrest the mafia boss and lock him up, said her life and the lives of everyone she cared about would be in jeopardy if he knew that the woman he'd killed along with Aaron — and then made it look like they'd both been killed in a car wreck — was actually a homeless woman they'd stopped to pick up off the side of the road in the rain.

Mikhailov thought Bailey was dead. But she was alive, thank you very much, ready to leap out of the shadows and testify against him as soon as they served the sealed indictments.

But Mikhailov vanished before they could put the cuffs on him. Returned to Russia. Left Bailey in Witness Protection Program limbo, unable to reclaim the life he'd stolen from her. She believed he still was in Russia. Apparently, the police did, too. And she'd have gone right on believing it if he hadn't decided to show up at the Nautilus Casino while she was there with her friends celebrating her birthday.

They'd caught his image in the background of their grinning group picture.

As soon as the implications of that sunk in — he was here in this country, they could lock him up and she could get her daughter back! — she'd reached for her phone to call her federal marshal contact in the WITSEC program and tell him.

That's when T.J. pointed out that it was Thanksgiving Day. The guy might not be in.

"Then I'll call his cellphone. And if that doesn't work, I'll call him at home."

Bailey's hands were trembling when she pulled up the emergency call list on her phone. She hadn't set it up, of course. Hadn't picked out or purchased the phone either. Things like that — her name, the city where she was parked until the mythical "soon" which never came, or the middle-of-the-night visits from the U.S. Marshal's Service to whisk her away into the darkness — she was only on the receiving end of such things. She didn't get to decide.

The day U.S. Marshal Bernard Jordan — probably Bernie to his friends, if he had any friends — had given her the phone, his face had been as expressionless as an eggplant.

"My office, my home and my cell numbers," he'd said, when he'd programmed it for her. "They're all on the 'emergency call list' in this phone."

Perhaps she was supposed to feel grateful that he'd given her all three numbers. Maybe she was supposed to feel safe and well-cared-for since she could reach Marshal Jordan no matter where he happened to be.

But at the time she'd felt neither safe nor well-cared-for. She had felt as desolate as barren wasteland a hundred thousand years removed from the ocean floor it had once been.

She punched in his office number first — just in case he'd decided to work on the holiday. But when she was sent to voicemail, she hung up. This was not a message she intended to communicate with a recording.

Home or cell?

Cell seemed less intrusive. He could be anywhere — at a crime scene, or in his car. Home conjured up images of a man watching the Cowboys play the Panthers, sitting on the couch in his underwear, and she didn't like that visual.

He picked up after the first ring.

"Marshal Jordan."

Bailey was momentarily speechless, had no idea how to convey the enormity of what she had discovered, a life-changing occurrence, the end of "soon" and the beginning of "now."

Her life back.

Her little girl!

"This is Jessie Cunningham." The name, her real name, came out effortlessly. She'd only spoken it aloud a handful of times since her name had been taken away from her along with her husband, her child and her life.

And one of those times had been when she'd blurted it out to T.J. the first day she met him, the day she'd put Oscar in her skull even after T.J. had pleaded with her not to.

She shot him a glance.

The old man was seated in the same spot he'd been that night. The image of him in the lantern light, with Sparky beside him soaking the couch with his wet fur flashed like a comet across her mind and was gone. He smiled what she was sure he meant to be an encouraging smile, but it hung on his face as limp as a surgeon's mask.

"I saw him! He's here. He's back."

If the federal marshal asked *"he who?"* Bailey would somehow reach into the telephone and rip his throat out.

"Mikhailov? Where did you see him?"

"At the Nautilus Casino."

"A casino — figures."

"He's standing in the background of a picture that was taken Halloween night."

"And you're just getting around to telling me about it."

"I've been busy!" she snapped.

She'd been recovering from near drowning in a flooded coal mine with half a dozen girls kidnapped by an international sex slave ring. But she couldn't tell him that. Because he'd ask how she'd gotten mixed up in a thing like that and the explanation wasn't one a man like Jordan would ever believe.

"I didn't see the picture until just a few minutes ago. It's him in the background. I'm positive. Pointed beard. Eyepatch." Her arms broke out in sudden gooseflesh. "I will never forget that face."

"All right then. I'm on it. I'll start lifting up rocks, see which one he's crawled under."

Bailey couldn't have said what she'd expected, but that response clearly wasn't it.

"That's all? You'll go 'looking for' him? Hope he turns up somewhere before he decides to spend another two years in Russia?"

"I know how you must feel, Mrs. Cunningham." Oh, how Bailey *hated it* when someone told her they knew how she felt. "We want this guy — bad. He's left a trail of dead bodies dating back thirty years and this is the first time we've had a shot at making a charge stick. We'll pull out all the stops on this one."

That made her feel better.

"So when can I—?"

"You stay right where you are! Don't say anything to anybody. You're only alive because Mikhailov thinks you're dead, and you'll be dead if he finds out you're alive."

Bailey wondered if he realized how convoluted that sounded, but she got the message.

"You've hung in there this long. Don't blow it all now. Let us find him, arrest him and *then* you come out of hiding."

"All right." She couldn't help the disappointment in her voice. But what had she expected — that she'd call the marshal and he'd go out and arrest Mikhailov before dinnertime so she could have her life back by tomorrow morning? Yeah, she kinda had. "I will remain a good little WITSEC bobblehead doll."

The marshal made some kind of grunting sound that might have been a surprised laugh. "You do that."

"But you'll call me, let me know what's going on, right?"

"I'll keep you informed."

Now was that natural place in the rhythm of a conversation where he said goodbye and hung up. But he didn't.

"So ... how have you been?"

Bailey was struck momentarily speechless by the non sequitur.

He sounded like he was her college roommate, had bumped grocery carts with her in the produce section and was trying not to look surprised that she'd gotten fat.

She opened her mouth to say, "Oh, fine. And you?" but could *not* shove the inane words out past her lips.

The federal marshal had no idea what she'd been through since she moved to Shadow Rock, West Virginia. He knew nothing about her suicide attempt, about Oscar, or her special "gift."

Or where that gift had sent her. Then she realized he'd asked the question because he had somehow sensed that she was no longer the pathetic, devastated woman he'd parked in a rental house in Albuquerque almost two years ago.

"I've been through hell in a dinghy, Marshal Jordan. If what doesn't destroy you makes you stronger, I'm ready to bench press a Hummer. I want my life back!"

She meant to say the rest just as forcefully, but all of a sudden she had only enough air to whisper, "I want my daughter back." The steel came back into her voice for the rest, though. "I am *counting on you* to make that happen."

"Yes ma'am." He said nothing more. Just hung up.

Chapter Two

You coulda heard a gnat tiptoeing 'cross a cotton ball in that room after Bailey ended the call to the federal marshal. The enormity of what had happened, how the world had shifted under Bailey's feet, must have left her reeling.

It'd left him and Dobbs and Brice knocked on they keisters, too. Yeah, they'd suspected that Bailey was in the Witness Protection Program ever since the afternoon T.J. had met her and she'd introduced herself as Jessie Cunningham, and then all her identification said she was somebody else entirely. A thing like that wasn't no accident. Other things, too — the way she looked so lost and desolate whenever she seen a child, 'specially a little girl, broke T.J.'s heart. The longing he could see in her eyes, the mama longing. The way she never wanted to talk about her past, likely 'cause she was afraid she'd forget key details of it, since the whole thing was made up.

They'd all known she'd tell 'em the truth when she was ready to do it. So they didn't ask, didn't pry. Still, wasn't a one among 'em expected the whole thing'd come out all at once, like the foul stuff in a boil when you burst it. She seen that guy with the eyepatch in the background of the picture, and her world literally changed in an instant.

"You look like a woman who could use a drink." Brice managed to keep his voice easy and conversational. He was good at that stuff, being the sheriff and all. Course T.J. knew his insides had got to be tangled like last year's Christmas lights.

She turned to him, looked at him but didn't really, then focused and she come back from wherever it was she'd gone, and the energy whooshed out of her.

"Make it a strong one, like strong enough to dissolve the swizzle stick." She sank down into a chair as she spoke, and T.J. seen that her hands holding that phone was still shakin'.

"Wine'll have to do," Dobbs said, turning toward the kitchen to fetch it. "Unless you've got a bottle of hard liquor stashed away you've been taking nips out of without telling us."

"Wine it is," she said.

"On your way in there, turn off that TV. Ain't nobody much interested in the Cowboys anymore."

They'd been preparing to watch the Cowboys play the Carolina Panthers when Dobbs had whipped out the picture that changed the world. Bailey didn't care nothing about the game. She was a Pittsburgh Steelers fan, said she bled gold, and that might just be one of the things T.J. liked best about her, that she had good taste in football teams.

It was quiet when Dobbs left, the sound of the distant football game cut off in mid-cheer. They's each thinking they own thoughts, but T.J.'s mind had been runnin' way out there in front of his headlights and he was sure Brice's was, too. As he had commented on more than one occasion, you don't get put in Witness Protection for seeing somebody cheat in a chocolate chip cookie bake-off. Even so, the revelation that the folks who wanted her dead was Russian mafia, was a conversation stopper. T.J. didn't have to ask to know that Brice was thinking the same thing he was, tryin' to figure how they could help Bailey stay alive long enough to testify.

Right now, the girl was wound tighter'n one of them wires on a piano that play the high notes.

"Feel like talkin', do you? If you don't, that's alright, too, but you gotta figure we got lots of questions about all this."

"Don't feel like you have to—" Brice began.

"No, it's alright. I owe you guys … all the times I've had to … make stuff up, shade reality …"

Brice tried to protest but she waved him off.

"I owe you guys the truth. But more than that, I want to tell."

T.J. seen the coiled spring in her begin to relax just a little. When she set the cellphone down on the table, her hands had just about stopped trembling.

"I want to talk about … it's been years since … there hasn't been anybody … I don't know where to start."

"The thing that most interests me," Dobbs said as he returned with a glass of wine and handed it to Bailey, "is that little girl of yours. Where has she been all this time? Who's been looking after her?"

Bailey's face hardened a little.

"I'll tell you who *hasn't* been looking after her — Claudia and Drayton Cunningham, Aaron's parents." The briefest smile caressed her lips, then was gone. "He called them Cruella and Dracula. As soon as I met them …" She shrugged.

"Spot on?" Dobbs offered. "The Brits have a way of nailing a phrase."

"Yeah. Monsters in human being suits … no, that's not fair. A monster is a proactive creature and they weren't that. They were just spoiled and narcissistic, born of privilege, flicked their genealogical ashes all over the peons — that would be me, by the way — who couldn't trace their ancestry back to Charlemagne. She's addicted to prescription pain meds, he's either senile or has dementia or Alzheimer's or something. That last Christmas—"

You could see how just them words — the *last* Christmas — took her breath away.

"We went to their house for a get-together. It was awful. Both of them barely functional, his brothers and their wives trying to put a good face on it. It was the memory of that Christmas that caused my Meltdown in Memphis."

Dobbs settled himself back into the big, overstuffed chair next to the couch. "There has to be a story there."

Bailey reached down and scooped Bundy — an acronym for Bailey's Un-Named Dog — off the floor into her lap and petted him as she described how she'd been — she called it "interrogated" but he suspected it'd only seemed like that when you was on the receiving end — by the police, told she had to leave her whole life behind, stuffed into a car and hauled off to Albuquerque.

"We were just about to cross the Mississippi River in Memphis when it hit me. What if Aaron's parents took Bethany away from María? They didn't really want her, of course, wouldn't know what to do with her if they got her. But they would certainly see it as the 'appropriate' thing to do. The thought of the two of them and Bethany … I lost it. Started yelling from the back seat. Scared the federal marshals to death. They thought I was having a stroke."

Bailey had demanded that the officers pull over to the side of the road and contact the agent in charge, the guy she'd called today, Marshal Jordan, and when she got him on the phone, she started screaming at him.

"I told him Aaron and I had named María Bethany's legal guardian if anything happened to us. She was the sole heir to our estate, which would include considerable sums in life insurance payouts for Aaron. We hadn't gotten around to buying life insurance for me."

Bailey told him that if he didn't keep Aaron's parents away from the child, she would come back, get Bethany and disappear.

"I was not rational at all, making stuff up on the fly, told him I'd say I'd been in drug rehab and Aaron was taking his girlfriend to the Bahamas behind my back. Mikhailov would assume he'd killed all the witnesses to the accident that day so I wouldn't be in danger ... but there would be nobody to testify against him for the murder of Aaron. Nobody for the feds to put on the stand, point a finger at him and send the monster away."

She paused, thoughtful for a moment. "After I heard it come out of my mouth, I realized I could probably get away with it. I could have had my life back ... but the price tag on that was letting Aaron's murderer walk free." There was enough steel in her eyes then to filet a fish. "Not happening!"

"So ... what'd this Jordan fella do?"

"I never did find out — what did it matter? He gave me the 'I know a guy who knows a guy' line, somebody in the Justice Department who was a good friend of Drayton's. I'm guessing he hinted that it would come out in court about Claudia's drug use and the pitiful state of Drayton's synapses if María had to go to court to fight for custody."

Bailey paused. He could tell she was fighting tears.

"It wasn't such a big deal at the time … was only supposed to be for a few weeks … that became months … that became years. I was supposed to get my life back … *soon.*"

Then she just stopped fighting them tears, let 'em slide on down her cheeks.

She lifted her wine glass as if she were clinking it against their own upheld glasses.

"Here's to soon … which has finally, finally become *now.*"

Chapter Three

"So your little sister, María, has … Bethany." Brice stumbled only for a second before he said her name, said Bethany, but Bailey understood. The poor man — well, all of them — were trying to get their minds around a whole lot. And her having a daughter, that had to be big pill to swallow.

Bailey was stumbling a little herself, as a matter of fact. She was talking about this, actually tacking words onto the thoughts she'd only dared have in secret for the past two years. It felt awkward. And freeing in a way that felt like chains had dropped off that had been wrapped so tight around her chest she could hardly breathe.

Which was what it must have been like for María most of her life.

"Actually, she isn't really my little sister. Not blood relative or anything. We just made that part up, but she couldn't be any more my sister if we'd had the same parents." She looked from Dobbs to T.J. Yeah, they got that part. "And her name's not really María, either. But *we* didn't make up that part. She did that all on her own."

. . .

It ought to have been no big deal, and Jessie certainly makes it look like it's no big deal that she has been moved to yet another foster home. It wasn't a bad thing this time, though. She was glad to get out of the Phelps's house, where the foster mother stayed drunk all the time and made the girls do all the work. And the father ... yeah, he was the touchy-feely kind, though she got out of there before she became a victim.

So she's not upset to be here, except, of course, for the normal upset of having to uproot herself from everybody and everything familiar and start out fresh with brand new parents and siblings.

This time, she'd be the oldest girl in the Anderson household, the harried social worker told her, giving her the plastic smile that looked like she'd learned how from a manual. There are four boys, and one other little girl and she's only eight. Jessie is twelve.

The car pulls up in front of a white frame house on the corner in a pleasant enough neighborhood — older homes but well-cared-for. There's a big live oak tree in the yard with one limb that sticks out straight from the trunk low enough for a kid to reach, which explains why there are three boys now up in its limbs with another on the ground shouting at them.

The social worker doesn't stop to introduce her to the boys — maybe because she doesn't know their names, though she was the one who placed them here, or maybe because she's in too big a hurry. She ushers Jessie inside for a perfunctory introduction to the Andersons, then sits at their kitchen table filling out and signing forms while Jessie "puts her things away."

She hauls her suitcase into the back bedroom that she will share with the little girl. It's dark and she starts to flick on the light, but even though her eyes aren't yet adjusted to the darkness, she can see that there's somebody in one of the two half beds in the room. She's sitting propped up on pillows, holding a flashlight and reading a book.

Jessie can hear the little girl breathing from all the way across the room. Wheezing. The social worker'd said the child had asthma, but Jessie had never heard anybody breathe like they were dragging every breath in through wet weeds on the shore of the river.

"It's okay, you can turn the light on," came a voice from behind the flashlight. "I like to read ghost stories in the dark. Scary stories are creepier if you have the lights off."

Only that's not really how she says it.

"It's okay" … wheeze … "you can turn the light on" … wheeze … "I like to read" … wheeze … "ghost stories in the dark."

She only has breath enough to form a few words before she has to draw in another, like maybe there wasn't enough oxygen in the gulp of air before.

But the little girl doesn't seem to notice. Clearly, it doesn't bother her at all.

Jessie feels along the wall by the door for a switch and flips on the overhead light. A bilious yellow glow from a single dirty fixture in the center of the ceiling. Since the curtains are drawn, it doesn't make the room a whole lot brighter.

But in the glow of it, Jessie can see the little girl sitting up in bed behind the flashlight. She has black hair like Jessie's, but not shiny like Jessie's. A kind of duller black. Not like it's unclean or anything like that. It's just that it's almost curly, a wavy kind of curl unlike the smooth, light-reflecting curls that hang on Jessie's shoulders. The little girl has her hair pulled back in a ponytail and looks at Jessie with large brown eyes.

It's hard to tell what her … what's the word, yeah, ethnicity, the little girl is. With a name like María, coupled with the black hair, you'd think Hispanic. In fact, the social worker'd said she was Puerto Rican. But Jessie's not so sure. She doesn't look Hispanic. She has large features, full lips and a nose that if it were even a little bit bigger would be unattractive. Now, it's noticeable, but nothing more than that.

Jessie has been around the block a time or two in her dozen years *on the planet, and thinks maybe the little girl is Indian, or maybe Middle Eastern … Lebanese, perhaps. Or maybe Jewish.*

The little girl has only stopped speaking in order to grab a breath to continue.

"My name's María. What's yours?" Followed by a wheeze. But before Jessie can launch words into the wheezy silence, the little girl continues. She quickly establishes a rhythm of words, wheeze, more wheezing, more words, and after a while, Jessie forgets all about the wheezing that punctuates the unending flow of one-sided conversation.

"I was named after the convent, St. Mary's Convent, you know the one downtown where the nuns still wear those black dresses all the way down to the floor so the bottoms of their skirts are always dusty, and dust makes me wheeze and that's how they found out I had asthma — that's what makes me breathe funny — because the dusty habits, you know, made me wheeze. They named me María Moses."

The little girl grins at that, showing teeth as white and straight as something off a Crest commercial. She has dark circles under her eyes, too, and Jessie can't tell if that's because she's sick, or she just has them the way some girls just have dark circles. Like the Indian girl who lived with the Phelpses, who always got stuck doing the dishes.

"Yeah, Moses, like the Moses who lead the tribes of Israel out of Egypt in the movie The Ten Commandments *that they showed once in school and Charleston Heston was Moses and he got in a chariot race. Have you ever seen a chariot race?"*

Jessie starts to answer. But it is surprisingly hard to break into the rhythm of words/wheeze, words/wheeze the little girl has going. So Jessie just hauls her suitcase into the room and hefts it up onto the bed where the little girl isn't propped up on pillows. The bed has a chenille bedspread that's probably pink, hard to tell in the yellow light. The curtains on the windows are lacy and look well-worn. That's easier to tell because the light shining through the pulled shade beyond the curtains shows where there are holes in the lace.

"The Moses part is because of the basket that Moses's mother put him in — did you know about that? — and floated it down the

river, but it's not like some people think that she just put it in the river and hoped somebody'd find it but she hid in the reeds and was watching since she knew that that place in the river was where the pharaoh's daughter took a bath and she wanted her to find the basket with the baby in it. Isn't that cool! That's where the reed part came from."

The little girl actually paused after "the reed part" … wheeze … "came from."

"The reed part?" Those are the first words Jessie has spoken since she came into the room.

"Yeah, my last name" … wheeze … "María Moses Reed" … wheeze … "get it?"

Jessie isn't quick enough on the uptake and María blows on through.

"Reed … for the reeds. But the basket I was in wasn't made out of reeds like they made baskets out of back then but was a plain old white plastic laundry basket and my mother didn't just leave me in the basket and shove me off down the river. She left me a talisman so she can find me when she comes back."

Talisman is not a word Jessie knows, and she's pretty good with language. But she doesn't have to ask, doesn't have to break in because the little girl continues in her speak/wheeze/speak/wheeze rhythm.

"This." She holds out a necklace that Jessie has trouble seeing in the dark. "See how it's a broken heart?"

Jessie can make out that it's one of those necklaces that has only half a heart with a jagged edge. To symbolize a broken heart, she's always supposed.

"She left me with this half and she took the other half and when she comes back for me, she'll hold up her half and I'll hold up mine and they'll fit together and I'll know she's my mother and not some imposter."

Jessie has seen necklaces like the one the little girl has in stores. They're all the same, all have the same jagged pattern. It's not like they're so unique you could use one to fit into another half for identification.

And it has also not been Jessie's experience that there's a line of mamas waiting at the door with necklaces, trying to claim themselves a little girl by tricking her into believing they're her mother. It hasn't been Jessie's experience that there are any mothers at all out there.

But she doesn't say that. All she does say is, "Copy that." Then she opens her suitcase and looks around for where she might be supposed to put her things.

"You get half the closet." Wheeze. "But you can have more than half." Wheeze. "I don't use up all my half."

She says Jessie can have the bottom two drawers of the chest of drawers, too, and that there are plastic boxes that slide out from under the bed where she can put things as well. Also, there is a chifforobe in the hallway they all share, where she can put bigger things if she has them.

"Did you bring anything besides clothes?" Wheeze.

"Yeah, a few things. They're in a box in the car."

"Barbie dolls? Oh, please, tell me you have Barbie dolls. I do!"

The little girl points to a dresser where there's an opaque plastic container stuffed to capacity with Barbie dolls and their assorted paraphernalia.

"I'm twelve, too old for Barbies." Jessie doesn't like that she sounds snotty when she says that. The little girl is cute and innocent, and Jessie doesn't feel so threatened by her that she has to hold up a cold, hard exterior. "I used to play with Barbies, though."

She turned toward her bed and the little girl saw the back of her shirt.

"You're Bailey."

"Jessica Bailey. Jessie."

"I like J's, Bailey. Jessica Joy. Of course, it could also stand for Jumping Jacks. I can't do jumping jacks because I can't breathe. Or it could stand for Jack and Jill, or jingle jangle. But Bailey's good. We'll go with that."

And from that moment on, the little girl calls her Bailey. And Jessie calls the little girl María — sometimes María Tortilla — though she soon finds out María is no more her first name than Bailey is Jessie's. That — in fact, everything the child has said since Jessie walked into the room — has been pure fantasy. No truth in a word of it.

BAILEY SMILED AT THE IMAGE, remembering the little girl with tousled, unruly curls and a big nose, sitting up in bed in babydoll pajamas, reading a book with a flashlight.

"That's why I told the WITSEC name-thinker-uppers I wanted Bailey as a permanent first name. I knew I could remember it because it had been on the back of my jersey when I played sports in school, but mostly because it's what María calls me."

Bailey discovered at supper that night what the other kids called María — *Dawn.*

"The foster parents called her Dawn, too. I found out later the true story."

María's mother had been a homeless heroin addict who had gone into labor in a laundromat. She'd been living in a box in the alley next to the dryer vent to keep warm. When she'd started bleeding badly, somebody called 911 and they rushed her to the hospital. Placenta previa. She and the baby almost died. She told the nurses the baby's name was Dawn.

"And the nurses said she must have read that off a bottle of detergent, that it was a good thing she hadn't named the little girl Tide."

She had said her last name was McKessen. But that was the brand name of a kind of syringe, and it was printed on the side of each one.

"The nurses said the baby'd been named after soap and a needle."

She had listed her nationality as Puerto Rican, and that was noted on the baby's birth certificate, but she could have made that part up, too. Who the mother really was, what her real name was, nobody ever found out. She disappeared from the hospital before the baby was twenty-four hours old, left behind a heroin-addicted infant who had to go through withdrawal.

"With a real story like that, no wonder she made up a tale that felt more palatable," Dobbs said.

"Yeah, that's what I thought. So I called her María instead of Dawn. That's what she wanted, how she wanted life to be, and I figured she hadn't gotten a whole lot of what she wanted in her short life. She could at least have the name she picked. And she always called me Bailey."

She smiled again.

"So WITSEC didn't give me my first alias. I had one going in."

Chapter Four

THE HOUSE still smelled deliciously of turkey, even in the rooms on the second floor that weren't even open when the bird was cooking in the oven. Bailey knew that because she went into each one of those rooms every night. It was part of her ritual. She checked every widow in the house every night, making sure it was locked.

She'd started it when she got out of the hospital, with the memory of the man who'd come for her in the night, the one she'd avoided by hiding under the bed until Fletch came riding to the rescue in his siren-screaming squad car.

Oh, she knew a locked window wouldn't have kept that man out. He was the Beast, a man she and the other girls had beaten to death with rocks, fighting him in the dark of the coal mine. At some point, that memory had gotten tangled up with her memory of Gandalf from *Lord of the Rings* fighting the Balrog. How the old wizard — Gandalf the White then, not Gandalf the Grey — had described his battle to Merry and Pippin when he ran into them in Fangorn Forest, saying that he had fought the monster in the darkness falling through the mountain. She and the girls had done that, not falling through the mountain, but buried deep under one. And just like Gandalf, they had killed "The Beast."

As she closed the last of the upstairs bedroom doors and headed back downstairs to take Bundy out to do his business, she found herself standing in front of the mantel, staring in fascinated horror at the photograph that had only a few hours ago changed her whole life. She'd asked Dobbs to leave it with her, had set it on the mantel intending to leave it there. Now, she picked it up and carried it outside with her, shivering in the cold November air.

"Hurry up, go potty."

She hopped from one house-shoed foot to the other, clutching the picture in her hand. Then she carried it with her as she made a circuit of the bottom floor of the house, turning off lights, then climbed the stairs and got into bed, patting the sheet beside her.

"Okay," she said and patted the bed again. She was trying to teach Bundy that okay meant she was allowing him to do something; in this case, hop into bed beside her. She had long since given up making the little mutt sleep in his crate downstairs. He got the okay part, but the "leaping part" was still more than his little short legs could manage. So she reached down, picked him up, nuzzled him and snuggled him into the bed beside her.

But she didn't turn off the bedside lamp. It was almost like she'd been waiting for this moment all evening, like the whole time she was describing to Dobbs, T.J. and Brice what'd happened that had stolen her life from her, telling them about María and calling Marshal Jordan, she'd been itching for them all to go away, for time to stop completely so she could stare unashamedly into the depths of this picture. To "look the monster in the eye." To confirm what she already knew to be true. The man standing with a group of people behind her chair in the birthday photo taken at the Nautilus Casino was the man who had killed her husband. He had shot Aaron — twice. She had watched. She had *seen.*

It had sounded like a firecracker. An innocent firecracker. But even at the time that didn't ring true. Who sets off a firecracker in the pouring rain?

Jessie had been trying to talk to the 911 dispatcher, but she couldn't seem to form the words. No, there weren't any words to wrap around the reality of the dead baby in the car seat, his eyes filling with rainwater, his blue sleeper slowly turning purple as it soaked with blood.

"911 dispatch. What is your emergency?" the voice on the other end of the line had said.

On her knees behind the open passenger door because she'd dropped her phone, Jessie'd had to lean over and look around the door to see the street signs so she could give a location to the 911 operator.

When she did, she'd seen two men hauling the young man from the red car back toward the gray car they'd arrived in, while Aaron stood in the street yelling at the third man.

Bailey put out her hand and touched the image on the photograph, then yanked it away like she'd touched something foul, something so unutterably disgusting that you'd want to wash your hands and then slather them in antiseptic. The man in the picture was not wearing a fedora, as he had been that night. But otherwise, he was as Jessie remembered him. A neatly trimmed beard, white now instead of gray, that came to a ridiculous point at the base of his chin. An eyepatch over his right eye. It was the same. It was him.

Jessie had opened her mouth to tell the 911 dispatcher

that there'd been an accident at the intersection of Akron and Baxter Streets, but that was when she'd heard the firecracker.

And the scream.

The homeless woman they'd picked up at the bus stop — what, five minutes before? No, it hadn't even been that long — was screaming. Not just once but in a continuous shrieking wail. Jessie'd been confused. What was the woman screaming about? Then she'd looked back at Aaron. He was holding his belly, then slowly dropped to his knees like he was praying.

The man with the eyepatch had been pointing a gun at him.

He had shot Aaron. Pulled out a gun and shot him.

When she'd sat in the anonymous room at some equally anonymous police station some unknown time later, wearing the orange jumpsuit they put prisoners in because she had to get out of the wet clothes and that's all there was to change into, she had learned the name of the man with the beard. Sergei Wassily Mikhailov. The police officers had told her he was the head of the Russian mafia, an utterly ruthless monster who had gained power and retained control over the troops by putting his own personal spin on horror.

They'd played a tape for her, a recording an informant had made of Mikhailov.

She was lucky to be alive, they'd told her. Fortunate that Mikhailov had believed the homeless woman was Aaron's wife. They'd said "nobody looks for somebody they believe is dead." So Jessie had to stay dead. Which meant she had to let everyone she loved believe she had died in that wreck with Aaron. If she hadn't done that, Mikhailov would have killed María and Bethany.

So she'd stayed dead ... while the monster disappeared

and went back to Russia. She'd stayed dead for almost two years.

But that time in limbo was over now.

She again touched the face in the picture as words so vile she couldn't believe they'd resided somewhere in the recesses of her mind bubbled to the surface, words that if she spoke them, she'd have to cover Bundy's ears.

She continued to run her fingers over the face in the photo. The pointy beard. The eyepatch. The face of a murderer.

A murderer who was now going to *pay* for his crime. She would see to that. She would put that monster in a little room with a needle in his arm. She'd watch him die and forever after cherish the image of him burning in hell.

Bundy whimpered and she realized she'd been hugging him to her chest so tight she was hurting him. She set him on the bed, then got up and went barefoot down the stairs in the dark to the chifforobe that Brice and Dobbs had moved to half a dozen locations in her living room before settling on a spot by the front door. She opened the top drawer and took out the yellow minion blanket, and took it with her back upstairs.

It was the same blanket as the one Aaron had bought for Bethany when they brought the newborn home from the hospital, the one that became the toddler's won't-go-to-sleep-without-it blankie. Bailey had searched every store in Albuquerque looking for a blanket just *like* that one. Not *similar. Exactly the same.* When she found it, she'd held it to her face night after night, crying herself to sleep.

It took months before the blanket became a source of comfort instead of grief, before she could hold it and conjure up memories of rocking Bethany to sleep cuddled up in it.

Easing back between the covers beside Bundy, who was

crashed out on the pillow next to hers, she put the picture down on the nightside table and held the blanket up to her face. She closed her eyes and began to rock back and forth, singing softly,

"Somewhere out there ..."

She and María had a favorite animated movie they watched so often they could quote the dialogue as easily as making up conversations between their Barbie dolls. Then came the night Bailey thought of ever after as the Great Pumpkin Pie Kerfuffle. In a foster home, special treats were religiously regulated and dispensed in painstakingly fair portions, even if the portions were miniscule. That day, Mrs. Anderson had baked a pumpkin pie. But the boys got to it while it was cooling and devoured it — their portions and the girls' portions, too.

Suitable punishment was meted out, of course, but that was small comfort when the two of them had to go to bed pie-less.

Lying in the dark that night, they'd made up new lyrics for the movie's theme song.

When Bethany was born, Jessie'd sung the child to sleep every night with the altered version. She'd cuddle the toddler up in the minion blanket and rock her in the old platform rocker she and Aaron had bought at a yard sale — not because they couldn't afford a new one but because it reminded Bailey of the rocker that'd been in the Anderson house.

"Somewhere out there ..." Bailey sang softly, "beneath a pumpkin pie ..."

Chapter Five

"... someone's eating my piece, and I'll have none tonight."

María rocked the little girl slowly back and forth in the platform rocker, singing in an admittedly off-key voice, but Bethany neither noticed nor cared.

Yeah, an almost four-year-old was too old and too big to be rocking to sleep every night. And the rocker did not go with the decor of the room at all. But María had found it in a pawn shop and hauled it home because it reminded her of the chair in the living room of the house where she'd lived when Bailey came into her life.

"Somewhere out there, someone's pretending to cry ..."

The platform rocker had the same squeak/clunk sound as the one where she'd grown up, where she'd sat next to Bailey watching television or reading a book — wheezing. Always wheezing.

"Saying they didn't eat it, but that's a big fat lie."

Bethany snuggled up next to her. She didn't put her thumb in her mouth, which was a good thing. Instead, she sucked on one corner of the minion blanket with its tattered and frayed edges. María had read a great blankie-sucking hack in a parenting magazine at the pediatrician's office when she took Bethany in for her shots.

You took the blanket the kid sucked, and you cut off a small bit of it every day. Like less than an inch. So the little kid didn't notice. And eventually there'd be no more blankie and no more sucking.

María hadn't started the process yet. Bethany so loved that blanket, María couldn't bring herself to start chopping it up. The little girl was only three and a half, after all; she had a whole lifetime to live not sucking on the edge of a frayed blanket. There was no hurry.

"'Cept they did, too, eat it," Bethany cried, "didn't they, Mommy!"

Mommy.

Oh, how María loved hearing that word, though every time she did she felt a pang of pain for the sister whose death had given her the precious gift of her child.

That's how she understood it now. The universe had orchestrated their lives like that.

At first, right after the accident, María had told Bethany Mommy and Daddy had gone on a trip, but they were coming back for her, because she couldn't bear to speak the words that made it real. Bailey was dead and she wasn't ever coming back.

But as soon as María got over her own stunning grief enough to think about it, she realized she couldn't keep telling the little girl that she'd only be here with her aunt María until Mommy and Daddy came home.

At some point, she had to tell her Mommy and Daddy weren't coming home. At least, she thought she'd have to tell her. But as the heart-ripping days became weeks,

Bethany stopped asking when Mommy and Daddy were coming back to get her. And María didn't remind her.

After that, time just flowed on. María had dropped out of school that semester, spent every hour of every day with Bethany. Loving her and grieving the gut-wrenching loss of her sister.

It was that next summer, on Bethany's second birthday, that she had first called María Mommy. She'd had a party for the little girl and her nursery school chums in the park. All the mothers held parties in the park when the weather was nice. No cleaning ice cream off the floor, lots of toys and playground equipment to play with — the perfect setup. They could even hose the kids down if they had to before they put them in the car.

It hadn't been some special, grand thing. One of the other little girls asked if she could go down the slide and Bethany had turned those gorgeous blue eyes on María and said, "Swing me, Mommy, peeeease. Make me go high as the sky."

Mommy.

None of the other women even noticed. They knew María's story, but they'd probably never noticed that María had insisted Bethany call her Aunt María.

But that day, María had said nothing. Just took the little girl's sticky hand and walked her out to the swing set on the playground, not swinging her anywhere near "as high as the sky" but high enough to make her happy.

It had been as simple as that. From that moment on, María was Mommy. It had been a journey through grief and denial to acceptance.

María had intended to show the little girl a picture of Bailey every night — the selfie the "sisters" had taken the day they went to the beach, fried lobster red and peeled for weeks afterward.

She'd intended to tell the child every night before she went to bed that "This is your mommy, Bethany. Her name was Jessie, but to the two of us, we were Bailey and María. She was the best older sister any kid ever had and she loved you so very very much."

She'd meant to say that. But in the beginning, she couldn't get through the first sentence without bursting out sobbing. And that upset Bethany, so she strangled her sobs, told herself she'd try again the next night. And she kept it up for a time — weeks, no, probably a couple of months. The thing was, by the time she was able to get through a recitation about Bailey, how she was Bethany's mommy and had left her with María because she loved her so much, by the time she could say the words without choking on her own tears, the little girl was not much interested in hearing them. At first, she'd looked longingly at pictures of her mother that María had set out all over her apartment. But after a while, the child seemed to forget all about her.

And wasn't that better, really? Was it good for the child to keep reminding her that her mother was dead?

That couldn't be healthy.

Of course, María talked to Bailey about it, as she had always talked over with her every important thing in her life.

"Bailey, I want her to know she has a mother, that *you're* her mother."

"I'm not there, María Tortilla. You are."

"But I'm not her mother."

"Define mother."

"I am not … ugh, you know what I mean. I don't want her to forget you."

"She won't forget me if you don't forget me. But that doesn't mean you have to remind her every day that her mommy, who loved her very, very much, burned to a crispy critter in a car wreck."

"Bailey!"

"Truth hurts, but it's reality."

"But—"

"When she's older, you can tell her more about me, about Aaron, too. Don't forget him, Tortilla Head, I know he intimidated you."

"He did not!"

"He did so. He almost gave you a coronary when he told you we were going to name the baby Webster."

"Okay, he—"

"Just make sure she knows — *someday*, when she's old enough to understand and handle it, when she's old enough for the subject not to be painful for her, make sure she knows she did once have two parents who adored her."

And so she had allowed Bethany to call her Mommy. Because that was, after all, who she was. She was Bethany Cunningham's mother. Bailey would have said, "The truth hurts, but it's reality." So she admitted it. As she gave Bethany bubble baths and played with her in the sandbox and read her stories and ... she acknowledged that Bethany was *her* child, *her* daughter. *Hers*.

She looked down and saw that Bethany was sound asleep. But she didn't stop rocking. Not just yet. She loved the warmth of the little girl next to her. The smell of her freshly washed hair, listening to the rhythm of her soft breathing.

Not singing now, just whispering the words.

"And even though I know there's not a crumb left in my cup ..."

"… it helps to think that they'll get sick and chuck the whole piece up …"

Bailey sang the words with a feeling in her chest she hadn't felt in so very long it was almost uncomfortable, like a pair of shoes you wore every day for years … then lost them for a time. Your feet had moulded them and shaped them and the foot still fit. But the fit wasn't perfect anymore. Bailey's foot wasn't the same size and shape as it once had been. The shoe would have to reform around the new — and maybe improved — foot of the new — and maybe improved — Jessie Cunningham.

The shoe, the *feeling*, had a name. It was called hope. She would not be rocking an empty minion blanket for many more nights. She wouldn't let herself go there, wondering how long. That was being greedy. Just knowing that soon finally, finally really did mean *soon* was something for which she should be so profoundly grateful she had no room in her heart for selfishness or impatience.

Soon … soon, there would be a baby in that minion blanket.

No, not a baby. A little girl. Bethany.

"Somewhere out there, with my very last breath, I'll get mine and their shares and they'll just starve to death."

For a moment, just an instant, it was like she could hear an echo of the words in her head, as if some other voice were singing them, too.

Chapter Six

Fletch opened the door to Brice's office without knocking.

"… knew you'd want to see——"

T.J. and Dobbs came into the room before he got the rest of the spiel out.

The two men settled themselves in the chairs that faced the huge cherry desk that Brice hated to sit behind when he talked to people because he thought his big office chair made the whole setup look like a throne and that was not conducive to putting people at ease.

But T.J. and Dobbs didn't need to be put at ease.

Dobbs looked good, better actually than Brice could ever remember seeing him. After getting shot in the mine flood that'd almost gotten all of them except Brice killed, and then battling pneumonia from all the water in his lungs, the big man had probably lost fifty pounds. He'd gotten new overalls that fit, Brice was glad to see. Buying new clothes was at least some indication that he intended to stay a smaller size, not to put the weight back on.

T.J., on the other hand, did not look good. He had looked like he'd swallowed a gym sock yesterday when

Bailey started telling her tale, and the old black man looked the same today, multiplied by losing a night's sleep.

"You look like death on a cracker," T.J. said, looking Brice up and down. 'You even bother to go to bed last night?"

"That'd be the pot calling the kettle black."

"I come by my black honest. You so roses-red with all them freckles, you had to earn yours."

The deputy stuck his head in the door and asked if Brice needed anything before he left.

Fletch had taken the early shift that morning at the Best Buy in town, it being Black Friday and they'd advertised the first ten customers in the store could buy a flatscreen television for a dollar — knowing full well they'd have two hundred people parked out front all night ready to fight over the ten available television sets when the store opened at nine.

Fletch had been there. Now, it was going on noon, and the worst of the grabbing, shoving and mayhem was over.

"Going home to the family Thanksgiving celebration this weekend," Fletch said.

Fletch's family was wealthy, old money, who Brice admired for their willingness to accept the shortcomings of their only son — and Fletch's limited mental capacity was a shortcoming alright — and be grateful for his strong points. Grateful that he was a genuinely good man, an exceptional law enforcement officer, and even if he didn't make the law review at Harvard like the sons of their friends, he had already been decorated twice for valor since he joined the Kavanaugh County Sheriff's Department and was, in reality, Sheriff McGreggor's most valued deputy.

"Don't eat too much and I'll see you Monday."

When Fletcher closed the door, the room was silent.

The whole building was quiet, of course. All the offices in the courthouse, where the sheriff's department took up most of the first floor, were closed.

Brice didn't have to come in today, but he hadn't shown up to get any work done, at least none that mattered to Kavanaugh County. Just work that mattered to him.

"Don't keep us in suspense," T.J. said. "Spill. I can tell by the greenish tint of your face you got something to report."

The three had arranged to meet here today after a hasty conference on Bailey's porch yesterday evening. A con-flab called in response to the staggering revelation at their Thanksgiving celebration yesterday that the man who had shot Bailey's ... husband, who had separated her from her little girl and landed her in the Witness Protection Program, was standing in the background of the group picture they'd taken at Bailey's birthday celebration on Halloween.

Brice had had the roughest time with the "shot her husband" part. He and the others knew she'd been keeping her past a secret and had figured out — *duh!* — that her bogus name and identity had been produced in WITSEC.

But somehow, whenever Brice allowed himself to speculate on what her past had been, and that wasn't often, he'd never put a man into the picture. Stupid. Ridiculous when you looked at the woman. How in the world would a woman like that stay single? Still, he'd never allowed his mind to go there, and when she'd said the h-word yesterday — husband — it had taken all Brice's self-control not to let dismay show on his face.

Standing outside in the chilly air last night on Bailey's porch, the three of them had agreed without even discussing it that they needed to find out more than Bailey seemed to know about the man whose sudden appearance back in the United States had changed Bailey's life in an eye blink.

He had told the other two that he'd see what he could find out about the Mikhailov dude in the picture and had sent them a text this morning that he had news.

"Wasn't hard to find out about the guy." Brice leaned back in his chair, reached for the cup of cold coffee on his desk, coffee that had tasted like battery acid when it was hot, and just kept talking instead. There was a burning sensation in his belly that he knew didn't have anything to do with the coffee, but he reached into his desk drawer and took out a packet of antacid tablets and popped a couple into his mouth.

"That bad, was it?" T.J. indicated the mints.

"Worse than a couple of Tums tablets can fix."

Brice felt cold, and could hear the ice in his voice.

"He's what Bailey said he was -- a monster in a human being suit."

"Most everybody I've run into in the Russian mafia flunked 'plays well with others' in elementary school."

"Who did you call?" Dobbs asked.

"I had a list of people to contact, but I found out everything I needed to know from the first one. Our very own beloved FBI Agent Haruto Nakamura."

That brought a smile to T.J., though he and Dobbs had only met the man briefly when they were giving their statements about what had happened at The Cedars three months before. Statements about the nightmare spiders' lair that had been created by a diminutive first-grade teacher, whose split personality had turned her into a killer.

"Helpful, was he?"

"Very, as a matter of fact."

Actually, Brice had called the man's Pittsburgh office

expecting to leave a message. He didn't think Nakamura would be working the day after Thanksgiving. But he had answered his own phone, had replied tersely that he was "on a case," and Brice figured he had probably been sleeping his office, if he'd been sleeping at all, from the moment he'd been assigned the case. That's what he'd done in Kavanaugh County after he was called in to investigate the kidnapping of one child and ended up finding the bodies of three others, and Brice had almost died in the effort.

"I told him what I was looking for and he didn't want to know why. An hour later he emailed me a whole file, with an equally Nakamura-blunt note at the top in his customary understatement."

It said: "I understand Mr. Mikhailov is an extremely dangerous individual."

The next part — from a man like Nakamura — had taken Brice's breath away. Nakamura had added, "Be careful."

Brice handed the two men printouts of what Naka-mura had sent to him, let them scan through it.

T.J. ran his finger down the list. "Assault, assault with a deadly weapon, assault with intent to kill, attempted murder, murder, manslaughter, kidnapping. Not a flavor of homicide he ain't sampled."

"This rap sheet goes back thirty-five years," Brice said. "But he's always a bridesmaid, never a bride — only gets charged, never convicted. Half a dozen RICO charges, too, that came up snake-eyes."

"And RICO is …?" Dobbs asked.

"Stands for Racketeer Influenced and Corrupt Organi-zations Act," T.J. said.

"You're a sucker for acronyms."

"It's a federal law that gives bigger sentences to perps

whose crimes was 'a part of an ongoing criminal enterprise.'"

"I can see why the feds want this guy so bad," Brice said, then dropped the printed sheets on his desk. "And along comes Bailey, the goose that laid the golden egg."

"She did tee this one up for 'em, for a fact."

"Get him, his son and two of his goons in one sweep — yeah, she teed it up alright. He'll never see it coming, thinks he got rid of all the witnesses."

"You two keep talking like they'll all get the death penalty," Dobbs said. "But this happened in Boston and Massachusetts is a state that outlawed that."

"That's where the feds come in. These guys won't be tried in state courts, they'll face federal charges and federal juries. And the feds can, *and will,* impose the death penalty in this case because it fits the statute."

T.J. picked up the ball there. "The federal death penalty can be imposed if you commit murder with the intent to prevent testimony by a witness or a victim. That monster killed Aaron Cunningham and that homeless woman so's they couldn't testify about seein' his son run that red light and kill that lady and her baby."

"There's something else I don't get." Dobbs literally scratched his head, covered in a thick shock of pure white hair. "If he doesn't have any idea there's a live witness out there, why did the Witness Protection Program keep moving Bailey around to all those different places? Why would they fear he'd find her if he wasn't even looking?"

"If I had to guess, I'd bet those moves didn't have anything to do with her and Mikhailov," Brice said. "In the past few years, there've been security breaches all over the FBI. I broached the subject once with Nakamura and got shut down quick, but it's happened to other federal agencies, too. If hackers got into their systems, they couldn't take a chance that the locations of the witnesses they've got stashed all over who knows where had been exposed."

"Like when the credit card company sends you a notice and says you have to change your password because your account's been hacked," Dobbs observed.

"Yeah, like that, 'cept for Bailey — and I'm sure she ain't the only one — it meant a lot more than comin' up with nine digits, one capital, one lowercase, a number and a symbol. It meant uprooting and moving."

"And they never told her why." Brice thought about Bailey's stories of marshals showing up in the middle of the night and whisking her off to somewhere she'd never been with a different identity. "Suddenly, she was somewhere new, being somebody new — no wonder after a while it got to her and ..."

He didn't finish. He didn't have to, of course. They knew as well as he did, better than he did, actually, how she had spiraled down, hit rock bottom and then put Oscar into her brain.

Dobbs looked down at the papers. "So how does this involve us?" He must have seen the look that passed between T.J. and Brice. "It's a police officer thing, right? I get it. You guys have this telepathy going on and the rest of us don't—"

"It's just we both know that soon's they arrest these guys, Mikhailov will know there's a live witness. When you charge somebody with murder, you got to *name* who it is you's saying they killed. Soon as Mikhailov finds out the woman his goon shot and stuffed into the car *wasn't* Jessie Cunningham ... but everybody in Jessie's life *thinks* she's dead ..."

"He'll go looking for her." Dobbs connected the dots.

"Under every rock and bush, scrape the gum off the bottoms of the picnic tables."

"And the two of you aren't convinced the feds can protect her when that happens."

Again, Brice shot T.J. a look.

"Let's just say we plan to hang around close."

"Make sure them marshals dots all they i's and crosses all they t's."

Chapter Seven

Sparklers.

Little kids on the Fourth of July, waving them in the air.

The light is pointed and looks like it's sharp on both sides and jagged, tiny swords that burst off the fiery center, flash out into the air and vanish without so much as the sparkle of a soap bubble.

Not just one sparkler. A dozen. A hundred. A thousand. All exploding with pointy lights so bright you can't look at them.

Or maybe it's welding sparks. A cascade of them, like a waterfall flowing thick and full and then the light's extinguished and it's gone. Poof.

Static.

White noise.

The sound that is what no sound sounds like. The opposite of sound, if sound has an opposite, like dark is the opposite of light. But silence isn't the opposite of sound. When there is no sound, there is the buzzing noise of static.

Sparkles and static. Like sparkles are maybe what static looks like, and static is what sparkles sound like. Bailey's head is full to bursting with both of them.

But there's something on the other side of it all. Images, a scene, feelings and thoughts that she could experience if it weren't for the constant interference.

Images seen through a white mesh screen. Horror images. The flames of hell. Tongues of red and yellow, licking the air above them like a kid licks a lollipop.

Smoke. Thick white and black smoke rolls out ahead of the flames that are creeping toward her. The smell of burning fabric and melting plastic slap her a heartbeat before the heat from the flames.

She's scared, oh so scared — the feelings muted by the static, music playing behind a closed door. You can catch some of the notes and a hint of the melody, but you can't identify the song.

Dear holy God in heaven, don't let the fire … don't let me burn to death! *That comes through loud and clear.*

Her heart makes a loud crash with every beat. The rhythm of waves hammering the rocks on the shore. Pounding. Pounding! Then the rhythm speeds up, gets faster and faster. It's a mortar slamming again and again into a pestle — pulverizing, hammering into dust what little courage there ever was in her heart.

The powder of it is as fine as talcum. The breath that explodes out of her lungs puffs it off into the air, fine white dust that dissipates, becomes motes that are incandescent, sparkling in the flickering light of the flames.

Flames!

Fire! It's coming for her.

She tries to grab her fear, hold on tight or it will wiggle free and eat her alive on the inside like the flames will consume her on the outside. But she can't grab her fear any more than she can quiet her heart or control her breathing.

There is no way to tame terror! No way to silence the scream that's crawling up her throat on little rat feet, eager to leap out of her mouth. But she doesn't have enough air in her lungs to scream.

The fire is coming. And it hurts!

It's licking at her leg and it hurts!

Images grow bright behind the white skein of static and sparks.

The images are blurred because her eyes cannot seem to focus. She is dizzy, the room's spinning, flames in a circle all around, a lioness leaping through a ring of fire in a circus.

Her cheek is against something cold. A floor. She looks out across the floor where the fire is oozing toward her. Flames flowing inexorably along the floor toward her face. She sees double images. Then just one.

And she can't turn away, is so tangled up in the huge skirt — all that fabric! — that she can't move.

Her mind turns and bolts away, explodes with stored images like birds scared off the limbs of a tree, flying away in all directions.

The sound of a child giggling.

The smell of coming rain on damp wind.

A ballerina, balanced on one long leg as the other points at the ceiling.

Music.

Tickets for opening night of The Nutcracker.

The fire ignites the edge of one of the tickets — not in the real world where she is burning alive — but in her mind, where she is going insane. The ticket bursts into flame—

She finds the air to scream, a shrieking wail that shreds her vocal cords, but cannot express her agony. The flames have ignited her skirt and the fire takes it. She draws her legs up to her body, away from the flame, but seconds later pain consumes her leg and she tries to pull away but she is bound and can do nothing but scream and beg for death.

It hurts!

The liquid flame has reached a strand of her hair lying out in front of her face on the floor. The stench of singed hair and burning flesh. The flame travels lazily up the strand of hair, closer and closer to her face.

So hot!

The fire is so close that when she tries to look at it her eyes cross and her already blurred vision smears red and yellow and black and gray together. Her other leg is burning now, the whole dress has caught. *Flames are moving up her body, so it doesn't matter, nothing matters, life is agony, pain she never dreamed existed, beyond her capacity to express it with screams that are raking whispers up her ragged throat and out between her blistering lips.*

She begs for the mercy of death. Pleads to die.

Now, please!

She breathes heat and flame into her mouth, down her throat to her lungs.

It hurts!

The world is filling with smoke. Not the churning black and white boiling up off the flames but a gray mist that obscures. She can see through it the flames eating up the world around her as if they were dancing ballerinas in the mist, making it swirl and eddy around them.

The world goes dark then, not because she has left it but because she has been blinded by the fire and can no longer see the flames devouring her. She tries to make some kind of noise, explode sound out into the inferno that is killing her, but she can control nothing anymore.

She can still feel the all-over agony, though. But that is graying out, too, as if it were melting into the mist. It is melting. She is melting.

She aches for black. Black will make the pain go away.

And then it does and she is no more.

Chapter Eight

Light grew behind Bailey's closed eyelids.

It started as just light, but then it became a golden glow.

She didn't actually will herself to open her eyes. She didn't yet have will, voluntary control over her body or her thoughts. They were running on autopilot, programmed, she supposed, by some mysterious node on a complex strand of a single DNA module.

Open your eyes when you wake up.

That command was in there somewhere. You didn't have to think about it, so it must be pre-programmed. You didn't have to wake up from a restful night's sleep and then think, "Okay, open your eyes now." So it had to be automatic.

Then her eyes were open.

Bailey was looking at a ceiling somewhere.

Since there was no familiar ceiling tile, the one that had become her best friend when she woke up in the hospital after she put Oscar in her brain, she must not be in the hospital. Good. That's where she *wasn't*. But the understanding didn't do much to narrow down the geography of where she *was*.

It came all at once. Not in pieces and bits but all at one time. Reality downloaded. As instantaneously as turning on a television and the show materialized.

Bailey was lying on the floor in her studio. Lying on the piece of plastic Brice had put under her easel because she had such a nasty habit of dropping paintbrushes onto the floor.

She hadn't dropped these. She ducked her chin; this time she willed it and it was so. Lifting her hands up, she could see that she had paintbrushes in both hands. Then she *did* drop them in the scooting motion that propelled her off her back and to her feet, looking at a portrait on the easel.

It was a portrait with a table on the front, but very small, totally out of proportion. On the table was … not a bowl of fruit or even a vase of flowers. There was a butter dish and a sugar bowl and salt and pepper shakers.

Above the table was a window that took up the whole canvas.

Bailey turned and ran. Slipping and sliding in bare feet on the splattered paint on the floor, she bolted from the room, slamming the door behind her. Now, what was on the shelf by the door was a rubber ducky. A big one, bright yellow, that she'd spotted in the back of the attic when she'd been cleaning it for a garage sale that never happened. She had, however, snagged the duck and set it on the shelf in front of the studio door after the day she'd slammed the door so hard she'd knocked the ceramic London phone booth off and it had shattered on the floor.

The rubber ducky tottered in place for a moment before it, too, took a swan dive — well, a duck dive — off the shelf. It hit the floor, bounced a time or two and lay still. Bundy leapt back when it landed in front of him. Now, he was yapping furiously at it.

She hadn't had her adorable puppy when she'd broken the phone booth. T.J. had given her the puppy for her birthday the night she'd met the beautiful teenager who was doomed to die just the way Bailey had painted her — strangled.

Bailey'd been strangled along with her.

She hadn't been strangled with this woman, though, hadn't drowned with her as she had Macy Cosgrove, either. The woman whose portrait she had just painted, with brushes in both hands that she had just dropped, had burned alive.

Bailey'd left without looking at her face. She would have to look at the portrait eventually, of course, but it didn't have to be right now. Her legs were still trembly, knees felt like bags of water that might just whoosh out from under her at any second.

FLAMES SINGEING the strand of hair on the floor ...
The stink of her own flesh burning ...

SHE SHUDDERED. *It had hurt so bad.*

But, of course, it hadn't really hurt at all because she hadn't really been burned. Except, of course, she had, too.

Bailey had never let herself consider all the different kinds of real-but-not-real brutal deaths that awaited her out there in the future, the pain and horror she would have to endure. But a dark foreboding chilled her soul now, like a hawk overhead casting its shadow on a mouse in a field below.

She stood, frozen by horror.

Yap, yap-yap.

Bundy was still barking at the ducky and she started to reach down and pick him up, but she had paint on her hands and she didn't want to slather the dog in paint or he'd smear it on the furniture.

Stepping around the duck on the floor, Bailey headed back toward the kitchen. She'd been there, making herself a sandwich for lunch with winter tomatoes that tasted like cardboard.

And then … BAM. Nothing. The next thing she knew, she was opening her eyes, looking at the studio ceiling.

She often wondered about that part. The part between her real life, getting the mayonnaise jar out of the refrigerator and examining the last two slices of bread in the bag for telltale green spots — and waking up holding dueling paintbrushes. Did she … what? Suddenly hear the theme song from *The Twilight Zone*? Get all glassy-eyed, turn and walk slowly out of the kitchen and down the hall, her arms out in front of her, looking like a recently killed walking dead that hadn't decayed too much yet?

Or did she just look normal? *Look* normal, while inside all her breakers had blown?

With every step toward the kitchen Bailey came more fully back to herself. Moving her legs helped. So did the feel of the rug on the bottoms of her feet. She'd learned that.

Wonderful. She was getting adept at dealing with a psychic curse she hadn't asked for and didn't want. But she was improving. Shoot, give her another three or four dozen grizzly deaths and she'd be a pro.

She had no appetite for the not-very-good-in-the-first-place sandwich. Coffee. Black. Strong enough to trot a mouse cross the top.

She'd only taken a couple of steps toward the kitchen

when she felt a sudden incredible joy bubble up in her belly that almost burst out her throat as a giggle.

It was so startling that for a moment she had no idea where or wh—

Soon.

Soon would really *be* soon now.

BETHANY.

It was like every time she thought the child's name it appeared in flashing LED letters in her brain, leaving bright red shadows behind when the letters blinked off.

Soon, she would see her baby … her baby!

That realization shined a rosy light into every dark shadowed corner of her soul and lit her world with the glow of it. The light made even the horror of painting a future portrait easier to bear.

The portrait.

Reality punched her in the belly.

See-saw. Up-down. Portrait-Bethany.

How in the world did Oscar abide all the commotion and stay put, snug as a bug in a brain?

Who was the girl in the portrait?

And what on earth was all the sparkling and static about? That had never happened before. It was almost like … she had a bad connection.

Then another emotion, as powerful as the bubbling joy, swept through her.

Anger.

Why *now*?

It wasn't like Bailey was in charge or anything, not like she got to decide when she painted the monstrosities. The only time she'd ever *decided* to do one she had led her friends on a fast track into hell.

But … *not now.*

Whatever it was, whoever this girl was, Bailey didn't

have time, didn't have the — what was the word the geeks in the computer store used? — the *emotional bandwidth* right now to deal with the absolute horror of another future painting and the absolute joy of getting her life back.

Not at the same time.

No, not now.

Then a thought that was every bit as horrifying as the still-wet painting that now rested on an easel in her studio stole her breath. *You don't suppose the two could be related — Bethany and the mystery woman who had burned to death?*

Bailey detoured around the kitchen door and took the stairs instead, two at a time. She'd left her cellphone charging on the nightstand by her bed.

Chapter Nine

Soon's he seen Bailey's number pop up on caller ID, T.J. knew. Oh, they was all kinda reasons she might be calling him. Everything from how-can-I-keep-Bundy-from-eating-my-shoelaces to I-can't-get-the-lid-off-this-jar-of-pickles.

This wasn't that, though. He didn't know how he knew, never questioned things like that anymore. He knew why she was calling and that was the beginning and the end of it.

"When'd it happen?" he asked without preamble.

"I'm fine, T.J., thanks for asking. And how are you?"

"The paint even dry yet?"

"No."

"I'll be over directly."

"No rush. I was barefoot and I have to take a shower to get the paint out from between my toes."

"*Wait until I take a shower?*" T.J. was incredulous. "You musta painted a future where didn't nobody die, everybody was out in a daisy patch chasing butterflies."

"No. A young woman burned to death."

Then T.J. got it. Bailey was distressed over the portrait.

Of course she was! She always was. Just like his mama had been. Didn't nobody in the world 'cept Bailey know what it felt like to die and yet not die. To feel all the horror of whatever cruel form of death you'd just been subjected to, but then wake up fine — make that "physically uninjured" — afterward.

But her distress was painted on a different canvas today. Wasn't painted on the bleak terrain of her life tucked away in hiding in the Witness Protection Program, aching to hold the little girl she hadn't seen in ... what was it she'd said? Twenty-three months, twenty-seven days and five hours. Something like that. It was even more now.

However horrible that painting was, the artist was a woman who was looking out into a future where soon really meant soon. Where it wouldn't be long before she was reunited with her daughter and the little sister who'd been taking care of her. Even terrible as a future painting could be, it was hard to dampen hope like that glowing in your soul.

"I'll give you time to get your drawers on."

He and the others hadn't made some pact sealed in spit that they wouldn't tell Bailey they'd got together on Friday to discuss the Mafia Monster, which was how he now appeared in T.J.'s mind. Sergei Mikhail-whatever-ov was too hard to pronounce. But there was a tacit agreement among them that wasn't no need to bother Bailey with that kind of thing. At least not until they had to. "Want me to swing by and pick up a burger on my way?"

"I'm good. There's a sandwich made out of cardboard tomatoes downstairs with my name on it. But would you mind ...?"

"I'll call 'em, see if they can drop by, too."

Brice's cruiser was parked in Bailey's driveway when T.J. pulled up out front. Dobbs pulled into the driveway behind the cruiser before T.J. got all the way to the porch, so he stopped and waited for his friend to catch up. Had to, really. Soon's Sparky seen Dobbs's truck he went barreling out to greet him. Dobbs spoiled that dog rotten. Ever since he'd given Bailey the puppy for her birthday, Dobbs had taken to carrying doggie treats in his pocket all the time and whenever T.J. wasn't standing there with a disapproving look on his face, he'd give one to Sparky without making him earn it.

"Sparky, sit," Dobbs said. Sparks instantly assumed the bum-on-grass position, and Dobbs popped a treat into his mouth.

"You think I don't know that little performance was all for my benefit?"

Dobbs just grinned.

Bailey met T.J. at the door with Bundy on the end of a leash.

"Would you take him out? It's freezing out there."

T.J. was wearing only a long-sleeved shirt. Just how he did life, no matter how cold it was. Bailey, on the other hand, thought it was cold if the temperature dropped below fifty-five degrees. He sometimes wondered if she slept under the mattress.

Once he was back inside, they dawdled much as they could, finishing coffee or hot cider, talking puppy antics, house training and Black Friday shopping. Bailey said she'd spent all day Saturday cleaning the house, top to bottom, which was quite a task for a place that big. Of course, they all knew what she was doing. She'd have scrubbed all the sidewalks in the whole neighborhood to pass the time between now and "soon."

Didn't nobody bring up Bethany/the marshal/Mafia Monster because then they'd feel bad for not telling Bailey they'd found out even more awful stuff about him than they already knew. And didn't nobody bring up the portrait or they'd have to stop procrastinating and go look at it.

Finally, it was time, though.

"Let's go have us a look-see."

They filed like a funeral cortege down the hallway. It didn't blow by T.J. that Brice was right next to Bailey the whole time. He wanted to be there to steady her when the hammer blow of seeing the dead woman she'd painted hit her.

It was always a shock, but none of them was prepared for the scream.

As soon as Bailey got a good look at the woman in the portrait, she shrieked.

Dobbs jumped back like he'd been shocked. Both Sparky and Bundy yapped. Brice looked like he'd been slapped and T.J.'s black face likely turned a whole shade lighter.

It was a surprised scream, followed by a longer wail, where she grabbed her own upper arms, hugging herself, while she shook her head no.

"Bailey, sugar—"

"Noooo," she cried, looked beseechingly into their faces like they could do something to change what she was seein'. Pointing to the picture with a trembling finger, she spoke in a tear-clotted voice.

"It's my little sister — *María!*"

Then she put her head in her hands and as Brice folded her into his arms, she sobbed.

Chapter Ten

In truth, Brice had almost been expecting something like this.

As soon as T.J. called, that's where his mind went. It seemed a logical conclusion.

Oh, sure, neither Bailey nor T.J.'s mother had any say over when the compulsion seized them, grabbed them by the throat and forced them to paint a nightmare and live it as they painted. Maybe Bailey would have painted the same portrait this afternoon even if they'd never taken a birthday picture, never captured the murderer in the background.

But Brice didn't believe that.

Bailey's reaction to the portrait was closer to a total meltdown than Brice had ever seen, and he had been through some of the most horrifying times in the woman's life. This was different from all the other times, though. She'd been "somebody else" when she'd painted the other portraits, not a young mother on her way to reclaiming a life that'd been stolen from her in an instant. The "before"

Witness Protection Program Bailey and the "after" were different people.

And Brice was certain that during all the lonely months when Bailey's present was empty and miserable, she'd clung to memories of "before" — that magical time when her life had been what it was supposed to be.

Now the present had invaded that past. Had assaulted that magical time. It was an affront, an outrage, like finding a roach in a bassinet. That brutal attack on the world in a bubble called "before" had multiplied the impact of the horror.

After they'd gotten Bailey seated, gotten her calmed down, she stared at the portrait, her eyes devouring every detail. Unlike the first portrait she'd painted, it wasn't someone's whole body as Macy Cosgrove's had been. This one was just a face, in profile. The face filled the right side of the canvas, with smeared colors on the other side.

And it was out of focus. Details weren't crisp, just suggested. It was all … blurry.

The agonized face was recognizable, though the features were contorted by fear and pain.

"She's … you know, older than I remember." Bailey burped out a bleat of laughter. "Of course, she would be. I haven't seen her since … you know in almost …"

She took in a deep shuddery breath.

There was a lot about this whole thing that they needed to unpack, but Brice was aware that the others were doing the same thing he was — holding the situation and Bailey like a fragile piece of blown glass. Careful not to shatter it.

"Last night, I was thinking … I was holding the minion blanket …" She saw their blank looks but didn't explain. "And, of course, I was thinking that *soon*—" She stopped and a trembling smile tried to capture her face but couldn't make it through the minefields on the beach. "There's that word. It's been redeemed now, though. Actually means something."

She pressed her lips together. Closed her eyes. When she opened them again, they were clearer.

"I was thinking that soon I'd be rocking my baby again. Only, she isn't a baby. Bethany's three. Three and a half. And she's frozen in my memory as a toddler." Bailey gestured toward the portrait. "Like María was frozen as a college student. She's a young woman now."

She paused, then added in a whisper, "A young *mother* now."

Bailey rose unsteadily to her feet. T.J. reached out to hold her back, but Brice shook his head and T.J. let it go.

She approached the portrait and examined it. She'd examined all the portraits like this that she'd painted, but never with the expression on her face she had now.

"What happened to her?" T.J. asked. Brice shot him a look and he added, "Unless you ain't ready to talk about—"

"It was different this time and not just because it was María." Bailey paused. "But maybe that *is* why."

She seemed to be considering, for the first time, that María's presence was a possible explanation for … what?

"The whole experience was …"

Brice watched her struggle to tack words onto images and sensations that mere words had never been designed to describe.

"There was … *static* and I couldn't hear. I was looking at everything through … like an old black-and-white television set in the 1950s where the picture is all whited out and you can't see it."

"That's called snow, sweetheart," T.J. said. "We was still

getting that kind of reception here in the mountains when the government was landing a man on the moon."

"It was like I didn't have a good connection." She paused. "No, it was more like the connection was too good. Too intense. It made sparks, like a welding torch. I don't know how to—"

"Feedback," Dobbs said and everyone turned to look at him.

"You know that awful squawking sound — from every high school graduation ceremony in the history of mankind. It's caused by feedback. And it happens because …" He paused. "This is a whole lot harder than describing a coal mine using sugar cubes."

"You got this," T.J. said, trying to be encouraging, though clearly he had no idea where his friend was going.

"The speaker on the stage is broadcasting the sound coming from the microphone. But if you get the microphone so close to the speaker that it picks up the sound the speaker's broadcasting, and transmits *that* sound *back* into the speaker … it's called closing the loop. Or feedback."

"What's microphones and speakers got to do with—?"

"Bailey is 'connected' to her little sister the same way the two of us are connected." Dobbs smiled at T.J. "Can't explain or define it, but it's undeniable—"

"Yeah, they's a connection."

"These paintings transmit some kind of connection between Bailey and the person she paints," Dobbs continued, in what Bailey called his "made for radio" voice. "But if Bailey is *already* connected to that person—"

"Maybe it's creating something like feedback," Brice finished for him.

"That's the most convoluted thing I ever heard," T.J. said. "Scares the bejeebers out of me that I understand what you mean."

"It's hard to describe what was happening to her because … besides the sparkling and static, it was like she was …" She looked at T.J. "The world was spinning around her. Maybe she was knocked unconscious, was just coming to and was still woozy. Maybe she was drunk."

"Just tell us what you saw, even if the images don't make sense," Brice said.

Bailey stared at the painting. No, stared through it, trying to see what all the interference had obscured.

"She was so scared. So scared. She …" Bailey swallowed before she continued. "She was in a fire and could see the flames coming."

A fire. The red-orange smears on the left side of the canvas — those were flames! No wonder Bailey was horrified — her sister *burned alive*!

"A fire where?" T.J. asked.

"I couldn't tell where she was. Could have been anywhere. The fire could have started … who knows? A chimney caught the wall or candles caught the curtains, or something electric sparked … I don't know all the things that can start a fire. She was lying face down on a cold floor and she couldn't move."

"Tied up?" Brice heard the warble in his own voice.

"*Tangled up.* She was wearing a dress like a ball gown or a prom dress and there was all this fabric, a big heavy skirt, and it was caught around her and she couldn't move."

The scraps of a smile touched her lips.

"María loved to play dress-up, loved the princess-in-a-castle look. I'm not surprised she'd have a dress like …"

Her words trailed off as the soft memories became images with razor edges.

"And fire was flowing across the floor toward her."

"*Flowing* — like a liquid?" Dobbs asked. "Alcohol? Like liquor of some kind?"

"If it was liquid, it wasn't gasoline — not flashing or exploding. Just … she was lying there, watching it flow toward her face."

Bailey's whole body shuddered. Brice gave T.J. and Dobbs a should-we-back-off look.

"Maybe we ought to talk about all this a little later, after—"

"No, now. While it's fresh in my mind."

Like it wouldn't remain fresh in her mind for the rest of her life.

"She … she burned to death." Another shudder, smaller. But more intense. "Her clothing — the skirt caught fire, her legs started to … to *burn*. And then her hair."

She stifled a sob. "She was blind before she died."

That was a conversation stopper. The silence in the room was so heavy it felt hard to breathe.

"Was there anything about you … or Bethany?" Dobbs asked.

"She wasn't thinking about us. If she had been, I'd have recognized who …" Bailey stopped and turned to Dobbs. "Get out your phone. Google the Boston Ballet website."

While he poked at buttons, Bailey said that María had pictured tickets.

"I didn't see them clearly because she didn't see them clearly. Nothing she saw was clear, but I can picture them now. They were Boston Ballet tickets." She paused. "Which explains the dress, why she'd be wearing something that formal. That's how people in Boston dress for the ballet."

"Got the website. What do you want to know?"

"When is opening night for *The Nutcracker*?"

"Wednesday, December second, eight o'clock."

Bailey's voice was barely a whisper. "She has tickets for opening night."

"Just 'cause she's got the dress on don't mean that fire is Wednesday night. She coulda—"

"Could have been buying the dress or having it altered — a fire in the dress store. Or just trying it on in her apartment. All I know is she didn't get to use those tickets."

Today was Sunday. Bailey's little sister would be dead, *would burn to death* sometime in the next four days.

Bailey turned and looked into Brice's eyes, as if she'd read his mind. And maybe she had.

"Not if we stop it from happening," she said.

Chapter Eleven

FUNNY how sometimes you didn't even know what you were thinking until you heard the words come out your mouth. That blew through Bailey's mind as she told Brice, T.J. and Dobbs that she was going to Boston.

"I have to go. I have to keep María from going to the ballet — from putting on the dress at all, anywhere, anytime! I have to get Bethany and María and bring them back to Shadow Rock where they'll be safe."

The words had the ring of absolute truth to them.

"That federal marshal told you to stay put," T.J. said.

"And you think I'm going to call him up and tell him where I'm going and what I'm doing?"

"Bailey, you can't—"

"Who says I can't? The Federal Marshal's Service that has jerked me around for more than two years? Or a particular federal marshal, singular? Only one thing in the world matters to my good friend Bernie Jordan — getting a conviction and putting Mikhailov away forever. He doesn't give a rip about María. Or Bethany — or me either, for that matter, except where I serve his purposes."

It did occur to her for a moment to consider that the Jessie Cunningham who'd hidden from a monster under a dumpster wouldn't ever have considered crossing a federal marshal.

"Bailey, be reasonable." Brice's voice was infinitely reasonable. "You're supposed to be *dead*. You've been *hiding* for two years! It's not safe for you to show your face in Boston until they arrest Mikhailov, get him off the street." His words didn't move her half a centimeter off center.

"If I don't do it, who will? Who else could convince María to run? Brice, we've only got *four days*!"

She realized she was almost shouting, so she dialed it back.

"Look, right now is the only safe time for me to go. Mr. Sergei Wassily Mikhailov has no idea 'Bailey Donahue' exists. He won't have a clue his ticket's about to be punched until they arrest him, charge him with murdering Aaron. That's when he's going to start scrambling around, trying to figure out how they could make a charge like that stick since he eliminated all the witnesses."

"When they charge him, he'll know 'xactly who he's looking for," T.J. said. "They'll charge him with murdering Aaron Cunningham and some 'unknown person.' Maybe they've figured out who she is by now, maybe not. But either way, they ain't gonna charge him with murdering Mr. and Mrs. Aaron Cunningham — which is who Mikhailov thought he was shooting. He'll figure out the bait-and-switch then."

"And where will he go looking for said 'Mrs. Aaron Cunningham'?" For a heartbeat, no more, she *ached* for that to be who she was, wanted it so bad her heart might break with longing. Then she moved on. "Well, duh, her only living relative is her daughter. Who is in the care of her sister because nobody's seen Mrs. Cunningham since the day of the car wreck." Bailey felt a renewed surge of horror. "So if María manages to survive the fire, Mikhailov will kill her! She has to get out of Boston and hide!"

"You need to talk to Marshal Jordan," Brice said. "You know he's already started the flywheel turning. He has some plan in mind to keep María and Bethany safe."

"Safe from *what*? You're a beat behind here, Brice. The worst danger my sister's facing doesn't have anything to do with the Russian mafia. She's going to die in a fire before eight o'clock Wednesday night. How am I supposed to make Jordan understand *that*?"

Brice was losing his patience. It was fear, concern, but it was coming out as exasperation.

"You're just going to — what, drive to Boston, walk up to your sister's house, and when she answers the doorbell tell her you're not dead, but she soon will be if she doesn't drop her life and run off with you somewhere she's never been?"

"You got a better idea? That part's going to happen anyway, the telling her that the sister she thought died is very much alive."

"It doesn't have to be dumped on her like a bucket of ice water."

"What's a better way?"

"Just about anything."

T.J. stepped in between them then.

"Every time Bailey's painted a portrait, it was real. Real past or real future, or real right now — but real, a real Bailey couldn't possibly have known about but somehow it come out through her brushes. We all in agreement about that part?"

She and Dobbs nodded, Brice didn't, but he didn't argue the point, either.

"And every one of them painting's been different from

every other one." He pointedly looked at Brice when he continued. "Like that one she done of somethin' that happened eighteen years ago. Or finding them girls in that closet." He turned back to the portrait on the easel. "This one's unique, too, cause this person ain't anywhere near here, ain't in West Virginia and maybe never has been." He looked at Bailey. "The connection is *you*. And it ain't no 'normal' connection if there is such a thing. All them sparks and static, everything a blur."

He paused for a beat and the argumentativeness left his voice. Now, he was merely pointing out the obvious. "Just 'cause we happen to know the person in the painting don't change nothing." He turned back toward the horror on the canvas that Bailey couldn't look at or her knees would fall out from under her. "This is the same's all the other paintings. We got to look at it like that. This girl is gonna die unless we do something to stop it."

Bailey let out a little squeak of a cry, didn't mean to, it just popped out. María had less than a week to live, and Bailey was the only person in the world who could save her.

They were still talking about it ten minutes later when Dobbs came back into the kitchen where the rest of them sat nursing cups of coffee none of them wanted. Bailey knew what she had to do, of course, but the specifics of how to do it … she hadn't screwed herself up to planning that part.

"I chartered you a plane, a Cessna Citation CJ2. It'll pick you up at Triple C Airport tomorrow whenever you set it up. Takes about two, two-and-a-half hours to get to Boston."

Bailey was so thunderstruck — what was the British word Dobbs always used? Gobsmacked. Yeah, so gobsmacked she couldn't speak.

T.J. didn't appear to be nearly as surprised as she was. Either he and Dobbs had talked it over beforehand, or he just knew his friend so well there wasn't much Dobbs could do that would surprise him.

"It's easier that way," T.J. said. "I figure Brice here will want to be packing and that's a hassle when you fly commercial."

Yeah, they'd talked it over.

"Do I get a vote here?" She tried for flip and chipper and merely sounded like a wounded bird. She had to swallow a couple of times before she could speak. "I ... are all of you ...?"

"T.J. and I are going with you," Brice said, trying to make it sound like it was no big deal when any fool knew it was a huge deal. "Dobbs will stay here dog-sitting. Do you know where your sister lives?"

"You could ask Marshal Jordan," T.J. offered.

"Riiiiiight. I'll get right on that. The only thing he's ever said is that she's still in Boston. I'll have to find—"

"Already got a call in to Al," Dobbs said. "He's on it."

Al Zankoski was the private investigator Dobbs had hired to track down the identity of the little girl in the only painting Bailey'd ever painted "on purpose."

"Dobbs, you can't ..."

"Can and did. My nickel. I decide how to spend it."

"What time?" T.J. asked.

"I can't leave before noon," Brice said. "Tight squeeze even then, but I'll make it work."

"Noon it is, then," Dobbs said.

"But ..."

"Don't you think it'd be a better use of your time to start gettin' ready than to stand here sputterin' and stammerin' about how we hadn't all ought to do what every one of us done made up our minds our own selves to do?"

"Don't you have some getting-ready to do?" Dobbs asked her.

"Ain't you gonna be bringing home two house guests? I know you got enough bedrooms here to house—"

She parroted the rest of it for him before he could get it out "… all the blond men in the Norwegian Army—"

"Yeah, and their significant others."

"One of them's a little girl," Dobbs said. "How about we all go into town and get … well, whatever it takes."

"A fooffy bedspread, maybe," T.J. said, then added, "Do not take that in any way as an endorsement of foof."

"Toys," Brice said. "That little girl's going to need something to play with, don't you think?"

Bailey's mind was spinning then, with glorious thoughts she hadn't even dared to think. She was going to see Bethany … *tomorrow*! The thought took her breath away so totally she could merely sit down in a corner somewhere and grin her gums dry.

The guys were right, she needed to get stuff. Lots of … well, things. She'd make a list.

She glanced up and saw them grinning at her and she grinned back.

Chapter Twelve

María McKessen looked out through the window at the huge flakes floating daintily on the wind. Big fat ones that quickly stacked up knee deep. Forecasters were predicting a blizzard. Every time it snowed, they predicted a blizzard, but she'd still gotten a call this morning not to come into work today at Damron's Dress Store. And María needed the money! This was one of only three shopping weekends left before Christmas and this seasonal job would pay for all the Christmas presents she'd been putting on layaway.

And there was the dress.

Just the thought of it put butterflies in her belly. It was so *beautiful*. A smile lit her face when she pictured the flowing gown she'd bought — using her employee discount or she never could have afforded it — to wear to *The Nutcracker*.

Well, María would just have to stop by the store tomorrow and pick it up. Maybe get the alterations lady, whose name she could never remember, to fix the hook that was missing an eye.

"Mommy, wook!"

She turned and saw that Bethany had padded into the living room and was standing beside her, looking out the window at the blur of white. It'd been snowing when María'd put the child down for her afternoon nap, but not like *this*.

The look of joy and awe and wonder on the little girl's face — María wanted her to see the world that way every day for the rest of her life.

"The snow is falling out of da sky up on top of da world."

The child's voice sounded just like the ringing of tiny bells. But not just bells, bells high up in the belfry of some chapel in some mountain range where the air was clear and pure and cold.

And then it didn't matter anymore that María wouldn't be able to do all the half dozen items on her to-do list. It was snowing and Bethany loved snow.

"Do we have any carrots?"

"Carrots?"

"For da snowman's nose. You have to use a carrot so he'll look like Frosty an' we need a hat an' a pipe."

Bethany was a bright, verbal child who had never spoken in baby talk, and though she was a fount of delightful mispronunciations of words and malapropisms, she spoke clearly. María liked to think that it was because she'd never spoken baby talk to the child. Had spoken clearly and distinctly.

And had spoken a lot of words.

Like, a lot.

It was what she'd always done because there were so many other things she couldn't do.

Bailey had always understood that.

. . .

BAILEY IS SITTING *in the middle of the living room floor, folding the towels from the huge pile of laundry Mrs. Anderson dumped there, still warm out of the dryer. María doesn't think it's fair that Mrs. Anderson always makes Bailey help her do things but the boys get to do whatever they want and never have to help.*

But Bailey says they would just mess it up anyway, whatever it is, and then she'd have to clean up after them so it was easier to do it right the first time.

María is sitting on the couch, propped up with pillows so she can see out the window, where the boys are busy building a snowman in the front yard. And throwing snowballs at each other.

"Why would you want to build a snowman?" Wheeze. "It's fat and white and" … wheeze … "just stands there." … Wheeze. "I'd make a snow castle!" Wheeze. "With ice turrets" … wheeze … "and a frozen moat—"

"What good would a frozen moat do?" Bailey is practical.

"There'd be guard walruses" … wheeze … "to keep people out." Wheeze. "It would be so beautiful."

She hadn't intended the longing to leak into her voice with that last part. She kept longings to herself, all the wanting of things she couldn't have, the ache to do things she couldn't do. Those wantings belonged to her and she kept them close to her heart and secret. But Bailey is so safe, sometimes they pop out when Bailey is around.

She stops folding the laundry.

"I have an idea." Then she gets up off the floor and runs into the kitchen, and María can hear things banging around in there, cabinet drawers opened and closed. Mrs. Anderson has braved the snow to go to the store for the extra food they'll need since school has been cancelled. Mr. Anderson is out shoveling the sidewalk.

Bailey appears in the kitchen doorway.

"Come and see."

Everybody knows it's hard for María to move around. It's not like she can't walk or anything like that, but movement takes air and she has to do everything slowly so she doesn't run out.

María gets up off the couch carefully. She loves it that Bailey doesn't come rushing over to help her like the "gushers" do. Gushers are people who make over her because they feel sorry for the "pitiful little thing who can't breathe." María hates gushers. Bailey just stands at the kitchen door, waiting.

When María makes it to the doorway, Bailey moves out of her way and points to the big double sink. It is piled high with crushed ice from the refrigerator ice maker, and from chunks of the fuzzy ice Bailey must have pried off the walls of the chest freezer.

"We're going to make an ice castle," Bailey says, and María sees where she has pulled up a tall stool in front of the sink for María to sit on. "We'll have to be fast, because it's going to be melting while we're building."

The whole experience is a glorious disaster, of course. The crunchy ice doesn't stick together at first … until Bailey thinks to go outside and bring in a bucket of snow to use as glue. Their fingers get so cold they can't move them … until Bailey thinks to get them both a pair of rubber gloves from under the sink, and sets a bowl of warm water on the countertop so they can warm their fingers in it.

The crunchy, not-sticky-enough ice cannot be transformed into the magnificent structure María envisioned, not even when they add ice cubes from the other side of the ice maker to build the walls. As soon as they construct anything fanciful, it either falls apart in seconds or begins to melt into nothingness. The best they have to show for their efforts by the time their fingers are too cold to keep working is a kind of lumpy mound of frozen ice-and-snow. One turret remains standing. You can't really tell it's a turret, but they call it that because that's what they were trying to build. The wall around the castle, made of ice cubes, is the most discernible feature of the structure. The rest … not so much.

Mr. Anderson comes stomping into the kitchen in his sock feet, having taken off his snow boots in the mud room. His cheeks are rosy from the cold and his nose makes María think of Rudolf the Red-Nosed Reindeer.

"*Whatcha girls doing?*" *He's a nice man. Too nice, really, so he is unable to command the respect of the herd of boys that Mrs. Anderson has to keep in line. He allows the household to be too loud, the boys to be too rowdy and the symphony of constant bickering to reach such proportions María sometimes wants to scream "shut up" at the lot of them.*

Bailey is standing behind María so María can't see her. But she can tell Bailey is mouthing something to Mr. Anderson.

"Why, that's an ice castle, isn't it?" he says and wins a permanent place in María's heart for the effort.

"It's where the ice queen lives," Bailey says.

"And the ice fairies." Wheeze.

María turns back to the rapidly dissolving not-structure and pronounces grandly, "But then the Meanies from the North" ... wheeze ... "come to plumber—"

"Plunder," Bailey whispers.

"Yeah, that, plunder" ... wheeze ... "and they destroy the castle" ... wheeze ... "and melt the queen and the fairies."

María reaches to the back of the sink and pulls out the spray nozzle on its black cord, points it at the castle and pushes the plunger. Water sprays out in a whoosh and whatever features the pile of ice might ever have had dissolve instantly and it becomes a formless pile of slush.

As María squirts water on the castle, Bailey pronounces solemnly: "And all the Meanies from the North grew up to be firemen."

María giggles. It's hard to laugh when you can't breathe and it comes out as a gulping, gasping sound that only resembles laughter enough that the people who know her no longer think she's choking to death. It wasn't an exceptionally clever remark, but María continues to cough and gasp out merriment anyway. It bubbles up from that place in her heart where she treasures a love for Bailey that she has never felt for anyone else in her whole life.

. . .

"Mommy?" María realized that Bethany had been tugging on the hem of her shirt. "Can we build a snowman?"

Bethany had just gotten over a really nasty ear infection and María wasn't keen on letting her play outside in the cold. She got down on one knee and looked into the child's eyes, such a startling shade of blue, the color of robins' eggs.

Pushing the child's black curls back behind her ears, she managed to keep her voice level and cheery. "I have a better idea. We're going to build an ice castle."

Chapter Thirteen

BAILEY'S FINGERS were instantly cold.

She was standing just inside the door of Walmart, waiting for Dobbs to park the Jeep, matching tooth for tooth the Walmart greeter's smile that clearly had been unloaded off a truck at the beginning of his shift.

All of a sudden, her fingers were freezing.

Not just cold as in it's-a-cold-day-and-you're-not-wearing-gloves.

Cold as in you-have-a-handful-of-ice.

Biting, numbing, painful cold.

She stared at her hands in disbelief for a moment, heard a bleat of sound, a burst of static and then the sensation was gone.

Dobbs and T.J. approached and she told them what had happened.

"I connected to María." There was a mixture of joy and terror in the words. Joy, of course, because she was somehow connected to her beloved younger sister in a way she'd never been when they were children, no matter how close they'd felt.

And terror because the connection was born of the portrait she had painted of María dead.

The image stole her breath and it must have shown on her face.

"How about we go have us a Starbucks and you tell us 'bout it," T.J. said.

"There is nothing so wrong with me that I'd have to suffer through a Starbucks coffee to remedy it." Coffee was coffee, for crying out loud. Why would you pay some ridiculous amount of money for it? She supposed it was so you could walk around sipping from the moon-face cup and the world would know you were cool. Dobbs loved Starbucks, though, so she never belabored the point.

"My fingers got cold. You know, like how I smelled breakfast that morning after I painted Macy, because *she* was smelling bacon and coffee. This was feeling instead of sight or smell."

Then it dawned on her what the cold fingers meant.

"María's building a snowman ... *with Bethany*."

The thought knocked the wind out of her. She had not allowed herself to think of Bethany so freely, or María either for that matter, in all these months. She'd walled off those thoughts because if she wallowed in them, in the pain of them, the loss they conjured up, then ...

Well, that's where Oscar had come from.

She had breakers on the circuits of her brain, and when her mind went to images of her daughter or dreams of her or fears for her, the breakers shut the circuits down.

That was the only way she could function.

But she didn't need the breakers anymore, didn't need to rein in her thoughts of her little girl. Because she would get Bethany back soon, and soon was a real time — *tomorrow!*

"Well, somethin' just lit you up like you just swallowed a flare. What was you thinkin'?"

Her smile was so wide, she had trouble talking around it. And around the laughter that bubbled up for no reason, like she'd just heard the most hilarious joke.

Joy. Pure joy.

"I was just thinking of Bethany. I never do that. If I did—"

"Yeah, Oscar," T.J. said.

She shouldn't have been surprised by his intuitiveness, but she somehow always was.

"Is everything I think and feel written on my forehead?"

'Nah." He took her elbow and began guiding her into the store. "Not on your forehead."

"In the sky," Dobbs said.

"In purple," T.J. said.

"In Hebrew," Dobbs concluded.

The toy department caused another crisis, not as joy-filled, more tinged with pain.

She looked up and down the aisles stocked with every imaginable thing any kid had ever wanted to play with, or didn't want to play with but some marketing director at Hasbro had figured out they could be manipulated into wanting to play with if the ad spend on the right kiddie television shows was adjusted properly.

"I don't … I have no idea what a three-year-old … three-and-a-half-year-old little girl might want to play with. What do I get?"

Dobbs looked down an aisle filled from floor to ceiling with dolls. "Just get her one of everything."

Bailey rolled her eyes.

"I don't want to overwhelm the child. And it matters

what kind of child she is. I don't even know. Is she a girly girl, who loves lace and pink and taffeta and Barbie dolls? Or maybe firetrucks. Or superheroes. Or dinosaurs. Or unicorns. Or …

Bailey was on such a rollercoaster of emotions she barely had time to feel something before she got hammered with the next feeling.

"You said María loved Barbie dolls so she probably got some for Bethany." Dobbs was ever the voice of logic and reason.

"Point taken. Barbie dolls it is."

Then she gazed with growing wonder/horror at the selection of Barbie dolls, clothing, accessories, vehicles, houses …

How in the world …?

T.J. took over then.

"This here one." He picked up a Barbie that didn't look in any way unique.

"Why that—?"

"'Cause you gotta pick somethin' and if you stand here looking at everything you ain't never gonna pick nothin'."

He dropped the doll into the basket and turned toward the accessories.

"Okay, we got the doll. Now, what do you want to dress her in so she's wearing somethin' 'sides her skivvies?"

And so it went. T.J. placed another Barbie doll in the basket.

"You don't want this here one to get lonesome, do you?"

And then a third.

"How they gonna have a Barbie party if ain't but two of 'em?"

Bailey managed to slam the door on memories of the

Barbie dolls that a little girl had left lying in the grass in a park …

When they had the group of dolls properly clothed, the basket was filled to the top.

"Now, don't we need something for them to ride in? Like one of them campers or vans with flowers on it? You can't let 'em walk wherever they're goin', not in them shoes."

"Enough's enough. We'll start here, and when we find out what she likes after she gets here—"

BAM, took her breath away again.

After she gets here.

After I meet my little girl.

"Oh, T.J., in just a few hours I …"

And all at once Bailey was scared to death.

"What's wrong?"

Dobbs didn't have to ask.

"You've progressed from thinking that you don't know your little girl to realizing she doesn't know you, either. She'll have no idea who you are. That's a scary thought."

It was indeed scary.

T.J. took her by the shoulders, turned her around and marched her out of the toy department toward house-wares. "Let's go find us some foofy sheets."

Back at home, the guys carried the purchases into the house and Bailey fished around in the sacks for the sheets she'd selected. They were from some movie about mermaids that she hadn't seen. True fact: Bailey Donahue had not seen a single movie since … Not in more than two years. She had some catching-up to do.

She left the guys downstairs unloading and throwing away boxes and sacks while she went up to put the sheets on the bed in … *on the bed in Bethany's room.*

She would take Bethany with her to the store and let

her pick out the curtains and the bedspread and if she didn't like the sheets, Bailey would get new ones she did like.

The smell of spices. Something cinnamon. And cookies baking. Chocolate chip.

... laughing all the way. Bells on bobtails ring, making spirits bright ...

The music was so loud and clear Bailey actually turned to look, though she knew even as she turned that she'd find no source for the music here.

The music wasn't in the Watford House. The music was in Bailey's head. And it was in Bailey's head because somewhere in Boston, *Maria and Bethany* were listening to that song.

~

"... a sleighing song tonight, ooooooooh." Singing was not María's strong suit, but what she lacked in skill she made up for in gusto.

Come for the off-key, stay for the tone-deaf.

Bethany sang along with the melody. She mispronounced the words but carried the tune better than María.

"Gendilc bells, gendile bells, gendile all the waaaaa."

As the little girl sang, María looked into the box of Christmas decorations and picked out a shiny gold one in the shape of numbers: 2012. Across the front it said: Baby's First Christmas. It had been in the box of Bailey and Aaron's Christmas decorations. María had cried over every one when she finally managed to go through Bailey's things.

When she looked at it now, her eyes welled with tears and she gave Bethany a squeeze before she hung the ornament on the artificial tree she had just set up in front of the apartment window.

"That smells good, Mommy. Is it cookies yet?

"Did you hear the ding on the timer?"

"No."

"Then it's not cookies yet."

"Soon?"

"Soon."

María flattened out a tree branch that'd gotten bent in the box.

"Would you like to go out into the woods and cut down a real tree next Christmas?"

Bethany's face — her whole face — beamed when she smiled.

"With a axe?"

María hadn't thought it through that far. An axe would be unwieldy, and she might end up chopping her foot off with it. Or Bethany might cut—

"No axe. Next Christmas, we will go to a tree farm and get the man who runs it to cut down whatever tree we pick."

"Trees grow ona farm? Like chickens?"

"Yes, but the trees don't lay eggs."

"Acorns not tree eggs?"

"Come to think of it, I guess they are."

The "real tree" was only one of the plans María had for after she graduated in June from Boston University. Anthropology/archaeology double major — because she was utterly fascinated by ancient civilizations. English minor because she cherished deep in her heart a yearning

to become a writer. And no, her degree didn't offer particularly stellar career opportunities. There was a reason why
the best place to find an archaeologist was in fiction, and
the Indiana Jones slot was already filled. She'd picked those
majors in the beginning with an eye toward finding something more practical down the line, but she'd been too
occupied with Bethany in the past two years to do more
than stay the original course. Bethany's financial future was
assured by the trust set up for her from her parents' estate.
So María wasn't being an irresponsible parent by picking a
less lucrative career path. In the past couple of months,
she'd been giving serious consideration to applying to law
school. With a 3.9 GPA, she'd likely make the cut and next
fall, Bethany would be four, ready for preschool.

"Look, Mommy, da angel's wing is broke." The plastic
angel María'd purchased at a yard sale last summer had
been on its last leg … well, last *wing*, then, but it was the
one Bethany'd picked out so María had bought it anyway.
"We needa take it to da doctor — for a shot."

"All she needs is a little superglue and she'll be good
to go".

María realized that her life plans were myopic,
centered around her and Bethany exclusively. But María
didn't have time for anybody else in her life. She'd had an
on-again off-again boyfriend when Bailey'd been killed,
and he'd faded into the woodwork then. Actually, she
hadn't even realized he was gone for months.

There had been other men along the way, but she
hadn't been interested. She'd had her hands full with
school and a toddler. It wasn't hard to stay single when you
were that busy. Besides, she was self-aware enough to
realize she wasn't a particularly pretty woman. She had a
nice face, nothing to write home about — her nose was too
big. She was nothing like the beauty Bailey had been. It

was almost like pheromones and insects. She wasn't attracting the attention of the opposite sex because she wasn't looking.

But someday. Yeah, maybe there'd be a man in María's life someday. After all, Bethany needed a daddy.

Chapter Fourteen

BRICE PULLED up at the Watford House a little before noon
on Monday. He was driving his own car, not a sheriff's
department cruiser, but he was still in uniform.

"You're not going to change clothes?"

"Planned to, but it got crazy. I've got a go-bag in the
trunk. Jeans and a t-shirt — that'll do.

"A t-shirt? Do you know how cold it is in—?"

"We're only going to be there a few hours."

"That's the *plan*. But who knows what'll—"

"I'm good." He dismissed the subject before she could
pursue it. She'd brought what she affectionately referred to
as her Nanook of the North coat.

"Do you know what you're going to say to her?"

"Kinda sorta. I was hoping maybe we could all talk
about that on the way."

The Cessna Citation CJ2 was sleek and comfortable.
Bailey didn't even want to think about what it had cost
Dobbs to charter it. As soon as the plane reached cruising
altitude, T.J. tacked words onto the thoughts that had been

chasing their tails around and around in her mind for hours.

"How you gonna tell your sister you still alive? You decided yet?"

Al Zankoski had texted Dobbs the address of María McKessen. Wouldn't even charge him for the information, said Dobbs could have found it with his phone. It was in a nice neighborhood with big red-stone houses that'd been converted into apartment buildings, usually three up and three down, but occasionally a single apartment had a whole floor.

Bailey shrugged and tossed the ball back at him.

"How do you think I ought to break it to her?"

"I can tell you what I think that federal marshal, the Jordan fella, was plannin' to do, the plan you're doin' an end run around right now."

Bailey gave him a be-my-guest gesture.

"If I's him, soon's I got that Mikhailov behind bars I'd pay a visit to your sister, explain that I was a marshal with the Witness Protection Program … and then spill it. It would be a shock, sure, but not as shocking as opening the door and finding you on the other side of it."

"The Marshal's Service, the badge — he could soften it." Brice had either come around to her view of the Boston trip or — more likely — resigned himself to the futility of arguing. "But he's not here and *we* are. Say one of us goes first to warn her — she'll think we're crackpots at best and nut-cases at worst and she might even call the police."

He was right, of course. He looked at Bailey when he continued.

"The only person who can approach María who isn't suspect is *you*. Shocking as that will be, it's better than the poor girl thinking somebody's playing some cruel joke on her."

No one spoke then, just looked at her.

"I can't think of any better way to do it, either. I'll just … *show up*, and hope I don't scare her to death." She took a breath. "And scare Bethany to death, too."

"Then you just gonna tell her, oh by the way, that she's got to drop her life and hop on a plane with you back to West Virginia — before nightfall?"

Bailey bristled. "What *else* can I do when I know—?"

Brice held up his hand.

"This is that battle plan that's going to fall apart as soon as the first shot is fired. If someone I knew and trusted told me there was a bomb in my house — I'd drop everything and run! If Bailey can convince her there's real danger … of course she'll run."

"Yeah … but truth is Mikhailov is a red herring here. Course it ain't safe for her to stay in Boston once Mikhailov finds out about Bailey, but right now, he don't know. If we b'lieve them portraits — and we all do — then *we* know it ain't Mikhailov's gonna kill her. She gonna die in a fire. Ain't no way in the world to pour out a story like that and x'pect somebody to swallow it all in one gulp."

Bailey had already figured out that part.

"Mikhailov, Witness Protection Program, *Bailey's not dead* — those are big enough body slams. The painting … nope, not going there. That's a story for another day. I'll convince her that she — *and Bethany* — are in so much danger from Mikhailov that she has to run."

They all sat back in their seats then, thinking their own thoughts. Bailey's bounced from María back to Bethany and back to María again like a tennis match.

If Bailey let herself consider that in — no, she absolutely

would *not* look at her watch again! She had looked at it so often today she was wearing the numbers off the face. In some *indefinite amount of time*, a few hours, she would see Bethany.

"... and I put the peaches she likes in the diaper bag with the rice cereal because there's only one brand ..."

Jessie is babbling. She knows she's babbling but she can't seem to stem the tide of words. Because when she stops talking, she's going to have to hand Bethany to María, turn around and walk out the door without her and she keeps backing up from that moment like drawing her hand away from a flame.

"Jessie, we need to go."

"She puts everything in her mouth now, everything she finds on the floor, so—"

"Look around, Bailey. I've stripped the whole apartment bare. I've put those plastic cap things in all the outlets, and those other things on the cabinet drawers in the kitchen so she can't open them, and there's not an object anywhere on the floor in this whole apartment smaller than a sperm whale."

María grins, the smile Jessie loves, showing her television-commercial white teeth. When she smiles like that, she's beautiful.

"I got this." María holds out her arms to Bethany.

The little girl leans out of Jessie's embrace with her arms out, too. She adores her Aunt "ee-ah." She hasn't yet gotten the M sound on the front of the word.

Instinctively, Jessie leans back, holding the child away.

"Jessie ..." Aaron turns his smile on María.

"I don't know if I told you, but I have this arrangement with the airlines. If I'm not there when the plane takes off, they leave without me." He turns back to Jessie. "We have to go."

María lifts Bethany out of Jessie's arms, and Aaron literally propels Jessie to the door. She turns and blows Bethany another goodbye kiss.

"I'll be back to get you soon, sweetheart. I promise."

That upsets the child. The note of something like desperation in Jessie's tone is unsettling. She senses her mother's reluctance and her face crinkles. She holds her arms out to Jessie and starts to cry.

"Will you two get out of here before she has a total meltdown. We'll be fine."

Aaron takes Jessie by the shoulders and literally shoves her out the door and closes it behind her.

She can hear Bethany behind the door crying. The sound breaks her heart.

BAILEY LOOKED out the window of the plane at the puffy white clouds below and the land so far beneath them there was nothing discernible on it.

"I'll be back to get you soon, sweetheart," she whispered under her breath. "I promise."

Chapter Fifteen

THE SIDEWALK HAD BEEN SHOVELED and salted, removing whatever remained from the blizzard-that-fizzled the day before, the storm that somehow missed Boston almost entirely, regardless of the weather forecasters' dire predictions.

The grit crunched under Bailey's shoes as she walked toward the last red building on this side of the block. María's apartment occupied the whole top floor of the two-story that had once been a family home, so it was a good-sized place.

She found herself walking slower and slower the nearer she got to the building.

She couldn't wait to get there. Every fiber of her being was screaming for her to break into a dead run.

Except, she didn't really want that at all. She wanted time to stand still, another few minutes to catch her breath, to still her pounding heart, to think of something better to say than, "Hi. I'm not dead."

She passed the house next to the one where María and Bethany — *Bethany!* — were inside *right this minute.* She was by then walking so slow she was barely making any progress at all. Finally, she stopped altogether and just stood there, staring up at the building. There was a Christmas tree in the front window.

María unloaded the sack of groceries hurriedly. She had stood in line a hundred years at the grocery store. You'd think all those people would have bought provisions before what the news was now calling the blizzard-that-fizzled, and that they'd have so much bread/milk/eggs/coffee/whatever on hand they wouldn't need to go to the grocery for a week.

Not.

All María wanted was her brand of coffee, Cafe Altura Ground Organic Coffee. It was an obscure brand that she couldn't get at the convenience store on the corner or she'd never have ventured into the supermarket in the first place. Apparently, the Rapture had happened and everybody on the planet *who could read* had been zapped up to heaven, leaving behind only those unable to grasp the meaning of "Express Lane," or fathom what "twelve items or fewer" could possibly mean.

Seriously?

She glanced out the window, hoping Mrs. Trimboni's husband hadn't pulled up and parked illegally on the street to let her and Bethany out early. Early was not a good thing today.

The street was totally empty. Not a person or vehicle anywhere in sight.

She'd better text the nanny and tell her not to come early. She punched the messages icon, then the little microphone. Unlike every other member of the human race with opposable thumbs, María McKessen couldn't type a text.

"Hi, Mrs. Trimboni …" she began.

There was a knock at the door. A soft, almost tentative knock. Clearly, not Mrs. Trimboni, who banged on the door like the Gestapo, would have walked in without knocking if María didn't keep the door dead-bolted and chain-locked.

She started for the door, hurrying to complete the text. "Early wouldn't be a good thing today," she said. "I'm running way behind."

She didn't bother looking through the peep hole, though parental programing was as sticky as gum on her shoe and she always heard the echo of her foster mother Mrs. Anderson's warning: "You find out who it is before you open the door, missy. It could be *anybody* on the other side. A serial killer, maybe. An axe murderer."

But the binocular lens in this door turned people into Fun House freaks with gigantic eyes and pointy heads. If the person on the other side of the door really looked like that, nobody'd let them in.

She unlocked the deadbolt and pulled the door open the distance of the chain as she finished the text. "Don't bring Bethany home until five-thirty. I'm wrapping her presents." She hit send and looked at the woman standing in the hall.

"Can I help you?"

❧

ALL THE PLANS Bailey'd made for what she was going to say went up in smoke the moment María opened the door, talking. Big surprise, that. Memories of María's adorable babble welled up in her chest and almost choked her.

"… bring Bethany home until five-thirty. I'm wrapping her presents."

Bethany's presents!

She looked up at Bailey then.

"Can I help you?"

Bailey couldn't speak. Her throat locked up tighter than a princess in a tower. All she could do was look, gobble up the adorable face.

Images flashed but didn't really register.

… so much older …

… lost weight, too thin …

… short hair, it's curly …

She saw only confusion on María's face, and maybe she was running away from what she was seeing that couldn't possibly be so. Bailey reached up and pulled her coat hood off her head, tried to smile and absolutely could not pull it off.

"María." Her voice was hoarse and tear-clotted. "It's me, sweetie. Bailey."

THE WOMAN in the hallway just stood there, didn't say anything. The light wasn't good out there. The super could pinch the Indian head off a nickel and only used 40-watt bulbs in the fixtures in the common areas. Twenty-five watt when he could find them.

She was familiar, though, even in the shadows. Then she pulled the hood back off her hair.

Black hair, hanging in soft curls on her shoulders.

Shiny black hair, sparkling even in the dim light.

Then she spoke, said a word, maybe her name, but María didn't catch it because a sudden roaring had erupted in her ears.

No … that was absurd.

"It's me, sweetie. Bailey."

Then María started to scream.

She was never able to order the sequence of events after that. She could hear someone screaming, but the person was down in a well and the sound was bouncing around and echoing.

She was suddenly hallucinating, had been dropped down into a dream world where there was a woman standing out in the hallway in front of her door, calling her name, calling her *María*.

She realized she was the one screaming when her throat felt raw and she clamped her hands over her mouth to stop the sound but it bled out through her fingers and went on and on.

Then Jason, a neighbor, was in the hallway beside the apparition. He wanted to know what was wrong, why she was screaming, but she couldn't tell him because she couldn't breathe. And then he was inside her apartment, but she didn't know how he'd gotten there unless she'd unfastened the chain but she didn't remember doing that and maybe he'd just used his pocket knife like he did that time on the door of the guy who used to live in 2C because he was drunk and had locked himself out.

Then María wasn't screaming anymore.

Jason was standing in front of her, talking.

The woman was still standing in the hall, looking in through the door at María.

María grabbed Jason's arm and yanked him back to the door. "That woman," she said, pointing. Her finger was shaking. She was going to ask him if he saw a woman there, but clearly he did. He was looking right at her. María saw her, too.

"I'm sorry to do this … show up like this," the woman said, "but I didn't know any other way …"

Then the roaring started again and she couldn't hear the words anymore.

But she recognized the voice who was speaking. Recognized the face — it was even more beautiful than she remembered. Then she collapsed on her knees in the floor and started to cry.

BAILEY DIDN'T KNOW what to expect so she hadn't expected anything at all, and María's screams seemed somehow a normal response. She'd have screamed, too, if she'd been María. She'd have screamed and thrown things and jumped up and down and …

When a young man appeared beside her and asked María what was wrong, she just kept screaming. He told her to open the door and she reached out and released the chain lock. And kept screaming. Backed away from the door, shaking her head, screaming.

But she was looking at Bailey now, really *looking* at her.

Seeing her.

Recognizing her.

When she folded up in the floor on her knees and began to cry, Bailey stepped past the bewildered young man, shooed him away with something like, "It's okay, she's my sister. She didn't know I … she thought I was dead." He looked shocked and she said, "Long story." Then she knelt on the floor and took María into her arms.

She was stiff one second and then folded into Bailey's embrace the next, was clinging to her now, clinging with a desperation, clawing at her, sobbing. Bailey was crying, too, holding her so tight it must hurt, but she couldn't let go.

María smelled of Eau d'Hadrien Annick Goutal, a knockoff, like the two of them used to smell on Saturday afternoons when they went from store to store until they went nose blind—

"Bailey?"

She pulled out of Bailey's embrace far enough to look at her. Tears slathered her face. Her hair had fallen into her eyes and her nose was running. She was the most beautiful sight Bailey had ever seen.

"How …?" She didn't wait for the answer before she grabbed Bailey in another hug and cried some more.

Into her hair, Bailey said, "It's a long, long story." She'd said the same thing to the young man, but now he was gone. "I didn't stay away because I wanted to. It wasn't my fault."

She held María, clung to her, *connected* to her. Not just to María-my-sister but to María-in-the-portrait. She had painted María and the instant Bailey touched her she felt the connection she'd felt to all the subjects of her portraits. Only bigger, deeper, louder than all the others. Maybe the connections just grew deeper with each portrait, but she didn't think that was the reason. This connection was not just incrementally more than she'd connected to Poli and to Jeni, the last two subjects of one of her what-hasn't-happened-yet paintings. It was some order of magnitude more. The portrait connection coupled with the sister connection was almost like climbing inside María's skin and living in there with her.

Chapter Sixteen

THEY SAT on the floor and held hands, like they had done when they were little girls playing Barbie dolls. Well, María was playing Barbie dolls. Bailey was just sitting there with her, participating in an odd way that the two of them had worked out without ever discussing it — where she didn't actually participate in the dressing of the dolls or the constant changes of clothing or the putting on of hats and carrying of purses and moving from one vehicle to another. That was what María did.

Bailey sat with her, a spiral notebook open on her knees, drawing. She was always drawing something. Playing with Barbies was during her "bird phase," which was the first and earliest phase, because it didn't matter if she made the legs too long or the beak too short, there was a bird somewhere that looked like the one she'd drawn. She wasn't concentrating on getting things right, though, wasn't giving it her full attention. She just didn't want to seem too interested in the goings-on with the Barbie dolls because she was, after all, twelve years old.

She did participate in the pretending part. She became

the voice of one or the other of the dolls, had conversations with whichever of the dolls María had chosen for that day. She planned parties, talked about what they would wear. She talked about the fabulous balls they would attend with billionaire single men who would fall immediately in love with them and haul them away in limos or Jaguars — though Bailey had only thrown that name out there because she had heard it but didn't really know what kind of conveyance it might have been.

But she didn't "play with" the dolls. She never touched them. She just drew birds on tree limbs or telephone lines and spoke sometimes, you know, to help her little sister play a game. But she wasn't playing with dolls. Not at twelve years old.

They sat together on the floor side-by-side like that now. They had never gotten up after María collapsed to her knees. They'd just somehow wound up on the floor leaning against the couch, holding hands.

They wouldn't let go of each other's hands. Each held tight while Bailey did most of the talking. She needed to explain, had to make María understand why — that was the single most important thing they had to talk about and after that they could get around to everything else.

Bailey glanced at her watch as she spoke. Bethany wouldn't be here for another ten minutes. Those would be the longest minutes of Bailey's life, but she needed them, too, was glad of this space of time in between for her to fill in the gaps of the past two years.

As soon as the two of them caught their breath, she told María what had happened to her in the half hour after she'd deposited Bethany in María's arms and drove off into the night.

All the awful details she hadn't even told the police.

Oh, sure, the part about the rats under the dumpster,

and Aaron's shoe on the street and the homeless woman's screams. But she even told María about the baby in the car seat that was lying face down in the puddle. How the blood turned the little boy's suit from blue to purple.

She told her about the orange jumpsuit and the police station, the ride to Albuquerque, putting the sheets on the bed there. Feeling desperately alone.

For once, María didn't have much to say. Her eyes were huge, devouring Bailey's face, her attention riveted on every word. Bailey wanted to know what had happened in her life for the past two years, too.

And oh how very, very much she wanted to know about Bethany!

She wanted to know … *everything* about Bethany.

And that would come, she would ask her questions — look at photo albums of … her heart almost burst in the anticipation of it. But she understood that she had to do the explaining first. She had to make María understand what had happened, why she had been lied to. Why she had been kept in the dark for two years.

Why she was allowed to believe that her sister was dead.

So Bailey told her about Sergei Wassily Mikhailov.

"He shot Aaron and the homeless woman because they … *we* had seen his son blow through the red light drunk. Mikhailov had been chasing him all the way from where they'd had a fight in a restaurant called Little Moscow, and he showed up — I don't know, a minute, two maybe after his son killed that woman and that poor little baby.

"So he shot him, *just shot him,* María."

She took a gulp of air because there didn't seem to be enough of it in the room. María had to understand about Mikhailov. Because soon … not now, oh, goodness there were other things to talk about right now, but *soon* they would have to talk about María and the danger she was in.

Not just the "generic" danger of being Bailey's sister when Mikhailov figured out Bailey was still alive — but the *specific* danger of a ball gown, flames and the opening night of *The Nutcracker*, about how it was that Bailey knew about that danger.

That was for later, though.

"When I was in the police station, they played me a tape recording that had been made by one of their informants in Mikhailov's organization."

She paused. "He died, the informant. They didn't tell me how or when, but they killed him. Mikhailov's accent was thick, but I could understand every word he said."

THE POLICE OFFICER picks up the phone and touches the screen and a gravelly voice issues from the speaker.

"Cross me and you die. A guarantee, I kill you." The voice is emotionless, not as if he were making a horrible threat but like he's telling the speaker box in a drive-through window to super-size his fries. "Any two-bit hood can say that, yes? But does anybody else guarantee to kill those you love, too? No, they do not, but I, Sergei Wassily Mikhailov, make you that promise. You cross Sergei and you die."

He pauses and his voice grows softer, but still there is no threat in it, no emotion of any kind. "Then your wife dies, your mother, your brothers and sisters, your children. I will find those you love and I will butcher them, one by one."

Bailey feels the voice slither into her ear like a poisonous serpent, coil through her head and down into her belly where cold fear begins to freeze everything it touches, ice spreading out inside her so fast she can hear the cracking sound it makes.

"It could take a week, a month, a lifetime. A fall from a high

window, yes? A hit-and-run driver. A car explosion. A gunshot from a dark alley. One by one, I will not leave breathing anyone who shares the same blood as you. Even after you are dead, you can look up through the fires of hell and watch me slice the throat of your baby son lying in his soiled diaper in your dead wife's arms and lick his blood off the dagger."

"Sergei Mikhailov is not human," says the other man at the table, not the one who had turned on the recording from his cellphone. "I'm serious, I really don't think there's a man in there anywhere. He is pure evil, has made his way in life by annihilating the competition and ruthlessly butchering anybody who stands in his way."

The woman speaks and her voice is hard-edged, not soothing.

"You have to understand what you're dealing with here, Mrs. Cunningham. His whole life is built on intimidation. He keeps the troops in line, and his enemies at bay, because they know he always … always keeps his promises. It's his trademark and he wears it with pride."

"If he knew you were alive, he would kill you," says the man who had played the recording. "Eventually he would kill every member of your family, too."

MARÍA'S FACE had grown deathly pale as Bailey told her the story. She could see shock and horror written on the girl's features. Empathy, too. There at the end, there was probably also fear.

"They told me about a family. The man had worked for Mikhailov and did something, stole money or something, and got caught. Mikhailov killed him and dumped his body with bullet holes … full of bullet holes … on the porch of his home."

The air was too thick again, hard to breathe, but she drew it with a struggle into her lungs to continue.

"The day after the funeral, there was a car bomb …

killed his wife and little girl. Within six months, his mother, two brothers and a grandmother were all dead, too. I don't know how. Didn't ask. Didn't want to know."

"So if this Mikhail-person knew you had seen and were alive, he'd have …"

"He'd have killed all of us. Me, you … *and Bethany.*"

María covered her mouth with both hands, her eyes wide.

"But why so long … and why are you here now?"

"The so-long part is because he vanished. The WITSEC marshals, they told me it'd only be a little while, that soon …" She couldn't even speak for a moment. The word *soon* did as it always did. It stole her breath. "They said they'd arrest him and I could testify and then … but he went back to Russia. He got away." She almost wailed the word "away," and grabbed her emotions again. Her hold on them was so very, very tentative. "They moved me from one city to another. It was a duplex in Albuquerque, then some other anonymous pace in some other anonymous city …"

María's face was awash with compassion, and confusion, with a large side order of shock. Bailey was babbling, knew it but couldn't stop, spewed words out in one long stream, pausing only to grab a breath now and then.

"Then on my birthday … we went to this casino restaurant and after dinner we had a group picture taken. And there he was in the background — *Mikhailov,* right there so close I could have touched him." She shuddered. "I called the federal marshals. Now that he's back in this country, they can arrest him. But as soon as they do, he'll know he missed one of the eyewitnesses. He'll know my name and he'll come looking for me."

Bailey burped out a bark of something like laughter. "All this time, I've been safe because nobody goes looking for somebody they think is dead. When he finds out I'm alive ..."

She squeezed María's hand so hard it must have hurt. "When he comes looking for me, he'll find *you,* too! You and Bethany. Right out in plain sight, and—"

At that moment, there was a thunderous knock on the door. It wasn't locked, and before either of them could move, it was thrown open and a large, broad-faced woman stood in the doorway.

Beside her was a little girl with long black hair that curled on her shoulders. Her eyes were the color of robins' eggs.

She smiled and her whole face lit up. A brilliant flare chased all the shadows into the corners of the room and created a golden glow around her head.

She held out her arms.

"Mommy!" she cried and ran into the room toward Bailey.

Chapter Seventeen

MARÍA COULDN'T DRAG her eyes off her sister's face. She heard what Bailey was saying, too, of course, but it was if she did it as two different people. One part of her was listening to the words, understanding them, grasping their significance, or maybe struggling to grasp the significance, while the other part of her did nothing but revel, bask in the miracle of her sister's presence.

Bailey wasn't dead. *Bailey was alive.*

Of course that was ridiculous, absurd.

Except it wasn't. She was sitting here, María could feel her next to her, could feel their hands, clasped together so tight that her fingers had grown numb but she couldn't let go, wouldn't let go.

She devoured Bailey face. She looked just like María remembered, like she looked in the half dozen pictures of her scattered around the apartment. At the same time, she didn't look like the Bailey María knew. Looked almost like someone else entirely.

There had been a ... softness to Bailey, a tenderness. She probably allowed María to see it more than she allowed others to see. She could be tender and vulnerable, and after she met Aaron … oh, my. It was almost like she had gone home. He gave her permission to be … weak. Sort of. In foster care, you learned early to build as much protective shield around yourself as you could because it was a cold hard world out there.

That's how Bailey had come to the Andersons, wearing that Foster Care Suit of Armor. She didn't wear it all the time, not once she relaxed, saw that it was an okay place, probably better than a lot of other places Bailey had seen. When she was with María, the armor was laid aside and she became real.

Aaron became that suit of armor for Bailey. Maybe she didn't see that, but María did. Bailey relaxed. She allowed herself to be vulnerable. To love … maybe too much. She set aside her shields because he was there for her, not to protect her in any real physical sense, exactly, but there to protect her heart. To love her totally and completely and fill up all the empty places inside her where she had needed love and it hadn't been there for her.

How utterly horrifying that he'd been butchered in the street while she watched. María's eyes filled with tears at the thought of that kind of pain. Watching him …

The person sitting beside her clutching her hand every bit as tightly as María was clutching hers was the product of that experience. That loss. That horror. She was who came out the other side. It wasn't that María could see the suit of armor again, like she had crawled back into it and stayed there confined, protected by it.

No, this person was someone who didn't need a suit of armor. Who had become strong enough — whether voluntarily or not — that she didn't have to hide behind anything anymore.

María's respect and admiration grew at the realization.

Bailey's pain at seeing Aaron shot down on the street, and losing Bethany ...

That thought stopped in the middle of her mind. Screeched to a halt and all the other thoughts behind it banged into the back of it one after another, bang, bang, bang, then toppled off the track and lay on their sides.

She had given up her daughter!

No, her daughter had been snatched away from her every bit as violently as Aaron had.

And that daughter ... had become *María's daughter*.

The little girl who now drew pictures of everything she saw, and talked about wanting a unicorn for Christmas and didn't suck on the edge of her minion blanket hardly at all anymore was no more the baby Bailey'd placed in María's arms than this Bailey was the woman who had placed her there.

That baby, Bailey's baby, didn't exist anymore. She wasn't there anymore, couldn't be conjured up any more than Aaron could be brought back to life. That baby had changed and grown.

Into *María's daughter*.

That's who she was now. Bethany Nicole Cunningham-soon-to-be-McKessen was María's daughter. She wasn't Bailey's little girl anymore.

The part of María's mind that'd been listening to Bailey's words heard Bailey say that the man named Mikhailov who had shot Aaron down would kill her if he found her.

"So if this Mikhail-person knew you had seen and were alive, he'd have—"

"He'd have killed all of us. Me, you ... and Bethany."

Killed Bethany.

The thought sounded in her brain like an ugly foghorn,

like the blaring of a train whistle, like the blatting of those backup signals on a forklift.

Bethany would be in danger if this man knew Bailey was alive.

María's little girl would …

Then she heard Mrs. Trimboni's knock on the door. As expected, she didn't wait to be invited, just opened the door.

There stood Bethany beside her. The moment Bethany saw her, she cried out Mommy, held out her arms and came running across the room.

Bailey was sitting on the floor beside María, closer to the door than María was. When she saw Bethany, her face … María took a picture of the look on Bailey's face with the cellphone of her mind. She would go back one day and examine the look there. The looks. The emotions that played across it. She would study that face, learn from it what loss and redemption looked like in human form.

She couldn't do that now, though, because there was no time.

Bailey leaped up to her knees and held out her arms as Bethany ran across the room.

"Bethany," she cried and grabbed the child as she ran by, clasped her to her chest and held her, sobbing noiselessly.

Bethany was thunderstruck, shocked at being violently grabbed by this stranger.

Note to self. Bailey is a stranger to Bethany now. I am her mommy.

The little girl let out a squeak of a cry and started wiggling, looking at María with surprise and fear on her face.

"Mommy!" she cried, and struggled to be free from Bailey's embrace. But Bailey wasn't in any space where she could attend to that. She was holding the child to her chest, crushing her, with a look on her face of absolute rapture, and tears pouring down her cheeks.

"Let me go!" Bethany cried, wiggling, squirming.

Before María could get to her she kicked out and caught Bailey in the leg, crying now, "Mommy! Make her let me go."

Bailey seemed to come to then, or at least came back to herself enough to lose her grip so Bethany could wiggle free. The child leapt back as soon as Bailey's hands let go and then launched herself into María's embrace.

"Mommy!" she wailed. *"Mommy!"*

She wrapped her arms around María's neck, buried her face in the crook of her neck and shoulder and clung to her with a death grip, sobbing.

Mrs. Trimboni stood in the doorway, too surprised by the scene to move.

Bailey looked at the child, her face a mask of misery and heartache. She reached out to touch her, then drew her hand back. She whispered, "I'm sorry, baby. I …"

Then she settled back against the couch. But didn't cry. Just wore a look of profound misery, far too deep to be assuaged by something as simple and cleansing as tears.

Chapter Eighteen

THERE MIGHT POSSIBLY HAVE BEEN a way that her reunion with the daughter she had not seen in almost two years could have gone more wrong, but right off hand Bailey couldn't imagine it.

Maybe there was a scenario of reunion that was more the polar opposite of how she had dreamed it would be, night after night, until she'd finally had to ban such fantasies from her thoughts or she would go mad.

She didn't think so.

She hadn't meant to grab Bethany like that. Would never have done such a thing. Had spent a good number of the hours since she knew that *soon* meant today considering how best to slowly become reacquainted with her daughter.

How to make a good first impression.

How not to put the child off by being too pushy.

Like with a dog you didn't know. You didn't rush up and pet it just because you thought it was adorable. People who tried to snatch Bundy off the ground because he was just the cutest dog Ev-er were not rewarded by tail-wagging and licks.

At the very least, he squirmed to be out of their grasp.

At the worst, he either bit them or peed on them.

She'd never have done a thing like that to her precious Bethany.

But that's exactly what she had done.

It had been knee-jerk.

It was that fantasy playing in her head, except this time it was real.

A door opens and there stands her precious daughter. She breaks into a breathtakingly beatific smile, holds out her arms, squeals "Mommy" and rushes into Bailey's embrace.

It had just been too much like Bailey'd always hoped and dreamed it would be. It was too perfect. She just fell into the narrative without thinking. So desperate to touch, to hold …

She looked at the little girl now, clinging to María, sobbing into the crook of her shoulder and she wanted almost more than she had ever wanted anything in her life to have a do-over of the past thirty seconds.

"Why what in the world …" said the broad-faced woman who had transferred into pit bull mode between one heartbeat and the next. A more rational Bailey would have liked that, would have appreciated how protective this woman — obviously her nanny — was of Bethany.

But right now all she could think was, "Butt out, lady, you don't have a dog in this fight."

She didn't say that, of course. Didn't say anything. Just sat mute, watching her little girl heaving sobs, wanting desperately to soothe them away instead of being the cause of them.

María said something to the woman. Bailey didn't attend to what it was. She mollified her with a couple of other remarks Bailey didn't listen to, and the woman harrumphed her way out the door, closing it a little too much like banging it shut.

Then there was no sound in the room except Bethany's sobs, which weren't ratcheting down in either volume or intensity.

"You don't understand …" María said. "Bethany is scared to death of strangers."

She could tell that María didn't like the way that had come out any more than she did, but the words hung in the air, a curtain between them, separating them in an almost tangible way.

María didn't say anything to ameliorate the situation, just began talking softly to Bethany. Saying all the things Bailey would say, wanted so desperately to say, but had lost the right to say by her own behavior.

She owned this one. Her bad.

"It's okay, sweetheart. Hey there, you can stop crying now. It's okay, sugar. Shhhhh. Do you hear me, it's okay. Now, stop crying. Everything's fine now. Mommy's gotcha. I've gotcha right here, hugging you tight. You're fine."

More words to that effect finally began to calm the child. She ratcheted down from full bore sobbing, to merely crying, to that hitching breath-in-and-out thing little kids did when they'd just had a good cry.

Bailey was devouring the child with her eyes.

She'd only gotten a glimpse of her face, but even in the glimpse, she was stabbed in the heart by the little girl's resemblance to Aaron. She had always thought the child was the image of her father, had said so on many, many occasions, to which Aaron had always replied that he sincerely hoped not because she would be far better off if she were the image of her drop-dead-gorgeous mother rather than her — his word — *schmuck* of a father.

Bailey ached to see her face clearly.

Finally, Bethany peeked out through her own hair in her face. Just peeked at Bailey, then buried her face again.

Meanwhile, María kept up a non-stop narrative about how everything was fine, that Bethany was fine, that Mommy was fine that nobody was going to hurt her.

Bailey didn't listen to the words. Because some of them cut to the bone.

What had she expected? In truth, what had she wanted? Had she wanted the little girl to pine away for her "real" mommy, to miss her every day, to love her and never forget her and long for her return?

Of course not. She had wanted her little girl to be happy.

Which meant, of course, that she would come to think of María as her mother. Bailey had always known and accepted that. Okay, she had known it, but some part of her had never accepted it and never would.

Some selfish, self-absorbed part of her had wanted Bethany to miss her and yearn for her *mommy*.

Clearly, she had not. She had bonded to María, and that was good, it really was — admit it, that was the very best outcome imaginable.

Bethany had a mommy who loved her and she loved her mommy.

It was just that Bailey wasn't that mommy.

"How would you like a glass of orange juice?" María asked.

Bethany nodded her head, which was only discernible because her black curls bounced.

María looked at Bailey.

"It's in a bottle in the refrigerator. Would you …?"

"Sure." Bailey leapt to her feet, crossed the room, rooted around in the cabinets until she found a glass, took the orange juice out of the refrigerator and poured it into the glass. She'd only taken a few steps back into the room when María told her.

"Not that glass. She can't hold that — it's too big. One of the small plastic ones on the lower shelf."

Well, duh … a big heavy glass.

So much she didn't know. So much … so much.

If she let it, she would be overwhelmed by how much.

She got the orange juice in the right glass, went back into the room, knelt in front of where María cradled the little girl and held it out to her.

Bethany looked at the class, shot Bailey a glance, shook her head violently and buried her face back in María's shoulder.

María took the glass from Bailey's outstretched hand.

"Here, sweetheart. It's the kind with pulp, you know, hunks of oranges in it the way you like it."

Bethany instantly sat up. She used the back of her hand to wipe the tears off her cheeks and then held out both hands and took the plastic glass.

Of course the other glass was too big. What was Bailey thinking?

She took a big drink.

"S'good, Mommy. The orange chunks tickle my tongue."

Bailey's heart almost burst out of her chest in love and longing.

But she grabbed her emotions in an iron grip.

She stepped to the couch, on the other side of María, not beside Bethany, and sat down.

"I like pulpy orange juice, too." She spoke to María, seemed to ignore Bethany. "What kind do you get?"

"Huber Farms. I liked Sun Gold better, but they don't carry it at the Super Save store where I shop now. This is the best I can do. Bethany, honey, hop down out of my lap so I can get a glass of orange juice."

"I wanna sit wif you."

"Fine, you can sit with me on the couch as soon as I get some orange juice."

María peeled the little girl out of her lap, set her on the floor, got up and started toward the kitchen. Bethany leapt to her feet and cried "Mommy!" while following on her heels, casting a fearful look over her shoulder at Bailey as she left the room.

Bailey had to get a grip, had to … Oh there was so much, so much. With Bethany, she had to get from here, which was roughly, "Don't get near me, Scary Stranger, or I'll cry" to "Okay, I'll sit in the same room with you if you don't touch me."

At least that far.

With María, she had to get from "My sister I thought was dead is alive and I don't even know how to think about that" to "Sure, I'll drop my life, quit my job" — did she have a job? — "and *run* because if I don't a psychopath will kill me."

And she had to cross all that distance now. Right now. There was a Nutcracker clock counting down — tick, tick, tick.

~

T.J.'s phone rang and caller ID identified Dobbs.

"You lonely?"

"Of course not. These two dogs are better company than you ever were. What's going on?"

Dobbs hadn't wanted to stay behind, probably felt a little guilty about "wimping out" on the rest of them.

"Me and Brice is sitting out here in the car waiting and Bailey's been in there with her sister for more than an hour now. Far as I can tell from here, the roof ain't blown off the building yet, so there's that."

"I just heard from Al Zankoski."

That was a non sequitur. Zankoski was a thorough investigator who didn't let complications like "private information" and "sealed records" and such stand in the way of him finding out whatever tidbit of information he'd been hired to collect. He wasn't cheap, but he had located María's address with so little effort he hadn't even charged Dobbs for the information. But what else—?

Dobbs answered the question before T.J. had a chance to ask.

"I asked him to see if he could locate one Sergei Wassily Mikhailov."

"You what?"

Brice looked up, surprised, at T.J.'s explosive response.

"Why would you do a danged fool thing like—?"

"Don't get your panties all in a wad. I just told Al to see if he could find the man. Not invite him to join the Rotary Club."

"Why?"

"What's the harm?"

"Harm? You're joking, right? If he finds out Bailey's—"

"The feds told Bailey they'd find Mikhailov, that they were 'all over it.' That was four days ago. Maybe it's just me, but that seemed like an awful long time — I was afraid he'd bailed again, gone back to Russia."

"Did he?"

"Nope. Mikhailov is in Boston. At least he was two days ago. It wasn't like he was in hiding or anything, either. Al said his operative saw the guy on Saturday, eating lunch with a group of people in that restaurant Bailey mentioned, Little Moscow. Right out in plain sight."

"If Zankoski could find him, why couldn't the feds?"

"I think that's a question somebody needs to be asking."

"At least he ain't been spooked, ain't got no idea they's a lion on the tall grass ready to pounce."

"That lion had better pounce quick. This guy stays on the move, a high-stakes gambler who goes all over the world chasing a game."

"Which explains the Nautilus." T.J. turned from the phone and spoke to Brice. "You's right about them private rooms where Mr. W. Maxwell Crenshaw charges a couple hundred grand for a seat at the table."

"As usual, this was a quick update," Dobbs said, "with a full report to follow. I'll send it to you when I get it."

Dobbs hung up and T.J. told Brice what he'd said.

"The federal marshal needs to know what Bailey's up to. He needs to know that his star witness ... his only witness—"

"We done been all through this. We here to keep that painting of Bailey's sister from coming true. Ain't no way to explain a thing like that to the law."

"I'd bet your pension—"

"Why's ever'body always so willin' to wager *my* pension—?"

"I'm betting there's a *reason* why Marshal Jordan hasn't busted the guy. If he's not even hiding, then why—?"

"That there's the good news. Means he don't suspect nothing. We got time to swoop in here, grab María and

Bethany and get them back to West Virginia. Then we don't have to tell that marshal what we doin'. We can tell him what we already done."

"And find out why he's dragging his feet."

With his phone still in his hand, T.J. sent Bailey a text.

Chapter Nineteen

WHEN MARÍA RETURNED to the living room from the kitchen, she carried Bethany on her hip and a glass of orange juice in her other hand. She didn't sit down on the couch, but in a recliner chair opposite it, so she was facing where Bailey still sat in the floor.

She had to let Bethany slide to the floor as she sat, but the child never let go of María. The moment she sat, Bethany climbed back up into her lap and looked at Bailey as if she thought Bailey might bite her.

The look broke Bailey's heart.

There was a beat of silence, then they both spoke at the same time.

"Bailey, I—"

"María, I—"

They stopped, and Bailey grabbed the conversational ball and headed downfield with it.

"María, honey, I know this has to be hard for you."

"Hard?"

Obviously, the word fell woefully short of what it had been meant to describe.

"And I'm sorry. I am so, so sorry. But *it's not my fault.* I didn't ask to watch a monster shoot Aaron down in the street."

Bailey hadn't realized she would choke on the words, but they were full of such anguish she could barely get them out. Clearly, her distress also upset Bethany. She cringed back into María's lap.

"Bailey, I don't think we ought to talk about—"

"I don't either. I don't *want* to. But we have to because you have to understand what's happening."

"Okay, I get it. The police or law or marshals or whatever kept you away, wouldn't let you come back, made you pretend you were dead, I get that part."

"Good, then—"

"But *you* don't get that walking in here like this … *poof,* 'here I am.'" She looked down at Bethany possessively and the child snuggled closer in response. "We, Bethany and I … we need to sort all this out, we need some time to—"

"That's just it. There *isn't* any time. There's a madman out there named Mikhailov who shot Bethany's daddy and would gladly kill her, too."

The little girl squeaked out a tiny cry and looked with terror-filled eyes at María.

"Somebody shoot Bethy? I don't want somebody shoot me."

Bailey never dreamed the little girl was that verbal, would understand something like that at three and a half. She'd stepped in it again. Bethany put her thumb into her mouth, huddled against María and began to cry.

"Bailey, stop it! You're scaring her to death."

"I'm sorry. I didn't mean …" Her emotions were getting the better of her again and she had to sound less like a raving lunatic and more like a loving sister … and mother.

"María, you have to listen to me." Clamping down on her emotions now made her sound cold and severe. Well, maybe that's how she had to sound to get María to listen. "Talking and discussing and explaining will have to wait until later. Later when … I have a beautiful home … there's a lake and a puppy and right now you have to pack a bag for you and Bethany — just the essentials, we'll get whatever else you need later. I have a chartered plane waiting—"

"A plane? Fly? Bethany can't fly anywhere. She has an ear infection, the change in pressure—"

"Fine, we'll take the rental car, then. How doesn't matter. The only thing that matters is you have to come with me *right now.* You are in terrible danger if you stay here."

Bailey could see María was emotionally backing up from the whole thing so frantically she was about to trip over her own thoughts.

"That's crazy. We're not going to … what, just pack up and leave? Just like that?"

María's reaction was transmitted with every syllable of her body language to the little girl. Her … *mommy* … was scared, and that terrified Bethany.

It wasn't supposed to be like this.

"I'm sorry I'm frightening you. I—"

"Then stop frightening us. Stop it! Stop all this talk about grabbing a coat and a change of underwear and dashing out into the night."

"But that's what you have to do. You have to—"

"I don't *have to* do anything."

"I didn't mean it like that. But you have to—"

The escalation of their voices hadn't yet reached shouting, but it was close. Bethany looked with huge, frightened eyes from María to Bailey and back to María. Then she burst into tears. Not just crying. Sobbing.

"Nooooo," she cried, shaking her head and squealing, "I don't wanna to go. I wanna to stay here. Mommy, make dat lady leave us alone."

Bailey watched María grab hold of her own emotions then. Hugging the child tight to her chest, she began to rock her back and forth, smoothing her hair out of her face as she did.

"It's okay, baby." She looked pointedly at Bailey. "*We're not going anywhere.*"

"Did you not hear a word I said about Mikhailov? You think he won't hurt you because … what? You think you can just put a Band-Aid on your navel and that'll keep you safe?"

María froze at the reference.

JESSIE WONDERS how she is ever going to get any sleep in a room with a little girl whose breathing sounds like a drowning water buffalo. She'd slept in houses where some of the other kids snored, but none of them had ever made a sound like María did just breathing.

After teeth brushing, good night perfunctory hugs — she hated that part, the awkward part in the beginning when you had to act like the foster parents and the other kids were your real family when the truth was you couldn't even keep all their names straight yet. The hugs were the worst. Two flagpoles, exchanging embraces.

She supposes in the foster parents' eyes they have to do the everybody-hug-everybody bedtime ritual to make the place seem warm and secure, like a real home. What they accomplished instead was making it seem phony and artificial. Later … weeks, months off in the future, such a routine would likely feel at least mildly comforting. The first night, it's awful.

So, she is glad to escape to the room she shares with María, whose bedtime is an hour earlier because she's younger and Jessie figures she'll already be asleep.

As soon as Bailey slips between the sheets, she hears the tiny, wheezy voice speak out of the darkness.

"Would you close" … wheeze … "the closet door?" Wheeze. "Please … I'm" … wheeze … "scared."

"Scared of what?"

"There's a … a suck-your-guts in there."

"A what?"

"A suck-your-guts." Wheeze. "It's a kind of demon."

Surprisingly, Jessie has heard the word before. All she knows about it is that it is some kind of scary monster thing, and that the word isn't "suck-your-guts." It's "succubus."

"A lady demon" … wheeze … "behind the clothes." Wheeze. "She waits until you're asleep" … wheeze … "and then …"

"Then what?"

"She comes out and …"

"And what?"

"She does it through your belly button." Wheeze.

"Does what through—?"

"First, she pops your belly button off."

"Like a lid on a soft drink?"

"Kinda."

"Then?"

"She's like a mos" … wheeze … "qui" … wheeeze … "to!" The more upset María gets, the more she wheezes.

"A what—?"

"Mosquito!" Wheeze. "She puts her nose" … wheeze … "in the hole" … wheeze … "and sucks out your guts!"

Jessie doesn't laugh. In fact, she doesn't even feel like laughing, though such a ridiculous little-kid fear is humorous. She just feels sorry for the little girl.

"Well, we better fix that!" She hops out of the bed and goes down the hall to the bathroom. She'd seen the box in the cabinet *when she'd gotten out the communal tube of — gag! — Crest toothpaste.*

Back in the bedroom, Bailey stands beside María's bed.

"Pull up your pajama shirt."

"Why?" Wheeze.

"So we can keep the succubus from sucking out your guts."

María's eyes are huge, but she slowly lifts up the shirt of her pink pajamas.

Jessie rips off the paper wrapping, pulls off the tabs and affixes the big Band-Aid over the top of María's navel.

"You're good now!"

María looks down at the Band-Aid.

"But can't she ...?"

"Oh, no. Band-Aids keep your blood inside you. That's why you put one on when you skin your knee or something like that. They're made to keep your guts inside, too."

"Oh," is all María says.

Then Jessie goes to the door, flips off the light switch and crawls between the cold sheets that smell pleasantly of fabric softener.

The voice comes from the darkness.

"Did you put a Band-Aid on your belly button?"

"I don't need one. When you're twelve years old, you're a big kid. Succubuses only go after little kids."

From that moment on, Jessie doesn't act like a little kid anymore. She's a big kid now.

The voice is so soft she can barely hear.

"Are you ... sure?" Wheeze.

"I'm sure. You can trust me, María."

INTO THE SILENCE THAT FOLLOWED, Bailey said as quietly as she could and still be heard over the crying child.

"You can ... trust me, María." She sobbed out the words. "I ... love you. You're in danger here. It's worse than ... there's more that I don't have time to tell you about right now. Please, please let me get you and Bethany somewhere you'll be safe."

She didn't say anything else after that. Felt suddenly flat, like all the air had drained out and there was no way to pump it all back in again.

María kept her head bowed over Bethany, rocking her back and forth, smoothing her hair, speaking quiet nonsense. When she finally did look up, her cheeks were again slathered with tears.

"I'm sorry ... I ... just *not tonight*, okay? It's too much. Too fast. I can't ... Bethany needs time to adjust. Please."

María took a deep, shuddery breath.

"In the morning. Tomorrow. Come back and get us in the morning. We'll be ..." She choked out the next words, making a sound like the familiar wheeze from years ago. "... *ready to leave* at nine o'clock."

Every fiber of Bailey's being wanted to scream, "*No!*" They couldn't wait. It was too dangerous. They had to go *right now.*

But did they? There was just one way to find out, and though she knew it would only add to the insanity, she said it anyway.

"Your dress for opening night of *The Nutcracker* — where is it?"

She might as well have hit María between the eyes with a wrecking ball.

"My *dress?* How could you *possibly* ...?" She couldn't finish the question because the rest of the words had fallen out of her head onto the floor.

"I'm so sorry, but I have to know. Where—?"

"I'm ... picking it up tomorrow. *Why* ...?"

"There's so much to explain and I'll tell you everything. There's just no time to do that now."

So they didn't *have to* come with her right this minute. T.J.'s text had said the police hadn't arrested Mikhailov *yet*. He still thought Bailey was dead. She was as safe from him now as she had been every day of the past two years.

Nobody goes looking for somebody they think is dead.

María and Bethany were still safe, too. For now.

The truth still in the husk was that Bailey didn't *want* to wait. Not a single second longer. She wanted them to come right now because she couldn't bear the thought of leaving them. Of seeing them both … *seeing Bethany* … for the first time since …

And then just walking away.

Leaving them and walking away.

It would be the hardest thing she'd ever done.

The part of Bailey that might or might not be related to Oscar's presence in her brain harrumphed loudly in her mind.

That's a load of crap.

Bailey Donahue had done a whole lot of things harder than this in the past two years. But none of them had hurt as bad.

"Okay, in the morning, then."

She knew if she didn't get up right then and walk out the door she would never be able to leave at all.

Then it hit her.

"No, *wait!*"

María looked shocked and Bethany was surprised into silence.

"I … please. I want to …"

She took her phone out of her pocket and tossed her coat back onto the couch.

"I … they took my phone, threw it into the car with the body of the homeless woman and … all my pictures were in it."

When she said the word pictures, the aching and longing and pain in the word came from the deepest recesses of her heart.

"I didn't have a single ... *not even one picture* of Aaron. Or Bethany. I want to ..." She lifted the phone up. "Can I take a picture. Please."

She watched emotions play over María's face and told herself that when she could, she would remember the moment, conjure up the image again and try to determine what all the emotions had been.

María leaned over and lifted Bethany's chin.

"Hey sugar, this nice lady wants to take our picture. Can you smile for her?"

Bethany shook her head and buried her face in María's chest.

"Aw, come on, honey. I know you have a smile. Remember the secret one I gave you? The one I told you to keep in your pocket so you could pull it out and put it on whenever you were sad? You have that one, don't you?"

Bethany looked up at María and nodded. She wiped the back of her hand across her nose, did nothing but smear it, so María used the hem of the little girl's shirt to wipe her face.

Bailey had punched the button on her camera as soon as she pointed the phone at them and it was recording it all, a video. Then when the two of them were ready, María looked up.

"Smile, sugar."

Bethany smiled and her whole face lit up like a rocket. A flare. A shooting star across the night sky.

Bailey switched from video to photo, punched the button, saved the memory safe in her phone.

She stood then, turned purposefully toward the door

and felt her knees turn to bags of water, unable to hold her up.

Oh, how she didn't want it to be like this.

She walked on legs she couldn't feel across the living room. If she turned around. If she turned back around …

Then María was beside her, holding the coat she'd left on the couch.

"… cold out there," she said. And something else about … "your pocket …" but her words were so tear-clotted they were almost unintelligible.

"Mommy!" Bethany cried.

She'd been left in the chair when María leapt up to get Bailey's coat and she sounded as bereft as if she'd been set on an ice floe and shoved out into the Arctic Ocean to be eaten alive by walruses.

"Tomorrow," Bailey managed to say, as María opened the door and stood holding it, openly crying now.

"Nine o'clock," María said, nodding. "We'll be ready to go."

Then Bailey was standing in the hallway, the closed door behind her, feeling as lost and alone as she'd felt that day when she walked from room to room in a featureless house in—

Stop it!

She shouted the words at herself so loudly inside her head she was surprised no sound came out in the hallway.

She had seen María and Bethany. She would see them in the morning … and then she would never … *never* be separated from them again.

Bailey shoved her arms into the coat María had handed her. Didn't button it or get her gloves out of the pocket, just rushed down the stairs and out the front door, wanting to get as far away as possible before she started to cry.

Chapter Twenty

"How many times, you think?" T.J. gestured with his chin to the closed door of the bedroom off the living room of the suite of rooms they'd taken at the Sheraton Plaza. They could hear muffled voices. The same muffled voices, over and over.

"A hundred, maybe." Brice considered. "More. Two hundred."

"Two hundred sounds about right."

Bailey had first played the video for them after she stumbled into the back seat of the car parked around the corner from María's apartment, and sobbed uncontrollably for maybe a minute.

Clearly, Bailey'd been devastated. But not freaked-out devastated. Not something-horrible-happened devastated. Just unutterably-sad devastated. Her first meeting with María and Bethany in two years had not gone well, but she *had* met with them. She had found them, seen them, spoken to them. They were all right.

If they hadn't been, Bailey would have been a whole other level of devastated. Brice knew her well enough to know from her body language the instant he saw her hurrying down the street toward the car, her hood thrown back, her coat unbuttoned, that she'd been through an emotional wringer. But it could have been a whole lot worse.

She'd calmed herself then. Literally grabbed hold of her emotions, clenched her fist around them, the way you'd put a clamp on a spurting artery to stop the blood flow instantly. Then she'd told them what happened.

When she'd described reaching out and grabbing the little girl as she ran to her "mommy" with her arms open, Brice had wanted to take Bailey into his arms and comfort her as much as she'd wanted to hug the little girl.

"I screwed it up," she'd said. "My bad."

T.J. reached over and used his thumb to wipe a single tear that was sliding down her cheek.

"The tears a mama cries for her child — them's blue tears. They's a special kind, got special healing power in 'em." He'd smiled what looked — to Brice at least — like a genuine smile. "It wasn't 'your bad.' You done good. Wouldn't a'made no difference what you done or said, wasn't no good way in the world to do what you had to do. It was gonna be too much for a body to take in all at once no matter how it went."

They'd both consoled her as best they could, made it clear they were sure her sister and daughter would be perfectly safe for one more night right where they were — both of them aware that though their safety was the most important consideration, it wasn't the only one. Seeing them ... and then leaving them there. That had ripped Bailey's guts out.

Then she'd shown them the video. The young woman consoling the child — a beautiful little girl who was the image of her mother. Of Bailey. No, of Jessie Cunningham. The little girl wiping her face, looking into the camera and smiling.

She'd shown them the still shot she had taken.

Brice was no good with a camera, always seemed to capture everybody with their eyelids at half mast, or their mouths agape, looking ridiculous at best and just plain unrecognizable at worst.

But the picture Bailey showed them, a single frame, taken with trembling hands, looked like it'd been taken by a professional photographer. The young woman's face was open, sincere and easy to read. She was upset but holding it together. Brice saw strength there that he instantly respected and admired.

The little girl was as adorable a child as he had ever seen. The lighting was shadowy, so her eye color was indiscernible, but he could tell her eyes weren't the dark hazel of her mother's. Bailey'd said she had her father's eyes. *Aaron's eyes.* Robin's egg blue. But she'd also said the little girl was the image of her father and that wasn't true. She looked just like Bailey. He could have picked them as mother and daughter out of a crowd of a hundred people.

That was the first time she played the video. She'd played it over and over again, staring at it mesmerized in the back seat of the car, while T.J.'d called around and gotten them a suite of rooms at the Sheraton and they'd checked in. Brice in his Kavanaugh County Sheriff's uniform had raised a few eyebrows. Though he wasn't about to admit that he'd been freezing in the car, when he'd stopped at the hotel gift shop to get basic overnight supplies for T.J. and Bailey — toothbrush, toothpaste, comb, etc. — he'd also purchased a ridiculously overpriced Boston sweatshirt. With that over his t-shirt and Kevlar vest, he'd be warm enough until they got back on the plane tomorrow morning.

They'd ordered room service. Bailey'd taken a bite or two out of her sandwich and now she was in the bedroom watching the images again and again.

"Tomorrow morning at nine o'clock can't come quick enough for that girl," T.J. observed, as he ate the remainder of his supper and all that Bailey had left untouched on her plate. Dobbs had told Brice once that T.J. could eat anything, anywhere, any time. Said it was a skill he'd learned growing up in a home where he wasn't sure where his next meal was coming from and honed during years of military service. Dobbs had nailed that one.

"She won't sleep a wink tonight, you know that, don't you?"

"Duh."

"You can go on to the room whenever you want. I'm going to crash here on the couch." Brice wanted to be there, near … in case she needed something.

"I'll stay for a bit, too."

T.J.'s phone pinged with an incoming message and Brice's pinged a few seconds later. Dobbs. Brice opened the message and found that it held an attachment of the full report from the private investigator, Zankoski. The message that accompanied the report was only half a dozen words long, but it chilled Brice to the bone: *You're not going to like this.*

Brice read the whole report through, beginning to end. Then read it again, slower this time. He had been impressed with how thorough Zankoski had been in August, when Dobbs had hired him to track down the identity of the little girl Bailey had painted. He'd gotten all the pertinent information, everything he'd been paid to collect. Then he'd provided even more, he'd dug deeper and unearthed the strange details of the case, the details that should have set off every cop's gut alarm Brice had. Eventually, he did piece it all together, but it was a heartbeat too late to do him any good.

This report was just as thorough and documented. It was their good fortune that Zankoski's law enforcement career in Milwaukie had been preceded by a brief stint with the New York City Police Department. He still had friends there and one of them had followed Zankoski's example, had set up a private investigator business — in Boston.

Brice smiled. Cops and former cops were a tight group. If you "know a guy who knows a guy," you can often dig out all manner of things. Like before, Zankoski had included information he'd hadn't been paid to find out, other details he'd gotten his Boston friend to chase down on his own. The basic information contained nothing Brice didn't already know about Mikhailov. The extra added attractions did.

As Dobbs had predicted, Brice didn't like it one bit.

When he looked up from his second perusal of the report, T.J. was looking at him. Brice said only one word, the only one necessary.

"Crazy."

"Yep. Just when you thought it was safe to go back in the water." T.J. shook his head. "Ain't bad enough the monster's a killer, now he's a lunatic killer. Of course, in my book that's kinda an oxymoron anyway."

The report had described conversations with members of Mikhailov's operation — not the higher-ups, just the foot soldiers, the minions. Even what little they knew had been chilling.

It seemed clear to the mafia boss's organization that something was very, very wrong with the boss. He'd always been vicious, but over the course of the last couple of years in Russia, his depravity had grown on some order of magnitude to a level intolerable even in the circles in which a man like a mafia boss traveled.

He'd always been totally devoid of morality or pity — or humanity — but he had been a disciplined man, rising up through the ranks of the organization because he was both ruthless *and* practical. He employed all manner of brutality, torture and murder as a means to an end. He got what he wanted, suffered not a peep of opposition, ruled with an iron fist. Did it all dispassionately.

Brice remembered Bailey's description of the tape recording she'd listened to in the police station, Mikhailov talking to an informant. She'd said he displayed no emotion whatsoever, described killing the family members of his enemies as if he were reading the assembly instructions for a backyard barbecue grill.

In the past two years, that had changed. He was seen in fits of violent rage, was so paranoid he literally had bodyguards whose job it was to protect him from his other bodyguards. He indulged in the most brutal violence *as if he enjoyed it.*

The single most chilling story had been the still unconfirmed tale of what had happened to his only son, Ivan, the young man who had gotten drunk and run a red light, crashing into a car, killing a young mother and her infant son. The crash that had led to the death of Aaron Cunningham, some nameless homeless woman, and had launched Jessie Cunningham into the desert of a seemingly endless exile in the Witness Protection Program.

The boy was not seen for months after the accident. Then he appeared — clean and sober — in Moscow. About two months ago, he vanished again, however, and rumor had it that his father had caught him drinking again and had beaten him to death with a fireplace poker.

Mikhailov also seemed to be suffering from intermittent hearing loss and vision problems.

"I'm thinkin' Zankoski's last suggestion sounds like the best guess."

"He *is* the kind of man who'd have to worry about a thing like that."

"Yeah, and the symptoms match, too. I seen it before, busted a guy once who was crazier'n a outhouse rat — sudden mood changes, paranoia, uncontrollable rage and depravity."

"Advanced stage syphilis."

"That'd be my read on it."

"He was dangerous enough as a simple mafia killer. Now, he's a mad dog."

"Had ought to be shot down like one, too — on sight."

"I'm not sure Bailey needs to know—"

"Bailey already knows," said a voice from the open doorway of the bedroom. The men turned and saw her standing there, phone in hand, her face a white mask.

"If you're concerned that report is going to upset me, don't be. There are no *degrees of monstrosity*. He murdered Aaron, shot him. Just … shot him. Twice. There's nothing he could do that's worse than that."

T.J. crossed to where she was standing in the doorway, her hands instinctively clasping her upper arms, hugging herself.

"How about you curl up in this here chair. I'll get the blanket off the bed. You ain't gonna go to sleep in that bedroom all by yourself anyway. Least in here, you got company."

She looked at him gratefully and nodded.

Brice went to the bedroom and stripped off the blanket, then wrapped it around her when she curled up in a ball in the chair.

"We'll both be right here," Brice told her. "T.J. already owes me the deed to his house, and we're going for double or nothing."

T.J. humphed. Bailey smiled a little, then closed her eyes. Cuddling her phone to her like she wanted to be cuddling her little girl.

Chapter Twenty-One

In the space of half an hour, María McKessen's life had gone from orderly, neat and tidy, planned out, happy and safe to unmitigated chaos. That fast.

Of course, Bailey's life had gone from happily married mother to on-the-run fugitive in less time than that.

Bailey.

María still had trouble believing it. So much trouble, in fact, that after Bailey left, she ran to the window, watched her come out the front door of the building and run off down the street, her coat unbuttoned, hood thrown back, black hair tumbling in the wind.

She had *run* down the street. María understood why. If she hadn't run, if she hadn't propelled herself forward, she wouldn't have been able to go at all. María had seen that, watched Bailey grinding her jaw as she got up off the couch to leave. Every step was lifting a thousand-pound weight.

María didn't want that! But she was as powerless to do anything about it as Bailey was.

Bailey had to force herself to leave and María had to force herself to let Bailey leave.

This was too much, overload, fried circuits. María had to get a grip, had to—

Bailey was alive.

Bailey wasn't … in the grave next to Aaron's in the Cunningham's private plot in the little cemetery down the road from their country home in Vermont.

Bailey was alive and she wanted her life back.

Wanted her daughter back.

When María thought about that, her heart took up such a mad beat it seemed to be trying to knock a hole in the wall of her chest.

Bethany was María's little girl. Except she wasn't. She was Bailey's little girl.

And Bailey wanted her back.

Oh, dear God in heaven, María was going to have to … *give her daughter up.*

No!

No, that wasn't … she couldn't … not precious *Bethany.* How could she?

María stood by the window of her apartment, looking at the empty sidewalk Bailey had run down and felt the whole world collapse out from under her.

Then, finally, she sank down on the floor and began to cry.

"Mommy …?" The pitiful tone of Bethany's voice broke María's heart. "Why you cryin'? Did that bad lady make you cry?" María swallowed back the sobs that were ratcheting up in her throat and managed to control her hitching diaphragm. She was scaring Bethany.

Water spiders.

María's thoughts were water spiders, skittering across the surface of her mind, moving so fast and so randomly she couldn't grab hold of any of them long enough to think it.

Bailey wasn't dead.

Bailey had watched Aaron's ... murder. A man shot him while she watched.

The look on Bailey's face when she pleaded to be allowed to take a photograph.

María's heart ripped out of her chest when she thought ... she'd had no pictures. All this time, two years, not one image to look at.

That's why María'd grabbed the little framed wedding picture — Bailey and Aaron — and shoved it into Bailey's coat pocket.

She hadn't seen Aaron's face since ...

"I need to go potty," Bethany said, taking her thumb out of her mouth only long enough to produce the words. As soon as the door had closed behind Bailey, Bethany had calmed down. But like every other kid on the planet, she was in tune with the mood of the grownups around her. She knew her mommy was upset, so she stayed close, clingy, wanting to sit in María's lap or hold onto her leg.

"Hey, kiddo, how about you don't chew it off — you're going to need an opposable thumb for something one of these days."

Bethany ignored her comment, kept sucking on her thumb.

"I need go potty."

"You forget where the bathroom is?"

"Mommy go wiff Bethy."

María got up off the floor, took Bethany's hand — to get her thumb out of her mouth — and walked with her to the bathroom. She helped her get her big-girl pants down and then back up again.

She made the child a peanut butter and banana sandwich. Wiped up the mess when she spilled her orange juice. Kept up some kind of running narrative with the little girl, who had recovered nicely and was now prattling on about everything and nothing.

She cleared off the table and set paper and crayons in front of the little girl — she wasn't up to the mess of paint, not now — told her to "draw me a picture," and when the child was finally focused, María sat down in the recliner and went chasing after the water spiders in her head.

Bailey was alive.

Some madman with a Russian name wanted to kill Bailey.

Wanted to kill María and Bethany, too.

María had promised that tomorrow morning she would abandon her whole life and run off to — where? She hadn't even asked.

How?

How could she possibly do a thing like that?

How could she *give up her little girl?*

Then she allowed herself to cry. Softly. So quietly Bethany couldn't hear, could only see Mommy's shoulders shaking.

Maybe she'd think Mommy was laughing.

Surprisingly, Bailey had slept after all. Hadn't expected to, but she'd closed her eyes briefly and the next thing she knew the light through glass doors that led to the balcony showed a pink-and-rose-colored sky.

She turned to the couch and saw Brice there, sound asleep.

T.J. was nowhere in sight, had either gone down to the room they'd rented for him and Brice or had arisen early and slipped out for coffee. The man was like a cat. He could sneak dawn past a rooster.

Bailey felt an unfamiliar sensation in her belly and for a moment couldn't even place it.

Hope.

Maybe just pure joy.

She'd had to smack herself around a little bit last night to get her head on right. Moaning and groaning about having to wait a few more hours to be reunited with her family when she had already waited twenty-three months, twenty-seven days and — she looked at her watch — five hours and fifteen minutes, not that she was counting or anything. She wasn't entitled to feel sorry for herself now.

She felt around for her phone, knowing she'd fallen asleep with it in her hand. When she located it in the blanket, she punched the button and a red battery icon showed up on the screen, informing her she was down to about three percent. She had forgotten to plug it in last night. With something like desperation, she leapt up and raced into the bedroom, dug in her suitcase for the charger cord and plugged it in to the nearest outlet — on the wall by the bedroom door. Then she knelt on the floor and punched the power button again.

She watched the video. Once. Twice. Then sat for some period of time staring at the photograph, until she felt her legs growing numb by her cramped position. She put the phone on the floor, closed the bedroom door and centered herself.

This was going to be a big day. She almost giggled at the thought, then picked up her overnight bag and headed to the bathroom.

An hour later, she sat with Brice and T.J. at the table in the room, warming their souls on cups of Starbucks that T.J. had brought them. Both men were showered and shaved. Brice was wearing the t-shirt and jeans from his go bag. The sweatshirt he'd bought and his vest were draped over a chair. His go bag didn't carry spare shoes, however, so he was stuck with the ones he'd been wearing with his uniform.

The men looked like they'd had a full night's sleep and she suspected that measure of alertness came from years of short nights and long days and getting by on whatever rest you could snatch here and there. She felt her heart swell with affection for both of them. Who didn't have to be here. Didn't have to do this for her. Could have been home, sleeping—

"It ain't like that," T.J. said.

"What isn't like what?" she asked.

"It ain't like me and Brice got other things we'd rather be doing and it is a mighty sacrifice for us to be here doin' this instead."

"How did you know I was thinking—"

"If you's considerin' a career change to riverboat gambler, I'd advise you not to quit your day job."

Brice nodded toward her watch. "If you look at that watch one more time there won't be any numbers there."

"Your eyeballs have just 'bout worn 'em down to nothing already."

If they could just about read her mind anyway, there was no sense holding back.

"Here's the thing," she said. "I know it's only eight o'clock, but I don't see any reason for us to sit here—"

"Where it's warm and comfortable—"

"When we could be sittin' in a cold car parked on the street staring at your watch, which by then won't have no numbers on it whatsoever."

Brice stood. "Let's go freeze." He was grinning, though.

"Bring a winter coat next time, dummy."

T.J. had gotten her *winter* coat out of the closet and was holding it out to her. She slipped her arms through the sleeves and put her hand into her pocket feeling for her gloves.

The room vanished.

Sparklers — bright, sharp sabers of stabbing light.

The white noise of static.

Cold air.

Her breath comes out in a puff of white in front of her as she hurries toward the big building that takes up most of the block. It's made of gray stone, with three archways in front, each with three sets of double doors beneath a bank of windows. High above the doors is an ornate cupola with a clock that says it's five minutes after eight, and when she sees it she hurries across the street.

She pushes through the doors into the cavernous open area beyond where big, black boards hang from the ceiling with rows of words on them.

Departures and arrivals.

The room blinks out of existence in a cascading waterfall of sparkling light and sound is muffled, words garbled.

An image slowly forms again behind a screen of snowy white.

"I need to go potty, Mommy." She looks down at the little girl beside her whose eyes are the color of robins' eggs.

"In a minute, honey. I'm looking for …"

She glances up at the black boards, then down at the piece of paper in her hand.

Chapter Twenty-Two

AMTRAK eTicket
Present This Document For Boarding
Reservation Number B0733A
BOS > NYP One-Way
Train 2260 Dec. 01, 2015. Seats 14A, 14B Departs
8:30 AM

"We're in a hurry, sweetie. Can you hold it?"

Bethany nods. María squeezes her hand, and pulls the child along beside her as she rushes across the station.

Bailey heard T.J.'s voice from a long way off.

"Come on back now."

She felt his hands on her shoulders.

The world of the cavernous room vanished. She was standing between Brice and T.J. in front of a half open hotel room door.

"What …?" T.J. began.

Bailey pulled her hand out of the coat pocket where she'd been digging for her gloves. What she clutched in her fingers wasn't a pair of gloves. It was a small framed photograph.

It was what María had slipped into her coat pocket as she was leaving the apartment yesterday.

A handsome man in a tuxedo with his arm around a black-haired woman in a white dress.

The man is Aaron.

The woman is Jessie.

It's their wedding photo.

Bailey looked at the picture and couldn't breathe. Couldn't think or be, was so overwhelmed she could do nothing but fall into the depths of it, awash in a sea of memories and random images.

AARON WHISPERS into her ear with a profound speech defect.

"Mar-widge is what bwings us togevver to-day." She stifles a giggle and pokes him with her elbow. "Wuuuuve, twoooo wuuuve …"

"Shhhhhh!"

"I bet ministers' robes are like kilts — they don't wear anything under them."

He takes her hand and squeezes. His hand is sticky.

"Is that icing …?"

"Cakes can be poisoned, you know. But unless I drop over dead, this one's safe."

"SHE'S RUNNING AWAY!" Bailey gasped out the words, her mind alight with a million synapses all firing at the same time as they're dropped from a great height into a blender. "María. She's taking Bethany and running away!"

Chapter Twenty-Three

BAILEY DIDN'T KNOW how they came to be in the car. The three of them were standing in the hotel room as she babbled out what she had seen when she pulled the photograph out of her pocket. The last person who'd touched the photo had been María. When Bailey touched it, she had *connected*, as she had connected so many times to the people whose portraits she'd been compelled to paint.

Then they were in the car, Brice driving, racing down the street toward the South Boston Amtrak station.

She had no memory of the events in between.

No memory of the events, but clear memories of the mental journey, the emotional one, far longer — in distance and time — than the one the three of them had taken from the hotel to their rental car in the parking garage.

Aaron.

She had not seen his face in more than two years. She had conjured it up in memory a million times. Two million. Then she felt her grasp on it begin to fade. She began to fear thinking about him too much. Like somehow his image, his *essence*, was like a candle, burning brilliantly, but finite. The image could burn only so long before it finally guttered out.

One day, it would be gone completely. One day, she feared, she would try to conjure up his face and it wouldn't be there. Nothing but blankness. One day she would not be able to remember what Aaron looked like.

She had gone through months where she literally did not dare think about him. Or about Bethany. She was afraid to call them to mind for fear they would not be there, their images gone forever.

She got over that period. It was one of the stages of … grief — yeah, stages of *grief* — she'd gone through. Now, she could call up his face, recall every plane and angle of it, could remember his eyes.

But she had not *seen* him, had not seen his image in two years.

And there he was. Smiling out of the frame. A moment from the past dragged into the present.

Not just any moment. Their wedding day.

For the first few seconds she stared at the photograph, she was afraid she was going to fall into it, fall out of the world and into that moment in time. That she would be consumed by the glory and wonder and love and aching and longing and *grief.* That it would take her, swallow her and she would never come back up out of it again.

Perhaps she would have. But …

María was leaving, was running away with Bethany.

The urgency of that held her in this world. As the storm of emotions, the tsunami of memories and feelings slammed down on her, she held tight to what she had seen out María's eyes.

María was at the train station. She was running away with Bethany.

Why? Why would she do a thing like that?

Even as she asked the question, Bailey knew the answer. She understood. She didn't want to. She wanted to feel a burning fire of anger at the woman who was at that moment running away with, was *kidnapping* her little girl, her daughter, her precious Bethany.

She wanted to hate that woman. Should have hated her. But she couldn't because she understood María's fear. María was terrified that Bailey would take away … *her* little girl. *Her* daughter.

María had loved the child, cared for her, rocked her to sleep, taught her how to button her shirt, held her hand when she crossed the street, cried when the pediatrician gave her shots, prayed over her and played with her — had raised her for two years.

Out of nowhere, a spirit returned from the grave to snatch the child out of her arms. *She* was Bethany's mommy now, and she flat out couldn't let that happen.

Bailey understood. She knew how much María loved Bethany, had always loved the child. Having been separated from the little girl for all these months, Bailey understood the stinging anguish of separation, knew what it felt like to have your heart torn out of your chest. She had to catch María, had to stop her, make her understand that she *wasn't losing Bethany.* The little girl would just be blessed with *two* mommies now instead of one.

Even more than that, she had to make her understand the horrible danger she was in.

SHE FINDS the air to scream, a shrieking wail that shreds her vocal cords, but cannot express her agony. The flames have ignited the hem of the dress and the fire takes it. Pain consumes her leg and she tries to pull away but she is bound and can do nothing but scream and beg for death.

MARÍA WAS GOING to die unless Bailey could catch her. And she might be putting Bethany in so much danger that she would die, too.

The connection had put her inside María's head, and though Bailey had been there for just a few moments, it had felt like touching an exposed wire in a lamp cord. It had shocked her, stunned her. There was enormous power in the connection because of the bond she already had with her sister who wasn't her sister, whose name was María only it wasn't, who had wheezed through her childhood and had been afraid a monster demon would suck out her guts.

She and María were linked as profoundly as any biological sisters — stronger than most. Which meant the connection went both ways. She could sometimes see out María's eyes *and* ... she could communicate with her, like she had communicated with Jeni and the other girls.

As the car careened around corners to a symphony of car horns, Bailey forced herself to relax, she settled back into the seat and concentrated, reached out with her mind to María.

BRICE WAS LOOKING AROUND FRANTICALLY for a parking place.

"Put it there," T.J. said.

"That's a loading zone."

"It's a rental. Let 'em tow it."

Brice pulled into the loading zone, threw the car into

park and the three of them bailed out of it and raced into the big stone building with the clock tower on top. The clock said twenty-five minutes after eight.

T.J. had been in the South Boston station a couple of times in the past. Once when he was a soldier returning from a mission that wasn't on the books, that never happened, and once when he'd come to Boston to talk to a Boston police detective about a killer who was stalking the streets of Chicago.

He tried to summon images of those previous times. The essential features of the station had remained the same but the trimmings had changed. Sprint ads on every surface not covered by some other cellphone provider's advertisement. Banners promoting movies he'd never heard of and sure as Jackson didn't intend to go see. There was even a banner advertising *The Nutcracker* at the Boston Ballet. Opening night tomorrow at 8 p.m.

Brice was studying the arrivals and departures.

"There. Penn Station, boards on Track 7.

Bailey pointed down the rows of numbered tracks and cried, "This way!"

The three of them ran toward the doors that lead from the station out to the trains, dodging through the crowd, around roller bags and strollers and old people with walkers. Brice was faster than either he or Bailey; a thirty-five-year-old man in prime physical condition, he left them in the dust.

He could hear Bailey. She was winded, but still had enough breath to cry.

Her little sister had taken her daughter and run off.

T.J. wanted to be compassionate about that, and he'd get around to compassion. It was on his to-do list. He'd cross that item off soon's they found the girl and got

Bailey's daughter back. Right now, though, he was madder than dammit.

Brice slowed just past a set of double doors. Trains pulled into the station between platforms so passengers could get on or off on either side of the train. Every car had doors on both sides, so you could step directly into or out of any of the fifteen to twenty cars behind the engine. That was a good thing, 'cause the first few cars was always First Class. If you could only get on the train through one door behind the engine, you'd have to walk sideways down the aisle between seats the length of three, maybe four cars before you find the seats for regular folks.

Brice had pulled up short and as he and Bailey arrived, panting, it was clear why. The train on Track 7 was closed up and pulling out, already halfway out of the station, gaining speed as it went along.

"No," was all Bailey could gasp. "Please, God, no …"

"We'll have to call the marshals," Brice said. "Jordan can have officers waiting to take them into custody as they step off the train in Penn Station."

"*Arrest* María?"

"Protective custody," Brice said.

"Kidnapping," T.J. said.

"That's absurd …"

"Bethany's your little girl, not hers," he said. "You can't let her just run off with the child."

The train had pulled all the way out of the station by then, out past the passengers who'd gotten off at the far end of the platform.

There were two figures standing there. Like they had gotten off the end of the train. Or had been waiting to get on there.

They stood by themselves, watching the train pull away. A dark-haired woman and a little girl. María and Bethany.

She let out a little squeak of a cry that could have been any emotion in the world.

María had Bethany by the hand and was walking slowly back down the platform toward the station. She was looking down, didn't see Bailey and the others on the platform on the other side of the empty track. Bailey turned and ran back up the platform, crossed in front of the #7 track, then began to walk slowly down the platform toward her sister and her daughter.

"Mommy, there's that lady again."

Bethany tossed the words into the hollow void that had opened up in María's chest and now stretched out endlessly in every direction inside her. The wind blowing through it was colder than the wind outside, colder that a breath across the polar ice cap. As cold as death.

"Mommy ..." The little girl snuggled up close, gripping tight to the hand María wasn't using to pull the suitcase. María looked down at the child, then followed the little girl's gaze ...

Bailey.

She had to be imagining ...

Where did *Bailey* come from?

How did she know ...?

She stopped walking. Stood as still as stone as Bailey approached, and Bethany snuggled tight to her leg and pulled around behind her.

Then María began to run. She dropped the suitcase and dragged a reluctant Bethany along beside her. When she got to Bailey, she threw her arms around her sister and sobbed.

"I'm so sorry, so sorry, but I couldn't do it, I couldn't. I was so afraid of losing Bethany, I was so scared. I …"

She was babbling and sobbing and making no sense because there was no sense to be made of any of it.

At some point in the darkness last night, as she'd sat up in the chair beside Bethany's bed and watched her sleep, María had snapped. Terror ambushed her. Not terror of the nameless Russian man with a gun, but terror of losing her precious daughter.

Terror took her captive, propelled her, herded her through the hours as she packed, ordered a ticket, called a cab. The terror was so great in her chest it left room for nothing else. It was as all-consuming as a wildfire through the brush. She had run before it. To the South Boston Station. To Track 7. To the train to New York's Penn Station, where she would … she had no idea what she would do when she got there. None. She had picked Penn Station because that had been listed on the example ticket on the website.

Don't leave, María.

She'd heard Bailey's voice in her head as she hurried across the station toward the track. She'd staggered, stopped, looked around.

Don't go.

She'd started running then, running from the words, dragging the suitcase and Bethany along the platform, down the length of the train to the last car.

She stood before the open door.

And she couldn't go through it.

No. She *wouldn't* go through it.

She wouldn't run away from Bailey.

Bailey's voice in her head wasn't the reason, though.

María had finally run all the way out to the end of herself. And somehow found herself there. Found María, the little girl with asthma whose big sister had kept the demons away with a Band-Aid.

Bailey was alive. She was *alive*.

Bethany was *Bailey's little girl.*

María would give up Bethany for Bailey.

To Bailey.

Chapter Twenty-Four

BRICE AND T.J. HUNG BACK, let the sisters have their cry. A train station was a good place for a couple of women to have a meltdown. Didn't nobody notice a thing, figured they was either saying goodbye or saying hello, paid 'em no mind at all.

Once the tears had ratcheted down, they talked. T.J. couldn't imagine what the conversation was like, them two women who'd been beat up by life and by events they didn't cause, by the evil of others, like they'd washed up together with that little girl on some island after they'd been shipwrecked at sea by a hurricane.

Finally, Bailey turned and beckoned to them.

The little girl was hidden so far back behind María it was hard to get a look at her. The young woman who was literally clinging to Bailey had a sweet, open face — which right now wasn't her best look, her eyes all swelled up from crying and her nose red. She wasn't much of a looker right now, but fixed up she'd be attractive. Not beautiful like Bailey, but pretty.

Then he reminded himself that they wasn't blood sisters anyway.

Bailey introduced them. He shook her hand. Didn't bother with his Thomas-Jefferson-Alexander-Hamilton shtick. Hers wasn't no dead-fish-on-a-stick handshake. It was strong and firm. He liked that. She looked him in the eye, too. He liked that, too. The little girl would barely peek out at him from behind her mama. No, not her mama. Bailey was her mama.

From her perspective, she'd just met a skinny piece of gnarled licorice and a redheaded, freckle-faced behemoth in a Boston sweatshirt.

Brice dropped down to one knee in front of the little girl.

"I'm Brice," he told her. "They won't let me wear green. Know why?"

She looked at him with the one peeking eye and shook her head.

"Then people would think I was the Jolly Green Giant."

"And you think that little girl got any idea who that is?" T.J. shook his head in disbelief. "That dude ain't been advertising frozen peas in a decade. You don't get out much, do ya?"

T.J. focused on Bailey and María then.

"Since appears you's all packed up, I s'pect we'd better get on down the road a piece. We got a long way to drive ..." He cut a look at Brice. "'Sides, we might not have no car to drive in."

"No car?" Bailey said.

"Brice was determined to park in that loading zone," T.J. said piously, cutting his eyes toward Brice. "I warned him, tried to get him to listen to reason, said they was gonna tow the car, but nooooo ..."

He kept up the banter as he gently herded the women and little girl out of the station. The GPS had said it was a twelve-hour drive. Best they could hope to do was get close enough so they could make it home with an easy drive tomorrow.

He watched the interplay between the two women as they walked along. Bailey and María was holding hands. *Holding hands!* They was talkin' about when they was little girls, silly memories. Safe memories. No landmines there, wasn't no dead bodies gonna surface, and right now that was definitely a prerequisite for any conversation.

Bethany was staying as far away from Bailey as she could get. He seen that Bailey was studiously ignoring the little girl, and he could tell with just a glance how it was cutting that girl all the way to the bone to do it. But she'd learned from her mistake, wouldn't go tacklin' the kid again.

The car was still sitting where Brice had parked it. Didn't even have a ticket.

"I'd call that the luck of the Irish if your last name wasn't McGreggor."

"There's no car seat," María said.

Car seat. Duh. They couldn't take Bethany anywhere without one.

"There's one in my car," María said. "We can stop by and pick it up."

T.J. didn't want to stop, would rather pull over at the first Walmart they seen and get a new car seat. But the women wasn't paying him no mind. He looked over their heads at Brice, who shrugged. T.J. had checked them out of the hotel when he went down at dawn to get coffee. Just one stop, wouldn't take long, and they could be on their way.

They pulled up beside María's car parked in a tiny lot

next to a wall of dumpsters at the end of the block. There hadn't been a whole lot of talk about logistics, he guessed because María was so totally fried by the circumstances her mind wasn't on a page where she was able to plan out what she'd ought to do about her car, or was the pipes gonna freeze and who was gonna water the plants while she was gone.

That wasn't no bad thing. If they got to talking about the needful things, they wouldn't never get on the road. Yeah, they was lots of loose ends. From the size of the suitcase María was packing, she hadn't brought much by way of belongings. They'd sort that out, too.

It didn't take María two minutes to unhook the car seat from her car and fasten it in place in the middle of the back seat of the rental. If it'd been left to T.J. to figure out how to get that contraption hooked up and that little girl in it, they'd all have to begin life anew right beside these here dumpsters.

"Wait," María said, and she turned to Bailey. "Pictures. I have albums full …"

You could see the yearning in Bailey's eyes. She needed to watch her little girl grow up.

"It won't take but a minute to get them." María turned down the sidewalk toward her building.

"I'm going with you," Brice said and strode up beside her.

The oh-don't-bother, I-can-manage froze on her face when she realized why he didn't want her to go alone.

"Mommy!" Bethany cried from the backseat, holding out her arms to María. "I go wif you!"

"Wait here for me, sugar plum. I'll be right back."

"Nooooo!" squalled the little girl and she began to wail, not in a kick-your-feet tantrum, just pure misery.

T.J. was proud of Bailey. She didn't leap into the back

seat of the car and start trying to console the child. Sat still in the front seat holding onto her emotions with her fingernails. Smart move. Which, of course, left him to deal with the situation.

"You ever seen anybody could take they thumb off and then put it back on again?"

He proceeded to demonstrate his one and only kid trick, but Bethany wasn't buying what he was selling. As María and Brice hurried up the steps and disappeared into the building, the little girl proceeded to engage in a full-bore emotional meltdown.

Goody.

Chapter Twenty-Five

THE BIG MAN in the bulky Boston sweatshirt and no coat was nice — what was his name? Brice? María was horrible with names. The man's size was intimidating, but it was comforting, too, if María let herself consider *why* he was accompanying her up the stairs to her apartment.

But her mind still couldn't/wouldn't go there. That there was somebody out there who wanted to kill …

No, that was a bridge too far. In a day or two, when it finally sank in that she had dropped her whole life and gone running madly away into the night … okay, mid-morning. Point being, she needed time for it all to become real to her before she'd be able to believe …

"I've got the albums stuck in a couple of different places," she told him as the elevator door closed in front of them. "One big picture album on the top shelf in the hall closet and there's a smaller one under my bed. There's also a box of loose pictures I haven't had time to … the ones of Bethany in her Halloween costume this year. She was a minion, you won't believe how—"

She realized she was babbling, but had a sense that

Brice was okay with that, might even be used to it. He was, after all, a friend of Bailey's.

How did somebody in the Witness Protection Program make friends when you couldn't tell anybody who you really were? But maybe they weren't friends. The two men — the old one was T.J, she remembered that much — acted like police officers. Both carried guns. That must be their connection to Bailey. They were part of the Witness Protection Program or something. But they called her Bailey — the name María had given her when they were kids. Did she drop Cunningham and go by Jessie Bailey now? You'd address somebody you were guarding by their last name.

But as soon as the thought entered her mind, she rejected it. These men were her friends. You could see it in every syllable of body language and in the easy way they had with each other.

So maybe they'd started out guarding her or whatever it was they did and then after a while they all became friends. She'd have to ask about that. She'd have to ask about all of it, so many things.

Where were they going? She didn't even know where they were going! How ridiculous was that? She hadn't even asked. Didn't know how long it would take to get there. If they'd chartered a plane or whatever to come to Boston, it must be more than a couple of hours away.

"—cute she was. I made the costume, got a diver's mask to put on her face, painted an eyeball on it so she could be the minion that only has the one eye in the middle, I can't remember his name."

The elevator dinged and María realized she hadn't given the man a chance to say a word since they left the car.

Where Bethany was probably hysterical by now.

"We need to hurry," she said as the elevator door opened.

The man continued her thought. "That little girl is *not* happy strapped in that car seat."

"Bailey scared her is all. She didn't mean to but—"

"She told us what happened."

"Bethy will … get used to her."

Will more than get used to her. Will become her …

No, best not go there, either. There were landmines barely under the surface all over her life right now and she needed to be careful not to step on one. Not until she was prepared.

They had gotten to the door of her apartment. She fished around in her coat pocket and pulled out her key ring. He took them from her before she could insert the key into the deadbolt lock at the top.

He moved her out of the way, put the key in the hole and turned it.

He looked at her quizzically. "The door's not locked."

María burped out a laugh.

"I blew out of here so fast this morning I'm surprised I remembered to *close* it."

She started to open the door but he gently shoved her to the wall beside the door. Then he turned the knob and pushed the door slowly inward with his left hand as he put his right hand on the grip of the pistol in the holster at his side.

The door was only halfway open when she saw something … movement inside … and Brice coughed. Somebody coughed.

After that, nothing in the world fit right.

The big man let go of the doorknob and staggered back as he began pulling his gun out of the holster. Another cough and he twisted around the other way. His pistol tumbled to the floor and he fell backward, slamming into the wall on the other side of the hallway.

Even before he went down, before he hit the floor, the movement she'd seen became a man inside her apartment. He must have been standing behind the door and when it began to open …

He wasn't as big as the red-haired man who now lay on his back at her feet.

But the gun in his hand made him look ten feet tall.

Gun.

He had shot Brice.

Killed Bailey's friend.

The man pointed the pistol with the long barrel at her, and María knew she had only moments to live.

"You are María McKessen, yes?" the man demanded.

She nodded. *Bethany!*

Squeezed her eyes shut. *Bailey would take care of her.*

Tensed for the pain of a bullet ripping into her chest.

But the man didn't shoot her. He grabbed her arm and propelled her ahead of him down the hallway. A second man had materialized out of her apartment and was following them toward the back stairs.

She glanced to the right at the door to Jason's apartment in time to see that it was open about an inch and Jason was peering out. Then he shoved it shut and they hurried past to the door marked "Stairs." The men were huge, but they moved so fast María had trouble keeping up. And quietly, their footsteps barely sounding on the steps.

The back door.

A blast of cold air in her face.

There was a gray van parked illegally right in front of the door. The side door slid open as they stepped out of the building and the two men shoved her forward. A fat man with a flat broad face inside the van grabbed her arm, the two men with her jumped in behind her, the door slammed shut, and the van sped away down the short alley, turned and pulled slowly out into the street.

There were no windows in the van, but as they drove past it, María caught a glimpse — out through the windshield — of the rental car parked in the tiny parking lot two doors down from her building.

The side of Bailey's face.

And a sound.

"Momeeeeee!"

But she must have imagined that part.

The man had thrown María on the floor of the van and she didn't move, just sat there trying to wake up. Because this had to be a nightmare. Had to be. Nothing like this was real.

Except it was.

There were four men in the van with her. Two sat in the back on a single bench seat that faced the back doors with her sprawled on the floor in front of them. Another drove, and the bald man with no cap who'd materialized out of nowhere in her apartment rode shotgun.

When the fat one with the broad, flat face had grabbed her and shoved her down, he had pawed her. She'd squirmed to get away from his rough seeking hands, disgusted and horrified. But when he found her phone in her coat pocket he snatched it out and let her drop to the floor.

They said nothing, to each other or to María. The silence was adding to the incipient panic that any second would explode. She wanted to cry but couldn't seem to get her vocal cords to engage. Couldn't do anything but sit here like a terrified rabbit.

What were they going to do with her?

Duh. They were going to kill her.

Then she did cry. Tears burst out, a sob like a grunt detonated in her throat and suddenly she was bawling so hard she could barely breathe.

Whap!

The man closest to her, the one with the pockmarked face who had shot the big man, Brice, hit her in the face. Slapped her so hard she flew backward and her head connected with the back door, making a jaw-jarring *thunk* sound.

"Shut up," he said. "I will put a gag in your mouth if you make another sound."

A gag in her mouth.

No, not that. If he …

If something covered her mouth and maybe her nose.

If she couldn't breathe …

She found herself whimpering despite her best efforts to keep silent. If they put a gag in her mouth, she would have an asthma attack. Breo inhaler or no Breo inhaler. She could feel the tightness in her chest now, just from the terror. If they gagged her, she would choke to death.

Her face was on fire, heat making her left eye water.

Nobody had ever hit her in the face. Nobody had ever … no one had ever hurt her. And so casually.

"Wipe your face," said the man who'd hit her, and tossed her a piece of paper, a McDonald's napkin. She didn't realize until he said it that there was blood dripping down her chin from a split lip. Maybe her nose was bleeding, too.

She inched up until she was sitting, her back leaned against the back door. Then she used the paper to wipe off the blood, terror clawing at her chest.

She'd reach up, open the back door and leap out.

They were going too fast for that, but she didn't care.

They were on a busy street, the car behind them would run over her.

A traffic light then.

The instant they stopped at a traffic light, she would leap out.

Idiot! You think they didn't lock the back door?

Of course it was locked.

Maybe she should just start screaming, wailing. Wouldn't somebody hear her and call 911?

If she made another sound, they would gag her. She would have an asthma attack and die.

She swallowed the scream with the panic.

She couldn't panic. She had to *think*!

Think what?

She had no idea.

Chapter Twenty-Six

BAILEY DIDN'T KNOW when Marshal Jordan had shown up. He was just there, talking to the other officers and she hadn't seen him come in.

Time had telescoped, like it had that day in the rain when Bailey'd stood looking at the car seat turned upside down in a puddle and Aaron held up the bloody guy from the other car by his lapels.

Call 911, he had shouted at her.

Were those the last words Aaron ever said to her?

No, the last words were *Jessie, run.* With his last words, Aaron had tried to save Jessie's life. Then another firecracker pop and the man with the gray beard and the eyepatch stood holding a gun as Aaron collapsed on the street.

Had he shot María, too?

Bailey could imagine it, could even picture it — as clear as if she had seen it. He is standing in the apartment. María comes in the door and looks confused. Yeah, she'd be confused that there was somebody in her apartment.

Then the one-eyed man points a gun and there's the

sound of a firecracker pop and María falls to the floor. Then he shoots her again. Just to make sure she's dead. After all, he had to shoot Aaron twice. Aaron had refused to die with only one bullet in him. He was stubborn like that.

Bailey shook her head to clear the webs of imagination.

The one-eyed crazy man — yes, crazy now, that's what the private investigator had reported to Dobbs. He'd been sane when he murdered Aaron. He'd been crazy when he kidnapped María.

Kidnapped.

He didn't shoot her down like he did Brice. Could have, but didn't.

Only it hadn't been the one-eyed man, but one of his goons. The boy down the hall — Jason — had talked to him, to both of them. They'd seemed nice enough, he'd said, just wanted to know about María. Only they called her Dawn, and he'd told them she wasn't home right now, he didn't think, and they'd asked where she went, and he'd said he didn't know, that this woman had shown up in her apartment yesterday and María/Dawn had started screaming and the woman said it was because María/Dawn had thought she was dead.

He'd heard the sounds in the hallway — Brice crashing into the wall — and peeked out, saw the men shoving María toward the back stairs.

"She looked so scared," he'd said.

Terrified.

More scared than squirming around in the mud under a dumpster.

Jessie'd been afraid the one-eyed man would find her.

The one-eyed man *had* found María.

And took her away.

Bailey swallowed hard. There was a lump in her throat and she didn't know what would happen if she didn't swallow it back. Maybe she would scream, or burst out crying. Maybe she'd throw up. But swallowing the knot in her throat was making it hard to breathe.

María was gone.

Mikhailov took her.

"Mrs. Cunningham ..." it was Marshal Jordan, the U.S. marshal with the Witness Protection Program. It had been so long since anybody'd called her Mrs. Cunningham. Not since that day in the safe house somewhere when she first met Marshal Jordan. He'd called her Mrs. Cunningham then, too. He'd spoken in that same tone of voice he was using now, the one she had come to loathe, the one that treated you like you were so fragile you might shatter into a thousand pieces.

Like you were weak and not possessed of all your marbles.

She wasn't weak now, and had every marble she'd ever had.

"I'd like the answers to some questions if you feel—"

"No, I'm the one who wants *answers.* You knew he'd come looking for me. Why didn't you get María and Bethany and take them somewhere safe before you served—"

"They didn't serve the subpoenas." Brice's voice sounded bitter as well as pained. He was sitting in the recliner opposite the couch with his sweatshirt, t-shirt and vest off and a paramedic was poking around two humongous purple bruises, one on his abdomen, another on his chest.

The one on his chest could have stopped his heart, she'd heard the paramedic say. The force of a bullet from a

Glock hitting a Kevlar vest at such close range had the explosive force of a sledgehammer blow.

Brice had been cold this morning, so he'd put on the vest under his shirt. He was alive now because he'd been cold. Big doors swung on such little hinges sometimes.

"Which means somebody leaked information to Mikhailov soon's you guys got arrest warrants." That was T.J. He was sitting beside her on the couch, holding her hand.

"Wait a minute …" Bailey's mind was not tracking, and she hadn't been able to get it to focus on much of anything after they heard the wailing of sirens and the Boston Police units came roaring down the street, skidding to a stop with officers piling out, guns in hand.

At that moment, the horror of it, hot and stinking, had overwhelmed her and she'd been carried along as relentlessly as the cold water in that coal mine had carried her and the other girls toward their deaths.

Now, all that remained of her fragmented memories were some snapshots. And those weren't even in color.

Black and white.

Snap.

T.J.'s face, contorted with emotion, gesturing at the officer on the street who absolutely would not let him go into the building.

Snap.

Bethany's face, contorted with emotion, screaming for her "mommy." Who'd told her she'd be right back. But who didn't come right back.

Snap.

Her own face, glimpsed in the mirror on the wall in María's apartment hours — maybe hours, who knew? — after she'd stepped inside and found a paramedic working on Brice and a Boston Police officer asking her if she was related to the woman who was renting this apartment and if she knew what …

Bailey had just stared at him, then past him at the mirror. She'd looked dead. The way her face had looked in the portrait T.J.'s mother'd painted of her thirty years before she was born. Dead, with a bullet hole in her temple.

"… just hold on here." Her voice was scared and anger-fueled and was every bit as strong as she didn't feel. She turned it full force on Marshal Jordan. "It's *your* fault? Somebody in *your* office or …?"

"That's not what I'm saying at all."

"Fine," T.J. said. "We'll all shut up now." He squeezed her hand. "And let you tell us what you *are* saying. 'Xplain how this Mikhailov fellow knew he was about to be arrested before it happened. So long before, in fact, that he had time to figure out that the wife of the man he was 'bout to be charged with murdering wasn't dead like he figured, so maybe he'd ought to go have a little talk with the family that'd been pretending for two years she was dead."

"There was a leak, yes," Jordan said, but held up his hands, placating. "But it wasn't in the Marshal's Service."

"What, you're playing CYA now? You think I care who—"

"We've been looking for Mikhailov ever since we got the call from Mrs. Cunningham."

Bailey doubted that, doubted he'd dropped his Thanksgiving drumstick and raced out his front door with his tie flapping in mad pursuit.

"He was seen on Saturday at a restaurant called Little Moscow. We were locked and loaded to take him down, but he was gone before we got there. I think that's when he found out about the indictments — on Saturday — because nobody's seen him since."

He turned and spoke directly to Bailey.

"Someone at the federal courthouse, a clerk, a bailiff — we'll ferret out who was responsible — was paid off. I'm not playing the blame game. I just want you to know *it wasn't us* so you understand that you're still safe while you're in our custody, that the Marshal's Service wasn't responsible for—"

She didn't let him finish. "I want to go back to that other part. The 'in your custody' part. What do you mean—?"

"Protective custody. You and your little girl. We need to get you out of here and to a safe—"

"*Safe?*" T.J. and Brice said the word together with the perfect unison of a chorus line.

Bailey knew the drill, knew what would happen next. She'd be hauled out of here to some anonymous place — with *Bethany!*

The little girl was in her room now with a woman from the Marshal's Service, maybe the same one who had held Bailey up so she wouldn't fall down in the shower and sat up all night watching her sleep that first night after …

But maybe it wasn't the same woman. Bailey wouldn't recognize her now if she found her under the bed. The woman reading a story to Bethany was an anonymous police officer who clearly had a way with children.

At some point during the police-officers-everywhere nightmare, Bethany had stopped crying, had fallen asleep in the car seat in the back of the rental car which was supposed to be bearing them all — *including María* — away to safety in West Virginia.

She'd awakened crying for her mommy, and Bailey had somehow managed to stay away from her while T.J. and the female marshal had taken her to her bedroom and tried to get her to play with her toys.

T.J. got down on the floor with her and some paints and a sketch pad.

Until then, Bailey hadn't even noticed all the little-kid art that decorated the apartment. Pictures of lopsided boxes that were either houses or wheel-less cars were stuck to the refrigerator with magnets. Free-form splashes of color — in watercolors and pastels and crayons. They all had neatly printed titles: A Bird in the Park. Jasmine's House. Flowers by the Stoop. Obviously, Bethany had inherited her mother's artistic flair.

But Bethany hadn't wanted to draw with T.J., so the marshal had picked out the most dog-eared of her story books — *Green Eggs and Ham* — and sat down with her in the rocker. Bethany had her thumb in her mouth and was clinging ferociously to a tattered minion blanket that was the wear-and-tear version of the one Bailey'd clung to just as ferociously as she'd cried herself to sleep for months.

Marshal Jordan was right now making plans to take Bailey and the traumatized child to some anonymous place with anonymous pictures of lighthouses or sailing ships — why was it that every place they'd taken her had been decorated in tacky ocean decor? Someplace empty. Profoundly empty and impersonal. Housing for an auto-mated attendant and her on-the-run robot child.

No.

"Bethany and I aren't going anywhere with you. We're going ... home."

Chapter Twenty-Seven

THE VAN finally pulled off the street and into a driveway. María heard the sound of a garage door opening and once they were parked in the dark interior of a building she finally had the courage to speak — for the first time since the man with the pockmarked face had hit her.

"I have to … I need to go to the bathroom."

The bald man who was sitting in the front seat turned around and glared at her.

"Piss yourself," he said.

The driver, a dark, swarthy man with a single thick black eyebrow and a heavy mustache, barked words in what María assumed was Russian at the man who had hit her. He pulled her to her feet and shoved her in front of him out the door of a van. They were in a large building, a warehouse, maybe, definitely bigger than a garage. It felt vast and vacant, not much warmer than it was outside and her breath frosted when she panted explosively out her nose. There were no windows to admit light and flickering fluorescents high overhead provided the only illumination, which left puddles of shadows around piles of something, boxes, machinery covered with tarps … something.

The driver spoke again and the man who had her arm continued walking with her, hauling her along beside him into a shadowed area, then shoved her between stacks of boxes about ten feet high.

"Go!"

"Here?"

"Go or piss yourself."

If she had not needed to go so desperately, she would have refused, but the pain of holding it overcame her shyness and she moved as far away from him as she could, turned her back and began unbuttoning her jeans. She kept her back to him, didn't know and didn't want to know if he, too, had turned his back or was standing there watching her. The stink of warm urine wafted up to her, making her briefly nauseous.

Nothing to wipe with. Duh.

She stood, buttoned and zipped her jeans, then turned back toward the man. He was facing her, surely had been the whole time. He took a step toward her, grabbed her upper arm and yanked but she managed not to step in the puddle she'd just made. As he dragged her back to where the other men were standing around the van, the garage door opened again and a big black car rolled in and parked on the other side of the van. She caught a glimpse of outside — gravel, concrete, a parking lot — before the door slid back down into place.

The driver of the car was a man in a tailored business suit and he hopped out as soon as he stopped and opened the back door of the vehicle.

The man who stepped out of the back seat was Mikhail-whatever. Unmistakable. Slender, immaculately dressed, a short white beard that came to a point on his chin. And a black eyepatch. She was looking at the man who had shot Aaron while Bailey looked on in terror. The man who'd believed he'd also killed Aaron's wife and now was looking to finish the job he'd started. They'd taken María to get at Bailey and it was a dark irony that they'd driven within a few feet of the victim they'd been seeking when they drove off with María in the van.

He gestured with a black-gloved hand and the man dragging María hauled her toward him and threw her down at his feet.

"You are the sister of Jessica Cunningham, yes? The legal guardian of her daughter."

His voice had an oily feel, unpleasant for some reason María couldn't identify.

She nodded.

The man who had thrown her grabbed her hair and yanked her head back.

"Answer the question."

"Yes … I mean, no, not really." The man still had her hair and he shook her head with it. She cried out and stammered. "I'm Bethany's guardian, but Bailey and I, we're not blood relatives. We just grew up in the same foster home and have always called ourselves sisters."

"Bailey?"

"Jessie … Jessica. We, I always called her Bailey."

"She came to visit you yesterday — as I am told it was the first time in a long time."

Panic was so close to the surface it burst out her throat.

"I can't tell you anything about her because I don't know anything. I—" The man standing behind her let go of her hair and kicked her in the back and she flew forward, landing with a grunt only inches from Mikhailov's shoes.

"You speak when you're spoken to," he said. He

sounded American, had no Russian accent María could discern.

She looked up, terrified, at Mikhailov.

"So you are going to tell me what I want to know about your sister and then I will not have to hurt you — not badly, anyway. I will give you a little demonstration that will make our conversation shorter and more profitable."

He nodded to the bald man who'd been sitting in the front seat of the van. He came forward, pulled María up off the floor and slammed her up against the back door of the big black car. The suit-and-tie driver of the car opened the front door and the bald man held María up against the car with his body, grabbed her right wrist and pulled her hand up to rest on the car door jamb. Then just held her there with her hand …

When the driver of the car began to move, she realized what he was going to do.

Nooooo!

She only had time and strength to yank backwards a little bit. But even so, when he slammed the car door shut on her hand, it did not catch all her fingers as he'd intended. Instead, it smashed down on two inches of her index and middle fingers.

She shrieked! The man holding her against the car stepped away and she tried … *her fingers were smashed* … to free them. She clawed at the door handle with her left hand, screaming her voice raw. Yanking, pulling. She tugged up on the handle, pushed the handle in, wrenched it out and shoved it down — frantic, desperate. She couldn't open the door to free her fingers! Didn't know how to operate the handle. She yanked and strained and shrieked and …

The men watched her struggle to free her mashed fingers, listened to her screams and did nothing.

Finally she did something that engaged the handle, the door came open, she grabbed her right hand with her left and crumpled to her knees, cradling her crushed fingers. It hurt so bad she felt instantly nauseous, couldn't stop herself, leaned forward and began to vomit violently on the ground, splattering the shoes of the car's driver.

He spit words at her, Russian profanity probably, as he leapt back. Then one of the men had her by the left arm, dragging her to her feet, shoving her away from the pile of vomit toward the van, where he allowed her to collapse beside it, crying and coughing, holding her smashed fingers.

Both fingers were flat! Had dents on them where the metal had crushed …

She didn't notice that Mikhailov had followed them to the van until she heard his voice above her.

"That was a little demonstration. Maximum pain, minimum damage. Probably didn't even break the fingers."

She was staring at her fingers, not trying to move them, trying to keep from vomiting again from the pain.

"Look at me when I speak to you."

She looked up.

He nodded and two of the men took her by the arms and sat her inside the open van door, on the floor with her feet on the concrete outside. She kept her eyes on his face as they moved her. Didn't want to watch her fingers turn purple and black.

"I can hurt you in ways you do not know, hurt you so bad you will beg me to smash your fingers in a car door instead because it would hurt less. Do we understand each other?"

She started to nod, then remembered.

"Yes." Her voice was hoarse from screaming and vomiting.

"Excellent."

Chapter Twenty-Eight

BAILEY WASN'T SURE, but she didn't think the marshal could force her to go with him. Maybe he could, and if he could, he would have to. He would have to drag her kicking and screaming out of here and off to Nowhere Land. She would not go gently into that good night.

She thought to explain it to him. But why bother.

Yeah, she needed to bother.

"I know where you plan to take us. Oh, not the specific place. I didn't know where the specific place was when I was actually there. But I know what kind of place, and I'm not doing that. Not ever again."

"Mrs. Cunningham, surely you realize the danger. Especially ... now."

Yeah, now. When Mikhailov had María.

"If you think María is going to tell him—"

"She might try not to, but there are ways to force—"

The hammer blow of the word *force* did what nothing else that day had been able to do. It dislodged the knot in her throat and she leapt up, raced to the bathroom, and was violently sick. Nothing but burning acid, coffee vomit.

Why was it she never threw up when she actually had something in her stomach to eject? Surely, that wouldn't be as unpleasant as acid burning the back of her throat and nose.

She kept her head hung over the toilet, dry-heaved a time or two, then flushed the noxious mess before the smell made her keep gagging.

She stood, shaky, turned to the sink, which was right next to the toilet. Tiny bathroom. It smelled like Chanel Grand Extrait. A knockoff, of course, all María could afford.

María.

Dear holy God in heaven, the monster who had killed Aaron now had María. He would *force* ... the word hurt so bad, razor blades through her soul ... force what?

He couldn't force her to tell him what she didn't know.

María didn't know anything that would be valuable to him.

In a horrible, soul-death way, Bailey realized that was the good news for Bailey and the bad news for María.

Bailey splashed some cold water on her face, wiped it with a towel that smelled like it had dried on a clothesline. That's when she saw the picture on the wall. It was one of who knew how many pieces of little-kid art all over the house. But this one was framed, though. Clearly, Bethany had drawn it. It had a little more shape than most of her artwork — you could almost tell that it was a tree. There was a small white splotch of paint in the green smear of tree limbs and leaves.

María had printed a title beneath it. The Barbie Tree.

JESSIE FINDS María on the front porch of the house, sitting in the porch swing that protests with a waaaa-ng sound so loud you almost don't want to swing in it. Mr. Anderson's always going to "put some WD-40 on it," but he never gets around to it.

As soon as she sees María's face, she knows something is wrong.

"I'd say you look like you just lost your best friend, but since that's me, something else must be wrong."

María says nothing, just points wordlessly up into the leaves of the big tree in the front yard. It is a huge oak tree, a perfect tree for climbing with that limb that sticks out at right angles to the trunk only a few feet off the ground. The boys clamber up and down it like monkeys.

Jessie looks where María is pointing but sees nothing.

"What?"

"There," María says. Her wheezing isn't as bad today as it is sometimes. She can get most of a sentence out. "The white at the end of that branch."

Jessie sees it then, something white and fluffy is up in the tree at least thirty feet off the ground, tangled in the smaller limbs.

"What is—?"

"It's Superstar Barbie. Kyle took it and he and Jake were playing keep-away with it."

Jessie seethes. She hates it when the boys tease María, and in truth they don't do it very often. Their own boy-on-boy aggression keeps them pretty busy and they know Jessie will leap to María's aid and they don't want to cross Bailey. She has a clear streak of foster-care toughness they don't want to mess with.

"Then Kyle threw it real high and it got stuck in the tree."

"I'll go get Kyle and make him climb up and get it."

"Can't. He and Jake went with Mrs. Anderson to karate class."

"Mr. Anderson can get it down when he gets home."

María looks at her disdainfully. "He's going to climb that tree?

Yeah, that was a stupid idea.

"Then we'll just have to wait until—"

"It'll be ruined by then."

As if to give substance to what María says there is a low rumble of thunder in the distance. The sky is full of boiling gray clouds.

"If it gets rained on … she's wearing that white gown."

Jessie remembers that particular garment, one of María's favorites, all ruffles and laces and tiny little snaps that Jessie always has to fasten for her.

A cool breeze rustles the leaves of the tree and carries with it the smell of approaching rain.

María looks miserably up into the branches at the splash of white fabric fluttering in the wind.

"I'll get it down," Jessie blurts out and is instantly sorry. She has never climbed a tree and there's a reason for that. Acrophobia. Fear of heights. Which, technically, she doesn't have. What she does suffer from is fear of acrophobia — she's afraid that she would be *afraid of heights if she ever looked down from something tall. She's relatively certain if that happened, she'd be terrified, but she has never actually put it to the test.*

"You could get it down?" María might as well have said, "You can leap tall buildings in a single bound?" She made it sound like it was a feat of derring-do unparalleled in human experience.

Which, of course, meant Jessie had to climb the tree.

"Sure. Piece of cake."

Thunder rumbled again. The sound was closer.

"Then … hurry, before the rain hits."

Rain. Yeah. The only bigger challenge Jessie can think of than climbing a tree for the first time is climbing it in the rain.

She rushes to the trunk of the tree and stands beneath the solitary limb sticking out at the bottom. From the side, it looks like it would, indeed, be a piece of cake to jump up and grab that limb. From below, it looks like it is at least fifteen feet off the ground.

"Use the chair," María says, and Jessie drags one of the wooden Adirondack lawn chairs to the trunk where she can use it as a ladder.

She climbs up the slats of the chair, holds onto the trunk and stretches out her hand as high as she can reach. Which is about six inches below the limb.

How did the boys get onto that limb?

They jumped for it.

She jumps, uses both hands, grabs the limb, then scoots her way up the trunk until she is straddling the limb. She looks at María, sitting on the porch.

Bad move.

Don't look down.

Above all other things, she knew she must not look down. So she turns and looks up. The doll is about fifteen or twenty feet above her, and she carefully begins to make her way toward it. Grabbing a limb, stepping from one limb to the next highest one. Moving carefully.

Finally she is positioned on the limb directly below the limb where the doll is caught.

Wind wiggles the branches, creating a sense that the whole tree is swaying.

"… almost there …"

The words are carried away by the accelerating wind and Jessie manages not to look toward the porch where María is shouting them.

She takes hold of the limb above, which she can barely reach, and begins to inch out on the limb she's standing on.

Which bends down slightly under her weight. The limb above bends too, though, and she doesn't have to go all the way out to the doll. She can pull the limb down to her and grab …

A gust of wind hits the tree, shaking the boughs. Jessie lurches, clutches the limb above, dragging it downward and the doll slips free and plummets to the ground.

María is probably moving slowly down the porch steps to get the doll out of the grass.

Probably, because Jessie refuses to look to make sure.

Then, of course, it hits her. Even at the time she realizes that this particular one of the great truths of the universe is one you can only learn by painful experience.

It is a simple task to climb up a tree without looking down. It is not a simple task to reverse that motion.

She froze in place.

Somehow María knew she was scared.

"Just look at your feet." Wheeze. "Your feet."

Jessie looks at her feet securely on the limb. Can see just beyond them the limb she'd stepped on before this one, and she watches her foot move slowly toward it.

By the time she makes it to the ground, it has begun to sprinkle and her arms and legs are trembling from effort, strain and terror.

María rushes to her, as fast as María ever moves anywhere. Hugs her. Tells her she saved Superstar Barbie's life.

Since the doll hadn't been alive to begin with, that negates some of the effort. But Jessie is okay with that.

BAILEY LEFT the bathroom and walked into a heated conversation going on between Marshal Jordan, Brice and T.J. Jordan was raking the two of them over the coals for bringing Bailey to Boston and they were hotly defending—

"María can't tell Mikhailov anything about me that'll help him find me because she doesn't know anything," she said.

"She can identify where—"

"No, she can't."

"Can't what?"

"Can't identify where or who or when. You don't understand what happened here. I showed up out of nowhere, did my back-from-the-grave routine and it totally hammered her. We didn't talk about anything except why I had pretended to be dead. I told her about Mikhailov and Aaron and ..." Pain momentarily stole the air from her lungs. "I told her she was in danger because he was back in the country and would come looking for me."

"That's what I mean, she will tell him where—"

"You're not listening!"

Her shout momentarily silenced all the other officers in the room, who turned to look at her. Good. She had Jordan's undivided attention.

"I did *not* tell her where we were going. Wasn't keeping it from her, we just never had time. I told her I had been taken by WITSEC to Albuquerque. And that's it. I never even mentioned Peoria or Omaha. I never said a word about Shadow Rock, West Virginia. Nothing."

"You didn't accidentally drop—"

"No, I didn't accidentally drop anything. I told her I lived in a big house with a big yard, a lake nearby and a puppy. That doesn't narrow down the geography a whole lot."

"Your name—"

"She's always called me Bailey. It's one reason I wanted the name. But I never gave her my WITSEC last name to go with it."

"You can't count on—"

"The Marshal's Service, to keep secret the location of one of their star witnesses? Because if I can't count on that, I'm already dead."

"No, the WITSEC program has a record of …"

"Save the brochure material, I'll read it on the website."

Jordan clearly did not know what to do with the new and improved version of Jessie Cunningham. He'd been expecting a mouse, not a mountain lion.

Then she turned down the heat, dialed back the belligerence she felt rising in the back of her throat like bile.

"In every one of the anonymous places you parked me, I died inside." The almost whispered words were more powerful than a shout. "I won't go back there. I absolutely will not take a traumatized little girl into a lighthouse-on-the-wall hellhole in Des Moines."

She could tell he didn't get the reference but she didn't care.

"I am going to take my little girl *home*."

Tearing up then, she didn't dare look at Brice and T.J., who had come to stand with her, one on either side. "I have a house with a yard. Bethany has her own room, with a pink bedspread and some kind of frozen-icy creatures from some movie I haven't seen on the sheets. There are toys. And soon there will be paints."

She took a big gulp of air.

"That little girl in there has just lost her *mother*!" The pain of those words came from so many wounds her whole soul was bleeding. "I'm going to take her somewhere she can ... heal."

Then Brice and T.J. took the ball and ran with it. They pointed out that if Shadow Rock, West Virginia had been good enough to hide their star witness last week it was still good enough this week. If the leak to Mikhailov hadn't come from the Marshal's Service, nothing had changed.

"Besides, the Watford House will be guarded like a fortress," Brice said. Jordan didn't get it, but she understood the grim tone. One of his deputies had been killed the last time he'd been protecting Bailey there. Brice would be ready for trouble this time.

"One of us will be with her and Bethany twenty-four-seven," T.J. said. "We won't even let her ... take the puppy out in the back yard to pee without an armed escort."

"Find my sister!" She spoke the words to Bernard Jordan softly but they conveyed a wallop that was staggering. "Don't let him ... hurt her. I'll be fine."

"We'll do our best."

He didn't sound hopeful.

"If, like you say, he can't find out from her where you are, then he will try to come up with some other way to use her to get at you."

"He's going to have to find Bailey to do that," T.J. said, "and that ain't gonna happen."

Chapter Twenty-Nine

THE MAN in the gray suit did not stand still in front of María. As he spoke, he paced. At first, she thought he had a limp. It seemed he favored his right leg. But the next few steps his gait was effortless, then he began to limp again.

"I will tell you what I know. You will fill in the parts I do not know."

He began to tick items off with his fingers.

"Your 'sister' was there the day Ivan ran the red light and ... had a little accident. She was a witness, but somehow I did not see her and she got away."

He stopped talking and María realized he expected her to say something.

"That's ... that's what she told me."

"If the woman in the car with the man I shot was not his wife, who was she?"

"I don't know. They left Bethany with me and drove away together. Alone. I ... I never saw Bailey again."

"So you are saying that sometime after they dropped off their daughter, they picked up this woman, the one I thought was his wife?"

"I guess so. I don't know."

"The grand jury issued sealed indictments, but Ivan and I went home before we could be arrested. So your sister went into hiding, stayed in hiding all this time, pretending to be dead. Just *waiting*."

He made the word sound sinister, like what Jessie had done was somehow a dishonorable thing, cheating, not fair.

"I didn't know she, I thought she was—"

"Speak when you are spoken to!" His soft voice had become the roar of an angry lion. He took two hurried steps toward her, his hand raised to hit her, his face a pinched rictus of rage. She cringed away, put her hands in front of her face to ward off the blow. But he didn't hit her and when she opened the eyes she'd squeezed shut, his face was inches from hers.

He cocked his head to the right, then the left, his eyes traveling over her face. "How do you do that?"

"Do what?"

"That thing with your face, the way it changes."

She had no idea what he could possibly be talking about, so she merely looked at him, almost as mystified as she was terrified.

"Stop doing it. If you refuse, I will cut off your ears and make you eat ..."

Something like approval spread over his face.

"Never do it again. Do you understand me? I know about your kind."

Was the right answer "No, I'll never do it again"? Or "Yes, I understand you"? She didn't know which so she said neither.

He stood and resumed pacing, limping badly now but totally calm.

"We spoke to the young man, Jason. He told us what happened yesterday when your sister appeared at your door. Then she left … and did not take her daughter with her. This Jason said you left early this morning in a cab — you and the little girl." He held out a hand and one of the men handed him a piece of paper — the Amtrak eTicket she had stuffed in her pocket. "One way, two people, Penn Station in New York. But then you came back home *without the little girl you took with you.* Explain all this to me."

He stopped pacing, turned to face her and folded his gloved hands in front of him, waiting as patiently as a brood hen on a nest.

She tried to respond, opened her mouth, but she was so sick and scared and in so much pain, she couldn't get her mind to put together a coherent narrative.

He was unperturbed, even encouraging.

"Take your time." Then an edge of menace crept into his calm. "*Make me understand.*"

María knew she had only a few moments to gather her thoughts. In the back of the van, she had thought about trying to protect Bailey, even had considered refusing to say anything at all. Now, she realized how preposterously absurd that was. He would find out everything she knew, make her tell him no matter how badly she didn't want to talk. He would hurt her and she would tell him everything. Gratefully, she didn't know anything that would help him find Bailey. She couldn't betray where the Witness Protection Program had hidden Bailey because she had no idea where it was. Now, she understood that her only hope of self-preservation was making him believe that she really didn't know much of anything.

"Bailey … told me why she had let me think … let everybody think she was dead. Told me that if … you … knew she was alive, you would kill her."

"And everyone else in her family, yes, that is true."

"She said the police had put her in the Witness Protection Program." She searched her mind for details. "They took her to Albuquerque. But then they moved her somewhere else. I don't know where."

"Why did she come out of hiding and contact you yesterday?"

"She said Bethany and I were in danger, that we couldn't stay here. She wanted us to … she wanted me to drop everything and go with her right then, pack a bag and get on a plane and just — run away."

"But you refused. Why would you do a thing like that?"

"It was too much … I couldn't … and Bethany was too upset …"

"That is not reason enough to refuse to run for your lives. What is the part you're not telling me?"

He was as discerning as a card shark.

"I didn't want her to take my little girl away from me!" María spit the words out with such emotion it verified the truth of them — she could see it in his eyes. "Bethany was … I was … I *am* Bethany's mommy. I couldn't just hand her over …"

"So your sister, Jessica is her name, yes? But you call her Bailey, why is that?"

"It's just something, when we were kids we … my name's not really María. We just—"

He'd heard all he cared to hear. "This Bailey just … what? Gave her daughter up and went away? You don't expect me to believe that."

"No, that's not how it happened. I told her to give me time. I said if she would come back in the morning, we would be ready to go. And then—"

"Then you took the little girl and ran away with her, instead of waiting for your sister. Yet you are here, the train ticket unused in your pocket and the little girl is gone."

"I got to the station and I couldn't do it. I couldn't do that to Bailey. And then … she was there at the station."

"Bailey?"

"And two men. The one …" The image of Brice flying backward into the hallway wall blew through her mind. "… your men shot. His name was Brice something. I don't remember his last name. And another man, an old man named T.J. I don't remember his last name either."

"How did she find out you had gone to the station?"

María felt her gut yank into a knot. He wasn't going to believe this.

"I don't know." She hurried ahead before he could protest. "Really, please believe me, I don't know how she found out. But she was there and we left, but we needed a car seat, that's why we came back, to get Bethany's car seat out of my car." She knew she was babbling but couldn't seem to stop the flow of words once they began to tumble out. "We had to drive because Bethany has an ear infection and she can't fly, and then I thought of the picture albums, and I knew Bailey—"

"Stop!"

She had to put her hand over her mouth to shut herself up.

"Where were you going, driving to because the little girl couldn't fly?"

"I don't know. She never … there was no time."

He looked so skeptical, she blurted out, "She said she lived in a big house with a big yard and there was a lake nearby." He said nothing. "And she has a puppy."

"You and the man, Brice, came back to get, what did you say?"

"Albums. Pictures. Bailey hadn't seen Bethany in almost two years. She missed her birthday and Christmas."

"The little girl and the old man, where were—"

"They waited in the car with Bailey."

She didn't see the explosion coming. It was as unexpected and as ferocious as a volcanic eruption. He turned on the man with the pockmarked face and began screaming at him in Russian, then aimed his tirade at the other man who had been in her apartment. She put it together that he was furious at them because they had missed the real prize, that Bailey had been there, waiting on the street, and they had let her get away.

He roared in fury and then she watched him grab hold of his emotions, climb back into the calm facade. He had been screaming so savagely that he had spit into the men's faces, and now he had spit in his beard, drips of it. María tried desperately to keep her eyes off it, to keep from staring.

When he began speaking again, he was totally in control. Except that his limp was so pronounced he stopped pacing and merely stood in front of her.

"Why now? After all this time, why did she come to you today?"

"Because the police knew you were back and she wanted us to get away before——"

"How did the police know I was back?"

"Bailey told them."

He grew very still, very intense.

"How could Bailey possibly know this thing?"

"She saw you in the background of a picture. You were with some other people but she recognized you."

"What picture? Where was it taken?"

"In a restaurant. But I don't know where. She didn't say."

"Just … some random restaurant. Somewhere."

Disbelief again. She could hear it in his voice. If he didn't believe her, he would use whatever force he thought it would take to convince her to tell him "the truth." He would hurt her. She scrambled to think of anything—

"It was in a casino, a restaurant in a casino."

"What casino?"

"I don't know."

"You don't know. She didn't mention where she was gambling—?"

"She wasn't gambling. She went to the restaurant in the casino to eat. Her friends took her out to celebrate. It was her birthday."

He took a step toward her, spoke softly.

"And what is your sister's birthday?"

"Halloween. October thirty-first."

He stared into the distance for a moment, then said a word that made no sense to María.

"The Nautilus."

Chapter Thirty

It was mid-afternoon before T.J., Brice, Bailey and Bethany left María's apartment in the rental car headed for the Massachusetts Turnpike and Interstate 90. T.J. took the first shift behind the wheel. Bailey rode in the back beside Bethany's car seat.

T.J. felt so sorry for the poor little girl. The child had to be totally exhausted. Disoriented and confused, in the company of people she didn't know — and María'd said she was afraid of strangers! Bethany had alternated between tantrums, meltdowns, sucking-her-thumb withdrawal and crying, makin' a sound like a baby rabbit.

He figured Bailey felt like doin' the same things as the three-year-old, strugglin' to wrap her mind around the reality that her precious little sister was now in the hands of a homicidal monster.

There'd only been one time since María'd hopped out of the car to go get picture albums for Bailey that T.J.'d seen anything but desolation in Bailey's eyes. Before they left María's apartment, Bailey'd taken a framed piece of little-kid art off the wall in the bathroom and tucked it under her arm.

"He didn't get Bethany," she'd told T.J. fiercely, her green eyes blazing, givin' off sparks like she'd seen in that vision. "If we hadn't come to Boston yesterday, Mikhailov would have her now, too."

"This ain't somethin' we can talk about in front of your marshal friend," he'd said, quietly, "and ain't a thing that's easy to think about. But you do realize, doncha, that this Mikhailov fellow done what we's tryin' to do. María sure as Jackson ain't gonna be gettin' all gussied up in a formal gown for opening night at the Boston Ballet tomorrow night."

It'd be ironic on steroids if the monster had *saved* María's life. Course, if he had, it was out of the frying pan, into the fire. He'd kept her from dying one way so he could kill her some other way.

They'd decided to drive straight through. It was a twelve-hour drive, but they didn't want to cut it up by stopping halfway, unloading Bethany and all that that entailed, and staying the night in some anonymous motel room.

Bailey wanted to take her little girl *home,* and Brice and T.J. were charged with getting her there.

The little girl had refused to eat, which meant that unless she'd had breakfast, she hadn't eaten a bite all day.

Exhausted, coupled with lack of food and a missed nap, they hadn't gotten a mile from María's apartment before she crashed out in the car seat. After only a little whimpering, she was sound asleep.

Brice sat up front in a t-shirt and sweatshirt with holes in 'em, trying to act like he wasn't hurtin' from where them bullets had almost come through his vest. He probably had a cracked rib, but he'd refused to let them paramedics take him to the hospital to find out. He was fine, thank you very much. Grim. Likely blaming himself for what happened, though wasn't nothing he could have done to prevent it.

Wasn't no reason to suspect Mikhailov was that many steps ahead of 'em.

The two of 'em didn't even need to exchange looks to communicate what they both knew, and what Bailey might know, too, but wouldn't look at right now: Mikhailov would do *anything* to keep Bailey from testifying.

Soon's it got quiet in the car, T.J. couldn't chase them demons away no more and all the possible scenarios reared they ugly heads.

Once that trial started, Bailey would have to come out of hiding. In this country, even a man like Mikhailov had a right to "face his accuser." Which meant she'd be in the courtroom with Mikhailov.

He and Brice'd see to it the monster didn't get to her before then, but wasn't nothing they could do once they's all brought together before a judge and jury.

If T.J. was to guess, he figured the madman would find a way to get a "piece" of her sister to Bailey. A finger. An ear. Make it clear that if she didn't keep her mouth shut, he'd send the rest of her a piece at a time.

T.J. didn't have no hope whatsoever that the feds or the Boston PD would find the girl. Rats like Mikhailov had too many hidey holes. All anybody could do now was what he and Brice was doin' — take care of Bailey and Bethany. Keep them safe.

When Mikhailov had finished interrogating her, his goons shoved María back into the van and drove her … somewhere. Maybe by the sea, the waterfront. She thought she detected a fish smell and could hear the squawk of gulls. But that could be her imagination. Right now, her senses had been so scraped raw by terror, every sensory input was suspect.

She was of no more use to them since she'd told Mikhailov everything she knew, so they were obviously taking her somewhere to kill her. Somewhere they could dispose of the body, maybe. Toss her into the water, and let the gulls peck out her eyes.

When the van stopped, the men hauled her out of it into yet another windowless garage, dragged her across it to a door on the back wall. The man with the pockmarked face opened the door, shoved her inside and slammed the door shut behind her.

There was no light. All around was absolute black darkness, and she panicked, banged once on the door in terror before the pain of her fingers stole her breath. Then she merely stood with her back against the door, trembling.

Sometime later — an hour, two minutes, a week — it occurred to her to feel along the wall by the door for a light switch. She found one, turned it on. Darkness was almost preferable once she made the connection, figured out that the room had been designed to hold *prisoners.*

A table, straight-backed chair, army bunk with a dirty wool blanket she would rather freeze to death than touch, a smaller door that she opened and quickly slammed closed. Either the toilet in there was backed up or a sewer pipe was broken. Gratefully, she didn't need to go, wouldn't likely need to for some time since she'd had nothing to eat or drink.

María stood in the center of the room, not wanting to touch anything, but her knees felt so weak, she knew if she did not sit down she was in danger of falling. The least offensive piece of furniture was the chair, so she eased herself down on it.

And waited.

Details about the room became clear even in the dull light. Details she had no desire to see but she had to look at something.

Someone had written on the wall. Gratefully, it was in a language María couldn't read. There were brown spots on the wall, too. Anyone who'd ever seen a television cop show knew what they were, that you could tell a lot about the nature of a wound and how it'd been inflicted by studying the pattern of those. Blood spatter.

Chapter Thirty-One

STATIC. *White noise. Twinkling lights, like sparks leaping away from a welding torch.*

Through white gauze, Bailey sees a room. It's small, lit by a single lightbulb dangling on a cord from the ceiling. No pull chain, though, so it must turn on with a switch.

Buzzing static fills her head and the image almost fades away.

A table and chair. A bed, a cot like in barracks.

It stinks. The smell of sewage is almost overwhelming, crisp and clear, not muted to a pale nothing by the static and snow.

There are spots on the wall.

Bailey knows what they are because María knows what they are. Drips of blood. Spattered blood. Dried there into dirty brown stains that would probably show through even if you painted the wall.

Spattered blood. A violent injury. Fear clutches at María's throat and the image begins to fade. Bailey struggles to hold onto it because it is a connection to María, but it's like trying to grab handfuls of smoke.

. . .

THEN THE IMAGE was gone and Bailey was sitting in the back seat of a car as night began to fold black batwings around it.

She started to tell T.J. and Brice about the connection … but didn't. After Bethany fell asleep, the adults only spoke to each other in necessary whispers, determined not to wake the child.

Besides, the connection told Bailey nothing useful, nothing that would help identify where María was, nothing that mattered.

No, that wasn't true. It had communicated something that mattered very much. María was still alive. A captive in some filthy room somewhere … but *alive*.

Bailey clung to that with a fierce grip as she listened to the soothing, mournful song the tire sang on the highway … and stared at Bethany.

Bailey remembered T.J. and Brice's comments about her watch before they left for Boston, that she was looking at it so often she was likely to stare the numbers right off it. If such a thing were possible, Bethany would have no face by the time they got to Shadow Rock because Bailey would have stared it completely off her head.

She couldn't stop looking at her. Or touching her. She reached over in the darkness and gently grasped the little girl's foot. María'd taken off Bethany's shoes to make her more comfortable when she'd fastened her into the car seat and now her little socked foot was warm and soft in Bailey's hand. So she held it. For hours.

She stared at the child's face for hours, too, devouring the details, the planes of dark and shadow in the play of approaching headlights and the glow from the instrument panel in the front seat.

Bethany Nicole Cunningham, age three and a half, was a stunningly beautiful little girl. Yeah, sure, Bailey wasn't exactly an unbiased observer, but she was certain even a stranger who saw her on the street would come to the same conclusion. Her hair was black like Bailey's. Curly like Bailey's, too. María's hair had waves, and could slide past both waves and curls into fuzzy if the air was damp. Bethany's shiny black locks hung on her shoulders in gentle curls. Her skin was alabaster, her features as perfect as the face on a porcelain doll.

Eyebrows that were delicate feathers, eyelashes so long they formed fans on her cheeks.

Her mouth was heart-shaped. Bailey realized sadly that she had only seen the little girl smile twice, that frozen instant when she stood in the doorway with her arms spread, squealing, "Mommy!" And when she posed with María for the photo.

Her smile transformed her face, pulled her heart-shaped mouth into a beautiful bow and made her eyes dance. Not hazel eyes like Bailey's. Blue, a striking shade of pale blue, like a summer sky. Or a robin's egg.

Oh, how many times in the past two years had she tried to imagine the face transformed by age. The toddler she'd told Aaron she couldn't stand to be away from for a whole week had been an adorable infant, but like all babies, her features were not yet defined enough to tell who she resembled, though Bailey had been sure she saw Aaron in them.

Now, Bethany's resemblance to Aaron was striking. Bailey could see it in the high, wide forehead and the strong chin.

This little girl looked like her daddy. A father she would never know. He had been shot down ruthlessly, pitilessly by the monster who ... now held María captive.

The long drive from Boston to Shadow Rock was an

enforced time of black silence where Bailey had no choice but to confront her demons.

In the past months, Bailey had become quite adept at not thinking about the awful things that had happened to her thanks to her gift for painting what hadn't happened yet. Gratefully, she was able to conjure up only a handful of memories about the time she and T.J. had spent in the monstrous second floor ballroom of The Cedars. Those memories had faded when whatever drug she'd been given had worn off. But she had no trouble remembering what it felt like to be held captive by a monster, the Beast, who had kidnapped teenagers and forced them into prostitution. She had known Jacko would hurt her, torture her to get information she couldn't give him, just like Mikhailov would hurt María to pry out of her information about Bailey that she didn't have.

The bullet named Oscar Bailey'd put in her brain last summer, wallowing in a pit of self-pity and despair on Bethany's third birthday, would have offered Bailey a get-out-of-jail-free card it she could have figured out how to dislodge it and send it off to bulldoze her brain tissue. María had no Oscar. She had no out. She was at the mercy of Sergei Wassily Mikhailov and he was a man who had no mercy.

Bailey had painted María burning alive, had lived through the death with her! Her portraits, just like the portraits T.J.'s mother had painted all those years ago, had never been wrong. María'd had tickets to the opening night performance of *The Nutcracker* at the Boston Opera House — at eight o'clock tomorrow night! — and she'd died before she had a chance to use them.

Maybe T.J. was right, that Mikhailov had saved María from her fate. Because he'd kidnapped her, she wouldn't be dressed in a formal gown for the ballet tomorrow night, wouldn't burn to death in it. It was hard to conceive that he'd "rescued" her, but if he had, it was a reprieve, not a pardon. She might not die in a fire tomorrow night, but Mikhailov would most assuredly kill her. Hadn't yet, but he would.

During that black drive through the night, taking her little girl "home," Bailey came to terms with the horror of her little sister's kidnapping. She could not allow herself to fall into the black pit of grief and despair that beckoned her every time she thought about it. She couldn't be so self-absorbed; she had to think of Bethany. She had to keep herself together to care for the little girl she and María both loved so desperately.

Bailey *had to* hold on. When Bethany asked for her mommy, Bailey would tell her that her mommy would be back soon. That horror word, *soon.* She'd been forced to believe in the eventual fulfillment of soon when the marshals in that anonymous house in some anonymous town had told her that's when she'd get her life back. She would cling to hope in the same soon for María's return.

María would survive.

She *would* come back.

She would return to Bailey's and Bethany's lives …
soon.

Chapter Thirty-Two

Sergei Wassily Mikhailov saw the world with absolute clarity. Like after a spring rain when the earth has been washed clean and sits warm and bright in the midday sun.

It was too crisp, of course, but he was used to that. All sharp edges with shadows behind to show what was flat and two-dimensional and what was not. The van was two-dimensional, lay on the flat surface of the garage floor like a leaf on the ground. The edges were sharp, outlined in shadow like a black Magic Marker. If he touched the edge of that image, it would cut his finger. But he would not do such a thing. He had learned, had been sliced open to the bone over and over until he accepted the reality that some things in the world were real and others just flat images with razor edges. When you understood that, you didn't get cut.

Volodya and Dmitri were real, of course. Their deaths would be real, too, and bloody, oh so very bloody. Mikhailov would slice their throats for their incompetence. Or maybe burn them alive. Oh my, yes. The intensity of that pain, their screams, the conjured image actually aroused him. But not now. Now, he needed his associates to implement the plan that had been forming in his mind ever since the sniveling slut revealed that the eyewitness he must silence had celebrated her birthday in the Nautilus Casino.

That was significant. A woman in the Witness Protection Program was not likely to make a big production out of her birthday. She would not do anything that would draw attention to herself. A birthday celebration would be something small, with a few friends.

Close to home.

If she celebrated her birthday at the Nautilus, federal marshals had her stashed away somewhere within, say, an hour's drive of the casino. That was a huge haystack in which to search for a pin — three states, West Virginia, Ohio and Pennsylvania, and the city of Pittsburgh.

The starting point was the Nautilus, owned by W. Maxwell Crenshaw, who had entertained Mikhailov and his associates and other high rollers who flew in from all over the country to play in his ten-thousand-dollar ante poker game. Only the best of everything — food, wine and women. Mikhailov was a masterful poker player. His face was immovable stone whether he was holding a pair of twos or a royal flush. He had no "tells," tiny movements or mannerisms that discerning opponents could use against him. He had won big, money that only mattered as an indication of victory.

Mikhailov considered how to narrow down the needle search, which would be complicated by the fact that he himself was now a wanted man. A fugitive from arrest warrants in Boston — which would mean nothing as soon as Mikhailov eliminated the only witness to the crime he was charged with committing. He thought he *had* eliminated all the witnesses, but this, this — even Russian expletives fell short of describing her — had hidden like a snake in the grass waiting for an opportunity to strike. His loathing of the *pig* was boundless. Hers would be a satisfyingly horrific death. He longed to watch her suffer and would squeeze delicious pleasure from her agony.

Dmitri approached him, the dead-man-walking who had let the Cunningham woman get away. Dmitri knew Mikhailov was displeased. Good. There was fear on his face. Excellent.

"I think you should see this." Dmitri held out a cellphone. "It was in her pocket." He indicated the slut who sat in the doorway of the van cradling her mashed fingers.

"What is it that I should see?"

"This morning, when she was on her way to the train station, she got five calls from a single number. She didn't pick up on any of them, said she didn't recognize the number so she turned off the ringer after the second call — telemarketers."

"Why is it significant that this young woman did not wish to purchase a time share in Florida, or 'consolidate her student loans'?"

"Telemarketing calls are computer generated. I don't think they keep trying the same number over and over if no one answers. The area code on the calls is 304. I looked it up. That's the area code for West Virginia."

"And your point?"

But Mikhailov knew the point, had already leapt ahead to the point.

"She was supposed to meet her sister but she didn't, ran instead. If I was the sister, I'd be calling to find out where she was, why she didn't show. I'd keep trying to reach her even if she didn't answer." He poked a fat finger at the list of five identical phone numbers. "I'm betting *that's* the sister's cell number."

Mikhailov did not smile, not on his face anyway. Dmitri did not know it, but he had just earned back his life. In fact, he would give Dmitri the privilege of killing Volodya for his incompetence.

Dmitri did something with the phone and held it out again.

"This is the woman you're looking for, the woman this one calls Bailey. I figured the sister'd have a picture."

Mikhailov stared at the photograph on the phone. A pretty black-haired woman holding a baby stared out at him. He memorized the face. He would never forget it. He could pick her out of a crowd of a thousand.

He dismissed the man with a curt nod, his mind clear, forming plans as fast as a spider spinning a web.

Perhaps he did not have to find Jessica Cunningham — *Bailey* — after all. Maybe he could give her a call and invite *her* to come to *him*, to a special celebration with her sister as the guest of honor.

He turned to the dead man Volodya. "Have the plane ready at the airport."

"Da ser."

"And I want to talk to Abi-Nadir. Find him and bring him to me."

Yes, it was good to kill Volodya. It had surprised him that Mikhailov wanted to talk to the Arab gun runner. Mikhailov could see it on his face, and any man who allowed others to see what he was thinking could not be trusted.

"Tell him I require his services. Have him call me before he comes, so he can bring with him all that is necessary for the task."

~

WHEN THEY CAME BACK to the room with blood spattered on the wall, María was certain they would kill her, had tried to prepare herself for death, but had no idea how to do a thing like that. But they didn't kill her. Instead, she was shoved into the black car with the tinted windows. Mikhailov sat in the back seat opposite her and she would much rather have ridden on the floor in the van or stayed in the room with the bloody walls.

But he said nothing. Absolutely nothing. He might as well have been a stuffed animal. She'd never been in such close quarters with another human being where the silence hung so heavy it was like it had substance. She didn't look at him, not even out of the corner of her eye. She eventually became aware of an odor. She had a pretty sophisticated olfactory system, primed as it had been for years by going from one store to another smelling expensive perfume she and Bailey could never afford.

What she smelled wasn't perfume, wasn't men's cologne. Wasn't aftershave or the odor of the shaving cream he used. It was some other smell, something darker and more noxious. It was *his* smell, the stink of the man himself, the reek of some dark, fetid pool scummed over with a glaze of filth. A pool alive with unidentifiable slimy *things* born of oozing decay, where small, furry creatures had been sucked down and drowned.

It was possible to see out the tinted windows. She'd never known that, had always assumed the people in those kinds of cars couldn't see out any better than the rest of the world could see in. They were driving down Boston streets. None she recognized. Then they passed through a gate and approached a big building she recognized as an airplane hangar.

There was an airplane on the tarmac and obviously they were all about to get on it. And go where?

Why were they taking her anywhere? They'd found out everything she had to tell them. What good was she now? Why didn't they just …

She watched the men who'd kidnapped her and held her captive load boxes into the hold of the craft, then stood around talking in a language she did not speak. It occurred to her then that she was not tied up and had not been tied up the whole time she had been a prisoner.

Should she … could she … make a run for it?

She looked around. There was nowhere to run, and when she turned back, Mikhailov was staring at her with a not-smile on his face and she had the sense that he knew what she'd been considering and was somehow disappointed she hadn't had the guts to go through with it.

Then they flew. She had no idea where they were going, wondered irrationally if they were taking her back to Russia for some reason. But she didn't think a plane this size could fly over the polar icecap and back down into Russia, and besides, what she could see out the windows was green, not white.

The change in pressure as the plane climbed into the night sky did something to her mashed fingers, that had been growing blessedly numb but now woke up and throbbed again in rhythm with her heartbeat.

There was food on the plane.

The fat man with the broad face whose name she thought was Maxim, shoved a sandwich at her and pronounced, "Eat."

It didn't sound like a request, so she choked the sandwich down.

The men were mostly silent, not a particularly gregarious lot. Four of them gathered and played some card game that was either one she did not know, or an ordinary game that seemed exotic because the men were speaking Russian.

Then they landed. It was the middle of the night now. She didn't know the time because she didn't wear a watch and they'd taken her phone. All she could tell was that it was a small airport, though there were a lot of planes parked outside and a long row of hangars.

Shoved into yet another car with tinted windows, they drove through hilly countryside toward a huge building lit up like a stadium even at this hour — the lights twinkling like the cut glass of a chandelier.

A private elevator. An anonymous hotel hallway. A room, a suite, with a living room and kitchenette and at least two, maybe more, bedrooms. She was shoved into one of them and the door was closed behind her. Not locked, though. She didn't think rooms like this had locks on the door. Not that it mattered.

This room was no cell where prisoners were tortured — for information or mere pleasure — with blood-spattered walls and a stopped-up toilet. It was a fancy hotel room, more lavishly appointed than anywhere she'd ever been. About an hour later a man returned with a plastic bag that contained basic toiletry items, toothbrush, toothpaste and the like.

After she saw what was written on the sack, she couldn't have slept even if her fingers hadn't ached. There was a logo that featured a periscope and the words The Nautilus Casino.

Chapter Thirty-Three

BETHANY WOKE up as they drove through the mountains —
out in the middle of nowhere, of course — and it was only
then that Bailey realized the little girl had wet her pants.
The car seat cushion was soaked.

"Where's my mommy?" she asked fearfully, only
removing her thumb from her mouth long enough to form
the words.

The haunted misery on her face broke Bailey's heart,
but she'd been steeling herself for hours to confront the
little girl's fear and she pulled it off rather nicely.

"She couldn't come with us on our trip, but she'll be
here soon."

"Where is she?"

"Wherever she is, she's thinking about you, sweetie
pie, and she told me to tell you how much she loves you
and that she will come home to you just as soon as she
can."

Bethany took her thumb out of her mouth again. "I
want Mommy." Then she put the thumb back snug
between her lips.

"So do I. I'm your mommy's sister; did you know that?"

Bethany shook her head.

"We used to play Barbie dolls when we were little girls. Did she tell you about that?"

Again Bethany looked at her with frightened eyes and shook her head.

"Well, she had one called Superstar Barbie that a little boy threw up into a tree …"

So Bailey prattled on, keeping the little girl's mind occupied while they searched for somewhere they could … then they found a general store right off the set of *Deliverance*, and once Bailey had Bethany cleaned up and dry, the child actually said that she was hungry.

They bought soft drinks and moon pies — breakfast of champions — and when they got back to the car, Bailey replaced the wet car seat cushion with a ridiculously over-priced handmade quilt she'd purchased in the 'West Virginia crafts' section of the store. It was beautiful, with intricate designs created by dozens of different pieces of fabric. Bailey planned to throw it away as soon as she got home; she wanted no reminders of this trip through hell.

Once in the car, Bailey continued her monologue.

Gradually, Bethany relaxed. She was nothing anybody could have mistaken for happy, but neither was she so utterly miserable she could do nothing but whimper and suck her thumb.

Bundy and Sparky saved the day.

Dobbs had stayed behind house/dog sitting at the Watford House while they were gone. He stepped out onto the porch as they pulled the rental car into the driveway.

Bailey was not surprised to see not one or even two but three Kavanaugh County Sheriff's vehicles — one parked down the street, one in the driveway and one out front.

Fletch got out of the car in the driveway and went to talk to Brice. Bailey walked along beside Bethany, thumb in her mouth, dragging her minion blanket, resembling nothing so much as a condemned prisoner on the way to execution … until Dobbs reached back and pushed the screen door behind him open just enough for fluff and fur to appear.

Bundy bounded down the steps and raced to Bailey, who knelt in the grass to accept his greeting.

Bethany looked at the dancing, wiggling ball of black and white fur … and *smiled*!

"Puppy!"

"His name is Bundy. Feel how soft his fur is."

As soon as she reached out, Bundy was all over her, jumping up and licking her and wiggling, his tail a blur.

Sparky was more circumspect. He ran to T.J., then to Bailey.

Then he approached Bethany, who was by then fending off Bundy's attack of delight … and giggling.

"It's cold out here," Bailey wailed, took Bethany by the hand and led the child trailing two dogs into the house.

Dobbs had wisely ignored Bethany — he was a big guy and she was a very small little girl — just mentioned casually to Bailey that he'd "fixed up the parlor" while she was gone and she might want to "go take a look."

The parlor was on the far side of the living room, opposite the door that lead into the hallway toward the "library" that Bailey had turned into an art studio. Like many other rooms in the huge house, the parlor had stood cold and empty the whole time Bailey had lived there, had only a few pieces of leftover furniture.

Yeah, Dobbs had fixed it up, alright. The room Bailey had left on Monday with a worn loveseat, a couple of random tables and a wingback chair with a broken foot had been transformed into a comfortable "den," so warm and inviting she couldn't imagine he'd managed to put it all together by himself.

"Oh … Dobbs," was all she could say.

Matching recliner loveseats covered in soft, "scuffed leather," sat opposite comfortable overstuffed chairs, one covered in a plaid fabric that featured the warm brown tones of the loveseats, another with a pattern that matched the forest green of the couch. There were end tables and coffee tables of glossy dark walnut, lamps with gold shades so the light from them was warm and soothing. Fluffy pillows and cuddly afghans were scattered randomly — all in subdued earth-tone colors that coordinated perfectly with the three multicolored rag rugs. Bailey was an artist; she understood color. The warm, relaxed feel of this room was intentional and deliberate, the product of dozens of decisions about furniture, fabric, color, texture and lighting.

Had Dobbs done all this on his own? Or had he hired a decorator? No sense asking him, he'd just brush it off, as he had her exclamation at the huge, flatscreen television mounted on the wall.

"Figured the little one would want to watch cartoons. I got cable."

Bailey teared up, tiptoed to kiss him on the cheek and whispered, "Thank you!" He turned and made a big show of pulling his gold watch out of his pocket, studying it as if it actually kept time.

Bailey looked at her watch. A Timex. It was 8 a.m. — give or take a few minutes. Then she turned to gaze again in wonder at the room.

Chapter Thirty-Four

Sergei Mikhailov looked at his watch. A Rolex. It was 8 a.m. *Exactly* 8 a.m. Then he turned to gaze again in wonder at the room.

He was standing beneath the huge archway that was the main entrance to the circular restaurant on the bottom floor of the Nautilus Casino, a room that was, in its present state, an obscene parody of style and good taste, but it would do for his purposes.

Directly across from him on the other side of the room were the doors leading to the kitchens. The wall to the right of them contained the huge bar, thirty, maybe forty feet long and three feet wide made of a lustrous teakwood with a deep, swirling grain. Behind the bar was a thirty-foot mirrored wall with glass shelves, displaying hundreds of singular bottles of liquor — everything from the finest cognac to the simplest bourbon whiskey.

Besides the main entrance where he stood, there were two additional restaurant entrances — the south entrance to his right and the north entrance at the end of the bar to his left. Gigantic Christmas trees decorated with colorful balls and bright lights stood sentinel on both sides of all the entrances. There were pointy-leafed holly wreaths at spaced intervals along the walls, connected by draped pine garlands across the fronts of the aquariums.

The aquariums were the room's finest feature. Inset so they were flush with the blue marble walls, they appeared to be windows out into the sea where colorful tropical fish in every shape and size glided gracefully through the sparkling water. Artfully placed lighting shone down through them, casting rippling reflections to dance on every surface in the room.

Now, they were covered up with ugly swags of tacky greenery.

The restaurant had no ceiling. A chrome grid supported white globe lights the size of pumpkins, pearls with clamshell shades, that hung down to light the room. Above the restaurant was a 360-degree observation deck where gamblers and party guests on the second floor could look down on the diners. As could the guests in the hotel rooms that faced the open atrium where the restaurant was located on the ground floor.

The railing that lined the deck was shiny chrome with an inset design — a pod of chrome dolphins cavorting in an endless circle. Attached to the railing around the whole circle of observation deck was a single strand of Christmas lights with bulbs as big as cantaloupes. Dangling from the railing directly above the main entrance where Mikhailov stood were half a dozen oversized Christmas stockings ten feet long with names stenciled on them, designed for feet that had twelve toes.

Mikhailov had lived among Americans for most of his adult life but he would never understand them. Oh, he understood that at this time of year, Christmas decorations were a cultural imperative. Themed decorations could be charming. Done tastefully they could convey a particular take on the Christmas traditions. Nothing wrong with that. But Crenshaw had gone a bridge too far when he'd decorated his beautiful casino/hotel complex using *How the Grinch Stole Christmas* as the theme.

Mikhailov loathed W. Maxwell Crenshaw but had once believed the man possessed at least a modicum of style and good taste. It appeared Mikhailov had been grievously mistaken.

On the archway beneath the words "Where your every desire is fulfilled," a sign had been added, "... in Who-ville style." A gigantic sleigh, piled high with Christmas presents, pulled along by Max with his tree-limb antler was outlined in neon on the top of the building — probably visible for miles.

But the co de grâs was the Grinch himself.

The green beast stood at the far end of the restaurant outside the kitchen entrances beneath the east side of the observation deck with its back toward the main entrance. All dressed up in a red Christmas jacket with white fur encircling the wrists and neck, and a Santa hat resting at a rakish angle on its head, the creature was looking back over his left shoulder toward the entrance. An evil grin twisted his already loathsome features. His left foot rested on a gigantic Christmas present wrapped in shiny green paper with a big red bow on it. The other Grinch foot, clad in a red felt slipper with white fur around the top, was on the floor.

Reaching with both hands above his head to the single strand of Christmas lights attached to the railings of the observation deck — it was clear the Grinch was *taking the lights down. Stealing them.* The portion he had already removed dangled to the floor by his foot.

A more disturbingly ugly creature Mikhailov had never

seen: Pear-shaped body with a huge round belly, a big head and skinny arms, supported by ridiculously spindly legs wearing red elf slippers. The creature had yellow eyes with red centers, and the predatory look on his face ought to give any normal child nightmares, and this was a children's story, was it not?

What kind of idiot puts a fifty-foot-tall furry green … *thing* in the middle of a stylish restaurant? It defied any logic Mikhailov could summon to apply to it. And that was only the most egregious of the decoration faux pas that littered the otherwise classically styled facility, so garish they reminded Sergei of those awful beads drunks on Bourbon Street in New Orleans wore around their necks during Mardi Gras.

"Do you have any idea what I had to pay to get that thing made?" Crenshaw had said of the creature when he'd escorted Mikhailov into the restaurant earlier that morning.

More than a nickel and the man had been pitilessly overcharged.

"Cost an extra ten grand just to make the fur flame-retardant. Fire codes, you know." It had been clear he was proud as punch of all the decorations. "The trees and greenery are real, makes the room smell like Christmas."

Crenshaw had pontificated about the nature of the clientele who patronized his establishment during the holiday season. High rollers could afford to jet off to a warmer climate with their families so he had to make do with the chaff, attract the locals, appeal to their more simple likes and basic appetites.

Mikhailov had watched his performance. It'd been quite a show. Crenshaw was a fool — not the buffoon he wanted others to think he was, but a fool nonetheless. He had managed to build an empire on Good Ole Boy, aw-shucks self-deprecation. Beneath that facade was a shrewd, clever mind and a character totally devoid of any moral hindrances — a fool, though, because he had not the slightest idea that those smarter than he was saw through his act. Crenshaw had somehow latched onto the notion that furry green monstrosities and a herd of ridiculous-looking Cindy Lou Who servers would seem charming and carefree — which was, after all, the atmosphere one wanted to foster in a casino where you made your money only when other people lost theirs.

As he spoke, Crenshaw's face had begun to melt.

Mikhailov had gawked at it in disbelieving horror.

The man's features had elongated as if they were made of wax. His chin had slid down his neck, dragging his lower lip with it to reveal teeth Mikhailov had not noticed were rotted, looked like the blackened chunks of foundation after a fire.

As his nose had melted, it pulled down his eyelids. As they'd begun to liquify, the eyeballs behind them — rock hard marbles — had popped out and slid down the goo of his cheeks like skiers on a slope, tethered by slimy red tendons and tissue.

"To what do I owe the honor of your presence on such short... actually no notice at all," he had asked, and Mikhailov had been amazed that he could speak at all given that he had no mouth or tongue ...

His skull had been exposed next and something green, like a sprout — no, *a worm* — had wiggled up through great fissures in the bone.

No. No, no, nooooooo!

Mikhailov's heart had started to hammer like a woodpecker trying to get out of his chest. All the oxygen had been sucked out of the room and Mikhailov had felt his lungs straining for air. He'd begun to gasp.

He could have demanded that Crenshaw stop. He'd stopped the girl — the sister whose fingers he'd mashed. She'd been growing boils dripping yellow pus on her face … he'd told her to stop and she had stopped. But if he looked at Crenshaw's melted face, he would vomit, so he looked away, past Crenshaw to two Cindy Lou Who servers spreading a cloth across a nearby table. Both had their backs to him.

"Excuse me," he'd said to them, and they turned. Their faces were not melting. They had no faces to melt, just blank spaces between their ears like the people in videos whose faces are blurred to obscure their identities.

"Mr. Mikhailov, are you …?"

He'd turned back to Crenshaw, whose face was perfectly normal now.

Mikhailov'd grabbed control and clutched it in an iron fist, showed no shadow on his face of his inner turmoil.

"I require nothing further from you."

He'd needed Crenshaw to leave him alone so he could take a casual, *solitary* walk around the facility. When he was at the Nautilus in October, he had seen little but a lavishly appointed private game room. Now, he needed to see the whole facility, plan where and how he would spring his little surprise.

"We will talk at … say early afternoon, a late lunch. Your office. A salad for me — just greens, no dressing, a sliced tomato and a hard-boiled egg on the side."

Crenshaw was not so dense that he couldn't tell he had been dismissed. He reached out to shake Mikhailov's hand but Mikhailov ignored the gesture. He shook hands only when not to do so would constitute a grievous breach of decorum in a situation that demanded it. This situation did not. The feel of someone's fingers grasping his — even though he never took off his gloves — was so abhorrent he always had to concentrate not to yank his hand back.

He was certain others could not tell, could not feel it through the glove on his right hand — the ropes of scar tissue that decorated his tortured flesh. He knew that *objectively,* but even so, he sometimes watched blood drip out the cuff of his glove and spatter on his shoes when someone squeezed the raw sponge of tissue beneath too tightly.

That's all his hand was sometimes — a raw sponge of tissue. Except when it wasn't, when it was his real hand, what was left of it. Sometimes the black leather glove became transparent, revealing the wreckage, the damage the best surgeons in Moscow had required half a dozen separate surgeries to repair. They'd told him how fortunate he was that the "dog" he'd said attacked him had only ripped off skin and the tissue beneath, had severed no tendons or ligaments, had bitten off *only* the little finger.

Fortunate, yes. Mikhailov had been fortunate, indeed, that the tsunami of clotted rage that had crashed ashore in his mind that day had receded before he'd chewed off his other fingers as well.

After Crenshaw left, Mikhailov stood for a time alone in the entrance archway of the restaurant, looking out over the sea of white tableclothed tables.

He turned to the potted Christmas tree to his right. Examined it. Then examined the one on the left. He circumnavigated the room, examining the garlands and wreaths and the other Christmas trees.

When he finally left the restaurant, he was wearing a look that approximated genuine delight.

Chapter Thirty-Five

T.J. KNELT on one knee in front of Bethany and imparted
to the little girl a significant piece of dog wisdom.

"If you run away, most times a dog'll chase you."

The next few hours were punctuated by the sounds of
a squealing child bounding through the house with
yapping dogs on her heels.

They quickly developed a racetrack that extended from
the newly appointed parlor-turned-into-a-den across the
living room, down the hallway, through the studio, back
down the hallway, into the kitchen through the doorway
off the hall and out of the kitchen through the doorway by
the breakfast nook ... and back into the den. Wash. Rinse.
Repeat.

The kitchen was the only room in the house with exclusively hardwood floors — no rugs or carpeting. It was a
show to watch the little girl race across the hardwood floor,
make a sharp turn around the big table in the middle of
the room — with the dogs trying to keep up, leaning in like
motorcycle riders in a tight curve, their claws scratching

ineffectually on the floor as they slid sideways instead of turning.

Bailey stood in the living room, watching the parade fly through as she talked to Brice about the protection he was providing to her — two deputies stationed by the fence in the back yard, one on each side. Fletch sat in a squad car out front.

"We've worked out a schedule." He glanced to include T.J. and Dobbs. "One of us — T.J., Dobbs or I — will be here every minute." He paused for just a beat, painful memories washing across his face. "*We'll* be taking Bundy out to pee."

The race ended when Bundy came bounding into the room sans Bethany and Sparky. Bailey and T.J. found Bethany sitting on the kitchen floor leaning up against the cabinet, not crying but looking like she might or might not, hadn't yet made up her mind.

"Fall down," the little girl said.

Bailey saw why. Bethany had taken her shoes off and when she tried to make the hardwood-floor turn, her sock feet couldn't get any better traction than the dogs' claws and they had slid out from under her.

The little girl rubbed the back of her head. "Hurted me."

That seemed to make the decision for her and her face puckered up, her lip stuck out and she tuned up to let fly. T.J. headed her off.

"Sit," he told Sparky, who was never more than an arm's reach from Bethany.

The dog obediently plopped his backside down on the floor.

"Sparky sit down!" Bethany said, surprised.

"Down," T.J. said.

Sparky plopped on his belly.

"Stand." Sparky was immediately back on all fours.

Bethany got to her feet. "I do it! I do it! Sparky, sit!"

Sparky sat.

"He knows all kinda other tricks," T.J. said, turned to Sparky and said, "Shake." Sparky offered his right paw.

For the next half hour Bethany gleefully ordered the dog around, told him to roll over, to play dead, to speak. She shot him with the imaginary gun of her thumb and index finder and he collapsed "dead" in a heap. Her favorite command was "dance." When Sparky got up on his hind legs and pranced around on them, Bethany danced with him.

Bundy was adorable, of course, in a fluffy-wiggling-delightful sort of way.

But Sparky was … *amazing.* It was almost like the dog knew that it was important to make the child happy, to give her reason to laugh, to help her relax and adjust.

At one point, Bailey caught T.J.'s eye and cocked her chin toward Sparky-and-Bethany, which quickly had become a hyphenated word. He nodded his head in mute understanding.

By midmorning, with some scrambled eggs, Captain Crunch cereal and orange juice *with pulp* snug in her belly, the little girl had dozed off on the couch in front of the television in the den. Both minion blankets were tucked snug around her. Sparky lay snoozing contentedly at her feet. He had not left her side since she got out of the car.

Just there, not demanding attention like Bundy. Just *there,* in the special way Sparky had of being there so it made you feel better just because he was.

The little girl had been confused when she saw the brand new, unworn minion blanket just like her tattered one, then she had grabbed both of them and dragged them behind her as she followed the dogs' sniffing progress around the new belongings in the den.

When she woke up from her mini-nap, Bailey showed her the studio and the little girl was fascinated with the paints and canvasses.

"Mommy lets me paint," she said, and a cloud of gloom settled over her.

Somehow, Bailey held it together.

"Then you need to paint her a picture, a surprise for her when she gets back."

Bethany brightened as Bailey set her up with a small pallet and dabs of color in front of a canvas leaned against the wall. Bundy had been banished from the room after he tried to lick the paint off the canvas.

By early afternoon, Bethany had turned whiny and quarrelsome, clearly in need of more than a mini-nap. Bailey hadn't even taken her to see her "very own room" yet. The first floor of the big house was intimidating enough, though she had chased the dogs around and around it so often she seemed to be comfortable there. That would do for now.

So instead of taking her upstairs, Bailey took her to go potty, then cuddled her up with both minion blankets in the rocking chair in the living room. Not like the one she and Aaron had gotten, like the one she'd seen in María's apartment ... like the one she would find to purchase somewhere, if she had to search the whole state of West Virginia.

This chair was a normal rocking chair, back and forth. Sparky and the puppy had each learned by painful experience to stay away from it, tails at the ready, when someone was rocking.

Bethany was half crying, half whining, rubbing her eyes, wailing her litany of "I want my mommy."

Bailey swallowed the lump in her throat and promised María would return "soon." Then she started rocking and singing,

"Somewhere out there, beneath a pumpkin pie."

Bethany looked up in surprise and delight.

"Mommy sings that song!"

Bailey almost lost it at that revelation. Of course María did! Of course she sang their special song to Bethany. But the image of her doing it so clogged Bailey's throat she was barely able to get the words out.

"I told you that your mommy and I were sisters, remember."

The little girl nodded, interested in that revelation now for the first time.

"When we were little girls, we made up the song because—"

"There was two boys who eated your pieces of pie and you didn't get any."

"That's right. Not a crumb."

"Mommy said you was mad."

"We were. And hungry." She began to sing again, because her throat was still too tight to talk.

"Someone's eaten my piece and I'll get none tonight."

"Somewhere out there, someone's pretending to cry, saying they didn't eat it—"

Then Bethany burst out, "But that's a big fat lie!"

The little girl looked up at her and giggled. Bailey kissed her on the forehead and continued to sing.

"And even though I know there's not a crumb left in my cup …"

Bethany sang along with her, "… it helps to tink dat they'll get sick and chuck the whole piece uuuuup …"

"Somewhere out deeeeer ..."

Bailey sang the song over and over. Bethany had relaxed in her arms and now was snuggling close.

So she kept singing.

Chapter Thirty-Six

SERGEI WASSILY MIKHAILOV stared out the window of Maxwell Crenshaw's outer office. He didn't see the placid waters of the lake reflecting the brilliant early afternoon sun and the piercing blue of the sky. He saw mist, colored mist.

The mind of Sergei Wassily Mikhailov had always been a very crowded place. He had been able to make his way through the teeming throng of ideas with speed, confidence and assurance, as one moves through a giant library, looking at the sections of books, the categories, seeking out a particular author perhaps and then selecting the book. Opening the book and going to a particular chapter, a specific page …

A single word on that page.

He was that laser focused …

Until he wasn't.

Until the day he went to the great library of his mind and found the crowd of ideas and thoughts and plans and memories shrouded in mist. A mist that swirled in whirlpools and eddies, changed colors like a kaleidoscope.

He got lost in the mist.

He could no longer see the book sections. They would appear out of the mist when he got near enough, but then he had to feel his way along the shelves, peering through the fog at the spines of the books, looking for … what?

The word or idea or plan he was seeking would blink out of existence, out of his mind with a little sparkle like a soap bubble.

Other days, there were great holes in the library, sections completely missing, gaping caverns in the floor, and if he was not careful he would step off into one of them and fall through, fall down into an endless blackness where darkness would gobble up his screams.

But it wasn't just the thoughts in his mind that would suddenly be in disarray, in ordered, linear logic one moment and a pile of scrambled confusion the next.

Not just thought, but emotions.

He had never been an emotional man. No, that was not accurate. He had always been an emotional man but he had harnessed the power of his emotions by suppressing them. He never showed anything he felt, learned how to keep silent as a second grader when the communists told him and his classmates that they must report their parents if they were dissenters.

His parents talked at the table at night in whispers about bad things, with wrong ideas, and wicked speech.

He told no one. Watched, waited, kept silent. His face expressionless.

His father was a kind, loving man. But he drank too much sometimes and when he did he spoke too openly about forbidden things. He watched his mother try to rein him in, but it was only a matter of time before his father would destroy their family.

Sergei would be taken away from them then, but he

would gain nothing in the exchange. That was not acceptable. He would find a way to take as much advantage as he could.

The morning after his father came home drunk, having said who knows what to who knows whom, Sergei went to the principal and reported him.

He was clear, concise. Did not overstate. Showed no emotion of any kind.

Showed none when they came and took his parents away, his mother crying and begging, his father's face the color of fireplace ashes.

Showed none when he was taken to the collective farm in a rural province and tasked with feeding the livestock, primarily pigs.

Showed none ever.

He had watched, listened, learned.

To be respected, you must be feared.

To be feared, you must be ruthless.

To be ruthless, you must have no feelings.

In all things, to gain great rewards, you must be willing to risk everything.

And far more important — you must be prepared to lose what you risk and gain no reward at all.

Learning that proved to be the most valuable and costly lesson of his life. It had toughened and hardened him as nothing else could have done. Indeed, it had made him the man he was today.

Sergei Wassily Mikhailov is thin and hollow-chested with sallow skin the color of the underbelly of a frog and eyes as dark and cold as a Polar ocean. At twelve, his voice is only now beginning to change and he is no bigger than the girls who sit in obedient silence in seats on the other side of the gymnasium. Though he is not as large and well-muscled as the other boys, he is smarter, more shrewd and clever, totally fearless and wholly unencumbered by the slightest shred of human decency.

He knows how this drill goes. The men in suits from the Central Committee, who sit with the headmaster at a table in the middle of the gym floor, have come to the commune farm to select the cream of this year's crop of young people, the best and the brightest to be trained for service in up-the-food-chain positions in the party.

The students here are those who have passed stringent qualifying tests that demonstrate not only their intellectual acuity but their dedication to the principles on which the Communist Party is founded and by which it governs the land. Mikhailov's scores were the highest in the commune school, but those will be overshadowed by today's display of brute force.

Since he cannot win this competition, he must change the rules of engagement.

The headmaster rises to describe the organization of the competition, the manner in which boys can challenge other boys in various sports and activities — weightlifting, wrestling, boxing — until a winner is selected who excels in them all. The last man standing.

Before the headmaster can speak, Mikhailov rises from his spot in the middle of this year's class of boys and makes his way down to the gym floor. It is such a breach of decorum, the headmaster is too surprised to object.

"I wish to issue a challenge, sir," he says. Some of the girls on the other side of the gym giggle.

"Return to your seat immediately," the headmaster rumbles, embarrassed by the behavior of a boy who clearly has not been properly disciplined.

Mikhailov holds his ground. "Are you not seeking the strongest boy here?" Then he turns past the headmaster and addresses the committee members directly. "These activities will not show you who that boy is."

The headmaster starts toward him, a blue fire of rage in his eyes.

If his plan is not successful, Mikhailov will not likely survive to compete again next year.

"I instructed you to—"

"Let the boy speak."

The words come from the man seated on the far right, his chair pushed back from the other two. He wears his suit a little too casually, sits with relaxed arrogance. Reaching into his pocket, he removes a crumpled package of cigarettes, taps one out across his finger and pulls out a lighter. When he speaks again, he breathes out the smoke he just inhaled.

"I'd like to hear what he has to say."

Mikhailov makes eye contact with the man and each instinctively identifies a kindred spirit in the other. This is the man he must convince — a broad-shouldered bear of a man with a thick black mustache and hair that falls over his forehead. No one else matters and Mikhailov turns and focuses his full attention on him.

"The kind of strength you're looking for has nothing to do with how many pounds of weights you can lift or who you can pin to the mat. You are looking for leaders who possess strength of character, tenacity and absolute determination. You want unflinching devotion and dedication. You are seeking one who risks much to gain more, who never flinches, never blinks. Sweat is not an indicator of character."

This is the speech he'd been practicing for months as he fed slop to the pigs and threw feed to chickens. He had come prepared, even down to washing his hands thoroughly before he entered the room, and touching nothing.

He pauses then, never taking his eyes off the man with the mustache.

"What does indicate character?" the man asks.

"Character is revealed ... by challenge."

That's how these competitions are organized. One boy challenges another. And the winner then challenges another.

Without waiting to be granted permission, Mikhailov turns his back on the adults and faces the rows of boys, most regarding him in smirking derision.

"I want to issue a challenge."

"To whom?" the headmaster asks, and all the boys sit up a little straighter, hoping to be the one selected to pound Mikhailov into the floor.

"To everyone." He makes an expansive gesture that includes all the boys. "Who among you has the courage, the determination, the strength of character to match mine?"

Then he drops his voice to a whisper, and not a soul in the room dares to breathe as he continues.

"Who among you is willing to do what Sergei Mikhailov is willing to do to demonstrate his loyalty and devotion?"

He sweeps his gaze once slowly across them, then turns back to the mustached man, executing his command performance for an audience of one.

He moves confidently, without a moment's hesitation — he has practiced a hundred times ... up to a point, that is. With his left hand, he reaches up to his face ...

This will hurt; how much he doesn't know, but it will hurt. He must not flinch.

... and digs his thumb into his right eye socket.

The girls gasp as one. Someone squeaks but doesn't scream.

In a single, unhesitating motion, Mikhailov shoves his thumb deep into his eye socket ... and pops out his right eye onto his palm.

The girls scream then, all of them. The boys gasp. Boris Stavanovich leans over and vomits onto the gym floor.

The pain is breathtaking. Blood pours down Mikhailov's face, but he's been as careful as he could be. He trimmed back his thumbnail so it would not damage the socket. His hands are clean to guard against infection.

The eyeball rests in his palm, still attached to the socket by tendrils of something. He can't see, what with only the left eye, and it is watering so profusely he can barely see anything at all.

With a final yank, he pulls the eyeball free and holds it out on the palm of his hand to the rows of horrified boys.

"I challenge you, any one of you, to be this strong, willing to sacrifice this much to demonstrate your loyalty and devotion."

No one voice can be heard above the hubbub of horrified reactions that do not require words.

Then there is a sound that silences everyone. It comes from the mustached man, his seat pushed back from the others.

He is applauding slowly.

Clap.

Clap.

Clap.

Mikhailov turns and looks at him with his remaining eye. The man is smiling. Then he leans his head back and bursts out laughing.

Chapter Thirty-Seven

BAILEY HAD GOTTEN ALMOST no sleep the night before in the car bearing her and her daughter through the darkness to the safety of the remote West Virginia mountains. As she sat rocking Bethany, reveling in the warmth of the child in her arms, she began to nod off herself.

ALL AT ONCE, the room and the child and the rocking chair vanish.

What appears instead is another reality. Like when she'd watched Macy Cosgrove get her hand stamped at the carnival. But this is different. The reality is strange. Everything is too bright and there are sparking flashes around the edges of her vision.

This time, she thinks of sparks flying up from a railroad track when an engine suddenly hits the brakes. Metal scraping against metal, fragments scoured off the surface. Though the sparkling lights are bright, the scene she can see is muted, wrapped in cotton.

A surface, wooden, like the top of a table. A hand appears, the hand of the person out whose eyes she is seeing the scene. María's hand, her right hand and her fingers are swollen and discolored, bruised — smashed. The index and middle fingers from the knuckle down are flat, the fingernails are black, and the throbbing pain of them shoots up her arm into her neck. Into that place in the jaw that reacts to something sour.

Then María picks up a straight pin and sticks the point into the base of the nail on her index finger. She spins it between her thumb and finger, in a drilling motion. Immediately, a gush of ugly bloody liquid pours out the hole she has dug. The pressure is less. The pain is less. She dabs a tissue on the fingernail, then places her hand back on the table and starts the same process on the middle finger.

The sparks have grown brighter and brighter, now they are so bright Bailey can't look at them, can't see the scene through the light. She blinks and the scene vanishes.

BAILEY'S HEART was pounding so hard she was afraid the movement would arouse the child asleep in her lap. She refused to gasp in air, knew her lungs were not really starving for oxygen, it just seemed like it. She gritted her teeth, tried to settle, calm.

Bethany didn't stir, was still sleeping soundly in her lap, her breathing slow and rhythmic. Bailey tried to match the rhythm of her own breathing to that of the child to calm herself.

Slowly, Bailey's heartbeat returned to something approaching a normal rhythm. Her mind was still in hyperdrive, though.

María had mashed her fingers. Badly.

Except maybe it wasn't María who—

The thought was so horrifying she gasped, and Bethany squirmed in her lap. Gritting her teeth, she willed herself to remain calm.

Somehow, María's fingers had been mashed. She would not, *could not* now allow herself to consider how it had happened. If she thought—

No, not now.

Now, she needed to try to remember what else she had seen in the vision, what there was that might help the Boston Police find María. But there was nothing. A wooden table top. Nothing more. Could be anywhere.

She grabbed her thoughts then, held tight, concentrated on the thing she knew now, which was that *María was not dead.* She was alive. Perhaps this was a "right now" vision or a "future" one. She couldn't tell the difference. But in the "now" of the vision, her sister was alive and mostly unharmed.

But the vision itself fascinated and frustrated her. What was happening with the sharp, fractured light, the flickering, sparks-flying effect? Was it what Dobbs had suggested, some sort of feedback because the connection was too intense? Maybe. It certainly hadn't happened during any of her visions of others.

She thought of what T.J. had said. "This time is different from last time. Next time will be different from this. You got to take each one as it comes."

For whatever reason there was, it felt like there was too much energy, a kind of pressure to the image that caused the sparking effect. It mattered, because if she got flashes from María, maybe one of them would be like Macy feeding her little brother. Maybe a reflection in a toaster

...

The child stirred, murmured something, and wiggled. So Bailey started singing softly again with tears streaming down her face and her breath hitching in and out in a wheeze almost as profound as María's had been when she was a little girl.

"Somewhere out there, with my very last breath, I'll get mine and their shares and they'll just starve to death."

Her heart broke for her little sister. What was

happening to María in Boston, a thousand miles away from Shadow Rock?

MARÍA STOOD at the hotel room window, looking out across the still water of Whispering Mountain Lake toward Shadow Rock on the other shore.

She was exhausted, had not slept, of course. The pain in her smashed fingers had throbbed so relentlessly she could not have slept even if there hadn't been an armed gunman outside her door.

She looked down at her fingers. Perhaps Mikhailov was right. Maybe her fingers had not broken, though she envisioned the bones in both of them from the joint to the fingertip pulverized. Not broken by the strictest interpretation of the word, but reduced to a substance similar to ground glass.

The fingers were double their normal size. The nails black. She could see that because she had taken her fingernail polish off Sunday night. She had been scheduled to have her nails done this morning.

Scheduled to have her nails done. A normal life event. Like taking her shoes to get the heel fixed that she'd broken off running down the steps. Normal, like getting Bethany up and dressed. While she put her makeup on, María always sang silly songs with the little girl, then she'd drop Bethany off at Mrs. Trimboni's on her way to class.

School. One more semester and she'd graduate. Might even start law school in the fall. Except, of course, she wouldn't. Wouldn't start law school or anything else in the fall. She would be fortunate indeed to see another sunrise.

She caught herself before she banged her fist in mute protest against the pane of glass. With two not-broken-but-crushed fingers, that would hurt. But the rage that filled her, fighting with terror for real estate in her tied-in-a-knot gut fueled a desire to hit something. Break something. This was crazy. She should be home oversleeping. Home burning the toast because that stupid toaster didn't turn off automatically at a particular setting but just kept getting hotter and hotter.

She blurted out a sound, some king of snort, cry, aborted scream. Some sound more feral than human, the cry of an injured beast, a cornered beast … a mother defending her cubs.

Bethany.

Thank God the child was safe with Bailey!

Right, safe with Bailey.

Like Bailey was safe.

María didn't know what Mikhailov was planning, how he intended to get at Bailey, but she was absolutely certain that bringing her here was part of some sort of plan to do that. Mikhailov had remembered where he'd been the night of October 31. Here. The Nautilus. That's why he'd hopped in a plane and flew half the night to get here.

Which meant he believed Bailey was somewhere nearby and he intended to find her, and María had been brought along and kept alive for that purpose.

Her fingers hurt. What a pathetic wimp she was to be caught up in that when …

But they *hurt.* The injury to them had been more than physically painful and Mikhailov had calculated all of it. There was such an offhanded brutality to deliberately smashing someone's fingers in a car door. It communicated a disregard for pain or injury. For a person's whole human-ity. It even communicated how efficient Mikhailov had become in his line of work.

Like he'd said, maximum pain, minimal damage.

The pressure under both fingernails was something approaching unbearable. She looked around, found two straight pins on a hanger in the closet affixed to the bag where you could put your laundry or dry cleaning. The light in the bathroom was soft — dim! — like maybe they'd figured out it was depressing for a woman to see herself in glaring light, especially first thing in the morning. Even María didn't like seeing those tiny lines around her eyes. She bet if you were over fifty, bright bathroom lights made you look like you were dying of pancreatic cancer.

But there was a gooseneck desk lamp on the bedside table and in that bright light she used one of the pins to drill a hole in the top of each fingernail. Bailey had taught her this little trick. Though María had never used it, she'd watched Bailey puncture her toenail after she dropped an iron skillet on it. Bailey'd said it didn't hurt. It didn't. In fact, the blood that spurted out relieved the pressure beneath the nails and the crushed fingers hurt less. She'd lose both fingernails.

She forced herself to try to move the index finger at the first joint and was rewarded with a lightning bolt of pain that threatened to return to her the sandwich she'd eaten last night. But she could move it and she thought maybe she should. She might need her right hand.

Throughout this whole adventure María had been a world-class weakling. A coward. So scared she could hardly get her breath. She didn't know how people survived fear like she'd felt. But they did. Whether she liked it or not, so had she. Maybe that's all courage was — surviving your fear. No, it was more than that. It was doing whatever you needed to do even though you were terrified.

She took a deep breath and let it out slowly. She had no courage, not a single shred of it. The monster who'd so casually ordered her fingers smashed was going to kill her

— that was a given. Bailey, too, if he got a chance. Even precious little Bethany.

Courage or no courage, María had to stop him if she could!

How?

There was only one way, of course. Simple, really. Easy to figure out, but the execution … not so much. The only way to stop Sergei Wassily Mikhailov was to kill him.

Chapter Thirty-Eight

Maxwell Crenshaw strode toward him, beefy hand extended before he remembered Mikhailov's refusal to shake his hand earlier. He managed to redirect the gesture deftly, reached out and clapped Mikhailov companionably on the shoulder, a charming smile stapled to his face and alert calculation in his eyes.

"So sorry you had to wait, Mr. Mikhailov. Please come in and sit down and I'll have your lunch—"

"No food, just water. Distilled. No ice. Let us do our business so you may go on about the rest of your day."

"Sure thing, Mr. Mikhailov." He instructed his assistant to bring water. It would, no doubt, be in a leaded glass goblet. Then Crenshaw led the way into his plush but admittedly tasteful office. "Please have a seat and—"

"I prefer to stand, but perhaps you might want to sit."

He loved watching fear leap into the man's eyes.

Loved it.

Maxwell Crenshaw had no idea what real fear was. How Mikhailov longed to — an icepick into his ear. Yes! Puncture his eardrum while he screamed and blood stained his shirt and —

Mikhailov felt himself slipping, sliding down a slick surface toward the darkness, a hole in the universe beyond which was nothing at all. Regaining control was getting progressively more difficult, required an effort of will that sometimes produced beads of sweat on his forehead.

"I require a table tonight in the back of your dining room, against the far wall."

"That'll put you behind—"

"Your green friend, I know." He decided to smile but couldn't remember how, didn't know which facial muscles to engage. His face merely shifted expressions, as if he had undergone a sudden assault of conflicting emotions. "His color is quite offensive. You do know that, don't you? The green of pus from an oozing sore."

Then he remembered how to smile and so he did.

The smile on Maxwell Crenshaw's face looked like he, too, had only just remembered how.

"A table for tonight. No problem. How many in your party?"

Sergei bleated out a sound that he managed to cover with a cough, though Crenshaw gave him a strange look.

Party. Yes, it would be a party!

"I want no other customers seated in that area. The six tables closest will be for my associates."

He saw Crenshaw hesitate, knew he would have scheduling and juggling to do.

"Certainly, Mr. Mikhailov."

"Because I will be in attendance, I require certain security measures. Instruct your staff that my associates are to be granted unlimited access and unquestioned authority in all such things."

Crenshaw started backing up.

"Well, now, security's a touchy subject in a casino. People come here to let loose, rock and roll, do things they'd never do 'back home.' If they showed up here and had to line up for metal detectors, or get patted down, or walk through a gauntlet of security guards — that would ruin their experience. An overt security presence is the opposite of excitement, impunity and dubious deeds. It's a ten o'clock curfew. It's the chaperones at the prom."

Mikhailov had no idea what was a prom, but it was clear that Crenshaw was not sufficiently intimidated.

"I am sure I don't have to remind you what … organization I represent. We have special interests in a … wide range of business endeavors, employ a security force unequalled in the private sector. My men are trained—"

He almost said assassins. Again, he made the strange sound and covered it with a cough. What was the sound? It was like a sneeze, came on him irresistibly, without warning.

Focusing again on Crenshaw, he saw that the man had gotten the subtext of his remarks.

"I can provide your associates discreet lapel pins that my staff recognize as … shall we say, trump cards. They will extend to them *every* courtesy."

Crenshaw reached for a smile but dropped it before he was able to affix it to his face. The man was rattled, unsure whether or not he had … what was the colorful way Americans put it? Oh, yes, not sure if he had stepped in it.

"Excellent. Our business is concluded." Mikhailov turned without another word and left Crenshaw's office, made it all the way out into the hallway and halfway to the elevator before he made that sound again. It was like aborted laughter, but more high-pitched. A sound like a frightened woman would make.

～

When T.J.'s phone rang at 4:30 that afternoon he looked at the screen and saw the name on Caller ID.

Leroy Burgess.

"Got 'er done," Leroy said without preamble.

"What's it gonna cost?"

"Oh, it'll run ye, that's a fact. But you're gonna have to crank it up in the water 'fore I'll know for sure."

T.J. was tired, bone weary, but it didn't have nothin' to do with not gettin' much sleep last night, taking turns driving with Brice as they drove from Boston through Hartford, Wilkes-Barre, and into the mountains in the darkness.

He'd missed many a night's sleep in his life and didn't feel like he felt now.

Ordinarily an optimistic man by nature, most likely to come down on the it's-gonna-work-out-fine side of a situation, T.J. had tried to jam this circumstance into the shape of good fortune he wanted it to fit into. But no matter how he tried to see it from another angle, it was clear's the nose on his face that things wasn't gonna end well for María Whatever-her-last-name-was. She wouldn't survive an encounter with a murderous maniac like Mikhailov. In fact, the best thing that he could hope for her was that she'd die quick. But she wouldn't. That wasn't going to happen and soon's Bailey was able to see anything else in all the world beyond the face of that precious little girl of hers, she was gonna figure it out, too. Brice and Dobbs already had.

That picture Bailey'd painted of María, the nightmare of fire and smoke and agony. T.J. didn't know what he believed about that. Maybe their trip to Boston had saved her from that fate. Maybe Mikhailov's kidnapping had. T.J.'s gut told him that somehow that 8 p.m.-tonight-ticking-clock still counted for something. Just about every time in his life that he'd failed to listen to his gut, he been sorry.

T.J. had been headed home, by way of the grocery to pick up a couple of little things, when his phone had rung and soon's he seen it was Leroy Burgess, he almost didn't answer it. Leroy was an old friend and a master mechanic. If he couldn't make it run, whatever it was — be it lawn-mower or Jeep Cherokee — you might as well sell it for junk because it wasn't never gonna go nowhere under its own power again. Leroy spent the winter puttering around on repair jobs that'd been left in his garage workshop and wasn't but one reason he'd be calling. The motor for T.J.'s jon boat was fixed. He didn't want to think about that right now.

No, actually, he *did* want to think about that right now. He wanted to think about anything else in the world besides the devastated look that was gonna come on Bailey's face when they found out the fate of her sister.

Leroy preceded to tell T.J. way more than he wanted to know or understand about the internal organs of a four-horsepower Evinrude outboard motor, and then explained that he had it in his truck and he'd be glad to meet T.J. at the Possum Trot boat ramp where T.J. had his old metal jon boat tied up.

"So's you can crank it up and see does it suit you."

It was not a particularly cold day for early December, but it still wasn't a day you wanted to go tooling around the lake in a jon boat. It'd be dark by five o'clock. But it was almost as hard to put Leroy Burgess off as it was to get him to agree to repair whatever it was you had broke in the first place.

"Fine," T.J. said. "I'll meet you at the boat ramp about five."

~

WHEN DOBBS'S phone rang at 4:30 that afternoon, he looked at the screen and saw the name on Caller ID.

Kavanaugh County Sheriff Brice McGreggor.

"I'm going to be a little late for my shift today," Brice said. "I'm going to go shake a tree and see what falls out."

Brice was scheduled to show up at about six o'clock and take Dobbs's place as the Bailey Watchdog. He'd spend twelve hours in the guest bedroom until T.J. showed up at six o'clock tomorrow morning.

Around the clock — Bailey wasn't going to be left alone in that house even for a second until Mikhailov and his son were safely arrested.

"Any tree I know?"

"A Maxwell Crenshaw oak."

Then Brice told him what he had figured out during the nonstop marathon drive from Boston the night before. Mikhailov had been at the Nautilus for an off-the-books poker game when he was captured in the background of Bailey's birthday picture. One of the games nobody was supposed to know existed, where high rollers from all over the world won and lost millions.

"Crenshaw knows Mikhailov or he'd never have allowed him in the game. How well acquainted are they? Maybe they're twins separated at birth or maybe they were introduced at the game a month ago. No way to know which. So I'm taking a shot in the dark."

It was at least conceivable that Crenshaw knew Mikhailov well enough that he could provide some tiny fragment of information about the man that would help police track the monster down before he butchered María, and if there was even the slightest possibility …

"I'm going to … explore the nature of their relationship," Brice said. "Pay a visit to the casino, have a little chat with Crenshaw."

"You be careful. You never know what might clock you over the head if you shake a tree hard enough."

Crenshaw was a criminal who had bribed and glad-handed his way out of trouble his whole life. He was dangerous.

Ending the call, Dobbs glanced toward the stairs. He thought he'd heard Bailey's phone ring the same time his had. Maybe it was T.J. who'd called her.

It wasn't.

Chapter Thirty-Nine

WHEN BAILEY'S phone rang at 4:30 that afternoon, she picked it up and saw the name on Caller ID.

María.

"I think we have a mutual acquaintance, do we not?" said a voice with a Russian accent. "Or perhaps I have a wrong number ... *Bailey.* Perhaps you do not have a little sister."

Bailey froze as still as a statue, unable to move or breathe.

Heaven to hell in a heartbeat.

Only minutes before – a mere *handful* of minutes -- she had been rocking Bethany!

She'd been reluctant to put the child down, reluctant to stop touching her, feared in that totally irrational way of psychotic fears that this part was just a dream. She had, after all, dreamed so often of being reunited with Bethany, of touching her, holding her, kissing her, and now the child was sleeping peacefully in her arms and it really did seem too good to be true.

Bailey didn't know if Bethany normally took a

morning nap — so much she didn't know! — but she surely took one in the afternoon. Given how disturbed her sleep had been during that awful journey from Boston, the child should be exhausted and Bailey hoped she'd sleep for hours.

She got up carefully, but movement didn't rouse the child. Then she recalled that Aaron had told her to stop tiptoeing around the house like a cat burglar while the baby slept. Bethany had to adjust to normal noises when she slept or every little thing would wake her up.

Aaron. He was always so reasonable. So wise.

He'd made a similar observation about carrying the sleeping child into the apartment after she fell asleep in the car.

Just put her in bed and take her shoes off. She'll be fine.

She smiled now, thinking of Aaron. It felt good to smile at the thought of him instead of the dagger of pain that stabbed into her heart at the memories.

She walked to the couch in the parlor, the brand new couch, thank you very much Raymond Dobson, and gently — but not carefully — laid the little girl down. Bethany wiggled, then put her thumb in her mouth and drifted back off. Bailey snuggled both the old and the new minion blankets around her and forced herself not to tiptoe out of the room. She didn't close the door all the way, wanted to be sure somebody'd hear Bethany when she woke up.

Dobbs was in the kitchen and the smell that wafted her way ... was he? ... Could it be ...?

Yes! Dobbs was concocting a pot of his legendary chili. Any other time, the smell of that chili would have transformed her in an instant into Pavlov's dog. Now, there was nothing in her stomach but a cold rock.

Opening night of *The Nutcracker*. Tonight at 8 p.m.

María wouldn't be there, of course, not because Bailey

had been able to bring her safely home to West Virginia, but because María had been kidnapped by a madman. Still … María *wouldn't be at opening night.* The future painting would not come true. How could it?

She felt weak at the thought, had to fight off a wave of despair that threatened to roll over her and carry her away, leaving a bare beach with all the debris swept out to sea.

While Bethany slept, Bailey had a chance to grab a shower and get cleaned up, so she stuck her head into the kitchen where Dobbs stood with what looked like twenty different ingredients in various stages of concoction before him.

"Listen for Bethany, would you?" she said. She almost couldn't form the next words. Such a simple thing to say. So ordinary. How she'd longed for ordinary so many times, yearned for … let it go. "She's napping on the couch in the parlor, should sleep for hours. I'm just going to run upstairs and take a quick shower. Fifteen minutes, tops."

He waved her on with a spoon dripping tomato sauce.

"I'll check on her … oh, maybe every three minutes or so." He smiled and she smiled back. Well, she pulled back the corners of her mouth into the correct position, but he wasn't fooled. Of course, his own smile looked like he'd learned how from a Smiling for Dummies book.

Sparky had curled up on the floor beside the couch where Bethany slept. Dobbs had Bundy in the kitchen with him — so he could pop out into the back yard with the almost-but-not-quite house-trained puppy. If he were allowed in the parlor with Bethany, he'd hop up on the couch beside her and slather her face with puppy-licks before anybody could stop him.

Bailey reached down and lifted Bundy — Bethany called him Bunny — into her arms and nuzzled her face into his soft fur. The little golden doodle puppy was probably the best birthday present she'd ever gotten. On the birthday that had started it all.

When she got to the top of the stairs, the phone in her pocket rang. She heard Dobbs's phone downstairs ring at the same time. Maybe this was a coordinated telemarketer attack.

Then she looked at the caller ID, sucked in a breath and touched the green icon.

If there had been a wire like those on old-fashioned phones that connected the receiver to the phone itself, the voice that came through it would have been slithering like a snake. Like an oiled worm with sword teeth.

"If you are nodding your head, I cannot see," said the voice. "So you must answer me, or I will have to hang—"

"Don't hang up! Please don't … Yes, I am who you think. I'm Jessica Cunningham." Even now, even standing there so shocked the breath didn't want to come back in, even now, she wanted to cry out. "And I know who you are. You're the man who murdered my husband." But she didn't say that, of course. She didn't say anything more.

What should she do? In all the police shows on television, the kidnapper called and the police were all set up to trace the call, find out where—

"There is no need to wonder where I am," he said, as if he had read her mind. "I will tell you so you do not have to track me down. I am at the Nautilus Casino, that floats in a body of water I believe is called Whispering Mountain Lake. And your lovely sister, María, is my guest here."

MIKHAILOV WANTED SO VERY BADLY to laugh. It took all his strength to keep his voice level and emotionless. Inside he was full of merriment and glee. Oh, to see the look on her face right now! He had seen the woman in pictures on her sister's phone, taken before she went into hiding—

Into hiding.

Lying in wait.

Ready to pounce.

The universe inside his head, the one that existed as a world unto itself behind his lone, remaining eye, began to change colors. It turned red.

The color started at the top of his vision and ran down it like paint dripping off the side of a building. No, like blood. All the way to the ground. Soaking into the dirt until it was spongey, made a squishing sound when you stepped on it.

The world was obliterated by swirling, bubbling, boiling red fog and if he looked at it closely, he could see the individual water droplets in the fog. No, not water. Blood.

The sight made him want to scream!

Without thinking, he put his knuckle into his mouth and bit down on it to keep from losing his grip, his hold on … everything. He felt blood dripping out the cuff of his black glove and looked down. He had bitten into his finger, through the leather and the flesh all the way to the bone.

A lone hysterical thought to make a break for it flashed bright and then was gone: he only had nine fingers left — if he wasn't careful, he'd be scratching his nose with a stump.

The pain brought him back from the edge and everything righted itself, like setting one of those old-fashioned videos in reverse. The blood stopped flowing out of his glove. The flesh of his knuckle knit back together, the leather reformed, the droplets of blood mist became smaller and smaller, too small to see. Then the fog was gone and he was in the library of his mind where the volumes appeared crisp and so clear they almost looked over-exposed.

The voice in his ear was saying, "Are you there? Hello. Oh, please don't hang—"

"Why would I hang up when it was I who called you?" His voice was as cold as an arctic ocean. This woman had been out there all these months, waiting, lying in the tall weeds ready to pounce. She would pay for that.

"Is my sister all right? I want to talk to her. Put her on the phone so—"

"Don't talk to me as if you were the one in charge!" A verbal slap in the face. "I am in control here. Do not believe for a second you have any power over me. I can lift a finger and your sister will have her throat slit … though that is a far more merciful death than I have planned for her."

"What do you want?"

"Why *you*, of course. I want you dead."

He heard the intake of breath on the other end of the phone when she gasped and he had to stifle a wave of hysterical giggling.

"The two of us have no time or energy for playing games. I took your sister. Now, I want to trade her for you."

"You're *here*?"

"Were you not listening to what I said? I will not waste time repeating myself. First, I should tell you to forget all the plans that are spinning like spiderwebs in your head. *He is here,* you think, *I will call the police, the federal marshals. They will find him. They will arrest him.*"

When he laughed, it was a genuine laugh.

"Don't be absurd. I will vanish, as I have vanished before. Marshal Bernard Jordan has not a clue where to look for me. Your sister will vanish with me. Are we clear?"

Silence.

"Do not nod."

"Yes, we're clear."

"Here is the deal I am offering. I will trade your sister for you. You come with me; she walks away free. End of story. Well, the end of the story for you."

"What ...? You'll *trade* ...?"

"I will tell you the terms of this arrangement and you will see that they are the only options you have. If you trade yourself for your sister, I guarantee she will be unharmed. She will walk free. I will further guarantee that I will not harm the little girl ... what is her name? Bethany ... Bethany Nicole, age three and a half — is that not right?"

She made some kind of inarticulate sound that he supposed was a strangled sob but it could just as easily have been a grunt of surprise, or a growl of anger.

"I guarantee the safety of your family if you accept the terms of this arrangement."

He paused, then sighed for effect.

"Do I have to explain this part? Surely, the federal marshals and the other law enforcement officials have told you about me. Who I am. What ... organization I represent. If they have told you, then you know that Sergei Wassily Mikhailov *never* breaks his word. He does what he says he will do. He *always* keeps his promises. Is that not what they have said of me?"

She said nothing.

"If you are nodding ..."

"Yes, that's what they told me."

"Excellent. Then you know you can trust me to uphold *my* end of the bargain. But should you strike a deal with me and not uphold your end, your sister will die a particularly painful and gruesome death."

The sound she made when he said that was something

like a muffled scream, so he knew he had her full and undivided attention as he described in some detail the drug-induced horror he would inflict upon her sister.

"The deal I am offering is the one and only chance your loved ones have for survival." He felt red rage seeping into his mind and his effort to restrain it pulled his vocal cords tight, made his voice strained and breathless. "The moment you told the police what you saw that day in the rain, you signed a death warrant for every member of your family and there is absolutely nothing you can do to keep me from … *executing* that warrant."

He paused for a beat, changed his tone from threatening to instructive, a professor explaining a particularly thorny math problem to a recalcitrant student.

"Surely, you are aware of how the American legal system functions, how long criminal proceedings can be postponed. With the proper legal representation — and I will have a team of the best lawyers money can buy — you can delay a trial for months … years.

"Do you know how long is the average stay on what you call Death Row? Seventeen years. You should google it, check to see if I tell you the truth. In other words, my dear, it will be *years* before you have a chance to testify against me and I will live for years after you do."

His voice dropped then to a dry, rasping whisper.

"Should you be so foolish as to come out of hiding like a jackal in the weeds, stand before a jury and point a finger at me, you will never live another moment of your life in peace. I will hunt you down, no matter where you go, no matter how long it takes."

In his own ears, his voice sounded like sand blowing across rocks in a desert, the scrabbling claws of scarabs scratching.

"I will pick my timing. I am in no hurry. Perhaps, I will

kill *Bethany* on her wedding day, yes? Slit her throat so her blood stains her beautiful white dress. Or no, I will wait even longer. Ah yes, that's it — I will wait until she bears a child. I will be there when she brings the suckling babe home, and I will kill the baby in front of her, dismember it while she watches. She will die an even more brutal death than the infant."

He stopped, allowed a few seconds for the images to form in her mind's eye.

"You will not know a moment's peace as long as you live. You will wonder *every day* if it is the day someone comes in the night with a garrote, the day your little girl does not come home from school. Do we understand each other?"

She said nothing, but he was certain he had so thoroughly knocked the breath out of her she could only nod.

He told her the specifics of the deal he wanted to make with her, what he had meticulously planned that morning as he had wandered around the restaurant in the Nautilus Casino — selecting just the right sites and promised that compliance would secure for her a "merciful death." A bullet in the back of her skull.

He said nothing else. Waited. He could hear that she was gasping for air. Then her breathing steadied. When she spoke, her voice was shaky, but level.

Chapter Forty

Bailey was sitting on the edge of her bed, the phone to her ear. She had been at the head of the stairs when it rang, when she answered it, when she heard the snake voice crawl out through the not-cord and into her ear, a serpent that slithered through her eardrum into her brain.

It was the most horrible voice she had ever heard.

For the first few moments he spoke, she couldn't concentrate on what he was saying. She was seeing him standing with that stupid Fedora hat in the rain, pointing a gun at Aaron. The firecracker sound.

Jessie, run!

Another firecracker sound.

The voice was talking through the phone but she couldn't grab the words with her mind. It was merely a serpent in her head, eating her thoughts with jagged teeth.

She heard silence then, and didn't know how long it had lasted. Had he stopped talking a minute ago, two seconds ago, an hour? Had he hung up?

"Are you there? Hello? Oh, please don't hang—"

"Why would I hang up when it is I who called you?"

The voice went on then. She listened. At some point she had walked into her bedroom and sat down on the bed. She had no memory of moving. Her mind seemed so very, very small.

The words he was saying, they were huge, each one too big to fit between her ears in her skull. And all of them … it was ludicrous to think she could jam them into her head and hear them, listen to them, understand them, assign them significance.

She caught fragments as the monstrous behemoths slammed into her mind through her ears. Heard pieces and listened to them.

He told her not to call the police. That he would vanish with María if she did. When he asked if she understood, she nodded.

"Do not nod."

"Yes," she said.

He offered her a deal. He would trade María for her. If she accepted, he guaranteed that María and Bethany would be safe.

"Sergei Wassily Mikhailov *never* breaks his word. He does what he says he will do. He *always* keeps his promises. He always keeps his word. If he says it, he will do it." The federal marshals who'd played the informant's tape for her in the anonymous room in the anonymous police station had said he kept his troops in line by always keeping his promise to kill anyone who crossed him and *all the members of their families, too.*

That's what had kept her cowering in hiding for two years.

Though her mind could not process all that he was saying to her, it was meticulously examining some of it.

Mikhailov always kept his promises to kill … therefore she was supposed to trust him to keep a promise *not to kill?*

No.

Every fiber of her being and soul understood with absolute certainty that this man could not be trusted about *anything.* He would kill when, where and how it suited him and it would make no difference to him that he had said some words, made some promise, some guarantee. Men like this monster had no rules of conduct except what got them what they wanted.

He *guaranteed* María and Bethany would be safe if she took his offer. No, they wouldn't. He would kill them out of spite.

If she refused his deal — "your sister will die a particularly painful and gruesome death. Clean and quiet on the outside, but an unimaginable horror from within."

"Do you know what is ketamine? It goes by many names — Kit Cat, Super Acid, Vitamin K. In small doses, it is an hallucinogenic drug used for recreation. In large doses, it will hurl you into an alternative universe from which you can never escape, where there are only crawling monsters, teeth and blood and fire. You have heard of PCP, too, yes? Angel dust causes bizarre, violent and psychotic behavior. Should you be so foolish as to combine the two, they will literally dissolve your brain matter and kill you with a cataclysmic stroke. But first, they will drive you completely mad."

He paused. "Crazy people are capable of anything. A … former associate of mine ate himself. He chewed off his own fingers, gnawed the meat and muscle and tendons from the bones of his arms, pulled out his eyeballs."

She gasped again.

"Another man I know set himself on fire. We provided the lighter fluid and matches, of course, but he was more than happy to do the deed.

He continued to describe horror but Bailey was not

listening. She was remembering being in María's body as she burned to death. Perhaps María had hallucinated the whole thing — she *had* seemed drugged — and the sudden darkness at the end was the blood vessels in her brain hemorrhaging, stroking out.

Or perhaps she had set the fire herself.

It made no difference, though. Whether physically real or imagined horror, the effect was the same. María had experienced burning to death. Bailey believed she — or Mikhailov — had saved María from *The Nutcracker* opening night fire Bailey had painted. But it didn't matter because Mikhailov would conceive a death for her that was equally horrifying.

If she remained Mikhailov's prisoner, María would die.

And she would raise Bethany on the run, constantly looking over her shoulder, always afraid. In the end, he would find them and kill them both.

He probably thought he was terrifying her with the description of what life would be like running from him. He could have saved his breath. She'd been living some variation of that for the past two years. The difference, of course, was that for the past two years he had not been trying to find her.

Nobody looks for somebody they think is dead.

Now he would go to the ends of the earth following her trail.

While he continued to hurl too-big words at her that would not fit into her head, she thought her own thoughts, smaller ones, a train of them.

They were quite simple thoughts, really.

As long as Sergei Wassily Mikhailov drew breath, she and Bethany and María would remain a single heartbeat away from discovery and death.

Only one thing would ensure their safety — Mikhailov had to die.

Bailey would have to kill him.

Some of the water-spider thoughts in her mind, that flitted around so fast it was almost impossible to think them, considered that the terrified woman hiding in the mud under a dumpster two years ago would not even have been able to entertain the thought. But *Jessie Cunningham* had died there along with Aaron, the homeless woman and the two innocents in the white Blazer. *Bailey Donahue* could do more than merely entertain the thought, she could perform the deed. Sergei Mikhailov wouldn't be the first man she'd killed. She had beaten a man to death with rocks in the absolute dark of a coal mine. It had been self-defense, of course. But killing Sergei Mikhailov was self-defense, too.

Some part of her was attending to his monster words. The rest of her had already moved on. From what Dobbs's private investigator had said about Mikhailov, his underlings believed he was losing his mind and they served him out of fear, not loyalty. They would not carry on some vendetta for him from the grave, avenging his honor. Once he was dead, they'd be well rid of him.

Except his son. What about Ivan?

"If I make a deal with you, how do I know your son Ivan will honor it?" She was both surprised and just a little glad that she had to bite her tongue to keep from saying, "You know, Ivan, the pathetic drunk who killed a mother and her baby, the son you murdered two people to protect."

She didn't say that. She heard what he responded.

"Ivan is no worry to you. He is dead."

"Your son is—"

"I killed him myself, tasted his blood, and then beat

him with the iron from a fireplace, buried it in his skull, hit him again and again until pieces of his alcohol-soaked brain splattered my shoes."

It was true, then. This man was insane. He wasn't just a vicious killer. He was a mad dog. He should be shot on sight.

Bailey had a gun, the one in the kitchen drawer she'd used to put Oscar in her brain last summer. She could kill Sergei Mikhailov with it.

"As a gesture of good faith, we will make the exchange in a public place, so there is no possibility of … treachery on the part of either one of us. María will be waiting for you in the restaurant of the Nautilus, where you took the … picture that began this little drama. She will be seated in the back corner by the kitchen, across from the bar, accompanied by two men, one on either side. It will not be noticeable that the men are restraining her. But both are prepared to inject her with the cocktail of madness I have developed. No gunshot, no blood, nothing that will draw undue attention. Clean and quiet. These men are … let's say they are similar to the weapon the Japanese used on you Americans during World War II. Kamikaze pilots. Both owe me debts. Performing this task will be payment in full. They are perfectly willing to risk death or imprisonment to protect their families from my vengeance."

She was sure they would. Just like she would be willing to die to protect hers.

"You will come into the restaurant through the front entrance under the archway at exactly six o'clock. Exactly. There are no clocks in casinos, so wear a watch. I respect attention to detail. It will be a sign to me that you intend to honor the rest of our agreement. Stand beneath the archway until you locate your sister, because you must walk *directly* to her, not a single wandering step. You will take her place; she will walk out unharmed. I will tell you the same thing I told her. If you make any attempt to draw the attention of others, any kind of scene, if you stumble, if you sneeze, if you do anything except walk immediately and directly to her table, she will suffer the horror of a melting brain.

"Once you have taken her place, she must leave the restaurant immediately, without pause or hesitation, go through the casino and out the front door and board one of those launches that are docked there. There will be eyes on her every second. Should she deviate from the plan in any way, a signal will be given, and you will be given the deadly cocktail I put together for her. A needle prick … devastation. But if she is obedient, if she lives up to her end of the bargain, I will … grant you a merciful death."

He paused and when he continued his voice was thin and reedy, as if he had himself on a tight rein.

"You should die the death dispensed to all who betray Sergei Mikhailov. You have earned a slow, agonizing—" He stopped again, took a breath and continued in the tight voice. "If she does as she has been instructed, you will be removed from the restaurant — under disguised restraint, of course, and brought to me. Somewhere private. There, I will put a bullet in the back of your head."

To match the one already in the front. A playmate for Oscar.

"I accept your offer."

There was silence on the other end of the line. Then a whispered, "Excellent."

"But I have one condition of my own."

A lion awoke on the other end of the phone and roared.

"No one sets conditions for Sergei—"

"You have to be there, or no deal. I have to see *you*."

"Oooooh," he said expansively, "that is not a condition! It is my pleasure. I wouldn't miss it for the world. I will not be seated with your sister, of course, but look around for me. I will be right out where you cannot miss me. Wait until we make eye contact, if you like, before you proceed.

"But should you decide to make some kind of plan to rescue your sister, bring with you other people, like those you brought with you to Boston … If you think perhaps to kill my men, to shoot them or somehow disarm them, you must forget it now and not think of it again. One second, less than a second and the drug will be coursing through her veins."

"I will come alone. I'll honor my end of the deal."

"And I will honor mine. You have my word."

Then the phone went dead.

Chapter Forty-One

BAILEY SAT LOOKING at the phone in her hand. Should she touch one of the handful of phone numbers on her favorites list, call Brice, tell him Mikhailov was at the Nautilus, let him handle it? That was the only safe thing to do — safe for Bailey. But if she did, Mikhailov would kill María. He had absolutely nothing to lose. He was already facing the death penalty for killing Aaron.

And what if, by some miracle, he managed to get away? That wasn't such a farfetched idea. He'd been eluding the police for years. He was an expert. As long as Mikhailov drew breath, she and Bethany would live in fear.

No, even if you could catch it, you didn't put a rabid dog in a cage. You shot it on sight. Mikhailov had to die now, today. She had to kill him. She was the only person in the world who could save her family.

Still, she sat, looking at her phone — the unreality of what her life had become washing over her. She should be in Boston making hot chocolate while Aaron took Bethany out to build a snowman. *How did she get here,* calmly contemplating murder? Bailey was an ordinary woman, not some too-pretty-to-be-real television-show cop with an attitude. She was *real*, a normal wife and mother—

Widow, not wife. And the mother of a dead child … unless *she* protected her.

The decision was made. What remained now was making a plan that would work.

Bailey had to have a gun, but not to shoot Mikhailov. She needed a gun as a red herring so she could get close enough to him to use her real weapon. One he wouldn't suspect.

Getting up off the bed, she found that her knees were strong. Her heart was not trying to pound its way out of her chest. She was scared, of course. But that was not the dominant emotion she felt. What she felt was an almost all-consuming rage.

Sergei Wassily Mikhailov's days of dispensing death were over. It was time he got a taste of the dish he'd been serving his whole life.

The gun … was in the kitchen. So was Dobbs.

She went downstairs wearing a look of determination that T.J. would have read instantly on her face. Dobbs, too, but his back was turned.

"I thought you were going to take a shower," he said over his shoulder.

"Was. Then it occurred to me that Bundy here might need to go out, and you're busy with the chili, no reason you should—"

"Oh, yes there is reason I should take him out! You *promised*, remember. You said you'd let us take care of you."

"Sure, I did, but this is just out into the back yard. I'll be right out there."

He put the spoon down on the counter and walked to the peg by the back door where the leash hung.

"Out into the back yard with the dog … not on my watch."

She knew he'd refuse to allow her to take the dog out, would demand to do it in her stead because she'd been snatched by a murderer out of the back yard when she was performing that particular innocuous task.

As soon as he closed the screen door behind him, Bailey whirled around and went to the drawer where she'd left the gun. Not a particularly safe or handy place to put a gun. She'd merely stuck it in there and forgot about it.

For a horrifying moment, she felt around in the back of the drawer and couldn't—

There it was! It was a Smith & Wesson Model 63 revolver. She wouldn't allow her mind to go to the night she had held the gun to her temple and pulled the trigger. That thought would trigger all manner of other memories she didn't have time to entertain right now. Brice had taken the gun away from her after she'd fit Oscar snug into the side of her skull, and he'd given it back to her with a handful of .22 cartridges.

The man in the gun store had shown her how to reload the weapon, but she hadn't been listening. Why did she need to know how to reload when she planned to use only the one round? She stuffed the pistol in its little nylon holster into the waistband of her jeans in the back and pulled her shirt out over it, deposited the cartridges in her pocket just as Dobbs swung the door open and brought Bundy back into the kitchen.

"First try," he said happily. "I said go potty, he looked at me like he knew exactly what I was talking about, then he sniffed around to make sure he'd picked a good spot, squatted and dropped a load. If you hadn't come down here to let him out, I bet he would have gone to the back door and scratched, like you've been training him."

"You're probably right. I should have given him the chance to earn a treat."

"Oh, I gave him a treat. Popped it right in his mouth as a reward as soon as he finished."

"You'd have given him the treat even if he hadn't done what you asked."

The big man beamed. "Give the girl a Kewpie doll. You and T.J. are in charge of the training part. I'm in charge of the make-the-dogs-happy part. A reasonable division of labor."

"I'm off to get clean. Listen for—"

"I've already checked on her once and you've only been gone ten minutes. I heard you on the phone. Was it T.J.?"

She stumbled. "No, it was a telemarketer."

"You talked to a telemarketer? Don't you know—"

"Yeah, but sometimes it feels good to yell at a robot."

She turned quickly and left the room before he could engage her in any more conversation. Hurrying up the stairs, she closed the bedroom door behind her and dumped the gun and cartridges on her blue flowered bedspread. It was called a revolver because it had a cylinder for the cartridges that revolved to deliver the next round. She remembered that much from what the gun store man had told her. What else she remembered was his dogged determination to talk her out of buying the gun at all.

"Ma'am, this gun is useless for self-protection. It's a .22." As if that alone should be explanation enough.

When she'd looked blank, he'd continued. "Say somebody comes after you, you could shoot the guy three times before he grabbed the pistol out of your hand and beat you to death with it. Then he'd walk away and die from blood loss two hours later. But you'd still be dead."

He'd told her you had to hit a vital organ for the gun to be effective and she'd figured, in error as it turned out, that the brain was a vital organ.

In its favor, the pistol was small. The barrel was only about three inches long. She remembered the "big hunking sight" on the end, which she hadn't used the one and only time she'd ever fired it, but she recalled Brice commenting once that you should *not* close one eye and peer out over the sight of a pistol. You kept both eyes open and looked down the barrel, and placed the sight on the target. She would have to hide the gun — somewhere that wasn't too obvious — and that would be easier, given that it wasn't a bazooka.

She found the catch and flipped open the revolving cylinder and loaded the cartridges into it. There were six holes and only five cartridges. The sixth was Oscar. She'd bought a box of ammo with the pistol, but they were somewhere in the kitchen … maybe, she wasn't sure. Five rounds was enough. Even if she'd been planning to kill him with the pistol, she wouldn't likely get to take half a dozen shots at him. She spun the cylinder, then snapped it shut and placed the weapon back in the holster.

Her mind had been leaping ahead of her at every stage of this plan, coming up with what she had to do next before she was finished completing the previous task. She would have to play the few cards she'd been dealt. Mikhailov had had bodyguards even before he went nuts. Now he was paranoid. She couldn't imagine he'd allow anyone close to him without searching them for a weapon.

But he'd picked the location — out in public. She'd carry a clutch purse and they'd immediately, though perhaps surreptitiously, search it. And they'd find the gun. That was the purpose of putting the gun in the purse — because they'd search it. And when they found the gun, they would smugly assume they had disarmed her.

At least, that was the plan.

All she had going for her was the element of surprise. You didn't expect a shark to bite you after you've taken out its teeth. You let down your guard. In theory, anyway.

How and when she would use the real weapon was something she'd have to improvise. She'd arrive in the slinky green dress and it would be clear — even without an in-the-middle-of-a-crowded-restaurant pat-down, which they surely would not be so crass as to perform — she carried nothing dangerous. Eventually, they'd leave the restaurant and take her to whatever non-public, private location Mikhailov had selected for her execution, and he would be there. Close. He had promised he would do the honors and she believed him. He wanted to kill her — it was personal. Though she didn't believe a syllable of what he said about a "merciful death," she did believe that he would be within striking range for her to use her real weapon.

For that, she would have to count on blind providence. A moment when everyone's back was turned. The dark interior of a back seat. She could stumble and fall and grab it as she got to her feet.

Besides, it didn't matter what she planned. It was T.J. who had told her that "no battle plan lasts after the first shot is fired." Battle was improvisation. She would have to wait for her opportunity to present itself, then take the opportunity when it did. The truth still in the husk, as T.J. would call it, was that her plan had almost no chance of success. But it was the only one she had.

And the other truth still in the husk was that there was almost no possibility she would survive the encounter. Say she got in close, struck and killed him. What next? Duh. His bodyguards would kill her on the spot.

BRICE HAD TURNED the Watford House into a virtual fortress, determined to keep her safe *this time*. Guards had been stationed all around to protect the occupants of the house, but their presence *imprisoned* the occupants at the same time. How could Bailey meet Mikhailov at the Nautilus restaurant if she couldn't even get out of her house?

Deputy Sheriff Raleigh Fletcher was stationed in a cruiser in front on the street. Her "nondescript blue Honda" was parked in the driveway. Two other deputies were positioned on opposite sides of her back yard.

She would have to get past "Fletch" out front or the two deputies out back.

Fletch. Definitely Fletch.

She wasn't actually aware of making plans, of figuring things out, basic trial and error. Try this, no, this would work better. She was following a plan that her mind was devising on the fly, staying just barely out in front of what she was implementing at that moment.

The Watford House was old, and attaching a functioning garage door opener on the heavy wooden garage door had been a challenge, and nothing former owners had tried ever functioned very well or for very long. She'd had it repaired only a couple of weeks ago and the man from Doors, Inc. pointed up to the complex weight and counterweight system, affixed to the door by a chain, and told her, "Ma'am, that's a clusterf—" He caught himself and coughed.

He proceeded to explain to her how it was a jerry-rigged system so temperamental the slightest "hitch in the git-along" would put it out of service.

"'Tween you and me, I'd park my car outside and use this for storage."

She had taken his advice. The garage door opened into the laundry room, which opened into the short hallway — T.J. called it a mudroom — between the laundry room and the door into the kitchen. No way to get there without passing Dobbs, who was bound to be wondering by now why she still hadn't gotten around to that shower. Picking up her hand mirror off the vanity top, she banged it a couple of times against the side of the bathtub until the plastic handle broke off. She took the two pieces downstairs with her and flashed them at Dobbs as she hurried past him to the garage.

"Superglue's in a box on the workbench," she said and didn't wait for his reply.

The door into the garage from the house was solid wood — not a hollow-core door anywhere in the building — with a knob lock and a sturdy deadbolt. She closed it behind her and went to the storage closet on the back wall. It was about fifteen feet deep but stretched the whole length of the garage with shelves lining both walls. The door was on the end close to the door into the house. There were two lights in the storage room ceiling, one directly above the door and another at the other end of the room. She flipped the switch — both lights came on.

There was a burned-out bulb in one of the four workbench lights. She unscrewed that burned-out bulb, took it into the storage room, and using the step ladder, swapped it out for the functioning bulb in the light at the end of the room. She put the bulb she'd removed out of sight on the bottom shelf of the workbench.

Looking around, she quickly found the other things she

needed — a big bottle of superglue and a pair of spring-action garden snips for trimming rose bushes. Using the snippers, she clipped off the whole top spout of the super-glue bottle, making an opening an inch across. Then she set it carefully out of sight beside the light bulb, stepped into the storage room, placed the snips on a shelf and went back into the laundry room.

Shoving some clean towels out of the dryer back into the washing machine, she turned it on. Then she picked up a couple of pairs of old tennis shoes, popped them into the dryer and turned it on. The instant clung-clunk-clunking of the shoes was deafening. Stepping out into the kitchen she gestured toward the noisy dryer in the next room.

"Sorry. They'll be dry in a few minutes."

"I thought you were going to take a shower." Without waiting for a reply, he continued. "Since you're down here, taste this. I think it needs more salt."

She forced herself to stop and take a taste. Somehow managed to keep a pleasant enough look on her face and her hands from trembling. The chili was probably deli-cious. She couldn't taste a thing.

"You can add salt at the table" — she affected a twangy West Virginia accent — "but ya cain't un-salt it."

He said something about her spending too much time around T.J. as she left the room, turned and raced up the stairs. She put her change of clothes, the gun, and her pearled purse into an old Walmart sack from the hall closet, hurried down the stairs and set it beside the front door.

Then she stopped, took a deep breath, and another.

Chapter Forty-Two

BRICE WAS POLITE, didn't go barging into Crenshaw's private office like Sherman marching on Atlanta. He did make sure, however, that the man's assistant knew he was here "on official business."

The office was as ornate-but-tasteful as everything else in the beautiful casino — well, except for the current Grinch Stole Christmas decor. Even to Brice's untrained eye, the gigantic green Grinch he'd seen in the restaurant when he came into the building was a swing-and-a-miss in the stylish ornamentation department.

The office nestled in the glittering punchbowl casino building, provided a view out across the lake which on a summer day would be crowded with the colorful sails of boats against the water reflecting the green forest hillsides. Even on this winter day, with the trees bare, it was still an impressive sight.

The walls were paneled with some kind of dark teak-wood like the bar in the restaurant, which had likely required the decimation of an acre of South American rain forest to acquire. You could get lost in the multihued swirls in the wood grain.

Crenshaw, a man who never missed an opportunity to grease the skids, kept him waiting in the outer office for only a few minutes before having him ushered into his private enclave, which was all glass, chrome, sharp angles and bright colors. The four pieces of original art on the wall were probably worth more than Brice's house. Each featured a different primary color, smeared and splashed around the canvas — the kind of art Bailey said was produced using the monkey-in-a-paint-fight technique.

The thought of her brought her face instantly to mind, along with a pain so layered and tangled he could never hope to sort it all out. He loved her, had tried his dead level best … but it had happened to him without his consent and he'd only admitted it to himself when he feared she had been killed. Now that he could no longer hide from his own feelings by lying to himself, he'd had to make some deeply painful adjustments in how he lived his life. He'd planned to begin implementing those as soon as the holidays were over. A slow withdrawal from her life. A conscientious rebuilding of the wall he kept between himself and all women, the one she'd come crashing through with a bullet in her brain and a magical gift.

Nothing in life was simple, but his relationship with Bailey had left simple in the dust months ago. It seemed that the moment she opened her eyes in the hospital, with Oscar in her brain, their every interaction was out-of-control turbulent and he'd merely been bouncing along in the back of the bus as it careened down a mountain road toward a cliff. Now, he was trying desperately to keep the woman he loved alive long enough for him to extricate himself from her life and walk away.

"Sheriff …?"

The voice came from behind him, in a tone that indicated this wasn't the first time he'd spoken. Brice turned around and stopped himself from burping out something like, "… lost in thought." He merely put out his hand.

"Mr. Crenshaw."

"Sheriff McGreggor, how can I help you today?"

Brice reached into his pocket and pulled out his phone. He'd put a copy of Bailey's birthday picture on it.

"What can you tell me about this man?" He held the phone out to Crenshaw. "The guy in the background with the pointed beard and the eyepatch."

Brice was carefully watching Crenshaw's reaction — his eyes, did they narrow? Did he blink? Since Crenshaw was a practiced gambler, he'd be more able than most to keep his feelings off his face, so his reactions would be subtle.

Except they weren't.

He literally whirled on his heel and turned his back to Brice, walking rapidly to his desk, tossing his next words over his shoulder.

"Don't believe I've ever met the man." He sat down in his office chair, ensconced behind a big desk that gave him a king-on-a-throne psychological advantage over the person he was talking to and looked up at Brice. Didn't meet his eyes, though. "Surely, you don't think I'm on a first-name basis with everyone who comes into my casino. Sorry I couldn't help you, but I'm really very busy. If you'll excuse me …"

The man was clearly rattled and off balance. A good place to have someone from whom you wanted information. Now, Brice needed to up the ante.

"Surely you don't think I don't know you have private card games for high rollers just like this guy."

Crenshaw was scrambling, struggling to get his mojo

back. He cleared his throat, stalling, trying to judge which route to take with the sheriff. Brice saved him the trouble.

"Don't bother to deny it. Don't think I wouldn't have landed on you with both feet if I had enough evidence to prove what we both know is true. I'm not on either of your payrolls, public or private. Right now I don't give a gnat's eyelash about an illegal card game. I'm only interested in what you can tell me about *this man*."

"I told you, I don't …" He didn't bother to try to float the rest of it because it was clear Brice wasn't buying what he was selling. "Say I do know this gentleman. An acquaintance. What could I possibly tell you about him that would help you in any way?"

Crenshaw's reactions were way over the top. He was massively freaked out that Brice had shown up with Mikhailov's picture. Why?

"This picture was taken in October. Has he been back to the casino since then?"

"No, I don't believe he has." Textbook lie.

Rudimentary deception detection: if you asked a right-handed person a question about a past event — When did you see the new *Star Wars* movie? — that person will look up momentarily, because that's what the human eye did when you were thinking. If he looked up and to the left, he was accessing his memory, and what he tells you is what he remembers. If he looked up and to the right, he was accessing the creative portion of his mind, because he was about to make something up.

So Mikhailov *had* been back here in the past month. Twice in five weeks. Brice broke out in cold chills. What could he say to keep Crenshaw off balance?

"Maybe you don't know that this particular junkyard dog's not just mean. He's rabid."

"What are you—?"

"He's crazy. Nuts. Psychotic."

"Mr. Mikhailov?" Crenshaw was incredulous. He was also *scared*.

"Oh, he's always been a killer. Just the price of doing business in his line of work. But at least in the past he was sane. Not anymore."

"Why would you say a thing—?"

"He beat his own son to death with a fireplace poker. Did you know that? Beat him until he wasn't just unrecognizable. It was hard to tell he was human."

All the color had drained out of Crenshaw's face and Brice was scrambling to put the pieces together. Why would it so upset him to know that Mikhailov was insane? Why would it matter to him that a man who'd been to the Nautilus at least twice to play poker … or was there more to it than that? More to their relationship than that?

"If you're engaged in any business dealings with Mikhailov, you're in way over your head. The man has dementia, a brain tumor, advanced stage syphilis … take your pick. Something's eating his brain and spitting out violence. He now kills randomly, irrationally, just for the pleasure it gives him."

Crenshaw rose unsteadily to his feet, had managed to crawl back into some semblance of a calm facade. The giveaway was the pen he gripped his hand, holding it so tight his fingers were white.

"I don't have any idea what you're talking about, Sheriff."

Brice leaned over the desk and spoke quietly,

"Oh, but you *do* know what I'm talking about. You've *seen* the craziness — haven't you?"

"I'm sure if Mr. Mikhailov is in need of psychiatric care he will seek it. Now, I really must ask you to leave. I have business to take care of."

Brice stood looking at him.

"You're hiding something, Mr. Crenshaw. You know a whole lot more about Sergei Mikhailov than you're saying." Brice held up both hands to ward off Crenshaw's protest. "Just know this — the man is completely, irreversibly *insane*. He kidnapped a young woman in Boston yesterday and is holding her hostage. There's a massive manhunt — federal marshals, FBI, local authorities. If you know anything about that, anything at all about where Mikhailov is or where he's hiding his hostage, when he goes down — and I guarantee he *will* go down — I will see to it you go down right alongside him. An accomplice after the fact to kidnapping ... maybe murder. You can't bribe your way out of this one, Crenshaw. Is that really what you signed on for?"

Crenshaw's voice did not waver, but it was airless and raspy, sand blowing across stone.

"If you're going to accuse me of a crime, I will not say another word without my lawyer present. I'm asking you to leave — now."

Brice found himself standing in the broad hallway in front of Crenshaw's office, his mind on spin cycle over the bizarre turn the conversation had taken, trying to figure out his next move.

The elevator doors on the other side of the hallway opened, two men got out, he crossed the hall quickly before the doors could close, got in and rode the elevator to the first floor.

If only he had a wire-tap on Crenshaw's phone. He'd bet T.J.'s pension that right this minute Crenshaw was calling Mikhailov.

Chapter Forty-Three

THE DISTANCE between the front door and the parlor where Bethany lay sleeping was roughly the space between the earth and the moon.

Bailey eased the door open. Started to tiptoe — thought of Aaron and didn't — to the couch where Bethany lay crashed out on her back, both minion blankets on the floor beside her. Sparky got to his feet when she approached. Then just stood, looking at her.

Sometimes — no, *often* — that dog was downright spooky.

She tried very hard to look upon the child with gratitude, with absolute love and gratitude that she had been granted this last time with her, this tiny space of knowing her before the end. But she wasn't that strong. Jessie Cunningham wasn't that strong and neither was the new and improved Bailey Donahue.

She couldn't find it in her soul to feel gratitude for being allowed to see her daughter again, touch her, hold her, sing to her, love her — and then have her snatched away again.

It's not fair!

She wanted to wail the words and wanted to tell the T.J. in her head that if he opined "the only fair I know gives prizes for livestock" she'd punch him in the face.

Bailey collapsed to her knees, heard the clunk of them on the floor and was afraid the sound would disturb Bethany. Wake her up. And if that little girl opened her eyes … Aaron's eyes. Aaron! If the child looked at her with the eyes of her father, Bailey could never leave her. She would never be able to do what she knew she had to do, make the sacrifice she had to make to ensure the little girl had a future.

She could do that. She would do that. But not if Bethany woke up. All bets were off if she woke up.

But she didn't rouse at all at the noise. Aaron had been right, of course. He had been right about everything. Bethany'd adjusted to noise. Bailey would *sooo* have coddled the little girl, wrapped her in cotton bunting and never allowed any harmful thing to get near her.

Aaron wouldn't have let her do that, spoil her. Aaron would have been at her side. Should have been at her side. But the monster with the eyepatch and the pointed beard had murdered him, had started all of this and now Bailey had to finish it. To do that, she had to find a way to walk away from Bethany.

She sat on her knees beside the couch where the little girl lay, watching the even breathing, her chest rising and falling in a steady rhythm. She wanted to reach out and push her hair behind her ears but that would surely wake her. As would kissing her. Even on the forehead, on the hand.

She couldn't touch her.

Bailey rocked back on her heels, tilted her head toward the ceiling and screamed a shrieking wail of savage misery and grief, so loud it shattered the windows in her soul … without making a sound.

Noooooo!

It wasn't supposed to be like this. She was supposed to get her little girl back, play with her, love her, kiss her boo-boos, teach her to ride a bicycle and fasten the hooks on her prom dress.

But she had to walk away from all that. Not just the right-now, the little girl lying asleep on the couch. She had to walk away from all the tomorrows out there stacked one on top of the other that she would never see.

Somewhere inside her crumpled. Her will left her and she knew she had only been fooling herself. She couldn't leave Bethany, couldn't give up the precious child. She was a fool to believe she'd ever be able to pull it off.

She flat out wasn't strong enough. The universe would just have to understand that.

No. Not Bailey.

Uh uh!

She could *not* give up all those tomorrows with her precious Bethany. Couldn't.

She took one breath.

Another.

But the expected blow of realization didn't come. She wasn't knocked off her knees by the power of understanding, acceptance and strength.

It was just somehow … there.

She would give up the tomorrows either way. On her terms. Or on Mikhailov's. She would kill him and save her daughter. Or she would keep her daughter … until the day he chose to come and murder them both.

Resolve stiffened her spine.

Was this what courage was? Yeah, probably. That thing you got right at the end when everything else in your whole life that mattered was gone. This was what was left when you scraped the bottom of the bowl of existence. The last spoonful.

She became aware of Sparky then, sitting beside her. Just sitting. Not angling for a pat on the head. Not licking her hand or her arm, just sitting, looking at her with his huge wise eyes. At that moment, she believed that Sparky understood on some level what she was doing, that she was telling Bethany goodbye. Then he turned and hopped up on the couch beside the child, stretched out beside her and laid his head gently across her chest.

And looked at Bailey.

I'll be here for her. I'll love her when you can't. I'll take care of her.

She couldn't kiss the child, but she could kiss the dog. And she did. She got to her feet, leaned over and planted a kiss on his snout between his eyes and his nose, held his look for a moment, then turned her back and walked with purpose out of the room, shutting the door behind her. She never looked back.

Chapter Forty-Four

Mikhailov listened to the semi-hysterical babbling of the man on the other end of the phone.

"Silence," he roared, and the three men in the room with him turned, but said nothing.

He couldn't let the red drain down over his vision now. When it did, he lost control, and while the violence was gloriously fulfilling, he had to be practical now. He had to hold it together.

Forcing his voice to remain level, he spoke again.

"Start at the beginning, Dmitri. Tell me what you saw."

"It's him, the guy I shot in that girl's apartment in Boston. He's supposed to be dead. But I just saw him get in an elevator in this building. He's a cop, a sheriff or something!"

"Where?"

"He was coming down the hallway from the private offices on the second floor."

A light on Mikhailov's phone started to blink, another incoming call.

It was Crenshaw.

"Find this man! Do not let him leave the casino. Send someone to catch up with him and ... tell him Mr. Crenshaw wants to talk to him. Has something important to tell him. Then bring him to me."

Nothing she was doing was an act of conscious will. She was just along for the ride in the body of Bailey Donahue, who was so hollow right now there was no substance to her at all. Nothing connected the pieces of who she was. A chilly wind was blowing through the tatters, the snippets of her personhood, and they danced gaily, like the little white seeds off the top of a dandelion.

If she stopped. If she paused for even an instant. If she asked for control of the body she had put on autopilot, with a flight plan filed and engaged, she would falter. If she faltered she would fail. Even a moment's hesitation and all was lost. If she so much as took an additional breath, she would not be able to walk away from the little girl asleep on the couch ... *and never see her again.*

She picked up the sack beside the front door and went out, closing it and the screen quietly behind her. Then she walked — was she walking, she couldn't feel her legs moving, it was like she was gliding along on a column of air — to her car.

She placed a smile snug on her lips, waved at Fletch in his cruiser, punched the button on her car key that popped the trunk, dropped the plastic bag into it and slammed it shut. Opening the driver's side door, she leaned in and took the garage door opener off the visor, then crossed the lawn to the cruiser, parked so the driver's side was nearest the house.

Fletch. By the book.

"Could I ask a favor?"

"Anything at all you need."

He smiled. He was such a dear man, good and kind and dedicated. She wondered to this day if it was her fault he'd gotten shot at the lake that day when she and the others were trying so desperately to locate and save Macy Cosgrove, who, it turned out, was nowhere near the lake. She also wondered briefly why some local girl hadn't snatched him up, with that square, Dudley Do-Right jaw and perfect-teeth smile.

Wondered those things with the disengaged part of her mind that was attending now to the plan while the rest of her wrestled with devastating, gut-wrenching grief.

"I need a box that's on the top shelf in the storage room. I could ask Dobbs to get it down for me, but with his back …"

"Glad to help."

Fletch was out of the cruiser in a heartbeat and walked along beside her as she aimed the garage door opener and pushed the button. The door slid grudgingly upward. He didn't ask why they weren't going in through the house. Once inside the garage, she punched the button again and the door went down. She offered an explanation this time, but probably didn't need to.

"It's cold in here with that door open."

On the top shelf in the back corner of the storage room — even Fletch would have to use the step stool — was a wide, flat cardboard box. It was filled with the left-over tiles from the bathroom renovation probably twenty-five years ago. She knew the contents because it had been in the attic and she'd convinced Brice to move it out of the way when she'd been getting ready for the yard sale that never happened. She'd been determined to dig all the way to the back of the flotsam and jetsam stored up there to find whatever'd been left by the original owners, the mysterious Sophia Watford.

Now, she had no real memory of being curious about Sophia Watford. Had no idea what it felt like to want … anything. She was alive for one purpose — to kill Sergei Mikhailov. That single-minded objective was a flamethrower that burned away all her desires, memories, thoughts and plans, everything that was not directly related to accomplishing her goal — saving the life of her little girl.

When Brice had lifted the box up onto the shelf, he had sworn he'd compressed his spine and made himself two inches shorter. He'd had to jam it in, wedge it between the wall and a pipe coming out of the ceiling. It would likely take two men Brice's size to get it out of there now.

She flipped on the light, walked to the back of the room and stood beneath the shelf.

"That's it. You'll need the step stool."

She'd left it leaning against the wall when she'd swapped out the lightbulbs. As soon as Fletch had it positioned beneath the shelf and had climbed it to the top, she said, "You need more light to see what you're doing. I'll get a new bulb, if you wouldn't mind putting it in for me."

She left him standing on the step stool. He'd have to climb down off the stool and cross the length of the storage room to the door to see into the garage, and she was counting on him just waiting where he was.

Stepping into the garage, she grabbed the bottle of superglue from the bottom shelf of the workbench, hurried to the garage door and engaged the manual lock — a handle in the middle of the door that shoved bars into tracks on both sides. She turned the bottle up and emptied almost all the contents into the mechanism of the lock, kept just enough to squirt into the side panels where the bars engaged.

Then she returned to the workbench, chucked the empty glue bottle into the trash can and picked up the lightbulb off the bottom workbench shelf. When she returned to the storage room, Fletch wasn't standing on the top shelf of the stool where she'd left him and her heart stuttered through a series of irregular beats. He'd moved the stool to beneath the burned-out bulb and stood waiting there for her. He climbed the steps, unscrewed the bulb and screwed in the new one.

"I'm sorry to put you to so much trouble. If you'd rather not—"

"Oh, no ma'am, no trouble at all. I'm glad to help."

This bulb produced light and Fletch climbed down off the stool, moved it to a spot beneath the shelf with the box of tiles. He climbed up again and tried to lift the box. It wouldn't budge.

"This is mighty heavy," he said, grunting. Anyone else would have asked her what was in it and why she wanted it down off that shelf. Fletch didn't.

"When Brice put it up there for me, he had to wiggle it around to get it to fit."

She stood beside him, watching him wrestle the box, making chit-chat as he pushed and shoved. She had to keep him occupied and engaged until the superglue dried. It wouldn't take long. The box moved back and forth on the shelf, but there was no way to get an angle to grip it to lift it. She suspected Fletch would stand there on that stool for hours trying to get that box down before he'd give up. But eventually it would occur to him — surely it would! — to go out into the back yard and ask for help from one or both of the deputies there.

She waited as long as she dared before she picked up

the rose clippers off the nearby shelf and stepped up behind Fletch.

"I think you're getting it," she said, encouragement dripping off the words like syrup off pancakes. As he shoved and grunted, she carefully lifted the cord that ran from the microphone on his shoulder, beneath the epaulet on his shirt, down his back and connected to a sending unit on his belt.

Snip!

"It's moving. I can see it!" she said and backed out of the storage closet, put the snips on the workbench and stepped into the house. She quietly closed the door behind her, locked the knob and engaged the deadbolt.

Stepping out of the mudroom into the laundry room, she closed that door behind her, too. The washer had filled and was making a grumbling slush-slush sound. She turned to the clumpety-clumpety dryer and opened the door. The drum slowed and the clumps ceased and Dobbs turned to look at her in surprise.

"Where'd you come from?"

She acted like she'd just come quietly into the kitchen behind him and he hadn't noticed. "The Marine Corps band could have marched through the kitchen and you couldn't have heard it." She took one of the shoes out of the dryer and examined it.

"Needs a couple more minutes." She tossed it back in, closed the door and switched on the deafening clumpety-clump again.

When she stepped from the laundry room into the kitchen, she closed that door behind her, too, muting the banging racket. "That'll help."

"Bailey … are you okay? You're acting—"

"I absolutely am *not* okay." She kept moving, couldn't let him pin her down. "I smell like the sweat-sock bin in the Steeler's locker room after a game, and this time I'm not going to think of 'one more thing to do' before I take a shower." She made it across the room so her back was to him and he couldn't see her face. "Listen for …" The word hung in her throat. If she said the child's name …

"I will. Sparky's in there with her. He'll set up a racket if I don't hear her."

She said nothing else, couldn't speak. If she were required to say a single syllable more she would dissolve in tears on the floor.

Dobbs turned back to his chili and she pretended to start up the stairs. She gave him a few seconds to re-engage, then slipped through the living room and out the front door. It took two tries to fit her key into the ignition of her car. She pulled out slowly, drove down the street with shaking hands on the steering wheel.

I'm sorry, Fletch …

Maybe she said the words out loud. Maybe just thought them. She was crying too hard to tell.

THE EVINRUDE OUTBOARD motor was humming through the water, making a sound like a sewing machine, ran better than it had the day T.J.'d bought it. He'd paid $25 for it to a fisherman at the marina who'd got disgusted and started selling off his gear when his jon boat started to sink. The guy's friend had tossed a cooler off the dock into the boat and knocked a hole in the bottom.

Takes a real special kind of stupid to do a thing like that.

T.J.'s jon boat was made of metal, couldn't knock a hole in the bottom with an ax. The boat was likely almost as old as T.J. He'd gone out fishing in it almost every summer day since he'd come back home to Shadow Rock.

It was almost dark, and T.J. turned the boat back toward the boat ramp when his phone rang. It was Dobbs.

No preamble. "Bailey's missing."

"How can she—?"

"Not missing, she ran away, tricked Fletch, locked him in the garage and—"

"Slow down, slow down, tell me what—"

"Fletch'd still be in that garage — I never heard him knocking and yelling — but he finally took an axe to the door."

"You realize you ain't making no sense whatsoever."

"All the sense you need to hear is that Bailey left. She got a call, told me it was a telemarketer, but I heard her talking. Half an hour later, she was gone, and I'm thinking that call is why she left."

T.J. was so floored at the news he didn't know what to think.

"There's more. Brice isn't picking up."

The sheriff always picked up.

"The dispatcher can't reach him either. He'd called in some number, I think ten-seven—"

"Means officer out of service."

"Whatever. Fletch got her to try to reach him anyway to tell him about Bailey, but he's not answering radio calls — because he's not in his cruiser."

"And you know that how?"

"He called me about forty-five minutes ago and said he might be late for his shift with Bailey tonight because he was going to the Nautilus to have a little talk with Maxwell Crenshaw."

"Why would—"

"Total long shot. Grasping at straws. Crenshaw obviously knew Mikhailov well enough to grant him a seat in one of his private games the night of Bailey's birthday party, so he thought maybe …"

"You saying both Brice and Bailey's in the wind?"

"That's what I'm saying."

What could possibly be important enough to Bailey to get her to leave that little girl of hers and go running off somewhere?

It wasn't like Brice couldn't get cellphone coverage at the casino.

T.J. needed to find Brice, tell him Bailey was missing, put their heads together and maybe figure out why in the Sam Hill she'd run off like that and where she went.

Looking out over the glassy surface of the lake, night shadows reaching out to claim the water, the decision made itself. Oh, he could go back to the boat ramp, tie up the jon boat, get in his truck, drive to the Joe's Hole Marina and take a launch to the Nautilus, or …

"I'm going to find Brice," he told Dobbs, stuffed his phone back in his pocket, turned the bow of his jon boat toward the Nautilus Casino and Hotel complex on the other side of Whispering Mountain Lake and headed out through the gathering night.

Chapter Forty-Five

BAILEY LOOKED out through the plastic window on the launch at a lone jon boat making its way across the lake in the darkening sunset shadows. Why would somebody want to be out on the lake on a winter night like tonight?

She had not been surprised by the small crowd waiting for the launch at Joe's Hole Marina. Wintertime pretty much shut down the big lake's recreational activities and she assumed the casino, too.

The rest of the crowd was as dressed up as she was. That was the kind of place the Nautilus was. She remembered how good-looking Brice, T.J. and Dobbs had been on her birthday, a month-long lifetime ago. That night, she had been distracted by her concern for the girl whose portrait she had painted, a girl being strangled.

Tonight, she was again distracted by the image of a girl whose portrait she had painted, a girl burning to death. Except maybe that was all in her head.

Bailey had not had a sufficient number of firing synapses to think about that particular piece of the puzzle after Mikhailov had called. She'd been concerned with escaping from the guards around her house ... and with telling Bethany goodbye.

BAM.

It was almost an audible sound, the banging shut of the door on all thoughts having to do with the little girl who should be waking up from her nap soon. If she slept too late, she wouldn't want to go to bed tonight and in a strange new place, she was going to have trouble going to sleep and ...

And maybe her ... *mommy* would be home by then to sing her the pumpkin pie song.

Maybe.

Stop it.

Let it go.

She pulled her mind back to consideration of the conversation she'd had with the monster murderer who held her precious sister captive.

His reference to drugs. PCP, angel dust. Was that what Bailey had painted — María's mind frying on the inside rather than her body frying on the outside? Had she been hallucinating the flames all around her? Maybe what Bailey had heard was the final scream of a mind melting, eating itself alive.

She shook her head so violently the woman standing next to her, dressed in the gaudiest flowered dress Bailey had ever seen, looked at her sharply and took a step away. Bailey stilled her body, and concentrated on the activity in her head.

She had "talked" to Jeni and the other girls after she painted them. Not long conversations, but she had put words into their heads. She'd told Jeni to "delay" the men who meant to kill them, and Jeni had swallowed the key that unlocked the electrical box with the switch to turn on the lights.

She had communicated to the other girls whose shadowy images she'd seen in the closet, told them to fight back. To use rocks. On her signal.

And they'd heard.

On the way to the train station in Boston, Bailey had called out to María with her mind, pleaded with her not to leave.

Had María heard her?

Bailey didn't know. She'd never had a chance to ask. But María had stayed. She hadn't run away. Maybe hearing Bailey in her head was part of what brought her to her senses.

If María'd heard Bailey then, maybe she could hear her now — even if the connection was a static confusion of sparkling images. Bailey had to try.

And say what? What could she say that would help María?

She looked up at the bright shining ball of the casino as the launch powered down in its approach to the docking slip, looked at the lighted windows of the upper floors that were exclusive hotel rooms.

María was there. In one of those.

She closed her eyes, cleared her mind and concentrated.

María, I'm coming.

Bailey formed the words in her mind without speaking them aloud.

Coming soon.

To set you free.

She felt nothing after she spoke the words in her mind. As she had felt nothing when she had tried to communicate with Jeni.

But feeling nothing didn't mean she'd been unsuccessful. Apparently, being aware of a message connection wasn't part of the process.

She turned and looked up at the bright lights of the hotel above the casino.

Had María heard?

~

T.J. REFUSED to shrink from the blast of freezin' wind off the water, told himself he wasn't cold and that he wasn't sorry he'd left his denim jacket in his truck. Told himself he wasn't grittin' his teeth to keep them from chatterin'. Of course, he didn't believe a word he said.

As he got to the west side of the lake, he spotted one of the Nautilus launches, making its round-trip route from Joe's Hole, the largest marina on the east side of the lake. No launches were running from Westbrook, Tucker's Landing or Blackfoot tonight.

It was getting dark. Sunset was about five o'clock out there on the flatland beyond the mountains, where the twilight of a slowly darkening sky would grant light for another fifteen minutes after the sun went down. Here, the mountain hid the sun on the western horizon and the pinkish-gold "sunset" sky above it. Real dark was quick and abrupt.

He wouldn't make it to the Nautilus before dark and his little jon boat had no running lights, meaning he was already breakin' the law using it. He could pull in behind the launch and follow it to the boat slips out front, but he wasn't making for the front door. The launch and houseboat slips there had no spaces for the likes of a plebeian jon boat. He figured to go around to the back of the facility, if a round building could be said to have a back side, to the space reserved for deliveries, and the ever-pleasant garbage pickup. He'd find a spot among the dumpsters to dock, slip in the back door.

Wasn't like there was a stated dress code at the Nautilus like he'd seen in places in Florida: No Shirt, No Shoes, No Service. Nothing like that. It was one of those understood things. Nobody spelled it out but everybody knew about it. Show up in this swanky joint dressed like T.J. — black corduroy pants and a checkerboard plaid wool shirt — and you'd stand out like a dog in a duck parade. T.J. did *not* want to stand out. He'd "borrow" proper attire once he got inside so he could make his way to the executive offices unnoticed. Not that he expected to find Brice there. The sheriff had told Dobbs he intended to go have a come-to-Jesus meeting with Crenshaw an hour ago. He'd long since left.

So where had he gone that he wouldn't/couldn't answer his phone? T.J. would start the search at Crenshaw's office. This wouldn't be the first time he had tried to find one person, one needle in the Nautilus Casino haystack. He, Dobbs and Brice had spent an evening looking for the girl Jeni, whose face peeking out of the shadows Bailey had painted. They'd found her, but it had taken hours and there'd been three of them. T.J. had considerably more going for him now than they'd had when they were searching for the girl. The casino/restaurant complex had been jammed with Saturday night partiers on that exceptionally warm Halloween night. Today was a cold Wednesday in early December. The establishment would be lucky to host thirty percent of the crowd they'd had that night. The girl had been small, elegantly decked out like every other woman. Brice McGreggor was six feet, six inches tall with red hair, wearing a sheriff's uniform. He stood out in a crowd.

Crossing the wake of the big launch, the bow bouncing on the waves, he glanced at the passengers, snug inside the canvas awnings fitted on the boat for inclement weather. Who'd want to cross the lake to a casino on a cold winter night like tonight?

~

María was looking out the hotel window high up on the side of the casino/hotel complex when words formed in her mind.

Sparkling words. That made no sense, but that's what they were. Words that sent out power, like a welding torch.

María, I'm coming.

Bailey.

It was uncanny how much it sounded like Bailey had spoken inside her head. That was crazy, but—

Soon. To set you free.

Without warning, María's knees turned to jelly and she leaned against the window sill of the bay window overlooking the lake.

Bailey's voice.

Like she was right here, whispering in María's ear.

María stared sightlessly at the progress of one of the launches across the lake. A smaller, unlighted craft came out of the darkness into the spill of light from the launch for a moment, then disappeared again.

Bailey couldn't possibly have—

Actually, she *could* have. She'd done it before!

That day Bailey had come to the train station to stop María from running away. María heard a voice that day, too. She'd dismissed it, wouldn't listen.

Don't leave, María, the voice had said. It had been like

now, like someone was speaking in her ear. Not just someone — Bailey.

Don't go.

María'd thought she'd imagined the voice. Of course, she had imagined it! But Bailey had shown up at the train station to stop her. Had known she was leaving. She didn't imagine that part. How?

María had never had a chance to ask.

The door to María's room burst open and a bald man came in. He'd been riding in the front seat of the van when María'd been hauled away. She thought the others called him Volo-da, or Volodya, something like that. He was carrying several bags and one large box, each embossed with the gold periscope logo of the Nautilus. Apparently, the casino had more than just a little gift shop, but high-end boutiques like those on the boardwalk in Atlantic City.

"I was guessing the size. But I'm pretty good at judging how a woman's body's put together."

He tossed the bags on the bed.

"Put these on. You're going out to dinner."

She didn't move, merely looked at him like he had grown antenna or a third eye.

"Do I stutter, lady? The boss said you were to get dressed in these clothes. You can do that voluntarily, or the boys and I can strip you naked and dress you by force."

He got an awful, lurid look on his face.

"If we get you naked, we'll have a good time with you before we put that dress on. All *three* of us."

She got up from the window seat, went to the bed, and picked up one of the packages with her left hand.

"The shoes were the only thing. Total guess. I got fancy high heels in a big size. If they're too big, stuff tissue in them to make them fit."

He smiled what felt like a very odd smile. A cat-that-ate-the-canary smile.

"Outfit comes with a fur cape. It's mink or ermine, one or the other. Very expensive. It will cover up *everything*."

He looked at his watch.

"You got half an hour to get ready."

He turned and left the room. When he opened the door, she could see that several men had gathered in the sitting room portion of the hotel suite and were standing around, talking softly.

She opened the dress box first and drew out of it an amazing evening gown covered in sparkling sequins. It was her style, alright — a Cinderella-at-the-ball dress with a swishy satin floor-length skirt, topped with yards of taffeta, and poofy sleeves. With all that fabric in the skirt, the dress was heavy — as cumbersome and bulky as a wedding dress.

The motive was instantly clear, of course. The extravagant evening gown had a purpose. The dress was to hinder her motion, slow her down. She might have been tempted to make a break for it in a public place. But she wouldn't make it three feet bundled up in this Marie Antoinette knockoff. All that fabric would make it easier for some guy standing next to her to conceal the weapon — gun, knife, dagger, icepick, whatever — he was using to hold her captive.

She went into the bathroom and tried to undress. It was an agony to do so with her mashed fingers. She could grasp the zipper on her jeans with her left hand, but had to pull the jeans down holding on with only her thumb, pinky and ring finger. They were skinny jeans and shimmying out of them one-handed took some doing.

Why was Mikhailov doing this? Why would he chance taking her out in public? How did he know she wouldn't scream her head off? How could he be sure that nobody'd notice, oh by the way, that the man standing next to her had a gun jammed into her ribs? Would they actually shoot her if she tried to get away — with people watching? The way she'd heard it, the Russian mafia boss had a real aversion to witnesses.

She stood in her underwear in the bathroom with 360-degree mirrors and looked at the dress that'd been selected for her to wear. Might have been her style, but it was definitely not her color. Black made her look like her kidneys were failing.

The dress fastened with a full length, up-the-back zipper which she would not have been able to fasten by herself if she'd had full use of both hands. So what was she supposed to do, holler through the door that she needed somebody to zip her up? She shuddered at the thought.

Dragging the skirt of the heavy gown across the floor, she went to the door, put her ear to it to see if there was still a room full of men out there.

There were only a couple and they were talking quietly, but it was in English and she could understand. She stood, listened and tried to piece together the fragments of the conversation she managed to catch.

"… better work or it'll be on us …"

"… the look in his eyes sometimes …"

From the vantage point of her own terror of Mikhailov, she could definitely spot it in others. His men were scared to death of him. No loyalty here. Only fear.

"… mouse coming to the cheese …"

"… both in the same trap …"

One of them made a sound, like something snapped, and the others chuckled with no real amusement.

All of a sudden, the door opened and one of the men

in the sitting room — a man she'd seen before, maybe loading the airplane, found her standing beside it.

"You eavesdropping?" It was the man from the airplane, alright, dressed now in an expensive suit. He reached out and grabbed her right hand, the one with smashed fingers. "Want me to smash the rest of them?"

"No! I wasn't listening." She turned her back to him, shuddered at the indignity. "I just need somebody to zip me up."

His fingers grazed her bare back as he pulled the zipper up and she only managed not to cringe with a huge physical effort.

"Do something with your hair. Brush it. Something. You look awful." He looked at his watch. "You got fifteen minutes." Then he closed the door.

María turned and dragged her skirts back into the bathroom, where the mirror did, indeed, reveal a woman who looked awful. Tangled hair and smeared eye makeup. Looked … oh, I don't know … like she'd been *kidnapped* maybe?

She dumped out into the sink the sack of toiletries she'd been given. There was a hairbrush, but the best she could do with her makeup was to wash it all off. None at all was marginally better than smeared. Spotting what was obviously a makeup kit, she opened it and found all the usual suspects, purchased from some woman at a makeup counter bent on selling a bunch of expensive products to a man who obviously didn't know what he was buying.

She scrubbed her face clean and applied the bare minimum. Base makeup, too dark. With the powder applied, she looked like she was wearing a death mask. As she struggled to make herself presentable, using her left hand instead of her injured right, she struggled to figure out why

Mikhailov would take her out to dinner. That was crazy. Why—?

The answer hit her with such force it staggered her and she smeared mascara on her cheek.

She was the cheese. They were planning somehow to use her to lure Bailey out of hiding. To kill her. To kill them both.

Chapter Forty-Six

BAILEY STEPPED out of the launch onto the deck of the massive casino and remembered how impressed she'd been when she first saw it, delightfully surprised by how tasteful it was. Not garish.

But the Christmas decorations she saw now … not so much. They clashed so completely with the style and dignity of the establishment it was hard to countenance that the management had been talked into it.

The *How the Grinch Stole Christmas* theme was on display everywhere she looked, from the gigantic lighted display on the top of the building, showing a ridiculously overloaded sleigh, the bulging bag of stolen Christmas presents, pulled along by the pathetic little dog named Max whose antlers consisted of two single sticks.

And, of course, the Grinch himself sat grinning on top of the bag of gifts.

It was ridiculous, and she assumed that was the point — to be amusing. To add a little lighthearted Christmas cheer to the flash and glamour of a place that could only afford to pay for all those lights and shiny things with the money the people they were "entertaining" lost at the games inside. Some marketing team somewhere had come up with this whole affair, probably tried it out before half a dozen focus groups.

Those groups' taste did not mirror Bailey's.

A view of the launch slips made it clear that this was going to be a slow night at the gaming tables. Black Friday five days before had ignited the Christmas shopping mania. The crowds were out Christmas shopping, not gambling.

She looked at her watch. A quarter of six. She had plenty of time to slide into one of those amazing bathrooms in the casino and change out of her jeans, chambray shirt and running shoes into the slinky green dress. And to slip into the six-inch stiletto-heeled shoes with which she intended to take the life of the man who'd killed her husband.

AARON REACHES his hand across the seat and takes hers. He squeezes and smiles that smile that puts delicious butterflies in her belly.

"Honey, we need this, we need you-and-me time. It's been too long. I miss you."

Thunder rumbles as the rain that had been a light drizzle ratchets up to a downpour.

His smile broadens. "Sunny Caribbean, here we come!"

FIVE MINUTES LATER, Aaron was dead. Sergei Wassily Mikhailov had shot him down in the street, had sent her into hiding, fearing for her life, unable to love and cuddle her own baby daughter for two years.

"It ends tonight," she said aloud, not meaning to, but not caring that she did, though the woman getting out of the launch beside her stepped sideways to put some distance between them.

Half an hour from now, one or the other of them would be dead — likely both. Mikhailov and Bailey. She had this single opportunity, one lone chance to save her sister's life and the life of her precious Bethany.

"It ends tonight," she said aloud again. She meant it that time.

She walked with purpose beneath the gold archway that now promised "Where your every desire is fulfilled … in Who-ville style."

The night she had been here to celebrate her birthday, the music riding the warm October air had been a Beatles, Rolling Stones, Simon and Garfunkel medley, played so softly you weren't even sure you were hearing it until you caught yourself singing along.

The music tonight was Christmas carols. The sanitized ones. The ones the Thought Police had deemed appropriate for the ears of absolutely anybody's *delicate* sensibilities — which meant they were so totally bland and colorless they were unpalatable to everybody.

"Here Comes Santa Claus" was piped out onto the deck, but as she crossed the threshold beneath the archway promise, the creepy Grinch theme song took over.

She passed into the ring of casino games that encircled the restaurant, ever tempting you to plop just one more token into the slot machine before you ordered your salad. There were vintage slot machines against the wall, ones made to look like the first of their kind in Las Vegas. She'd watched a lovely girl put tokens into one of those machines a month ago and the girl had lived only a few hours after Bailey saw her there.

The people all around who glanced at Bailey were likely seeing the last few moments of her life, too.

She paused just inside the door to the bathroom, stood momentarily in the "parlor" adjacent to the facilities, as richly appointed as any luxury apartment she'd ever seen pictured in *Better Homes and Gardens.* Tasteful wingback chairs, loveseats, delicately carved tables with Tiffany lamps. There was a maid, whisking up imaginary trash off the immaculate carpet.

She'd paused because her mind had yanked her to a halt. It had been ping-ponging all over the map, going from Aaron to the Grinch to the music selection in a gambling casino.

Self-preservation, of course, she realized that. The true horror of her situation and the magnitude of the act she was about to perform were such that thinking about them might paralyze her with horror.

But the ping-pong match ended now. She'd lost.

It was time to put her game face on.

Every thought and act from now … actually, for the *rest of her life* … was about freeing her sister from the monster, and then — *please, God!* — getting an opportunity to kill him.

And then …?

Oh, she'd been herding her mind away from such considerations, but in reality she harbored no illusions about her own chances of surviving the evening. If she were granted an opportunity to pull off one of her shoes and bury the icepick stiletto heel into his neck, Mikhailov's henchmen would gun her down on the spot. Why would they let her go free? The possibility that she could kill Mikhailov and somehow get away from his murderous henchmen … that was a fairytale. His bodyguards might even be the same men who'd been with him that day on a rainy street, who'd on his command pulled out guns and shot the homeless woman as she ran terrified up the street.

Those weren't the kind of men who'd let her continue to draw breath after she'd killed their boss. Even if the boss was certifiably psychotic and all his men hated and feared him. Even then … no, she would die soon.

T.J. had said that successful people made a decision, stuck to it and didn't waste time looking back.

T.J. Dobbs.

And Brice.

She'd never see any of them again if this went south and it was definitely pointed toward Tennessee, not Ohio or Pennsylvania.

Brice.

She sucked in a little gasp as it occurred to her that … she loved the man. She did.

Well how about that.

Amazing what popped to the surface when you let down all your defenses and got real — for the last time. Bailey wasn't surprised by the revelation … bemused, maybe. She'd never let herself go there. The list of reasons would stretch from here to tomorrow morning. None of them mattered now.

In fact, it felt good to admit it to herself — in a way she didn't pick at.

Yeah. It felt good.

Chapter Forty-Seven

MIKHAILOV STOOD in the shadows for a moment before he went all the way into the room, studying the man Dmitri and Volodya held at gunpoint.

The name tag on his shirt said he was Brice McGreggor. Mikhailov's men swore this was the same man who'd gone upstairs to help María gather up the picture albums — the man they'd shot and killed. Except he wasn't dead. The bullets they had fired at him had knocked him across the room but did no other apparent damage.

Some kind of law enforcement officer, a West Virginia county sheriff or some such, he must have been wearing a Kevlar vest yesterday afternoon — why? That was one of oh-so-many questions Mikhailov planned to ask him.

Then his mind began to fill with mist. Red mist. Different this time, thicker.

The whole world around him began to turn red.

It was a genuinely odd sensation and he watched it with keen interest.

The ceiling was a bubbling, boiling red, like lava in a volcano. It wasn't lava, though. It was not blood, either. It was red light. *Boiling light.* It flowed in every direction from the center of the ceiling until it reached the walls, then the light became liquid and flowed down them. Now, it *was* blood, a deep red with a delicious copper smell like wet pennies. If he stepped to the wall and wiped off some on his finger, it would taste gloriously salty.

His son's blood had tasted salty. When he'd slit Ivan's throat, blood had squirted into his face, into his mouth, and Mikhailov had tasted the salt in it. His men believed he had beaten the worthless drunk to death with a fireplace poker. Not so. He had beaten his lifeless body until it was unrecognizable *after* he was already dead, after he had choked and gurgled, spewed out drops of blood in a fine mist as the front of his white shirt turned crimson.

What would it be like to rip a man's throat out … *with your teeth?*

Mikhailov began to breathe hard, gripped in an unnamable emotion, and it took every ounce of strength he possessed to keep from leaping forward and sinking his teeth into the throat of the man whose hair was the color of the boiling light and the dripping blood all around.

He backed up from the man, from the emotion. In his mind, he backed out of the room with boiling light and dripping blood, backed away into eternity.

His back hit the closed door behind him and all the men in the room turned to look at him.

He blinked once. Twice. He could see now. Red mist covered everything but he could see. He could think, too, and questions filled his mind as bloodlust filled his soul.

Why had this country bumpkin West Virginia sheriff traveled all the way to Boston for a woman in the Witness Protection Program?

What was his stake in all this?

What had the red-haired sheriff said to that idiot,

Crenshaw? Mikhailov had ignored repeated calls from Crenshaw, which likely were to warn him about this man. What had he said that so upset the sniveling fool that he wouldn't stop calling?

Mikhailov would find out.

He stepped out into the light from the shadows by the door.

"Good evening Mr. … no, it is sheriff, is it not? Sheriff Brice McGreggor?"

Mikhailov walked around the man and stood in front of him. The room was full of shadows. He liked shadows. Things lived in shadows that licked up the blood you spilled sometimes.

"Give it up, Mikhailov. I've called the federal marshals—"

Dmitri slammed a club into the sheriff's belly and he grunted out the rest of the air in his lungs and doubled over.

"I speak, you listen," Mikhailov told him. "Later, you will speak and I will listen. I am curious to know where Jessica Cunningham has been hiding all this time in the weeds, what has been her life as she waited to be Judas. How she came to make your acquaintance." He leaned closer. "What was the nature of your relationship with her … *before her death?*"

Even in his present state, the man tried to straighten, but didn't yet have his wind back. He was a big man.

His throat. Right there so temptingly close.

Mikhailov almost groaned aloud with longing.

"Take him downstairs and restrain him," he told Dmitri. "I have not the time to deal with him now. The show I have so creatively and carefully orchestrated will start very soon and I will observe it from the best seat in the house."

Then he made a sound he didn't intend to make. It burped out his lips before he could grab it back. Almost like a giggle. He coughed to cover the sound, but he saw the looks on his men's faces. He did not like those looks, saw them more and more often and his loathing grew.

Maybe he would rip their faces from their heads. Just the skin of their faces off the bones.

That was for later, though. Now, he had other business to attend to.

"I want him to see nothing when I question him, only to hear my voice." Mikhailov turned and strode out of the room, tossing the next words over his shoulder as he left. "Gouge out his eyes, blind him."

MIKHAILOV DIDN'T BOTHER to put in an appearance to prep María for her venture out into the world. A blond man the other called Emile did it for him.

"Show me your shoes."

She obediently pulled up the long skirt and showed him the black high heels. She had jammed toilet paper into the toe so she wouldn't walk out of them.

"They are too big, but that's no excuse for tripping. Do. Not. Trip."

Then he laid out the rules of engagement. Simple: no engagement of any kind with anyone. She was to speak to no one, make eye contact with no one.

"Do not think that the crowd offers you safety, that you could enlist the help of some stranger, make a scene and draw attention to yourself. There will be a knife inches from your back every second." He showed it to her, a vicious dagger with a sharp point and razor edges on both sides.

"You so much as sneeze, and I will jab it between your ribs directly into your heart. Such a wound will bleed very little, with no heartbeat to pump out the blood and that small amount will not be visible on a black dress. You will merely stagger, look drunk. I will hold you upright, appear concerned that my wife is unable to drink responsibly."

He smiled, held up the fur wrap for her to see. It looked like Batman's cape. As big as a tablecloth, it was mink or ermine or the fur of some other small wooly creature and she knew it must be very expensive. Then he fit it around her shoulders — her whole body disappeared beneath it.

"This will cover a multitude of sins."

There were slits on the sides for her hands and when they walked out into the hallway, she was instructed to take Emile's arm and not let go.

"Look like you're having a good time," the blond man whispered down at her as they walked together through the hotel hallway.

That part … she couldn't pull it off. Not even if they killed her.

"Smile!"

The single word was slathered in threat.

She pulled back the corners of her mouth. To keep them in that position for any length of time would require roofing nails.

With a dark, brooding sort whose name she didn't know walking along casually on the other side of her and Vladimir only a step behind, they proceeded into the elevator, out again, crossed the glossy floor of some sort of atrium. It was made of what looked like a single sheet of pale blue marble, shined so you appeared to be walking on water. She slipped on it once, but Emile kept her upright with his grip on her arm.

From the atrium into a casino. Through the casino to a restaurant, where the *How the Grinch Stole Christmas* theme met its zenith in a gigantic figure of the Grinch, stealing the Christmas lights off the railing of the observation deck above their heads.

The man on her arm had only to make eye contact with the maître d' and they were shown to a table in the back corner of the room between a side entrance and the doors leading into the kitchen. They had to walk around the gigantic sack of "stolen" presents and Christmas decorations that stretched out across the floor in front of that section of tables, a lumpy sack where the monstrous Grinch had been stuffing all his stolen Christmas goodies.

Clearly, it was a slow night. The crowd they passed through in the casino had been small, most of the slot machines sat empty and silent, and when she was seated between Emile and Vladimir at the table, she saw that the waiter had quarantined them. There was a swath of empty tables, two deep, all the way around theirs. They were completely isolated.

No one offered to take her Batman cape — clearly, prearranged. None of the other women seated in the restaurant had worn their coats in. But when they got to the table, Emile graciously removed it from her shoulders and draped it over the back of her chair.

He sat down beside her, picked up the carafe of water and poured some into a glass. Handing the glass to María, he held out two pills in the palm of his other hand.

"Take these."

She looked at them, horrified.

He smiled at her when he spoke so it'd look like they were just having a pleasant conversation. His words didn't match his facial expression.

"You need to relax ... look like you're enjoying yourself. These will help. Don't be an idiot. If I wanted to poison you, why would I dress you up like a Barbie doll and drag you to a restaurant to do it?"

She didn't move.

"Take the pills, sweetheart, or …" He casually pulled open his suit jacket to reveal an inside pocket. Sticking out the top was what appeared to be the top of a syringe. "This stuff is a nasty cocktail of chemicals you absolutely do *not* want in your bloodstream. It's the pills or this. Pick."

She held out her hand and he dropped the pills into her palm. She popped them into her mouth, tried not to swallow them, tried to use her tongue to tuck them away behind her lip. But that was probably a skill you had to practice. The pills slid down her throat and she tensed. Nothing happened. Yet.

He reached over and took her right hand as if he wanted to hold it. Instead he eased it down off the table and she felt cold plastic digging into her skin. A plastic zip tie, like for a garbage sack. Quickly and efficiently, she was affixed to the chrome bar that encircled the back of the chair, the whole act hidden from view by her mink Batman cape. The man sitting on the other side of her did the same with her left arm, zip-tied to the chair back.

She jumped when she felt the knife prick in her side, looked at Emile fearfully. He merely nodded. She bobbed her head in response: message received and understood. *You can kill me right here, right now, and I won't even fall face-first into my food because there isn't any.*

Task accomplished. She marveled at the audacity. She'd been kidnapped and here she was in plain sight, tied to a chair in a public restaurant, with dining families making soft conversation, couples holding hands across the table, and servers — looking like Drew and Cindy Lou

Who — gliding to and fro, taking orders and delivering food to tables.

Obviously by prearrangement, the servers ignored them. They sat together in silence, three stone statues. That seemed the most egregious insult of all. Nobody noticed three stone-faced people sitting alone at a table in the back of the room, not speaking, not even looking at each other.

Who didn't notice a thing like that?

Dmitri looked at his watch, then leaned past her to speak to Vladimir.

"Five minutes. You ready?"

Vladimir nodded, and cocked his head toward the observation deck in front of the gigantic Grinch. Mikhailov stood at the railing. But he was smiling. Yes sir, he was positively grinning his gums dry.

Chapter Forty-Eight

No one was in the restroom, so Bailey selected the stall on the end.

These were complete restrooms. The toilets were concealed inside actual *rooms* with actual doors, the floor-to-ceiling variety, that locked with a knob lock, which popped up a dainty red flag on the other side that said "occupied" when you engaged it. This was not a place where you looked beneath the stall walls, searching for feet. Bailey would have total privacy.

She took off her jacket, shirt and jeans, stripped to her underwear and then pulled on the black tights she'd put in the sack with the dress and shoes. She'd worn pantyhose under the dress at her birthday celebration. But tonight she'd be wearing the floor-length version of the gown and nobody could see her legs. Tights were warmer.

The dress was jade green, what María would have called "slinky" but which Bailey preferred to call "form-fitting" — down to the knee. From the knee to the floor were rows of big poofy ruffles. Like the train on a bride's dress, you could remove the ruffles if you preferred the short version of the dress. Bailey'd picked short for her birthday because the all-the-way-to-the-floor ruffles completely hid the high heels and she'd definitely wanted them to show.

She'd picked the long version for tonight because she definitely did *not* want the shoes to show. The perfect coup de grâce that sealed the enchantment of the outfit, the shoes were an exact match to the distinctive green of the dress, and featured *six-inch stiletto heels*, thin as an icepick, made out of shiny chrome with a green rubber tip.

The sales lady had admitted she'd never sold a pair of the shoes because most women couldn't walk in heels that high. Maybe it was being a runner with strong calf muscles, but Bailey had no trouble at all.

Ping-ponging again, her mind getting up too close to the white-hot stove of her intent, the reality of what was going to happen in the next half hour, and her mind skittered away to dresses and shoes and keeping her legs warm with tights. Shoot, she'd be dead in under half an hour. Her legs wouldn't have time to get cold.

That stopped her. Washed the random thoughts away that'd crowded into her mind to keep reality at bay.

Yes, it was very likely that she would not be alive an hour from now. She tried to think that, but it was hard to conceive of not existing. She had come very close to dying in a flooded coal mine with some Eastern European teenagers and she remembered how badly she had wanted to live then. How hard she struggled to survive.

Well, she would struggle with no less determination and strength now. Recognizing that it wouldn't likely do any good wasn't the point. It was the struggle that mattered.

Gratefully, Mikhailov had backed himself into a corner with this public place. He had to keep *both of them* alive, each to silence the other, while he made the exchange. He couldn't chance that the two of them would start screaming about kidnapping and murder in the middle of the soup and salad course of the salmon special on the menu.

She would walk through the main doors of the restaurant at six o'clock just like she'd agreed. He would be there. He wouldn't stand her up. He wanted her too badly to renege on that part of the deal. She would walk to the table in the back of the room between the south entrance and the kitchen. María would be there, accompanied by men who would kill her at the whim of their boss. María would stand up; Bailey would sit down. María would walk back out the way Bailey had walked in. And then …

Then the men seated at the table might pretend to eat. Or they might give her the bum's rush out of the room at once. They surely would search her purse as soon as she stepped up to the table. They'd find the gun. They'd assume they'd taken the sting out of the wasp.

After that, she'd be taken to Mikhailov. She believed with the strength of all her intuition that he would confront her *up close*. That he would want to get in her face. He was not the kind of man who would allow others to perform this task.

Not since he'd gone crazy and developed a lust for blood.

He would get close to her …

Then somehow, *somehow,* she'd find a way to plunge the pointed stiletto heel of one of her shoes into his neck.

That was all she had going for her. An unlikely weapon and the element of surprise.

Her mind flashed to the night of her birthday celebration, Brice standing in her living room all dressed up in a suit and tie. Six feet six inches of muscle, topped with a face that only missed Pierce Brosnan perfection because the features were stronger than that, the bone structure of his face more angular.

He'd looked her up and down until his gaze landed on the shiny stiletto heels.

"How on earth do you walk——?"

"Balance," she'd told him confidently. "It's all about balance."

"You know, those shoes would be considered a deadly weapon in some states."

Deadly weapon. Exactly what Bailey needed.

SHE'D POP off the cap and plunge the icepick sharp shoe heel into his neck under his right ear, right into his jugular vein, the place she'd be most likely to inflict a *lethal* wound. The heel point would not have to pass through the fabric of a suit coat, maybe even a vest, a shirt and an undershirt. Directly into his skin the full six inches. The point might even come out the other side of his neck.

And afterward? She might draw another breath. Maybe even two. Then Jessie Cunningham aka Bailey Donahue would be dead.

But María and Bethany would live on.

She pulled the gun in its holster out of her Walmart sack and slid it snug into her pearl-studded purse with the little silver strap that fit around her neck, allowing the purse to swing stylishly low on her hip. She snapped it shut. Then she picked up the green shoes with the silver icepick heels, popped off the plastic caps, then gently snapped them back on ... loose.

That cap comes off, you gonna poke a hole in the bottom of the boat, T.J.'d said the night of her birthday party.

She studied the wickedly sharp heel, pricked a small

hole in her thumb … enough to draw blood, so she put it in her mouth and sucked on it.

The image of Bethany sucking her thumb blazed across Bailey's mind like a giant meteor, flames behind it like the tail on a kite.

Suddenly, the iron fingers of fear grabbed her belly and squeezed.

THIS WASN'T GOING to work!

It was a fool's errand. No way could she plunge the stiletto heel into him fast enough … before one of his bodyguards stopped her.

What was she thinking?

This was insanity.

Stop it!

The panicked thoughts screeched to a halt on the track. All her other thoughts slammed into the back of them and then fell over on their sides.

Yeah, maybe it was a fool's errand, and if it was, they'd picked the right girl for the job. It was insane, but so was everything else in her life. Painting pictures of things that hadn't happened yet. Now, *that* was insanity!

It occurred to her then, as it had when she'd come up with the plan, that Jessica Cunningham could never pull this off. Would never have tried. But she was Bailey Donahue now and Bailey could and would attempt it. She'd sacrifice her life to make it work.

Bailey leaned over the little sink-ette in the toilet stall, ran some cold water and splashed it into her face. Then she slipped into the slinky dress, put her feet into the ridiculously high-heeled shoes. She'd have blisters in … no, she wouldn't live long enough to form blisters. Then she stepped out of the stall into the bathroom. A woman was standing at the sink washing her hands. She turned to Bailey and stopped.

"Oh my," she gasped.

Well, *that* screwed the pooch.

The first person who got a look at her had noticed the stiletto heels the dress was *supposed* to hide.

"I'm sorry, I didn't mean to gawk," the woman gushed. "It's just … that is the most *beautiful* dress I've ever seen. The color green. It's the same color as your eyes. Would you mind if I asked where you got it?"

So Bailey stood there for a few moments chitchatting!

It was surreal.

Bailey told the woman about the little dress store. The woman said she'd seen the place but had never shopped there. Bailey suggested she give it a try. She said she might just do that. Then she left the room.

Well, if the woman noticed the dress but not the shoes, Bailey had leapt the first hurdle.

She went into the bathroom stall and stuffed her clothes and running shoes into the bag that had contained the green dress, shoes and gun.

Back in the bathroom, she shoved the sack down into the trash receptacle on the wall. Then she looked at herself in the mirror. What was it T.J. said? Yeah, her face looked like death on a cracker. Shoot, she never had taken that shower! With fear sweat added to her aroma now, she likely smelled pretty gamey.

Nothing to be done about that.

She leaned over and splashed more water in her face from the full sink. She took a comb from the clutch purse she'd brought along for the goons to search and find the gun in it, and ran it through her hair. Then she stepped back.

A month ago, she had worn this dress to a birthday

party in this casino. She'd looked lovely. She had. She was self-aware enough to know the green dress fit in all the right places, and her face had been glowing.

Tonight, her face looked like she'd just escaped from a concentration camp. Her eyes were black holes in her face. Like cigarette burns.

But that was self-analysis. The woman who'd wanted to know where she'd gotten the dress hadn't seen her that way. Bailey needed to walk out of here with that woman's view of herself snug in her head.

She was a beautiful black-haired woman in a stunning green dress.

She looked at her watch.

Showtime.

Chapter Forty-Nine

Cheese.

Bait.

Five minutes and the trap would snap shut.

Bailey was coming.

… and you know that how …?

The maddeningly rational voice in her head that always pleaded her case before the High Court of Common Sense had put in an appearance.

Because Bailey had said so. Had told María she was coming to rescue her.

That's crazy.

Crazy? Yeah, absolutely crazy. But it was true. Bailey *had* told her. Just like she'd pleaded with María not to run away the morning she'd taken Bethany to the train station.

How?

How should I know!

Great. Now, María was yelling at her *own* voice in her head. Then she felt her head swim and a wave of dizziness seized her. The pills. She shook her head, concentrated. It *was* true, real. It *had* happened. Now, she remembered!

Everything that had happened in between had shoved the memory out of the spotlight into a corner of her mind.

It stood centerstage now, spotlight glaring.

They'd only had that one tiny snippet of conversation about it, before they'd left the subject for some other time, for the long car ride that never happened.

"How DID you know I was here?" María had asked through her tears, standing on the train platform with Bethany glued to her side.

"I … saw the Amtrak ticket. One-way, New York Penn Station."

"But *how* …?"

"Later, there'll be plenty of time—"

"I heard you! You begged me not to run away. You did, didn't you!"

Bailey had grinned, in a tired, sad, knowing sort of way and nodded.

"Yeah. After all, you botched it the last time you tried, too, remember?"

María had been nine, Bailey thirteen. They'd watched the 1998 Winter Olympics on television and the women's figure skating had captured María's whole imagination. For an entire rainy Sunday afternoon she'd concocted an elaborate fantasy — she and Bailey would run away, learn how to skate like that. María wouldn't have asthma, breathing the cold, pure air of — Nagano, Japan — which was a fairyland of white snow and bright blue sky.

Bailey, of course, had spent the day trying to convince her it wouldn't work. None of her logic put the slightest dent in María's determination. She even went so far as to start deciding what to take with her. To start packing. And that's what sunk the ship.

Snow boots.

"Where there's ice, there's snow," Bailey had told her. "You don't have any snow boots."

"Well, I'll … I could … maybe there's …" Wheeze.

The fantasy had collapsed in on itself then. From the weight of all the arguments, but tipped over the edge by her lack of proper footwear.

The conversation at the station had banked left after Bailey's revelation that she had *seen* the Amtrak ticket and taken a turn into their shared past. There was safety there. Pain and fear and mystery were for another day.

The "another day" never happened. María hadn't ever had a chance to ask Bailey about it.

Bailey said she "saw" the ticket. She'd described it. That was impossible, but there wasn't any other explanation for how she knew.

Impossible didn't matter. Not yesterday at the train station, anyway. It didn't apply to her and Bailey. And maybe not now, either, as death exhaled its cold breath down their collars.

Bailey had … seen what only María could see.

Bailey had … spoken words only María could hear.

She felt the men around her tense, was distantly aware of the stupid Christmas carol in the background clatter of plates and silverware in the restaurant.

… Bells on bobtails ring. Making spirits bright …

She didn't have a watch but knew some horror clock was ticking down toward a deadline.

Bailey had spoken to *her* … Maybe *she* could—

… fun it is to ride …

Trap!

María screamed the word in her mind. Willed the words to communicate to Bailey.

For a single frozen moment, she heard the stupid Christmas carol *through someone else's ears.* Through Bailey's!

… in a one-horse, open sleigh …

It's a trap, Bailey! Run!

THE BEAUTIFUL WOMAN in the green gown glided across the casino toward the main entrance to the restaurant.

As soon as she got to a point where she could see into the room, she saw the huge, decorated Christmas trees on both sides of the fifteen-foot-tall entrance archway. Grand as those were, they paled in comparison to what was behind them in the back center of the restaurant. The Grinch who stole Christmas. Holy moly. At least fifty feet of lime green fur wearing a red velvet jacket and a Santa hat. His back was to the doorway, but he was looking over his shoulder at it with an evil grin on his face. His left foot rested on top of a huge Christmas present with a red bow.

On the floor to his right lay a long lumpy sack, full of the Christmas presents and decorations he was stealing. The sack stretched out fifty feet behind him in front of the back corner of the room. The furry green behemoth was reaching up over his head to a string of glowing Christmas lights the size of cantaloupes that lined the railing of the observation deck stretching out over the restaurant. The glowing light string he was stealing hung down from the deck and vanished into the sack by his right foot.

The Grinch would have been an amazing sight even if her senses hadn't been turned up to maximum volume.

Everything was on overdrive. She seemed to be aware of every sensation so keenly it was overload. It was like she could hear the individual notes of "Jingle Bells" piped into the room. She could smell the potpourri of perfumes and aftershaves and men's colognes, noticed small details like the garlands and wreaths on the walls were real, not artificial greenery. The whirring sound of the spinning numbers and symbols on the slot machines buzzed in her head.

Got louder and louder, morphed into that white noise sensation that had plagued her ever since she'd painted María's portrait. White noise and white static in her mind, with bright sparkles and twinkling light. The sparks grew brighter. Her mind was filling up with them, like there was a welding torch just out of her view and the sparks from it were cascading down in front of her.

There was the sensation of a voice she couldn't quite hear. Like looking into a snowy 1950s-era television set and through the snow, there was an image. But it was almost not there.

The stupid Christmas carol was instantly muted, like the volume had been turned way down.

… fun it is to ride …

Then the brilliant sparks coalesced into a single pulsing twinkle that exploded with a pop. María's voice burst through, like it had substance and had exploded through a barrier.

"Trap!"

María screamed the word so loud in Bailey's mind it knocked Bailey back a step.

For a single frozen moment, she heard the words of the song through María's ears.

… in a one-horse open sleigh …

"It's a trap, Bailey! Run!"

This time, it wasn't Bailey talking inside someone else's head. This time, someone was talking in hers. Screaming a warning.

Run!

DOBBS WAS PACING, which was what T.J. did when he was upset, and there'd been so much turmoil in their lives in the past six months that Dobbs had taken up the practice. Of course, it didn't matter now, didn't even look like he was pacing. When you were looking after a three-and-a-half-year-old child and two dogs, it was a good thing to stay on your feet.

Gratefully, the hurricane/tsunami combination of Fletch hacking his way into the house from the garage with an axe — and the discovery that Bailey was missing — had already crashed and receded before Bethany woke up from her nap. She hadn't cried, had just come sleepy-eyed into the living room, dragging both minion blankets behind her and announcing that she needed to pee … and she wanted her mommy.

And she meant María, who'd been kidnapped by a madman — not Bailey, who had taken it upon herself to go to an extraordinary amount of trouble to sneak out of the house. The whole garage door unit would have to be replaced, with the lock mechanism and the release bars frozen in superglue.

Where had she gone? And why? It had something to do with the phone call she'd received, but what could possibly have enticed her to leave Bethany behind?

After he helped the little girl do her business, she had wondered around forlornly, asking alternately for her mommy and for the "singer lady." That had to be Bailey, though Dobbs didn't know why the little girl called her that. He had to tell the poor child that this other grownup she was growing to trust had vanished, too, just like her mommy.

Dobbs had a way with kids. Like dogs, they sensed the

essential gentleness of the man and responded with trust. Bethany'd been introduced to a pot load of strangers in the last twenty-four hours and Dobbs had the least history with her. But Bethany wasn't whiny because she minded being with Dobbs. It was that she wanted her mommy and the Singer Lady, and was justifiably confused and upset by the revolving door of adults — her mother was there, said she'd be right back — and vanished. Then she'd been hauled halfway across the country in the company of strangers, to an unfamiliar environment, and another adult who'd popped up in her world like a target in one of these carnival arcades had vanished just as suddenly.

Even with his essential charm, Dobbs would have had "a hard row to hoe" with the little girl if it hadn't been for the dogs — one so intuitive and smart it was downright spooky, and the other exuding such "adorable-fluffy-puppyness" he was irresistible.

A game of sorts had evolved around Dobbs's pacing and the "run-away-and-a-dog'll chase-you" line T.J. had explained to the child earlier.

Bethany took off down the track they'd made in the morning — from the den across the living room, down the hallway, through the studio, back down the hallway — in the doorway at the front of the kitchen and back out the one on the back by the breakfast nook. Bundy bounded after her but Dobbs kept Sparky at his side. Bethany would stop at whatever corner where she was about to go out of sight, turn and look, and Dobbs would release Sparky to follow her. As soon as Sparky disappeared from view, Dobbs lumbered along behind. When he caught up to Bethany, he'd motion for Sparky to sit until Bethany turned to look, then he'd release him. It only took a couple of rounds before Sparky knew the rules. He stopped, sat beside Dobbs, then raced to the next corner, where he'd sit again and wait for Dobbs to catch up.

The game got Dobbs up and moving, gave him an excuse for his pacing, and was so mindless he could allow his mind to wander — ticking through one unanswered question to another.

Where was Bailey?

Why had she left?

Why was Brice not answering his phone?

He was considering possibilities when he became aware that he was merely lumbering along behind Sparky, who ran to each corner, sat, and as soon as Dobbs joined him, he ran to the next corner.

Bethany was not up ahead at the corner, looking back. When he got to the corner, she wasn't at the next corner, either.

"Bethany!" he called out.

The name echoed in the sudden silence in the big house.

"Bethany, where are you?"

Nothing. Not a sound.

Reality hit Dobbs in the chest so hard it stole his breath.

Bethany was gone.

Chapter Fifty

Bailey didn't trust Sergei Mikhailov, knew he wouldn't keep his end of the bargain. He would go after María and Bethany as soon as he'd killed her even though he'd sworn they'd be safe. Bailey had come to the rendezvous at the Nautilus restaurant — not because she believed the monster would keep his word but because it was her only chance to get close enough to Mikhailov to kill him.

That was the only thing that would keep her family safe.

But she'd walked into a trap. He'd lured her to the restaurant to kill her there, on the spot. There would be no exchange. No freedom for María. He intended to kill them both here, now, tonight.

Then he would kill Bethany.

A trap.

The words reverberated in her head with individual booms, like the pimply-faced kid in the marching band hammering the padded sticks on a kettle drum.

What kind of trap?

What was his plan?

Think!

She felt a little like scales had fallen off her eyes and she could see reality clearly. Everything he'd said to her on the phone was an elaborate ruse to gain her trust and compliance. He'd picked a public place because she'd never have trusted a private exchange, would never have agreed to one. But the whole elaborate exchange plan was all smoke and mirrors. Details to grant the lie credibility. And the fry-your-brains drug cocktail — was that real or a con? What difference did it make? He *would* kill María, using some method or another — *that* was the point. He'd never for a millisecond intended to let her walk out of the restaurant alive.

Duh! María was as dangerous to him now as Bailey was! What had Bailey been thinking? He'd *kidnapped* María. He'd couldn't let her live to tell police *that* tale.

He'd selected the restaurant to give Bailey a sense of safety — a big crowd, people all around her. He knew she'd believe he wouldn't *dare* kill her there, couldn't just gun her down the minute he saw her.

But why not? Public shootings happened all the time. Mikhailov wouldn't be the one taking the fall for it. Some flunky would do the deed and he'd never have to get his hands dirty.

Mikhailov *was* here, though. She believed that much of his elaborate deceit was true. He was somewhere in that restaurant right now because *he wanted to watch* it happen.

He hadn't been faking his pleasure when she'd demanded he be present as part of the agreement.

You may wait until we make eye contact if you wish — before you proceed.

The impact of the words rocked her.

Stand beneath the archway and look around.

That was it, wasn't it?

Can you say "*sitting duck?*"

Out in the open. A clear shot. The target even standing obligingly still between the lighted Christmas trees. A single headshot would leave almost no blood at all. She could testify to that from personal experience.

There'd be a sound — how loud? Depended on the weapon, she supposed. She'd fold up in a heap. If he played it right, it would be awhile before somebody noticed and figured out what'd happened. For her, it would be *game over*.

The only thing that didn't ring true in her new interpretation of reality was that Mikhailov was granting her what he'd call a merciful death. *That* was out of character.

Ah, but María would be watching. Perhaps that was part of the juice he got out of the squeeze — that María would see her sister die.

He'd kill María, too, of course. Maybe tonight, right here in the restaurant. No, not likely. He'd save her for later, in private, where he could take out his rage on her.

Bethany, too. He would take his time killing Bethany.

The thought ripped Bailey's beating heart out of her chest.

Nooooooo!

But how could she stop him? What could she do?

María and Mikhailov were both here, within rock-throwing distance from where she was standing.

She had to save one and kill the other.

How?

She looked at her watch. She had only ninety seconds to figure it out or she'd be late for Mikhailov's party.

~

Sergei Mikhailov strode with delighted anticipation through the winding hallways from the room in which the sheriff had been brought to him to the observation deck overlooking the restaurant from which he would watch the show.

He neither knew nor cared how the devices that would create the show worked. He did not understand the structure and function of an internal combustion engine, either, and he could still get into a car and go where he wanted to go.

Abi-Nadir had tried to explain it all to him when they were loading the supplies onto the plane but he had brushed him off.

"I told you what I want to happen and you have assembled a proper device to make it happen, yes?" he had asked.

"Yes. But I have never worked before to the particular specifications you require and—"

"Do not angle for a higher fee!"

The Arab gunrunner retreated like a mouse back into its hole from the edge of menace in Mikhailov's voice.

"Oh, I am not. I would never. I just want you to know that I am not certain what the result will be." Before Mikhailov could protest he hurried on. "It will be *at minimum* what you specified. But it is possible there will be much more … damage than you are perhaps expecting."

Mikhailov didn't give a fig how much damage there would be because damage was not his objective. The devices he had demanded from the Arab were not WMDs — weapons of mass destruction. They were weapons he intended to use for a specific task. All that was required was that they kill the people he wanted to kill. Anything beyond that, well, that was icing on the cake.

"Tell the others how it works if you're intent on explaining. They will be the ones installing them."

No, installing wasn't the proper terminology. There was nothing to install. Each device was a self-contained unit that functioned independently of the others. But they shared the same detonation programs, so they could join each other in gay abandon if he punched the proper codes into his phone.

As soon as Mikhailov's men had taken charge of restaurant security earlier in the afternoon — with their lapel pins that trumped the rank of any of Crenshaw's employees — the devices had been distributed to the spots he'd indicated.

Disguised as they were to look like micro "speakers," they were not the least suspicious looking. Ahhh, the wonders of nanotechnology — that something so powerful could be rendered into such a small package.

Mikhailov shook his head in amazement. He shouldn't have. He should have held his head steady, perfectly steady. When he shook it, red mist like that smoke they used at rock concerts poured out of his skull into the world. It flowed in a soundless rush from his ears, nose and eyes. It muted every color, stole shapes and replaced them with lurking shadows. The world all around him filled with mist, seeping out from under doors and out of crevices and vents, flowing down from the ceiling and up from the floor.

He would never be rid of the mist now, never be free because it would be everywhere before him, in the rooms where he was going before he opened the doors, out in the world obscuring the trees and blotting out the sun. He would breathe it in and breathe it out and ...

Stopping abruptly, he closed his eyes. Calmed himself. Took hold of his mind and held it in firm hands. When he opened his eyes again, he was certain he would see the world cleared of mist and —

No. It could not be. The dragons had joined the mist *outside* his head. They had escaped. Watching in horror, he saw the dragons — a sparkling gold one he had named Rage, a purple one he called Brutality and a red one, Bloodlust. The beasts lumbered toward him down the hallway, knocking aside the people they passed with a flick of their horned tails.

They were ugly beyond conception. More horrifying by half than the human mind could endure. He had conceived them, birthed them and when they were inside his mind, he controlled them.

Now, no one controlled them.

No! Wait.

He was suddenly horrified.

Not *today.* Some other day — destroy all of creation some other day. This was *his* party. He was the dragon here that breathed fire and destroyed. He would not have the glory stolen from him.

Mikhailov advanced on the nearest dragon. He would throttle the beast with his bare hands.

THE LAYOUT of the back of the casino/hotel complex was pretty much as T.J. had pictured it. Back here out of sight were the loading docks for supplies and the huge green dumpsters that contained the mountain of garbage the place generated.

T.J. prided himself on bein' indifferent to cold and for the most part he got away with that little self-deception. Not tonight. The cold wind off the water had sliced right through his wool shirt and t-shirt and by the time he got to the back of the complex, he was so cold his fingers was growing stiff.

A four-horsepower Evinrude outboard don't make a whole lot of noise and what little it did was masked by the noise coming from the building. Big sodium lights brighter'n streetlights illuminated the facility and he'd have been visible in the water but wasn't nobody looking.

The "floating island" might have been only a hundred feet from shore, but all the deliveries still had to be loaded on something that floated to be transferred to the facility. A big loading dock that connected the building to the shore — that'd make the island a peninsula — wasn't in keeping with the floating casino image.

Nobody was working the loading docks on a night like tonight and he was able to pull his little jon boat snug up against one of the pontoons the deck floated on in the shadow of one of the barge slips, and tie it up. He climbed up onto the deck and hurried to the building, where over-hangs over the doors and loading bays provided at least some shadows where his black face and dark clothing could blend in. He walked down the loading docks, carefully testing all the doors, hoping he could find one that some-body'd not bothered to lock.

That didn't happen. Finally, he settled on the loading bay on the end, as far away as possible from the sodium light. There was a light in the overhang above the door, but he picked up a piece of slat from a supply pallet and broke out the bulb. Then he took out his pocket knife and began to go to work on the lock.

Most locks wasn't terrible hard to pick if you knew what you were doing and had the right equipment. He did and he did. Oh, he didn't have all his lock-pickin' tools, didn't carry them around with him just in case he decided he wanted to break in somewhere. But Dobbs had given him for Christmas a Swiss Army knife that had more gadgets on it than the tool shelf in his garage. A bottle opener, magnifying glass, hole punch, two sawblades, wrench, scissors, hacksaw blade, corkscrew, pliers, tweezers, ruler, fingernail file, screw driver — both flat and Phillips head, and a compass. He'd long ago removed the useless fingernail file, ruler and magnifying glass and used the space they'd occupied to insert half a dozen small picks in various sizes.

He had the lock disengaged in less than a minute, stuck the knife back in his pocket and eased the door open an inch. It was dark inside, a storage room or warehouse. He slipped inside and closed the door noiselessly behind him. Then he stood still where he was for five minutes. That'd been one of the hardest things for him to learn in Special Forces training — allowin' his eyes to adjust to low light by standin' still while they did. Patience.

A patient man would always be rewarded in the end. He believed that, just was often unable to apply the principle to his own affairs. Within five minutes, was able to see shapes emerge out of the gloom and that was good enough. It was a big storage room with a high ceiling. He spotted a forklift parked nearby and began to make his way down the aisles of boxes and pallets of industrial-size green beans to the glow of light at the other end of the room.

Chapter Fifty-One

"Begone!" Mikhailov shouted at the dragon lumbering down the hallway. "Leave me!"

A bellhop passed by and looked at him when he spoke.

"Kill him," Mikhailov screamed at the dragon. Now the bellhop walked faster, looking at him the way you looked at a poisonous snake you almost stepped on in your garden.

He continued to issue commands at the dragon.

"Hurt him first. Pull out his guts and make him eat them. Make him chew off his fingers."

Mikhailov snatched at the glove on his right hand, but it was tight, hard to get off. He wanted to show the bellhop the hideous result of chewing off your own ... but by the time he'd removed it, the bellhop was halfway to the end of the hall, looking over his shoulder, his eyes wide with fear.

Holding up the scarred horror of his right hand, he screamed at the bellhop to look, to come and see, but he spoke in Russian. He didn't mean to, thought the words in English but they came out his mouth Russian.

The bellhop dropped the tray of dishes from somebody's room service order and bolted through the door marked "stairs" and was gone. The dragon looked at Mikhailov. Mikhailov nodded and the beast followed the bellhop. The dragon would make him pay.

So Mikhailov *did* still control the beasts after all. He smiled at that. Loosing dragons on the world that you could bend to your will, that was a good thing.

When he breathed out, a tongue of flame left his mouth and heated up the air in front of him.

Oh, my!

How spectacularly glorious! He could *breathe fire*. He looked at his watch but could not read the dial through the red mist. It didn't matter. It would be soon, only a few minutes, and after tonight he would not have to employ the Arab gunrunner. He could breathe fire on his own! This was the last time he'd be a spectator. He would watch. Applaud. Laugh at the agony of his enemies.

After tonight, he would destroy all who opposed him. He would burn them with his breath … starting with the bumpkin sheriff, McGreggor. The *blind* sheriff. Mikhailov would see how long he could drag out the man's death, burning him a little at a time.

That was for later, though. Right now, he had a job to do, a show to watch, an enemy to destroy and he must not be late. He felt in his coat pocket for his phone. Abi-Nadir had already programmed into it the detonation number for the devices — one after the other.

The first one … a pause to allow the emotional agony to strike its blow, and then the second. All he had to do was touch the screen lightly and the hateful, hiding witness would *die*.

It was a shame he had forgotten to bring marshmallows.

OF COURSE, there was no plan Bailey could devise, in ninety seconds or ninety years, that would miraculously whisk María out of harm's way and stop Mikhailov in his tracks.

She wasn't a superhero, some secret agent with a black belt in karate and a fountain pen that turned into a bazooka. This wasn't a movie or a comic book. This was *real life.* She was a thirty-year-old widow who'd come here with her pitiful little amateur plan, thinking she could outsmart a professional killer, a murderous psychopath. All she'd gotten for her effort was blisters on both heels.

So what *could* she do? Because she *had* to do something. She couldn't just run like María'd said, throw her sister under the bus and condemn Bethany to a lifetime of fear and eventual murder. Bailey would fight to the death to prevent that.

Fight with what? She'd once fought with lumps of coal and had beaten a monster to death.

Her weaponry now consisted of what? Two icepicks and a cap gun.

What else did she have to fight with?

What would T.J. do?

Or Brice?

Think!

But she couldn't because her mind was in such chaos—

She stopped breathing.

That was it — *chaos.*

Confusion.

Disruption.

Do *something,* even if it's the wrong thing. That's what T.J. would say. Action is always better than inaction.

When in doubt, do the unexpected. That's what Brice would do. Kick up dust.

Throw as much mud as you can in every direction and hope some of it sticks.

When Bailey'd heard María's shout in her head, she had frozen so abruptly in place that an older couple who'd been walking behind her bumped into her.

"Oh, I'm so sorry, dear," said a white-haired lady with bright blue eyes and skin like cracked porcelain. "I didn't mean to—"

"Get out of here!" Bailey screamed the words inside her head but her voice said them in something like an urgent whisper.

"I beg your par—" began the old man with a cane at his side.

"*Run*! There's a bomb in the restaurant!"

A look crossed over his face Bailey had seen before. It was the one that had been on the face of Macy Cosgrove's mother when Bailey had tried to get her to run from the flood. Incredulity. Confusion. Disbelief.

All morphing toward anger.

She brushed the sputtering old man aside. Mere words would never work. Her eyes raked the walls of the casino. There had to be one somewhere. It was a requirement. She took several steps, shoving people out of her way, looking around frantically. Desperately.

About thirty feet away a small group of people all moved along together and the red box appeared on the wall behind them.

She ran to it, stumbled into a fat man in a red jacket, spilling his drink on his coat. She banked off him, shoved aside a couple of middle-aged women with badly dyed hair and too much makeup and literally slammed into the wall beside it.

The red fire box was incased in a plastic box that had to be removed.

Pull to open cover, then activate fire alarm.

There were white arrows pointing upwards from the words, apparently indicating what direction you were supposed to pull down. She clawed at the plastic cover, realized she was whimpering.

A man appeared beside her.

"Lady, what are you trying to—?"

Without warning, the plastic cover came open in her hand. An ear-splitting shriek squalled out of the box.

The man leaped back and put his hands over his ears. Bailey ignored the "prank alarm" on the plastic box.

Inside the cover was the red fire alarm box.

Pull down, it said on the lever.

Bailey pulled down.

Chapter Fifty-Two

BRICE HAD WALKED into the trap like a lamb to the slaughter.

When the man stopped him as he was getting on the launch and said Crenshaw wanted to talk to him, he was too thrilled to be suspicious. He had put the fear of God in Crenshaw and the fear had been eating at his guts ever since Brice left. Apparently, the fear had eaten all the way through his tough-as-rawhide exterior to the coward beneath.

But he was a businessman, and if he had seen Mikhailov in the past month, surely he'd seen signs of his mental deterioration. He'd noticed, alright, but didn't know what it meant until Brice told him. Now, Crenshaw knew Mikhailov couldn't be trusted, that whatever business arrangement they'd forged together was about to go seriously south.

And he'd decided to fess up, save his own precious backside and help Brice corner Mikhailov and find María.

Brice believed that lovely little fairytale right up until he stepped into the room where the guy said Crenshaw was waiting to talk to him — privately, away from prying eyes — and found not Crenshaw but two clearly-mafia-esque goons with guns drawn.

One of them was the pockmark-faced man he'd caught a glimpse of in María's apartment, before the man had shot him. Twice.

He saw recognition on the man's face, too, behind his blank stare. He knew Brice was "the one that got away."

Brice was quickly relieved of his weapons, both the one in the holster at his side and the backup on his ankle, and held at gunpoint waiting for … *Mikhailov?* Of course! Brice's mind became a washer on spin cycle. He, T.J., Bailey and Bethany had driven from Boston; these guys had flown. But the method of their travel didn't matter. How they had known where to come did. How had they found out? María couldn't have told them because she didn't know.

Maybe that "there's-no-leak-in-the-U.S.-Marshal's-office" line was a crock of the warm, sticky substance you found on the south side of a horse going north.

Even that didn't matter right now. What mattered was that Mikhailov was here. Brice was sure of it. If he was here, *so was María.* He intended to use her as bait for some kind of trap for Bailey.

The mobsters said nothing. Efforts to get information, insight, anything from them were met with a stony silence these guys had perfected over a lifetime. They didn't give a rip that he was a law enforcement officer. He was prey, their boss was the predator, Brice had been caught and it would likely soon be their jobs to dispose of him.

He'd heard Mikhailov enter the room, had not observed the unwritten rule that you only looked at the boss when he allowed it and was rewarded with a gun to his temple.

The fat guy had jammed something like a nightstick into Brice's belly when Brice tried to talk to Mikhailov. Then the old man had stood in front of him so clearly losing it that Brice couldn't believe the guy's flunkies didn't pick up on it. Maybe they did, but just didn't have the guts to do anything about it.

Mikhailov was as monstrous as Bailey had described, all the more chilling for his lack of passion, the offhanded nature of life and death he dealt out on a whim. He'd been like that two years ago. But the old man with white hair who stood before Brice now was even more dangerous than the man who'd shot Bailey's husband in the street. That man operated with sequential thinking, weighed cause and effect, had reasons — though certainly not justifiable reasons — for doing what he did.

What stood before him now was pure evil wearing a thin veneer of humanity — like a kid in a Halloween costume.

There was unhinged madness in his eyes, chilling insanity. Mikhailov had said he wanted to know what Brice's relationship *had been* with Jessica Cunningham. *Had,* past tense. Speaking of her as if she were dead.

But she was at that moment under the watchful care of Dobbs and three of his deputies, so what was he talking about?

What was the show he had orchestrated and couldn't be late for? It had something to do with María and Bailey and that thought froze Brice's heart in his chest.

As did Mikhailov's direction to his men to tie Brice up … and *blind* him.

They'd screwed this up last time. They'd be more careful now. Two of them. One of him.

Not good.

He took note of his jailers as they marched him out of

the room. Pock Face was on the right, holding a gun on him. A bald guy walked beside him, armed but his weapon wasn't drawn.

They began to pass through a labyrinth of interconnected passageways, consulting with each other in Russian at intersections. Brice quickly figured out they were as unfamiliar with their surroundings as he was.

That was good.

He assumed the destination, the room where he was to be tied to a chair, couldn't be very far away. Once in there, it was over. Escape was only possible while they were en route.

Brice had deliberately raised his hands in the universal "I surrender" position when the man pointed a gun at his back. If the man had known anything about tactical defense, he'd have told Brice to lower them. Apparently, he didn't.

Now, Brice gradually slowed down. The men behind wouldn't realize that they were slowly getting closer and closer to him.

"Hey, get the lead out," Pock Face said. "Move it along."

Okay, they did notice, were more watchful than he'd hoped. If they noticed the slow-down, they were too observant for him to execute the maneuver he was planning, the one card he had to play. There was only one way to disarm the man holding a gun on him. But Brice would need a distraction — a second of inattention — to pull it off.

The distraction came from an unexpected source seconds later.

Chapter Fifty-Three

EVEN THIS UNHEATED storage room was at least twenty degrees warmer than it was outside and T.J. felt his tensed-for-cold muscles begin to relax.

As he approached, he detected kitchen sounds — pots and pans banging, plates rattlin', silverware jinglin'. The kitchen was at the back of the restaurant on the first floor. He needed to get up at least one floor and maybe more'n that to find the executive offices of Mr. W. Maxwell Crenshaw in the flesh.

Light shone around big garage doors that opened into the building, but he found a smaller door at the other end of the room, opened it and peeked out, then stepped into an unlighted, deserted hallway he was sure was located between the warehouse and the stockroom of the restaurant.

And would wonders never cease!

There was coats and jackets hangin' on the wall on pegs. About halfway down, one of the waiters or someone on the kitchen staff had hung up his white jacket. It belonged to a man or woman considerably shorter than

T.J., which meant the sleeves were too short. Otherwise, it worked. He was wearing black corduroy pants — not standard issue, but would pass in a cursory glance better than a pair of jeans would.

After he slipped the jacket over his wool shirt, he went to one of the doors he figured led to the back of the kitchen. The key to disguises was not so much lookin' the part but assumin' the body language inherent to the part. Look like you b'longed somewhere and most folks assumed you did.

He needed to navigate the kitchen into the restaurant, cross it and out into the casino. Beyond that'd be a bank of elevators.

He squared his shoulders, lifted his chin, tried to look as condescending as possible and walked into the kitchen. Gratefully, it was every bit the madhouse it had sounded through the door. Chefs stood at stoves around all the outside walls, other cooks in white coats but with the funky little flat hats that meant you wasn't good enough to be a chef, was cuttin' up vegetables on wooden tables. A blast of cold air hit him as someone exited the huge walk-in freezer where he caught a glimpse of sides of beef hanging down from hooks like suit coats in a dry cleaners. Steam was everywhere. The clatter of dishes was deafening, but it was still possible to hear the shouts of waiters calling in orders or order changes, the former greeted by the chefs with grunts, the latter by streams of obscenities.

Looking not only like he belonged there but like maybe he was in charge, T.J. made his way through the throng toward the OUT doors. Restaurant kitchens had traffic laws much more strict than the State Department of Motor Vehicles. Waiters went *out* with orders, carrying them on trays balanced on one and sometimes both hands, with a third tray resting between the crook of their arm and their chin, through the two sets of doors *on the right*. The ones with OUT painted in gigantic green letters above them and on them.

Waiters came *in* to place their orders through the two sets of double doors on the left, the ones with IN painted in red above them and a gigantic red X across them.

T.J. picked up a tray with a bottle of expensive brandy and Kahlua for somebody's coffee and balanced it on his hand, heard someone shout "Hey you!" behind him and knew he'd been made. But he hurried toward the out door, had almost made it when the whole world lost its mind.

A DEAFENING BUZZER SOUNDED SOMEWHERE. Everywhere. The sound came from every direction at the same time.

A voice proclaimed in automated-attendant indifference:

"Please exit the building immediately. Do not stop to gather your belongings. Follow the lighted signs to the nearest stairwell. Do not use the elevators."

Into the stunned shock of aborted conversations that followed, Bailey shrieked at the top of her lungs, her voice clear above the din of the smoke alarm. She sounded terrified. She was.

"*Bomb*! There's a bomb. *Run!*"

Instant *panic*!

The word "bomb" ignited terror quicker than a match thrown into a puddle of gasoline.

Those who'd been considering what they should do in response to the smoke alarm leapt up now, knocking their chairs over behind them, shoving tables out of the way, colliding with all the other people doing the same thing. The stampede toward the exits was thunderous, punctuated by shouting and women screaming. It was true what they said about panicked crowds. Most people blindly ran back out whatever door they'd come in, even if they had to pass half a dozen other open doors to get there. There were exits on the north and south sides of the round restaurant as well as a bank of swinging doors into the kitchen. People in the back of the room made for the kitchen. But everybody else ignored the side exits and came thundering out through the main arch.

A human bottleneck.

That's what Bailey'd counted on.

When the crowd came running out, Bailey went running in.

Bent over so she was hidden from view, she swam upstream in the crowd, bumping into people, getting shoved to and fro, almost falling. She crossed under the archway and into the restaurant unseen. Jammed into the crush of people going in the opposite direction, Bailey knew only that she was headed in the general direction of the back of the room between the south exit and the kitchen, so she plunged onward, bent at the waist, bulldozing her way through the crowd of people rushing toward her.

With no plan, running on pure instinct and adrenaline, Bailey's forethought only got as far as "find María." She had to locate her sister, get to her somehow. What she would do when she got there … she'd figure that out when she got there.

She was unprepared for how abruptly the crowd of people ended. One second they were rushing toward her in what seemed like an endless flow, and the next instant Bailey was standing by herself among overturned chairs, spilled drinks and uneaten plates of food as the crowd of people thundered on behind her toward the front entrance.

Bailey was the only person in the room who wasn't leaving. No, that wasn't true. One other person remained where she was. *María.*

As soon as Bailey stood upright, she discovered she was about dead center of the room and she could clearly see María seated at an empty table in the back. On the other side of the Grinch's bag of stolen goodies.

Alone!

Whoever had been sitting beside her, whichever of Mikhailov's goons had been guarding her, had beat feet for the door when the alarm sounded. María remained seated, didn't rise. She probably *couldn't.* She'd been tied up in some way — plastic zip locks, duct tape, rope — something bound her to the chair where she sat.

Bailey had to get to her and untie her, get her out of here.

But she'd had only taken one step in that direction when she heard a sound from above her. Heard it clearly above the din of the fire siren and the automated voice directing her to stay out of the elevator. It was hard to describe what the sound was. It was a cry, more feral than human, a cry huge and Jurassic, full of rage and torment. And madness.

Chapter Fifty-Four

T.J. HEARD a fire alarm squawk to life with a mighty buzzin' howl, just about the most unpleasant sound there was — musta tested it on lab rats and picked the sound that made 'em eat their young. An automated voice urged people to make for the exits.

"Do not stop to gather your belongings. Follow the lighted signs to the nearest stairwell. Do not use the elevators."

Most fires in restaurants started in the kitchen. This one, if there really was a fire and not just some kid's prank, had originated somewhere else, and T.J. downshifted into police officer mode between one heartbeat and the next. Had to get them people in the dining room out of the building, and right now they was likely standin' around wonderin' if this was a drill.

He set his swiped drink tray down on a nearby rolling dessert cart and headed to the *out* door. Just then, a woman's screaming voice rose above the sound of the alarm, shrieking words, but he couldn't make out what she was sayin'.

As he put his hand on the out door, it swung suddenly inward with a mighty force, slammed into T.J. and knocked him backwards through the air. He landed on his back and shoulders, his head whacked into the tile floor and the lights went out.

The stampede of exiting people trampled him in their panicked flight.

His prone body was partially blocking the doorway and people tripped over him in their frenzied flight. The mob had to step over him, or on him to get by. Most stepped on him.

Shoes kicked him in the side, the leg, the ear.

A big man's shiny thousand-dollar Italian leather shoe came down with all the man's weight on T.J.'s left forearm. A woman's high heel punctured his corduroy pants and hung, tripping her. Off balance, she came close to crashing down on top of him before she pulled out of the shoe, stepped barefoot on his face and kept running.

Someone kicked him in the eye. A big man fell on him and somebody fell on top of him. Both scrambled to their feet. The man on the bottom used his knee on T.J.'s abdomen to push himself up. A woman's high heel stabbed into the top of T.J.'s hand, the pointed toe of another woman's shoe jabbed him in the thigh. Someone tripped over his leg and came down knee-first on his upper arm.

The rush of people forced the door inward in their mad dash through the kitchen to the hallway behind it, slowly shoving T.J.'s body out of the way.

A BUZZER SOUNDED that blotted out all other sound in the world, a from-everywhere buzzing cry accompanied by a maddeningly calm voice instructing the crowd to exit the building.

That's what María's two guards did. They both got up and bolted away, but she wasn't sure it had anything to do with the buzzer. It seemed like they'd already started to get to their feet before it sounded, as if they were responding to an entirely different signal. Either way, they leapt up and were gone in an instant.

People were running out of the room, women were screaming and then the world cranked down pudding-slow, molasses-slow, the seconds thick and ponderous and unhurried.

The crowd ran.

Gone.

Bailey was there.

Bailey!

All of a sudden, she was standing in the center of the room in front of the Grinch, stunning in a slinky green dress, form-fitting to the knee and all puffy ruffles from the knee to the floor. It was breathtakingly beautiful. Bailey was breathtakingly beautiful.

Bailey saw her. They locked eyes. Then Bailey looked upward toward the observation deck.

IT WAS ALMOST UNIDENTIFIABLY HUMAN, but that wasn't surprising given that the man who'd given voice to it wasn't human.

Even before she lifted her eyes, she knew who she'd see. Mikhailov stood at the railing of the West Observation Deck above the kitchen, a few feet from where the Grinch's fingers were removing the oversized Christmas lights.

He was dressed in a gray suit, vest … and a red tie.

Festive, in celebration of the season. His beard still came to that ridiculous point at the base of his chin, but it was no longer gray. It was pure white. So was his hair — in a cut a little longer than was stylish. She hadn't seen his hair that day because he'd been wearing a fedora.

Aaron is yelling at the man wearing a fedora, standing in the rain in the middle of the street in the intersection. The man is older, has to be. Nobody but older men wear hats like that, older men with money.

There is a popping sound, almost like a firecracker, but with a sharper edge.

Jessie looks at Aaron. He's holding his belly and he slowly drops to his knees like he's praying. The man, the older man wearing the fedora is pointing a gun at him.

"Jessie … run!" Aaron's voice cries.

Another gunshot rings out. The fedora man has shot Aaron again. Shot him! He flies backward onto the wet street and lies still.

Mikhailov's cry of impotent rage and madness seemed to last forever, seemed to last longer than a single breath, like the aria of an opera singer goes on and on and on. His face was flushed and twisted into such a sickening mask of loathing fury that it, like the cry, was not even identifiably human.

There stood the man who had stolen Bailey's whole life, casually, like flicking a piece of lint off the sleeve of a suit coat. He had murdered her husband, *butchered* him, taken away her child and kidnapped her sister.

Yet *he* was yelling at *her* in rage.

He was also sputtering out words, either so angry he couldn't pronounce them, or in Russian. Or so insane he had lost the power of human speech altogether.

He stopped in mid-screech. Like you'd taken the batteries out of his remote controller. Then he turned slowly, moving his gaze from Bailey to María, who sat in the corner tied to a chair.

He looked back at Bailey, nodded and smiled. Sudden terror that froze her breath, stopped her heart, turned it into a chunk of black coal in her chest. He lifted his cell-phone. Without ever taking his gaze off Bailey's face, he pointed down at the phone and in exaggerated precision lowered the finger to the face—

There was a whump sound. It wasn't a foreign sound, but familiar, a normal sound that had been amplified, multiplied, ramped up until it was way, way too big. It was the sound from a backyard grill when you toss a match into the lighter fluid on the coals.

WHUMP!

The world became red flames.

Chapter Fifty-Five

MIKHAILOV WAS IN POSITION. Waiting. His moment of glory was only seconds away ... if the woman was prompt. Given how convincing he had been that he was honest and dependable, he was sure she would not be late. She would walk into the doorway and—

Suddenly, a deafening buzzer began to bleat, a ragged cry that seemed to come from every direction at the same time. Then a voice that sounded like baggage claim at the airport instructed calmly, "Please exit the building immediately. Do not stop to gather your belongings. Follow the lighted signs to the nearest stairwell. Do not use the elevators."

He stood in staggered surprise as the people in the restaurant froze, confused. For one beat. Then two.

A woman's voice out in the casino screamed, "Bomb! There's a bomb. Run!" The bubble of communal indecision burst and the people below him became a herd of panicked animals, stampeding toward the exits.

Not exits. Exit.

Almost no one went out either of the side entrances. He couldn't tell for sure what the people in front of the kitchen did, but it appeared that the entire restaurant emptied into the casino through the front arch. The one with the sign, "Where your every desire is fulfilled," with the addendum, "in Who-ville style."

This was wrong, *all wrong*. This wasn't the plan at all.

An image appears out of nowhere in his head. It is a full-length portrait of him, exquisite in every detail. He is standing alone on a pedestal, dressed in his traditional three-piece suit and always, always, always a dark red tie. His white hair and beard are the color of snow, his cheeks flushed, his eyes steely with determination. The focus begins to narrow, as if the painting were viewed by someone walking purposefully toward it.

He begins to see it then, appearing slowly. It is not a painting at all but a mosaic, intricately formed from hundreds — thousands of pieces of colored glass. It is an even more impressive work of art in that form, with such detail—

Clink.

It's a small sound, barely audible.

He looks around to see what could have made—

Clink. Clink.

Then he sees them, tiny pieces of colored glass lying on the pedestal, fallen from his image. Slivers of colored glass so small, it's impossible to see where—

Watered-down American coffee in a ridiculous Styrofoam cup with the words The Nautilus—

Poof. The image, the memory vanishes and he cannot remember what—

. . .

CLINK. Clink-clink.

Clink.

More pieces are falling now. He understands that each piece is some part of him that is no more. The memory of the cup of coffee this morning is gone. No longer exists. He could struggle for twenty years and never remember it, what it looked like, the smell, the taste. The whole memory has come loose, broken off from who he is and has left a hole there where it once was.

Sudden panic almost overwhelms him.

The clinking sound is no longer individual sounds. It now resembles the sound of raindrops. A shower.

The shower becomes a storm. The storm a torrent. The torrent a monsoon.

A hundred pieces. A thousand. Ten thousand.

... SUN SPARKLING off the water in the Black Sea as the boat ...

... pipe is cold in his hand and he brings it down and blood spatters ...

... eyes going sightless as life leaves the body of ...

... warm breeze that smells of ...

... blind mice, see how they run. They all run ...

HE GRABS at the mosaic pieces frantically, gathers up handfuls, but where do they fit? How can he put them back if he doesn't know—?

THE WHOLE SCENE vanished with a tiny sparkle that reminded him of a soap bubble and the automated voice in Whoville below was telling people to leave the building.

Noooo! This wasn't the way. He was here to watch his two enemies die! *Burn,* and now—

The cry again. The sound he had been making more and more often. A sound as unexpected and uncontrollable as a sudden sneeze. It was a cry from his innermost being, from his soul, voicing … what?

Why, madness, of course.

The automated attendant voice:

"Please exit the building immediately. *You really are quite mad, you know.* Do not stop to gather your belongings. *Pieces of you are falling off.* Follow the lighted signs to the nearest *stairway to hell where you will burn for all eternity.* Do not use the elevators."

Then he saw her.

Crouched, running into the room while everyone else was running out. A woman in a green dress. It was Jessica Cunningham. The traitorous jackal in the grass who had been slinking around for two years, hiding with the dregs of humanity, waiting to bring him down. He sputtered profanity in Russian. But no word in any language captured the rage and hatred boiling in the volcano of his soul.

She had stopped when the crowd passed and was gone, and now she was looking around.

And saw her sister.

Oh, how touching.

His anger was an atomic reactor with all the bars removed.

Hotter and hotter.

He clamped a lid on it, left it boiling there. And he was quite calm.

He looked at the woman and she at him. They made eye contact. Just as he had agreed to do. He looked from the woman to her sister and smiled. Then he touched the surface of his phone and set off the incendiary device —

two of them, actually — that had been placed in the Grinch's bag of stolen presents and Christmas decorations on the floor. One at each end.

It claimed its life in glorious flames.

Chapter Fifty-Six

THERE WAS NO *BOOM*, no sound of an explosion or a bomb. Only a horrifying whump sound and the room erupted in a fireball that reached up thirty feet in the air. The bag of stolen gifts and decorations on the floor beside the Grinch's foot became an instant inferno. The red-orange flames sounded like the fluttering wings of a flock of birds startled into flight.

María forgot for an instant she was attached to the chair and tried to rise. Instead of standing up, the motion toppled her over on her side on the floor, awash in yards of black satin.

From her vantage point on the floor, all she could see was flame, the heat hitting her like a wave of hot water, the smell of burning fabric and cardboard curling up from the blaze in a haze of gray-white smoke.

Mikhailov had sprung his trap, had done what he set out to do. He'd killed the only eyewitness to Aaron's murder. Now, he would walk free. Bailey was gone. The flames had eaten her alive.

THE BLAST of heat was intense, blistering. It staggered Bailey, didn't knock her off her feet but knocked her backward a step. She squeezed her eyes shut at the heat but could see through her closed eyes the blazing red.

She opened her eyes to a world gone as mad as Sergei Mikhailov. The elongated bag of the Grinch's stolen Christmas presents and decorations was a blazing inferno. From one end to the other it licked flames up into a rising pall of sickening dark gray smoke.

Two pearl lights with clamshell shades dangling from the chrome grid above the fire exploded with loud popping sounds. Sparks spewed out and the rest of the globe lights linked off. Ambient light from the atrium shone down, but it seemed that the huge room was lit only by the dancing red flames.

The whole back corner looked like hell itself had opened a crack in the world right there in the Nautilus Casino Restaurant.

The back corner.

María.

Bailey sucked in a gulp of smoke-filled air, staring in horrified disbelief. That whole part of the room, from the south entrance on one side to the kitchen entrances on the other was bubbling, boiling flames. Looking at it was like looking into a fireplace on a cold night.

María was ... *gone!*

The painting had not been a drug-induced hallucination. It had been reality.

There was a sound from above again, but not like the first one. This one was much softer, with no hard edges. There was nothing sinister about it. It was wrapped up snug in soft wool on all sides, warm, cheerful laughter.

She dragged her eyes away from the conflagration in front of her and saw Mikhailov standing there on the observation deck. He was leaning on his elbows on the railing, his face lit by the flickering flames, grinning down at her. He looked from her to the flaming back corner of the room and back to her.

He laughed again.

Then he performed the same motion as before. He held out his cellphone and slowly lowered his finger to the surface.

Another blast rocked the room, the whump every bit as large and overwhelming as the first one had been. But the smell was different. This one smelled like a forest fire. It was. She turned toward the sudden blast of heat and saw a solid wall of flames across the front entrance to the restaurant. From one side to the other was an inferno, from the floor to the quickly blackening arch above.

All the other restaurant entrances looked the same.

Bailey instantly understood. That fire was meant *for her.* She was supposed to be standing there.

Stand beneath the archway and look around.

She was supposed to see María, then seek him out to make eye contact.

Wait until we make eye contact before you proceed.

Once he'd gotten her attention he would set off the first blast.

He would … *kill María* before her eyes.

Then he'd set off the second fire and she would become a torch of flame where she stood.

She'd been right to be suspicious of the "merciful death." A gunshot, a sniper, a headshot. Oh, no no no. He wanted to set her on fire and stand there on the observation deck and watch her screaming and writhing in agony as she burned to death.

Bailey turned back to the flames devouring the corner where María had already done just that — *burned to death* — and was staggered by a blow of grief.

She looked up at the observation deck and grief took a back seat to a stronger emotion, a consuming rage for Mikhailov so intense it took her breath away. She didn't just want to kill him. She wanted to *rip him apart* with her bare hands.

Mikhailov's happy laughter was gone. The rage was back, but it was no longer a boiling passion. It was rage as cold as a polar ocean and a loathing beyond human description. Greater than her loathing of him only because his mind was unhinged. She was sane. He was mad.

But in that moment, Bailey stepped out of sanity like a too-big overcoat. Left it in a heap at her feet. Her only thought, her only reason for existence was to kill Sergei Mikhailov. She would willingly, gladly, *cheerfully* die in the attempt.

There was no second place here. She would kill him or he would kill her.

No participation trophies.

THE SMOKE SMELLED like a forest fire. It mingled with the general stink of "something burning" that billowed in the open *out* door where T.J. lay sprawled on the kitchen floor.

Blood seeped out of T.J.'s nose and dripped down his chin from his split lower lip.

The shadowed floor of the restaurant was littered with debris left behind in the panicked stampede — upturned tables, chairs, dishes, silverware, bottles of liquor and carafes of water. The Christmas-tree torches bracketing the exits ignited nearby tablecloths and pieces of the flaming trees rose up on the hot air, then settled down on other tabletops, spreading the blaze.

The tray loaded with after-dinner drinks that T.J. had set down on the rolling cart had been upended. T.J. lay in the ruins of broken glass, spilled liquor and crushed desserts — a piece of cheesecake and a strawberry tart were smashed on his chest, a "sharing-size" bowl of Death by Chocolate coated his left leg.

Overturned and broken bottles on the restaurant floor poured Bacardi, gin, bourbon and vodka out across the blue marble with its swirling pattern that provided the illusion of walking on water. When a flaming piece of tablecloth lit the alcohol, it became a puddle of fire. The puddle became a pond. The pond became a river, moving, spreading out, flowing in every direction.

The river of fire advanced on the kitchen doorway, blue tongues of smokeless flame flickering up from it — toward the puddle of brandy and Kahlua where T.J. lay unconscious, sprawled amid the broken glass.

Chapter Fifty-Seven

THE LOOK on the face of Jessica Cunningham when she saw the fire eat up the world around her sister was almost payment enough for her betrayal.

He laughed then, glorious genuine laughter. As if he had just heard the best joke of his entire life.

But even as the laughter bubbled up from his soul, the lid on his rage bounced up and down, the thunderous beast beneath demanding to be loosed on the world.

The pressure built and built.

Then a bomb went off inside the confined space of Sergei Wassily Mikhailov's skull, the instant, white-hot glare of a nuclear warhead. One beat, two, and the concussive force hit and destroyed everything in its path.

The agony was more fierce than any pain Mikhailov had ever felt. He put the heels of his palms to his temples to contain the force of the blow but it rocked him, staggered him.

He looked out at a disintegrating world through the one-eyed vision he had imposed on himself at age twelve. It had, indeed, been a great risk for a *great reward*, but it was years before he understood his reward. That day taught him so many valuable life lessons they were worth the price he paid for them.

Trust no one.

Depend on no one.

Allow no one power over your life.

Repay every betrayal, no matter how long it took. Exact a payment ten times what you suffered.

It took Mikhailov twenty-three years to find the man with the thick black mustache from that day in the gymnasium. With the aid of a doctor, he kept the man alive for four days of nonstop torture, crushed the bones in his feet and legs with sledgehammers, cut off his fingers and hands with a blowtorch, then sent his body home in pieces to his family before he killed them, too.

Memories of the man shrieking in agony filled Mikhailov's mind now as he stood on the observation deck above the burning restaurant and he felt again the joy and gratification the revenge had granted him.

Then the world was all red mist and white smoke, mingling, swirling. He could hear dragons roaring in the mist and he became one of them, was transformed into a dragon, a hideous lumbering beast that breathed fire and desolation.

THERE WAS A GREAT BUZZIN' sound, seemed like it come from a distance, from another room or another world. An unpleasant sound, annoying. T.J. thought it had to be some kind of danged alarm clock. What'd he need an alarm clock for? He'd been waking up just shy of four o'clock in the morning for thirty years. Them things had snooze buttons on 'em, didn't they? On the top — hit it and shut the thing off.

But he couldn't move his arm to reach. He didn't feel his pillow under his head. Felt like he was lyin' on something hard and cold, not in his bed.

The sound was gettin' louder.

It was gettin' hotter, too.

T.J. wanted to wake up from this dream, shut the alarm off and go back to sleep. But the dream wouldn't let him go.

People was screaming in his dream, women and men, and the sound of runnin' footsteps.

He felt himself come up nearer and nearer the surface of the dream waters now, a bubble dislodged from under a rock on the bottom of an aquarium that floats lazily up to the surface to vanish.

T.J. was floatin' up to the surface. But it wasn't the quiet surface inside an aquarium.

It was hot, noisy, the stink of burning — a bonfire or a forest fire. A voice was speaking distinctly over the buzz, about going to the exits and elevators and the like.

Confusion clouded T.J.'s thinkin', makin' it hard to concentrate. But thoughts was ordering now, beginning to leap into place after reveille when the soldiers all ran to their individual places in the line.

Backs straight.

Chins out.

Eyes forward.

T.J. opened his eyes. What he saw made no sense so he closed them again. Then they popped open and he really looked, focused, *saw*.

A slab of tile stretched out away from his cheek. At eye level was flame.

Moving flame. Like a candle comin' his way only

wasn't no candle. It was liquid fire … no, it was liquid *on fire.*

Awareness began to light his mind and with awareness came pain. Pain from a dozen sources raced to register their complaints in his brain. His arm, upper arm. His face, his eye and cheek. His nose was broken, surely — he recognized the nature of that pain. Lip split. His left arm was its own particular agony demanding that he attend to it and ignore the others.

He moved the arm and the stab of agony was the smelling salts that brought him the rest of the way back to consciousness.

Consciousness was awareness of himself and his surroundings. It didn't yet factor in explanations of why he was here and what he was doin'.

Lying on his back on a tile floor. Left forearm likely broken. Pain points everywhere. Broken ribs for sure.

The *whoom, whoom, whoom* sound in his head was signaling an injury of some kind there, too, but the buzzin' he could hear was comin' from outside his skull, not inside.

Some kind of alarm was going off.

Then it come to him — it was a fire alarm.

WITHOUT WARNING, water began to squirt out of the fire suppression spigots on the ceiling of the hallway deep in the bowels of the Nautilus Casino and Hotel complex.

Surprise provided the second of distraction Brice McGreggor needed.

In an adrenaline-fueled blur of motion, Brice pivoted on his right leg and spun around. With his hands raised in the "I surrender" position, the motion sent the back of his right hand slamming into the gun the goon had pointed at his back, knocking it to the side.

Brice instantly leapt forward, grabbed the gun, and wrapped the weapon in what training officers called a "catcher's-mitt hold" — right hand encircling the gun barrel, left hand on top of the other man's grip.

In a single fluid motion, Brice pulled the weapon that was still in the guy's hand up tight to his own chest, then spun his whole body back left. The motion used the torque of Brice's body to wrench the weapon out of the gunman's fingers.

Before the man could regain his balance, Brice brought the gun upward and slammed it into the back of the man's head. As the man collapsed, Brice grabbed his shirt to keep him upright and crouched behind him. Two gunshots rang out and the man dropped out of his grip.

The second gunman didn't get the chance for a third shot, though. Brice pulled the trigger on the gun he'd taken from the man who now lay dead at his feet — shot the second gunman in the face.

The man dropped on the floor beside his companion. The whole confrontation had taken less than five seconds. The spewing spray of water from the spigot in the ceiling hadn't even gotten Brice's shirt wet.

He took a moment, forced himself to let out the breath he was holding, made himself draw another breath slowly, then let it out. The adrenaline rush of a life-or-death struggle provided extraordinary strength, speed and sensory acuity. But the price tag on that was dealing with the after-affects — difficulty concentrating and a feeling of exhaustion.

To help him shake them off, he turned his face up into the squirting water to clear his head.

Why had the sprinkler system come on?

A fire alarm could be a malfunction, a prank or a drill. But the fire suppression system was activated by heat and smoke. There had to be a fire somewhere in the building.

Did fire have anything to do with the show Mikhailov had "the best seats in the house" to watch?

Brice turned and sprinted down the corridor toward the stairs door they'd just passed, making for the second-floor observation deck.

When he opened the stairs door, smoke flowed into the hallway along with the buzzing shriek of the fire alarm. He could hear the distant sounds of people screaming.

Chapter Fifty-Eight

So ENRAPTURED BY her own rage, Bailey was barely aware that fire was all around her now, 360 degrees. The Christmas trees at the doors had exploded in flames. Literally exploded, blowing flaming branches out in every direction. The fire from the remains of the trees had spread, raced around the walls of the room along the decorative garland of live greenery, pausing only to ignite each wreath as it passed, a flame chasing a fuse to a stick of dynamite.

The walls in the restaurant and in the rest of the casino were the same blue marble as the floor, with inset aquariums full of tropical fish to grant an illusory underwater experience. Though the walls and floor were not flammable, the decorative cornice where the walls joined the floor of the overhead observation decks would soon be ablaze.

Tablecloths, napkins, and centerpieces of pine cones and holly were burning, giving off a thick black smoke. The chrome and glass tables, and the chair backs, cut metal in a classic Hepplewhite shield design, wouldn't burn, but most of the seat cushions were smoldering and some were already in flames.

Since the restaurant had no ceiling, the open-air atrium above it now formed an effective chimney, sucking air through the doors the panicked crowd had thrown open as they scrambled out onto the deck, up through the fire in the restaurant, feeding the flames, and out into the huge open space above.

Bailey didn't give a moment's consideration to escape. Her only purpose in life was to get to Mikhailov and kill him. He had to *pay* for what he'd done! He had to die before he vanished again, only to return in a week or a month or a decade to massacre the rest of her family.

Boiling smoke obscured the observation decks above the restaurant, but the gray was a live thing, swirling and eddying, blowing away in tatters in places to reveal a portion of one of the decks for a moment, then rolling back in like fog off the sea.

Mikhailov had been leaning on his elbows on the railing looking out into the restaurant below. He'd been laughing merrily, but the laughter had turned off abruptly, like he'd closed a spigot. Bailey's last sight of him was when he stood up unsteadily, pressing the heels of his palms against his temples and shaking his head.

He was up there. She was down here. How could she get to him when the exits were blocked with flames?

It was almost as if María spoke to her mind again. Not as it had been earlier, when her psychic voice had blasted through the static barrier and told Bailey to run, that it was a trap. This voice was soft, spoke to Bailey out of the mists of memory. It was even … wheezing.

*"Y*OU COULD GET IT DOWN?*" María might as well have said, "You can leap tall buildings in a single bound." She made it sound like it was a feat of derring-do unparalleled in human experience.*

Which, of course, means Jessie has to do it.
"Sure, I can climb it. Piece of cake."

She'd climbed the tree to get María's doll out of the branches.

The next words were María's, too. Somehow, she'd known that day that Jessie had locked up, had frozen there on the tree limb, too scared to move.

Wheeze. *"Don't look down!"*

As Bailey stood in the burning restaurant, smoke filling up the corners, the fire coming at her from every direction, she did as María had directed all those years ago. She didn't look *down*. She lifted her eyes slowly *up*, instead.

Looked at the Grinch.

And said softly under her breath.

"Sure, I can climb it. Piece of cake."

If that blasted buzzer T.J. couldn't manage to turn off was a smoke alarm, that would explain the river of flaming liquid that was now about two feet from his nose and coming his way.

He reflexively jerked back from it. Bad move. Seriously bad move. Jerking was not a motion that was readily received by an injured body, and clearly his was. He'd been in a wreck maybe, or hit by mortar fire. Something like that.

Whatever it was had set something on fire and flames

was comin'. He didn't jerk this time, just tried to move away, the only motion he wanted now was away from the fire coming at him. Easy, solid, non-jerky motion.

But as soon as he raised his head off the floor …

All the marbles he had carefully arranged in some semblance of order in his skull flew off in all directions. The room spun around him. He felt his face settle back gently — how could it settle gently on cold tile? — and T.J. Hamilton left the building.

The fire was as relentless as a flood when the river'd left its banks. Made it to his shoe. Caught the shoelace on fire on its way to the sole. The stink of burning rubber rose in a black pall, while the rest of the fire began to find purchase in clothing. The cuff of his corduroy pants. The sleeve of the white jacket he'd stolen off the hook.

Fire was comin' to eat him up.

BAILEY KICKED off the ridiculous heels, the stilettos she'd been foolish enough to believe she could use as weapons to kill Mikhailov. She still had a gun zipped up tight in the clutch purse on a strap around her neck, though. It would have to do, even if she had to beat him to death with it.

She unhooked the ruffles on the dress that extended from the knee to the floor. Looking around, she spotted a steak knife on a nearby table, grabbed it and used it to make a slit in the center of the bottom of her dress. Dropping the knife, she ripped the fabric of the dress upward all the way to the waist, revealing the tights she'd worn … because it was cold.

Then she studied the fifty-foot-tall Grinch. The only place on it that resembled the one and only tree she'd ever climbed was his left leg. With his foot resting on the

Christmas present, his leg from the knee to the body was like that limb that stuck out on the bottom of the oak tree. To get to that leg, she'd have to climb up on top of the gigantic box wrapped in shiny green paper with a red bow the size of a chest freezer.

Amid the flames all around, she found what servers called a "two-top" table. It was small enough that she could shove it up next to the giant Christmas present where the Grinch's left foot rested.

She climbed up on the table, then climbed from the table to the box. The leg from knee to body, like the oak tree limb, was too high above her to reach. She had no Adirondack chair to use as a ladder this time, so she grabbed hold of the green fur above the elf slipper and used it to pull herself up the leg. Handfuls of the fur were easy to grasp. She dug her toes into the fur beneath her to shove her body upward.

Once she got to the knee, she crawled out on top of the thigh, stood and walked down it to the body. The Grinch was wearing a red velvet Santa coat so there was no green fur to grab on his body. The coat was loose, though, baggy. Maybe she could grab a handful of fabric and pull herself upward ... but there was nowhere her bare toes could get purchase on the velvet.

The *front* of the coat had a strip of white fur running up the middle. She could climb that, just had to get around to the front of the creature. The black belt of the Santa suit that encircled the creature's bulbous belly was a piece of molded plastic about four inches wide. She could climb up onto it, the way you'd climb onto the top of a board fence, then balance on the top of it and inch around the body. Like moving from one window to another on a three-story building with your feet on a four-inch ledge.

Well, a building didn't have a loose coat to hold onto. There was that.

Bailey climbed to the top of the belt and carefully got to her feet on top of it. Holding onto handfuls of the baggy velvet coat in a white-fisted grip, she began inching along it around to the front of the creature.

She glanced at the floor, twenty-five feet below.

Bad move.

Don't look down!

A wave of vertigo swept over her and she was dizzy, the world spun, she felt her grip loosening, her weight shifting.

And then Bailey was falling.

Chapter Fifty-Nine

THE LIGHT WAS ... weird. It was flickering, different colors. The restaurant's overhead lights had gone out, but the lights in the aquariums that lined the walls had not. The glow from them was like sunlight filtering down to the bottom of the ocean from the surface. It sparkled and shimmered, twinkled in the shiny chrome of table and chair legs.

Only the ocean was on fire. The twinkling water was red and orange, too, writhing and gyrating, casting grotesque shadows on the floor and filling the air with the gray haze of smoke.

The flames that had killed Bailey were stalking María now, moving in like jackals around a wounded antelope. From all sides, closing in. Tablecloths were going up in balls of yellow flame — made of cotton, not linen. Linen took longer to ignite and was easy to put out. Cotton smelled like burning paper, burned like paper, too.

She knew that because ... one of her many part-time jobs when she was going to college was at a daycare center. There were all kinds of fire codes for the place, and as she sat one afternoon rocking a cranky child to sleep for a nap, she read the required warning posters on the walls. Fire drills, fire prevention, meeting points, how to put out a fire. There'd been a chart listing, in order of most flammable down, various fabrics — what not to allow for curtains or seat cushions in a facility with small children.

Her head was spinning — what had been in the drugs they'd given her? Whatever it was, it made her dizzy.

She concentrated on picturing the chart to clear her head.

Her dress was satin topped with acres of taffeta — both made of silk and some other synthetic stuff. Silk burned slowly and curled away from the flame, smelled like burned hair or charred meat.

An instant image flashed in her mind's eye — the black dress on fire. With her *in* the dress, there *would be burned hair and charred meat.*

Dear God, she didn't want to burn to death. *Don't catch the dress on fire, please no!*

The heat from the nearing flames was intense. She struggled in vain to free her hands, but they were secure. The guards had wound the zip ties through the spindles on the back of the chair, so there was no getting rid of the chair!

Her feet weren't bound, but without hands, she couldn't stand up because her legs were tangled in yards of black satin.

Did Mikhailov actually plan that part? So he could stand up there on the observation deck and *watch her burn?*

She couldn't rise. Might have been too dizzy to stand up if she'd been able to get to her feet. But she could scoot, and she scooted as best she could away from the flames, back toward the wall. When she reached it, she'd be trapped, fire coming and nowhere left to run.

BAILEY LANDED on her side on the Grinch's furry thigh where she'd been standing, a drop of five or six feet, with a solid *thump* that knocked the wind out of her. Her momentum sent her rolling toward the edge of the leg, for another drop to the giant Christmas present or all the way to the floor.

Squeezing her eyes tight shut to quell her dizziness, she grabbed handfuls of green fur and held on, stopped rolling and lay face-down in the green fur of the Grinch's leg panting and crying in terror and rage.

She got to her knees, her breath hitching in and out, sobbing.

Don't look down! María's wheezing voice spoke from her memory.

María. Mikhailov had *killed* Bailey's little sister.

Crying turned off so abruptly she was momentarily strangled, coughing in the growing smoke.

Getting to her feet, she crossed to the belt and climbed back up to the top. When she got to her feet this time, she listened to María's voice in her head, a continuous loop … *don't look down … don't look down.*

She didn't.

When she came to the strip of white fur up the front of the coat, she grabbed a handful of the fur and then dug her big toe firmly into it, tested to be sure it would hold her before she shifted her weight onto it. Up one step, test again. Wash, rinse, repeat.

Hand over hand she climbed up to the fur trim on the velvet coat around the neck, and then grabbed handfuls of the green fur on the creature's head to continue upward until she could dig her toes into the top of the fur trim on the coat neck. Balancing on the ridge of fur, she edged along it to his shoulder, stepped out onto it, then leaned back against the Grinch's furry head, panting, more from fear than exertion.

At least forty feet off the ground now … but she didn't look down.

Both the Grinch's hands were reaching up to the railing of the observation deck, removing the string of lights. She would have to climb up the right arm, clad in the velvet of the Santa jacket. The angle would get steeper and steeper the closer she got to the hand.

She studied the Santa hat. It appeared to be part of the head, not just sitting on it. Grabbing the white ball at the end of the hat for balance, she crossed the shoulder to the right arm.

Because she couldn't get a grip on the coat-clad arm, she'd have to shinny up it like climbing a flagpole, which she had never done, by the way.

Wrapping her legs around it, she grabbed hold of the velvet fabric of the too-big coat and used her knees to shove her body upward. The white fur lining the coat cuff was the objective. When she reached it, she grabbed handfuls of the green fur on the hand above and pulled up until she was standing on the coat sleeve trim.

The Grinch's skinny fingers wrapped around the string of lights he was stealing off the railing of the observation deck. The fingers were furry … and fragile. The thick fur made them look more substantial than they were. She'd planned to crawl across the fingers to the railing, but they'd never hold her weight.

Up higher into the smoke that was at last beginning to fill the atrium and back up into the burning restaurant, her eyes watered and breathing deep resulted in a spasm of coughing. She had last seen Mikhailov standing with his heels of his palms to his temples. Shaking his head from side to side, he reminded Bailey of a video she'd seen of a bull suffering from mad cow disease.

Now, Mikhailov was nowhere to be seen. She'd find him … as soon as she got to the observation deck to start looking. Desperation put steel in her spine, and before she had time to consider what she was doing and chicken out, she crouched on the hand and launched herself across the space between it and the observation deck railing, pushing off as hard as she could. The railing caught her in the belly and she grabbed hold, hoisting the rest of her body over it to plop ungracefully on the floor.

Scrambling to her feet, she unzipped her purse and took out the pistol she'd put there as a prop for Mikhailov's flunkies to find and think she was unarmed. With only that gun, she actually was mostly unarmed. It was a .22, after all, and would likely take more than one bullet —

Fine, then! She'd shoot him six times.

Or five, however many rounds were in the thing. She'd just keep shooting until he was dead. She gripped the gun firmly and headed off into the swirling smoke — totally unaware of the chain reaction of destruction she had left behind her.

THE GRINCH WAS a creature designed as a comic, not as a live being. The proportions were all wrong — a huge head and a big bulbous body atop ridiculously spindly legs.

When Bailey pushed off to jump to the railing, the motion shoved the whole figure backwards abruptly, throwing it off balance. Since its left foot was resting atop the Christmas present, all the weight of the figure shifted to the other leg — one skinny appendage ending in an elf shoe on the floor.

The leg instantly buckled and the whole figure came tumbling down in a collapse of green fur and red velvet, crashing on top of tables and chairs, landing on the floor behind the bag of stolen Christmas presents where the incendiary device had been set off.

It lay there, stretched out along the floor between the flaming sack of presents and the spot where María lay tied to a chair in the corner, cringing away from the coming flames.

Chapter Sixty

Climbing up the stairs, against the flow of terrified humanity racing down, Brice stepped out into the Nautilus Casino on the second floor and found himself in a strange world of swirling shadows and smoke. The lights were out, but there was a red glow from the first-floor restaurant, and a weird shimmering luminescence from the lighted aquariums that lined the walls.

The air was thick with smoke — not unbreathable yet, but getting there fast. People were running, women were screaming, trying to get out, not sure where "out" was, following the lighted EXIT signs that glowed as red beacons in the gloom. Roulette tables were overturned, one-armed bandits lay on their sides, chips worth thousands of dollars lay scattered on the floor.

Mikhailov was up here somewhere. Brice was certain that the Russian was responsible for all the carnage. It had been his little show. To what end and for what purpose, Brice didn't know, couldn't fit all the pieces of the puzzle together. But he was convinced Mikhailov had brought

María with him to West Virginia to use in some way against Bailey.

Find Mikhailov and he would find María.

Brice had come out onto the observation platform from the south side. When he got to the railing, looking down into the burning restaurant was like looking into a barbecue grill. The overhead pearl lights were out and smoke rose from a dozen fires. Though the floor, walls and furniture wouldn't burn, the tablecloths, seat cushions, centerpieces, Christmas trees and decorations would. Flames were chewing greedily into those and lighting little streams on the marble floor of burning alcohol …

Brice literally stopped breathing.

He swept his gaze in what seemed like horrified slow motion across the width of the restaurant. Directly across from him, on the north side of the restaurant, was the bar.

The bar that had thousands of bottles of alcohol.

The bar that probably had barrels of booze stored under the floor.

Brice had read about the Heaven Hill Distillery fire in Bardstown, Kentucky, the rivers of burning bourbon that flowed down the hillsides, the warehouses full of whisky aging in white oak barrels exploding like small nukes.

This fire hadn't gotten to the bar yet, but when it did …

The explosion might be powerful enough to blow the whole floating casino out of the water.

~

NOT THERE.

There.

That was how Mikhailov appeared out of the swirling smoke about twenty feet away from where Bailey stood.

Smoke stung her eyes. Her throat was raw from coughing.

How long had she been wandering around the smoke-filled observation decks, searching for him?

Knowing she must get out of the inferno or she would die.

Knowing she would rather die than leave him here alive.

In the strange flickering light from the fire below, the shimmer of the aquariums and the fog of smoke swirling around him, Mikhailov was an apparition, the Ghost of Christmas Past. Gray suit, red tie, white hair, black eyepatch.

She found herself smiling.

He had shot Aaron. Now, she would shoot him.

She leveled the gun at him.

And suddenly, there was silence.

The chainsaw buzz of the fire alarm and the insistent voice of the not-person giving directions "… lighted signs to the nearest—" abruptly cut off.

There was a stutter of additional noise, then nothing. No, not nothing. Without the blatting alarm assaulting her hearing, Bailey became aware of the sounds of fire — the crackling and popping, the indistinct cry of frightened people, all painted on the canvas of flames that sounded like the fluttering wings of ten thousand birds.

When Bailey cried out in rage and loathing at Mikhailov, her voice rang out crisp and clear above the muted fire song.

"This is for Aaron!"

Mikhailov hadn't seen her but he heard her shout. His head snapped up.

She pulled the trigger.

Bang!

Mikhailov staggered backward from the force of the bullet striking him, but didn't go down.

The pistol was, after all, only a .22. It might take two or three shots from it to kill him.

Then Mikhailov vanished again in the smoke.

Bailey ran toward the spot where Mikhailov had been standing, but he was gone. There was blood on the floor there, a small puddle of it. A trail of blood drops led away into the smoke. She followed the trail.

~

T.J.'s return to consciousness was abrupt this time and more or less complete. Not foggy, in and out, confused. He became aware of a far-off buzzing … that became a close buzzing … that became …

Sudden pain raced up his leg and he pulled instinctively away.

His pants was *on fire*, was burning!

Wasn't no way to stop, drop and roll, 'cause he was already on the floor. That's where the fire was.

He scrambled to his knees, his burning leg an agony, and his obviously broken left arm refusing to do anything but scream. He managed to bat at the burgeoning flames in his corduroy pants with his right hand, burned it some, but got the fire out.

Wouldn't be out for long, though. Not if he toppled back into the flames, and he was swaying on his knees, a drunken world around him of fire, both distant and close. There was smoke up here, much worse than it'd been when his face was on the floor.

He began to cough, felt his head begin to swim again, knew he had one shot at seeing another sunrise and he better get it right.

With the self-discipline born of months of training and years of execution, he managed to do several instinctive and cognitive things at the same time.

His brain ordered his body: *get outta here, fool!* And his body obeyed.

Lurching upward, stumbling, falling, slamming into the wall, he staggered away from the river of burning liquid flowing in the door from the restaurant.

Door.

Restaurant.

Kitchen.

Memory returned. Sorta. He'd been goin' out the kitchen door into the restaurant when that buzzer, that fire alarm sounded. The panicked people crashed *in* the *out* door, knockin' him down and … people stepped on him, but he may have imagined that part. No, he wasn't imagining the pain. *Everything* hurt, people coming in that door had trampled him like a herd of spooked buffalo!

He only remained upright by holding onto the wall, trying to make some sense out of what he was seein'. The restaurant of the Nautilus Casino was in flames. Christmas decorations, tablecloths, Christmas greenery. A pall of swirling multi-colored smoke seemed to pull past him from the kitchen and into the burning restaurant.

Like a wind …?

There was no ceiling on the restaurant, only them observation decks that stuck out over it all around. The atrium above it was a chimney, pulling the flames and the smoke upward.

God help the people in that hotel!

Then he realized the squawk of the fire alarm had stopped. That's why he heard so clearly the sound that come from directly above his head.

Bang!

A gunshot.

~

A FIGURE APPEARED in the swirling smoke and disappeared just as quickly. Mikhailov!

Bailey squeezed off a shot but had no idea if the bullet had landed true.

It was like chasing a ghost. The smoke was making her head swim. She thought she was hurrying to the spot where she'd seen him. But after two steps every direction looked the same.

Now she was totally disoriented, spinning in circles. How would she ever find him in this blinding smoke?

Movement off to the right, the smoke swirled around something and she fired. She heard no cry. Had she missed? Had she imagined he was standing there? She couldn't keep firing at shadows.

Crying now, swinging her gun in front of her, searching, desperate for a target.

He couldn't *get away*. She couldn't let him get away. Every moment she spent looking for him was a moment she wasn't trying to find a way out of the fire and save herself.

If she didn't get out soon, she would die here. But he was here somewhere. If she couldn't kill him, maybe the fire and smoke would.

Then there he was. The smoke swirled away from him as he staggered forward. Maybe she had landed more shots than she thought. She took careful aim this time and pulled the trigger.

Chapter Sixty-One

BANG!

T.J. knew a gunshot when he heard one … usually. But right now, his head was swimmin' so bad it coulda been a firecracker or a bazooka. The firing was comin' from right above his head. Somebody was up there on that observation overlook … shootin'.

Brice?

Well, T.J.'d come here looking for him and he was around here somewhere — packing. The offices of Mr. Maxwell Crenshaw and the other high mucky-mucks was up above the restaurant. T.J.'d been plannin' to start at those offices in his effort to track down Brice.

That wasn't happenin' now.

Bang!

T.J. heard it clear that time. No mistaking the sound. It was a gunshot but it wasn't Brice. The sheriff packed a Glock service weapon and the shots from above were comin' from a much smaller weapon, like a .22.

A thought dropped into his mind like he'd downloaded it off the internet. Bailey had a .22.

Why would … Bailey *here*? Well, she sure as Jackson wasn't home where she was s'posed to be! Dobbs'd said she tricked Fletch and vamoosed.

What on earth would possess that girl to come here?

Wasn't time to figure out the why. They was lots of people in the world shooting .22 pistols, but right now, he had to find out who was shooting that one on the observation deck above him.

Or beat feet outta here. One or the other.

Smartest thing was Door Number Two. When they'd come here for Bailey's birthday party, T.J.'d admired the mirrored wall behind the bar with liquor bottles on glass shelves. Soon's the fire out there got to that alcohol, it was gonna get ugly quick. A smart man'd make sure he wasn't around for that show.

But might be the person firin' those shots up there was Bailey. And if it was … T.J. had to find out one way or the other. He turned and tried to take a step and the floor threatened to smack him in the face. He had to get up to that observation deck and the shape he was in, he wouldn't make it up a flight of stairs from here to the top of a bunk bed.

All the elevators was on the *other* side of that fire.

BANG!

Bailey fired and Mikhailov went down on one knee. She advanced slowly toward him, saw there was blood on his shoulder as well as his upper chest and leg, so she'd landed more shots than she thought.

She was close now. Five feet of swirling smoke separated them.

There was so, so much she wanted to say to the

monster before she dispatched him to hell. Things she'd rehearsed in her mind in the midnight dark when the blue fire of rage urged her out of bed to pace the floor in some nameless house in some nameless city — where she'd been banished *because of this man.*

But now, the words wouldn't come.

"Murderer." The word was slathered with every shade of loathing.

He looked her full in the face, a crazed animal, a brute beast incapable of human understanding. The eyes were open too wide, bottomless depths of inarticulate fury, windows on a mind gone completely mad. Then his features slowly morphed and she saw recognition on his face, momentary sanity in his eyes.

"Where did you hide that I did not see you that day?"

When he spoke, blood spewed out with the words. She'd hit a lung.

He was down on one knee, in the will-you-marry-me position, unstable, swaying drunkenly. Any second now, he would topple over. Blood from his wounds formed ever-widening splotches on his meticulously clean suit coat and pants.

His face was as devoid of emotion as the face of an action figure doll, molded in plastic, a permanent blank look affixed to his features.

She stood over him now, three feet away, the gun aimed at his head.

SMOKE WAS GETTIN' so thick T.J. was gaspin' as he staggered to the food elevator on the far wall of the kitchen, the one that delivered food to the snack bar above. He'd a'been a big man, he couldn't have managed it. But skinny as he was, he folded right up inside it. That burn on his leg was an agony he managed to ignore only by concentrating on how bad that broken arm hurt.

He pushed the button, then used one hand and one foot to shove the door closed after he was inside, and the platform rose up slowly through the floor of the casino into the mini-kitchen above. Opening the door, he dropped his legs out and just sat for a moment, his head spinning.

Bang!

He got down and did his best imitation of hurryin' in the direction of the shot, which was coming from the observation deck right in front, the one over the back portion of the restaurant and the kitchen.

Swirling smoke.

A figure.

Dear holy God, it *was* Bailey.

She was wearing that green dress she'd wore for her birthday, 'cept it was split right up the middle of the front and she was barefoot. She was holding a gun on a man, who had fallen to one knee in front of her.

Smoke rolled in and obscured the view.

T.J. staggered forward, toward where he'd seen them.

When the smoke swirled away again, the scene had changed so dramatically, T.J. was afraid he was hallu-cinating.

~

Bang!

The sound came from Brice's right, from the smoke-filled observation deck directly above the restaurant kitchen. It sounded like … No, it couldn't have been a gunshot. But it could have been a bottle exploding as the fire got to the kitchen.

There'd be more than a popping sound when the fire got to the bar!

Standing at the railing on the south side of the observation deck, Brice traced the leading edge of the fire as it stitched together the tablecloths, seat cushions and centerpieces, fueled by the spilled alcohol all around.

Wait a minute. Something wasn't right. Where was …?

Where was the Grinch?

The huge green creature that had stood in the back of the restaurant in front of the kitchen doors was … gone. Where did it go?

He squinted down into the restaurant, the smoke swirled, cleared briefly and he spotted it. The huge green creature had toppled over on its side, and now lay on the floor, at an angle, from the kitchen out toward the front entrance. The bag of stolen gifts and decorations had likely been the other ignition point of the blaze in addition to the entrances because it was a wall of fire on the other side of the Grinch, which must have been mostly fireproof because its green fur—

What was *that?*

He'd seen something in the swirling smoke directly below where he stood and his heart seized up in his chest. Then it was gone, erased by smoke — gray, white or black, depending on what was burning. Had it really been—?

Yes! There. The pall of smoke shifted, cleared away momentarily and he saw it. Lying on the restaurant floor was a woman in a huge black ball gown. Had she passed out? She lay on her side with the chair … like she was still seated. Something didn't look right …

It hit him all in a rush. The woman was lying on her side as if she were still sitting in the chair because she was *tied to it.* She didn't get up because she *couldn't.*

Was that *María?*

He wasn't sure. He had barely set eyes on the girl before she was kidnapped and carted off. Why would Mikhailov tie her to a chair and then set the restaurant on fire around her?

But whoever she was, the Grinch that stole Christmas had saved her life. The fire from the flaming sack of stolen presents would have gotten to her already but the furry green creature had served as a firebreak.

Not for long, though. The Grinch's clothing didn't appear to be as fire resistant as its green fur. The elf slippers were burning and the bottom of the coat was catching. More important, fire was edging around the creature's feet, leaping from one tablecloth to the next, moving toward that back corner of the room.

As he turned and bolted toward the stairs to the first floor, an image flashed through Brice's mind of the portrait Bailey had painted of María, and he realized he was experiencing what T.J. and Dobbs had seen dozens of times — the horror of a painting coming true.

Bailey had described the sensation of burning to death.

María was only minutes away from that.

The instant before he turned away from the railing, the huge skirt on the black evening gown caught fire.

Chapter Sixty-Two

MIKHAILOV'S VOICE was ragged and hoarse. His breath wheezed in and out like María's used to. "Your husband deserved death. He was weak and pathetic."

Mikhailov twisted his face and mimicked another voice in a ridiculous falsetto. "'Jessie, run!'"

He coughed, spewing out fine droplets of blood with his words.

"Who was she, that woman I thought was you, who lies beside your husband's mouldering corpse in the family crypt?"

He was goading her, trying to manipulate her. Still in charge. The puppeteer pulling the strings to make others dance.

Some part of Mikhailov's syphilitic brain understood that to kill him like this was to become him. That would be his parting shot, striking out at her in the only way he had left. He had failed to take her life, but he could in his final act on earth take her soul.

Bailey owed her precious Bethany a better version of herself than that.

She suddenly felt all used up. Empty. Without her realizing it, her rage and loathing had grown, crowding out who she really was. The Essential Jessie. The woman who had sat in the very back row of herself in the Watford House kitchen a six-month lifetime ago, put this same gun to her temple and pulled the trigger. Since the moment she'd seen Mikhailov's image in that photograph, hatred had squeezed into insignificance the Jessica Bailey whom Aaron had married, the big sister who'd gotten a wheezing little girl's doll out of a tree before it got wet.

When she let go of her hatred, the space where it'd been was empty and hollow, with a chilly wind sighing through it.

She slowly lowered the gun.

"I hope you burn to death here in the fire you started. Burning's not good enough for you. But if you somehow manage to survive, you will find a ring of police officers three feet deep waiting to arrest you, and when they put a needle in your arm and send you to hell, I will be watching through the glass. Smiling. But *I* won't kill you."

He looked at her with an expression she couldn't read. He swayed, almost went down, but remained upright. "That's such a shame, my dear, because ..."

It was not possible that he could move that fast, strike like a coiled snake. One second, he was swaying drunkenly, weakening from the loss of blood, about to crumple to the floor. And the next he was launching himself at her. He didn't stand all the way up, but dived at her, caught her around the waist and knocked her backward onto the floor and was instantly on top of her, pinning her down.

He glared down at her with his one eye and finished what he'd started to say.

"... *I* will kill *you*."

She still had the gun in her hand and twisted it toward him, pulled the trigger.

Click.

The gun was empty, which struck Mikhailov as enormously funny. As he grabbed her throat, encircled her neck with strong, thick fingers and began to squeeze, his laughter was lazy and real. The laugh of a man who was totally enjoying himself, engaging in the one activity he had completely mastered, at which he was singularly proficient.

Killing another human being with his bare hands was what Sergei Mikhailov loved more than anything else in all the world.

T.J.'s mind had to be playin' tricks. He'd seen Bailey — he had! She'd even been wearing that green party dress, standin' over a man, pointin' a gun at him … They both vanished in smoke and when the smoke cleared, everything had changed.

Bailey now lay on her back on the floor with the man on top of her, his hands around her neck. Strangling her.

T.J. gave orders to his body parts, but they'd already mutinied and taken over the ship and he wasn't the captain in charge no more. He tried to *run* to Bailey, to help her. But "run" just flat out was *not* hap'nin.

Shamble, maybe. On his burned leg with a broken arm.

Stagger was in there somewhere, but even stagger seemed to require somethin' for him to lean on and without it, he was off balance.

The scene disappeared in smoke.

He had to get to her! Get that man off her.

Mikhailov. Had to be. Somehow he'd got her to come out here, lured her out here. Now he was killin' her.

Coughing, choking on the smoke that had changed color from white to gray, T.J. lurched in the direction where he'd seen the figures.

Where was they?

Seconds ticked away.

It only took seconds to strangle the life out of somebody.

T.J.'d been staggerin' around up here seemed like an hour.

Where'd they go?

~

SERGEI MIKHAILOV WAS A BIG MAN, heavy, as solid as a refrigerator. His weight was crushing. The instant his fingers dug into her neck, Bailey couldn't draw in another breath.

She knew what it felt like to be strangled to death. She had been murdered that way with Poli, the Romanian teenager Bailey'd tried to save by passing the girl a note written on the back of the receipt for this dress — outside the restaurant below that this madman had turned into an inferno.

The darkness at the edges of her vision came rushing at her.

Darkness.

She didn't have the strength to get away, but maybe she could do one last thing, strike one final blow. Maybe she could sentence Mikhailov to darkness.

He had only one functioning eye. If she could somehow put out the other ...

With the last bit of strength she possessed, Bailey

slammed the gun still in her right hand into the left side of his face, jamming the barrel of the pistol with its huge sight into the eye not covered by a patch. If the blow had enough force to destroy his one good eye, she would blind him, sentence him to live the remainder of his days in darkness.

~

BANG!

There was another shot from the smoke, now turned dark gray. T.J.'d been going roughly in that direction, now he staggered forward with renewed force, felt like one of them little kids just learnin' to walk, the way they stand up and stagger forward, leanin' forward until momentum runs out and they fall on they faces.

He broke through the smoke. Could make out bodies on the floor, not movin'.

Two bodies.

Chapter Sixty-Three

As Brice ran from the first-floor stairs to the south entrance doorway and into the restaurant, he could hear the sounds of a symphony of sirens and knew that help was on the way.

María would be long dead before they got here.

He could see trees burning on both sides of the entrance archway but he didn't slow down — he ran *faster*. Then he bent low, tucked his head and dived through the wall of flames, like he was a tackler trying to get to the running back before he made it into the end zone. He didn't dive *into* a fire, because nothing was burning beyond the trees. Diving through it, he was barely singed. Turning his fall into a forward roll, he came to rest up against an overturned table.

He leapt instantly to his feet — that dress was *burning!* — and made his way through the burning seat cushions, tablecloths, and piles of flaming *whatever* from the Grinch's sack on the floor.

"María! María, where are you? Help me find you."

He thought he heard something off to the right. Then it was clear. She was screaming.

He burst out of a cloud of smoke to see her lying on the floor ten feet away, the skirt on her black dress flaming. Without slowing down, he grabbed the back of the chair she was tied to and flung it across the floor. Even before the chair and María hit the wall, Brice had grabbed another chair. Swinging it like a baseball bat, he slammed it into the inset aquarium.

Glass exploded outward with a flood of water that poured over María, drenching her and dousing the fire in her dress.

Brice knelt beside her, as tropical fish flopped on the floor around them.

She looked up at him, seemed to be struggling to focus.

"Please ..." It was all she could say, and even that was slurred. She'd been drugged.

Looking around, he kicked dishes aside, found a steak knife. Then he rolled over the chair with María affixed to it so he could see where the plastic ties bound her wrists. He tried to be careful, didn't want to cut her. But the clock was ticking on the alcohol bomb on the other side of the room.

If that bar went up, there wouldn't be enough left of either one of them for a DNA sample.

THE .22 PISTOL Bailey was jabbing into Mikhailov's left eye went off with a muffled *Bang!* and Mikhailov collapsed in a lifeless heap on top of her.

The sound of the gunshot shocked her and the gun dropped out of her suddenly numb fingers.

The pistol had been *out of ammo!*

How had—?

The empty chamber.

One of the gun's six bullets was Oscar, who now resided in her brain. She'd loaded the five remaining rounds into the pistol before she came here, *five* cartridges into *six* chambers. She'd spun the chamber and snapped the gun shut, not putting it together at the time that now she was playing Russian roulette, that eventually the hammer would come down on the empty chamber. The first shot, maybe? The second? Third?

It had been the fourth chamber that was empty. The bullet she'd just fired into Mikhailov's brain was the last of the five.

She pushed the monster's lifeless body off hers and lay where she was for a moment, gasping.

A face appeared above her, looking down through the smoke.

T.J.!

Then he collapsed to the floor beside her, blood dripping out of his ear.

~

Maríá gasped and began to cough. The world was swimming in and out of focus, but the fire was out. She had drawn her feet up tight to her body when the skirt of the gown caught fire. She'd screamed, shrieked, knowing that in seconds the flames would reach her legs.

Then the chair — with her in it — was sliding across the floor. She slammed into the wall and a sudden rush of water poured over her, left her gasping and sputtering, totally drenched. But the fire in her dress was out!

María saw him then. The big redheaded man who was Bailey's friend, the one who had been shot that day in her apartment. But he'd been killed, was dead. Did that mean she was dead, too? If she was, then something else had killed her before she burned to death and she was absolutely okay with that trade.

He was talking to her, but she was having trouble focusing. She was coming back, though, no longer felt like she was wrapped in the cotton of whatever drug they'd given her. She was struggling to concentrate, connect with the real world.

She felt him turn the chair over, cut the plastic ties that bound her to it, and she fell free into the puddle of — were those *fish* flopping on the floor? She had to be hallucinating.

"… get out of here … you stand?"

The man pulled her up to her feet and she promptly folded back up like a broken marionette on the floor. But she managed to sit upright, wobbling but sitting.

Then he cut her dress, tore the fabric off the skirt. Was he trying to get her out of the mounds of wet fabric so she could move? No, because he draped big pieces of wet fabric over her head.

She heard "… you out of here," and focused on his face. That's when María saw that he'd draped pieces of the wet fabric from her dress over his own head and shoulders.

He took her wrist then and started dragging her across the wet floor. She slid easily.

Suddenly, heat hit her like a blow, took her breath away. There were flames all around her, licking at the wet fabric. A red and yellow inferno of fire!

He'd dragged her into the blaze, into the flames. Noooooo!

She screamed, or tried. But she couldn't make a sound.

María really was going to burn to death after all.

Chapter Sixty-Four

T.J. HAD APPEARED out of the smoke like some figure out of a horror movie, some monster from the deep rising up out of a foggy swamp.

He looked pretty monstrous, too.

Bailey rolled off her back and got to her hands and knees, leaning over him where he had collapsed on the floor next to the body of the now gratefully dead Sergei Mikhailov. Wearing a white jacket with a burned sleeve, his leg obviously burned, too, he looked terrible — nose bleeding, cuts and bruises, split lip, and quite obviously a broken left arm.

"T.J. what … what are you doing … what happened?"

"We kin sit here chattin' like we's composin' some idiot Christmas letter if you want, but if it was up to me, I'd say we'd ought to get outta here."

He was hurt. But he was fine.

She stood, reached down and pulled gently on his uninjured arm. He groaned. Something about the movement hurt, but he staggered to his feet with her assistance.

Then the weight of her loss hit her, and she almost staggered under it. She stifled a sob.

"What?"

"María's *dead*." The words coming out her mouth made it real. "Just like in the painting. She ... she burned to death."

"Sugar, I'm so sorry. I—" T.J. stiffened. "Ain't time for grievin' now or won't be nobody left to look after that little girl. Bethany needs you."

He nodded in the direction of the north entrance to the restaurant, but she wasn't sure what she was supposed to see there. "We got to boogie."

"How do—?"

"Down to the kitchen, out the back."

"Okay. Lean on me." She put his good arm over her shoulders and walked/carried him back toward the snack bar until he motioned toward a metal opening in the wall.

"That there's the pumpkin we's going to the ball in."

She had no idea what he was talking about, but he turned their staggering procession that direction and explained how the food elevator worked.

"Wouldn't it be easier just to go out—"

"We ain't got time for a debate. That there's gonna blow."

Again he indicated the north side of the restaurant ... *where the bar was located.*

She got it. The liquor. When the fire hit there ...

"Get in, T.J. I'll send you down, you send it back up for me."

"Ain't no way I'm goin' first. *You* get in."

She mimicked his West Virginia accent. "We ain't got time for a debate!"

Then pushed him into the opening. He didn't have the strength or the unbroken bones to keep her from doing it.

She closed the doors with T.J. sitting curled up inside. She was glad it wasn't Brice. He'd never have fit.

She found only a moment, but it was a moment, to be glad that at least he was safe, nowhere near this conflagration.

Two walls of fire stood between Brice and escape.

The clock was ticking.

He grabbed María's hand and began dragging her as fast as he could. They'd have to blast through. He'd already done this once. Except this time, the fire wasn't a hoop of flames like a lion jumps through in a circus. This fire was deep. They'd be bulldozing their way through the pile of burning debris from the exploded Christmas gift sack along with whatever other flammable items might have been in the vicinity.

The wet fabric should protect them. Should. If it didn't, Brice was about to join María in the death Bailey had predicted for her.

Beyond that fire lay the restaurant entrance, which was also on fire.

In the heartbeat before Brice plunged into the flames, a single image flashed across his mind like a comet. Bailey.

With some kind of inarticulate yell, he took a mighty leap and jumped into the flaming debris of the Christmas sack, dragging a soaked María behind him. He didn't draw a breath, couldn't, the air was too hot. Hot enough to burn. Even without touching a flame, the heat was blistering his skin. He could feel his face, the skin tightening like a sunburn. Had to close his eyes. He couldn't see, was stumbling. Couldn't fall down, couldn't — and then they were through and he was running across the blue marble floor toward the second hurdle.

He had María's small hand clutched tight in his big one. He felt pain on the back of his hand as they passed between the burning trees, knew the piece of wet fabric had fallen away there, but was pretty sure he'd protected María's hand with his.

Brice continued to drag María until they were well into the casino that encircled the restaurant. Then he stopped, pulled the wet — *steaming* — piece of satin off her head and asked if she could stand.

She nodded and actually managed to stay upright when he pulled her to her feet, but he didn't depend on her walking, just put her arm over his shoulder and carried her to the doors leading outside.

When they passed beneath the archway that promised their every desire would be fulfilled "in Whoville style," a blast of cold, fresh air revived them both. María took two or three big gasps and her eyes cleared. She might even have been able to stand on her own, but they weren't safe yet.

A single launch was still parked at the dock, motor running, the captain motioning with come-on gestures, shouting "Hurry!" Brice made for it. It would be a long run around the casino to the boardwalk and then to shore … dragging/carrying María along beside him.

The two of them leapt aboard and the captain hit the throttle and they were flying through the cold black night out into Whispering Mountain Lake, away from the ticking bomb that would blow at any second.

María sagged down on a seat, put her face in her hands and burst into tears.

Brice sat down beside her, knew she had to get out of

that wet dress quick or she'd develop hypothermia. But right now, it was enough just to be alive.

"We made it. We're good."

"Bailey didn't."

Brice felt a lead ball form in the pit of his stomach.

"What about Bailey?"

María nodded toward the fire.

"She's gone. In there. Mikhailov … he …" Then she couldn't speak, broke down in heartrending sobs.

"María, are you saying Bailey's … *here?*" He stared horrified at the burning building behind them. "In there?"

She looked at him and could only stammer, "She's dead. I watched him kill her."

Brice continued to stare at the fire, the flames lighting the red of his face.

Bailey was in there?

Bailey was … *dead?*

Chapter Sixty-Five

Once Bailey uncurled herself out of the food elevator, T.J. directed them through an almost solid wall of smoke. She had to help him walk and he'd have protested if he hadn't been convinced of the need for speed.

He led her out into a hallway, where she stumbled over a woman's shoe.

"B'longs to one of them people stepped in my face," T.J. said. Someone in the panicked crowd he'd said had trampled him.

T.J. directed the way through a door, down through a warehouse to the other end and out another door.

The smoke hadn't made it to the warehouse yet. So the air there smelled fresh and clean.

When the two of them staggered out the back door of the building onto the deck outside, she dragged great heaving lungfuls of fresh, cold air into her lungs, which sent her into a coughing fit but that was fine, thank you very much, just fine.

"Come on, stop your lollygagging!" T.J. motioned for her to help him down into a small jon boat tied up beside the dumpsters. She followed him into the boat, untied the line and pushed the boat out into the water.

"You gone have to crank that motor, sugar. It takes two arms and I am temporarily short one." He took a breath. "How you do it is—"

She put her hand on the top of the little Evinrude outboard, grabbed the handle of the pull cord and yanked. The engine burst into life instantly.

She pushed him gently down onto a seat and took the handle on the motor.

"Where'd you learn a thing like that?"

"I got skills."

"That way!" T.J. pointed to a spot about seventy-five yards away where a rocky cliff jutted out from the shore into the lake. "We best hunker down behind that 'cause when this baby blows …"

It was a near thing. The stern of the little jon boat had barely snuggled in behind the rock face before the blast.

The explosion was cataclysmic. It really did sound like a bomb had gone off. The building had a convulsive seizure and vomited a tower of flames up into the black velvet sky and rained down burning liquid onto the water.

The rumbling became the solid roar of a consuming fire while the debris was still settling out of the sky onto the water — that had a layer of burning alcohol floating on the top.

It was a manifestation of a horrible truth. T.J. and Bailey had leapt out of the frying pan into the fire. Flaming water was all around them. They couldn't just sit where they were … and *cook*. They couldn't have climbed that cliff face even if T.J.'s arm hadn't been broken.

Bailey looked at T.J. with frightened eyes. He patted her hand.

"Sugar, this here jon boat's made out of *metal*."

"So's a frying pan."

He looked back at the inferno of the casino, and all of a sudden his face was full of emotional pain that was way out beyond fear.

"I didn't say before, but," he began, then stopped and started over. "You need to know ..."

She didn't like the sound of that. Oh, how she didn't like the sound of it.

"Spit it out, T.J. What?"

"Brice come out here this afternoon to have a sit-down with Maxwell Crenshaw, get him to fess up to what he knowed about Mikhailov."

Her mind leapt ahead, knew where he was going. No. Oh, please no.

"He's in ... there?" Her voice sounded so small, so childlike. "Brice is in there?"

"Yeah, sugar, I think he is."

Brice stood beside the captain of the launch, looking back at the conflagration. Everything was on fire. Even the water.

Bailey was gone.

That was impossible. Not now. Not when she finally had her sister and her daughter back. Not now.

And what ... what was he going to do ... *without her?*

María was remembering the day Bailey had helped her dress up as Princess Leia for Halloween. She had sneaked two honeybuns out of the box in the kitchen, poked holes in the middle of each, then pulled María's hair through the holes, spread it around on the outside of the buns and pinned it in place with bobby pins.

María didn't think she'd be able to go trick-or-treating at all because she couldn't quit giggling. Laughing gave her asthma.

"Don't think about it," Bailey'd told her.

But how could she *not* think about the two honeybuns on the sides of her head? Whenever she did, she started to giggle.

And wheeze.

She was wheezing a little now — not bad, not like it was when she was little and had asthma. The smoke and the coughing. Even the fresh air on the launch hadn't helped. Her mashed fingers were throbbing painfully, she'd bumped them against—

None of it mattered. Bailey! María had already lost her once. Grieved her death once. Staggered under the weight of it once. *Not again.* Not dead after she had just come back to life.

Come back to life like the man who had saved her own life. The big redheaded sheriff who'd come into the flames and dragged her out. She'd *watched* him get shot. But he was alive.

Bailey wasn't, though. Bailey was dead.

María was crying, she supposed, because her cheeks were wet.

So were the cheeks of the big man standing beside her.

THE FLAMING water was about to lap up against the side of the jon boat stuck up against the rock face. The heat was almost unbearable, the air scorched Bailey's throat when she breathed. They had to make for open water. It was their only chance.

T.J. had told her how to do it, what to do. He'd have done it himself, but he'd deferred because of his broken arm. But also, Bailey thought, because he believed she could handle it. He believed in her.

She *could* handle it. She would point that jon boat out into the waters of Whispering Mountain Lake. It was dark and cold there now, not like the July day she and Brice had ridden out across the waves together, the first day after Oscar that she was glad to be alive. She shook her head — not now. Right now, she had a job to do. She had to crank that throttle full open and sail out through that burning water to safety.

They'd make it!

Or they wouldn't and they'd burn to death.

She had already done that once, with María when she painted the portrait. Today, María's death had happened in real life. Bailey didn't know how to think about the fact that over and over again, she painted portraits of people and they died anyway. Or her desperate effort to save them ended up killing them.

She didn't know how to think about any of it.

María, back in her life! And then gone for good.

And Brice.

There wasn't anywhere in her head or heart where she could think about that right now, either. If she tried, something would break or come undone or fall apart and the whole of who she was would come loose. Loose pieces would fall off. Pieces that'd be gone forever.

All she could do was think about Bethany ... *who had lost her mommy today.*

T.J. nodded.

Bailey nodded back, her eyes watering from the heat.

She cranked the throttle and the two of them flew out into the flames like phoenixes who would somehow come out the other side alive.

BRICE AND MARÍA turned to look when somebody on the launch beside them pointed. At first he couldn't tell what … then he could see. It was a metal jon boat roaring out over the flaming liquor on the water, hurling through it, bursting out of the flames and continuing on, full throttle away from the flames toward the handful of launches parked in the lake a safe distance from the disaster.

María saw her first.

She shrieked "Bailey!" and then started laughing and crying at the same time, yanking on Brice's arm and pointing at the jon boat, where a black man …

Bailey. It was T.J. and Bailey.

Suddenly, the night was no longer cold. It was as warm as the July day he'd seen Bailey's black hair shimmering in the sun. The day he'd fallen in love with her.

BAILEY SAW Brice and María on the launch. She gobbled up the sight of them with her eyes and her heart, and began to laugh. She didn't throttle back the little Evinrude, though. She merely piloted the jon boat around and around the launch as the cold night air carried her laughter away to the stars.

Chapter Sixty-Six

IT HAPPENED four days after the fire, when T.J. finally pitched such a fit that the doctors at the hospital threw up their hands and said fine, go home, if your concussion and punctured lung kill you, good riddance!

At least that's what T.J. told Bailey they said.

It had taken the combined efforts of Bailey and Brice to get him into an ambulance at the marina in the first place.

He did *not* want to go to the hospital. But it was more than just that. He didn't want to leave the others and Bailey understood that. None of them wanted to separate. Each of them had for a time believed they'd lost someone they loved. They all were reluctant to let the others out of their sight. Bailey couldn't take her eyes off María. Or Brice.

Tonight, they'd ordered huge "kitchen-sink" pizzas — everything but anchovies — and T.J. was set up on the couch in Bailey's new "den" with a pillow under the cast on his arm.

"If I'd knowed you was gonna fuss over me like I was a

still-wet chick out of the egg you just laid, I'd a stayed in the hospital." He looked at Sparky. The dog refused to get more than eighteen inches away from him. "And if that mutt don't get out of my way, I'm gonna trip over him and break the other arm."

It was amazing how T.J. could say one thing and mean exactly the opposite — and somehow communicate it so you understood.

Bethany was a bubbly, delightful, happy little girl, the world brightened by her presence, chasing Bundy — Sparky refused to play, wouldn't leave T.J.'s side — and soaking up the warmth of having her Mommy back. And her *new* mother.

"Don't be ridiculous!" Bailey had said when María corrected Bethany for calling her Mommy, said she was really Aunt María. "Of course you're Mommy. And I'm … Mama or Mom — whatever Bethany decides. We've picked our own names our whole lives, and it's worked out fine so far. The kid's got two mothers. When she's a teenager, she'll wish she didn't have any."

Which prompted Brice to ask if the rest of them should start calling her Jessie. Bailey didn't even have to consider it. "I'm Bailey — Bailey *Cunningham*, not Donahue — but Bailey. I was Jessie in another life." Her voice grew quiet. "I'm not that person anymore. Jessica Cunningham died with Aaron." She hadn't meant to cast a pall over the evening, so she continued in a cheery voice. "Which means a new driver's license — *again*. I'm thinking about wallpapering my bathroom with the old ones."

Brice advised her to wait a day or two before she went to the Department of Motor Vehicles in the courthouse. The dust hadn't completely settled there after what'd happened at the Nautilus, a disaster everyone agreed could have been a whole lot worse.

Bailey's decision to "create chaos" by pulling the fire alarm had cleared the restaurant before Mikhailov detonated his devices. Otherwise, 150 people would have been trapped by the flames. Mikhailov didn't care how many innocents he had to butcher to get what he wanted.

The marble walls and marble flooring had slowed the spread of the fire beyond the restaurant and most of the crowd had raced down the gangplank to safety in the parking lot.

A single launch captain named Hoppelmeijer had waited, loaded up the stragglers — which included Brice and María — before pulling out into the middle of the lake to join the little armada already there. The death toll could have been staggering. As it stood, three people had still been in the building and were killed when the alcohol bomb went off, six died from smoke inhalation in the hotel and another two dozen people were injured. Bailey, Brice and María all had burns and poor T.J. looked like he'd been dragged through a forest fire behind a team of Clydesdales and the Budweiser beer wagon.

Of course, none of what had happened was the fault of W. Maxwell Crenshaw III, "Billy" to his friends if he'd had any. As usual, he'd skated. If he'd admitted to Brice that Mikhailov was at the hotel, Brice could have summoned an army of law enforcement officers to take him down — though, in truth, María would not likely have survived his arrest. But Brice had no proof that Crenshaw had knowingly harbored a fugitive or was complicit in a kidnapping. The casino employees who'd seen the two of them together earlier in the day had developed a severe case of group amnesia. Meanwhile, Crenshaw was preening in front of the media, professing his absolute innocence — not my monkeys, not my circus — and playing the heartbroken victim. He'd lost his whole business, after all. There was nothing left of the floating casino and hotel complex but a pile of charred rubble.

"I'd bet T.J.'s pension the place was insured for two or three times what it was worth," Brice had said, goading T.J. into his predictable "why's-everybody-always-bettin'-*my*-pension?" response.

Mikhailov's flunkies — the ones Brice didn't kill — had slipped away into the crowd. Local, state and federal authorities were searching for them. María could identify them and would gladly testify but Brice and T.J. both believed that once the roaches had crawled back under the baseboard, nobody would ever see them again.

Bailey had explained to María about the painting, and all the other paintings, and what kinds of situations they'd found themselves in because of them. It had taken hours — *days*. The look on María's face must have mirrored the one on Bailey's the day T.J. and Dobbs had told her the fantastic story of their childhoods. She'd thought it'd be easier for María to swallow since Bailey, Brice, T.J. and Dobbs could contribute to the story.

Riiiiight. *Easy to swallow* that Bailey could paint the future and because she could, the four of them had almost been washed away when a dam exploded. Had almost been killed by a human spider. Had almost drowned in a flood in a coal mine.

That story would win the gold medal in the Couldn't Possibly Be True Olympics.

María was still reeling from the psychological blow. She hadn't seen the painting of her yet, said she wasn't ready. But she didn't want it destroyed until she did.

Then Bailey noticed a splotch of paint on Bethany's shoe.

"Where did she get that?" she asked nobody in particular.

"I can tell you *when* she got it," Dobbs said. "That child almost scared me into the middle of next week. I was pacing the floor, worrying about all of you. She was chasing Sparky and Bundy. And then she wasn't. She was just gone."

"Hard to lose a child big as she is," T.J. said. "Did you try looking where you left her?"

"You want the other arm in a cast?"

"Ain't no need to get your panties in a wad."

"I did find her, thank you very much. Actually, she found me, running around from room to room calling for her."

"Where was she?" María asked.

"I guess in the studio. She must have been there because she had that paint on her shoe."

Bethany perked up at those words.

"It drip-ted," she said, and held out her shoe to display the mostly scuffed off paint on the tip of it. Green paint. An odd shade of lime green.

"You painted a picture?" María asked. "You know I have to spread out newspapers so you—"

"Wasn't my picture. It was already painted."

The adults looked at each other. For some reason, Bailey got a queasy feeling in the pit of her stomach.

"Can you show me the picture?"

"Uh huh."

Bethany hopped off the couch and ran into the studio. The glorious north light was not in evidence on this overcast December day. But the overheads granted plenty of light to see. By the time the adults got to the room, Bethany was standing beside a canvas resting against the wall.

Bailey stifled a gasp when Bethany leaned it away from the wall to show the front.

"See, I painted," Bethany said.

There was silence then, everyone taking in what they saw and processing it in their own way. It was the portrait Bailey had painted of María — watching the flames come at her before she burned to death. The one María hadn't wanted to see yet.

At least that's what the portrait had been before Bethany took a brush to it. Now, the portrait showed María with the fire coming at her. But a great glob of lime green paint was smeared on the canvas *between her and the flames.*

"How did …?" somebody asked. Didn't matter who. They all wanted to know *how did …?*

María was the only one of the group who wasn't feeling the full impact of what she was seeing. It was shocking to see herself there, like that, of course. But she hadn't seen the other portraits and wasn't connecting the dots.

"Bethy, where did you get the paint?" she asked the little girl.

The child pointed to a pallet that lay on the floor between the portrait and the wall. It was covered in dry paint — yellow, blue, burnt umber and some other colors, all mixed together to form lime green.

"Bethany …?" Bailey heard her own voice and paused, started over with less tension in it. "Honey, how did you know what colors to mix together to get …?"

She shrugged.

"I gotted the paint and the brushes … and then it was just there."

All the air was sucked out of the room, but Bailey found enough to say, "Brush-*es*?"

"Uh huh." Bethany pointed to two brushes with dried paint lying on the floor where the pallet had been. "Dose brushes. Boff two of 'em."

"She bumped her head *in the kitchen*." There was no emotion in Bailey's voice because she was feeling every emotion in her whole being at the same time and they cancelled each other out.

"*What?*" María asked, looking from one person to the next. "What am I missing here?"

"The day before … you weren't here. She was running with the dogs and took her shoes off. When she hit the hardwood floor in sock feet she slipped and fell."

T.J.'s voice was emotionless, too, maybe because he was too stunned to feel anything at all.

"I got Sparky to sit for her, so she wouldn't cry."

"So she fell in the kitchen and bumped her head …" María was totally confounded. "What does that have to do with the Grinch-green paint on this picture?"

Bailey didn't know where in the world to start to explain it to her.

Dobbs wasn't trying to explain it. He was trying to understand it.

"Did Bethany paint that Grinch on the picture because she somehow knew it fell and saved her mommy?" Profound silence rushed in to fill the void left by Dobbs's made-for-radio voice, a voice tight with a kind of fear Bailey'd never heard there before. "Or did that Grinch fall and save her mommy because Bethany painted the picture?"

Not a person in the room had an answer.

THE END

If you loved reading *Black Water* and want more Ninie Hammon right now, you're in luck! Right now you can get *The Jabberwock* and start reading Ninie's new *Nowhere USA* series today!

Get The Jabberwock Today

A Special Request

Thank you for reading *Blue Tears*.

If you enjoyed this book would you please consider writing a review of it on your favorite bookseller's website so other readers might enjoy it too. Just a couple of sentences would mean a lot to me.

Thank you!
Ninie Hammon

About the Author

Ninie Hammon (rhymes with shiny, not skinny) grew up in Muleshoe, Texas, got a BA in English and theatre from Texas Tech University and snagged a job as a newspaper reporter. She didn't know a thing about journalism, but her editor said if she could write he could teach her the rest of it and if she couldn't write the rest of it didn't matter. She hung in there for a 25-year career as a journalist. As soon as she figured out that making up the facts was a whole lot more fun than reporting them, she turned to fiction and never looked back.

Ninie now writes suspense--every flavor except pistachio: psychological suspense, inspirational suspense, suspense thrillers, paranormal suspense, suspense mysteries.

In every book she keeps this promise to her Loyal Reader: "I will tell you a story in a distinctive voice you'll always recognize, about people as ordinary as you are--people who have been slammed by something they didn't sign on for, and now they must fight for their lives. Then smack in the middle of their everyday worlds, those people encounter the unexplainable--and it's always the game-changer."

Cornbread Mafia

Fire In The Hole

Blown' Up A Storm

Ridin' For A Fall

So Shall The Tree Grow

Nowhere, USA

The Jabberwock

Mad Dog

Trapped

The Hanging Judge

The Witch of Gideon

Blown Away

Nowhere People

Through The Canvas Series

Black Water

Red Web

Gold Promise

Blue Tears

The Taken Saga

The Taken

The Changed

The Hidden

The Saved

The Unexplainable Collection

Five Days in May

Black Sunshine

The Based on True Stories Collection

Home Grown

Sudan

When Butterflies Cry

The Knowing Series

The Knowing

The Deceiving

The Reckoning

The Fault

Stand-alone Psychological Thrillers

The Memory Closet

The Last Safe Place